IMPROPER
GENTLEMEN

D0863268

IMPROPER GENTLEMEN

DIANE WHITESIDE
MAGGIE ROBINSON
MIA MARLOWE

BRAVA

KENSINGTON PUBLISHING CORP.
www.kensingtonbooks.com

BRAVA BOOKS are published by

Kensington Publishing Corp.
119 West 40th Street
New York, NY 10018

Copyright © 2011 Kensington Publishing Corp.
"Talbot's Ace" copyright © 2011 Diane Whiteside
"To Match a Thief" copyright © 2011 Maggie Robinson
"A Knack for Trouble" copyright © 2011 Diana Groe

All rights reserved. No part of this book may be reproduced in any form or by any means without the prior written consent of the Publisher, excepting brief quotes used in reviews.

All Kensington titles, imprints, and distributed lines are available at special quantity discounts for bulk purchases for sales promotion, premiums, fund-raising, educational or institutional use.

Special book excerpts or customized printings can also be created to fit specific needs. For details, write or phone the office of the Kensington Special Sales Manager: Kensington Publishing Corp., 119 West 40th Street, New York, NY 10018; Attn. Special Sales Department. Phone: 1-800-221-2647.

Brava and the B logo are Reg. U.S. Pat. & TM Off.

ISBN-13: 978-0-7582-5109-1
ISBN-10: 0-7582-5109-2

First Kensington Trade Paperback Printing: August 2011

10 9 8 7 6 5 4 3 2 1

Printed in the United States of America

CONTENTS

Talbot's Ace

DIANE WHITESIDE

Chapter 1

Silver and black spun through the man's fingers in deadly pinwheels of steel under the lead-grey skies.

Charlotte Moreland froze in front of the Silver King Hotel, unable to take another step even though the young man was more than a dozen paces away.

Three years of playing poker in the West's worst gambling dens had taught her much about the narrow margin between great shootists and the dead. She had no desire to join the latter near an establishment called Hair Trigger Palace.

Handsome and harsh as a Renaissance angel, he was utterly absorbed in weaving patterns of light as he spun his revolvers. His black broadcloth frockcoat, black trousers, and black boots were as finely made as if they too bore homage to the death-dealing implements he worshipped.

Her fellow stagecoach passengers streamed into the closest saloon to warm themselves with beer or whiskey. One headed swiftly into the hotel to claim his clean lodging, more priceless than a good meal in this hastily built town. A few pedestrians glanced at the effortless display of gun tricks, then walked swiftly past.

He flipped the heavy guns between his hands and they smacked into his palms like a warrior's salute. He immediately tossed them high and spun them back into the holsters at his hips.

Last spring in Denver, she'd seen a shootist testing his pistols. He'd shot a can of peaches until it had exploded its innards across a wall, just like a person would. She'd been wretchedly sick in her hotel room afterward.

This man slapped the leather holsters and, an instant later on a ragged beat, death looked out of the guns' barrels.

His expression hardened to that of an angry fallen angel leading armies of destruction. He shoved his guns back into place, clearly ready to teach them another lesson.

Charlotte gave a little squeak and trotted onto the boardwalk in front of the hotel. No matter how flimsy its roof and planks were, it still offered more protection than the open street. Men, equipped with guns and a temper, were dangerous to both themselves and everyone nearby.

The shootist whirled in surprise and his gaze drilled into her.

Heaven help her, it was the same *pistolero* she'd seen in Denver—Justin Talbot, the fastest gun in Colorado.

Recognition flashed across his face. But not greed, thank God. Perhaps he hadn't recognized her photo, flaunted by those skulking Pinkerton's men throughout the mining towns.

Why had she dreamed about him for so many months?

He bowed to her with a flourish and she froze. Her heart drummed in her throat, too fast to let her breathe or think.

How should she acknowledge him—formally, with a bow or a curtsy? Heartily, with a wave inviting affection or perhaps intimacy? Or coldly, with an averted shoulder and gaze, as befitted such an experienced death-dealer, no matter what skills living in this town required?

He frowned and anguish slipped into his eyes. A man whistled from behind him.

Talbot's mouth tightened and he bowed to her again, far more coldly. She gave him the barest of nods in return, all her drumming pulse would support.

He disappeared into the Hair Trigger Palace an instant later, his expression still harsher than an ice-etched granite mountain.

Truly, she should not feel bereft, as if she'd lost a potential friend.

She slapped dust off her carpetbag and silently castigated herself for standing outside on the hotel porch like a wilted daisy. In order to dodge any Pinkerton's men on the lookout for her, she'd given herself very little time to claim her hotel room after arriving in town. She'd be a damn fool to lose her chance of playing in the tournament by not making it out of her hotel room and down to the Crystal Saloon.

The Silver King's brightly lit lobby was even more crowded than she'd expected. Smooth-talking gamblers jostled elbows with rough miners under stuffed and mounted antelope. Buckskin-clad mountain men and sober businessmen shouted at clerks, who hovered over an immense mahogany bar.

A little boy weaved his way through the room, pulling his mittens on with his teeth. His respectably dressed mother followed him, all the while admonishing him not to go outside until both hands were covered. The second mitten dropped out of his grasp just before he reached Charlotte, but he kept on running for the door.

Charlotte snatched up the bright red lump of red wool an instant before he escaped into the fresh air, and offered it to his mother. "Ma'am? I believe this may be his."

The woman's patient, weary face brightened when she saw the worn mitten. Then her gaze traveled upward to catalogue the newcomer's attire, especially her diamond brooch, the telltale mark of a professional gambler.

She gasped in audible horror and yanked her child's glove out of Charlotte's unresisting grip.

"Ace Moreland," she hissed.

"Ma'am." Charlotte bowed formally, the same way she would have greeted an ancestral enemy at a ball overlooking Boston Harbor. The only use for that nickname was as a disguise.

Her stomach tightened in sickened resignation, but not surprise. She should have known better than to stay at a respectable hotel. But Wolf Laurel was such a young settlement that females traveling alone had very few options.

The woman grabbed her son by the ear and hauled the protesting child away, without a backward glance.

Charlotte laughed silently, mirthlessly, at herself. She should have learned not to approach a respectable woman by now, although not being allowed to aid a child hurt worse than any previous slight. There was nothing left to do but keep moving on.

She headed for the front desk and the hotel manager, who should treat her with the courtesy due a guest. She needed to earn a bigger fortune soon, if she wanted women to be polite to her face.

The men there were, as ever, friendlier than the so-called gentler sex, but they didn't push the bounds of propriety. Any hints of that would probably come later at the poker table. Her famed ice-maiden visage should keep them at a distance. Or at least, it had always sufficed until Holbrook.

She readily located the manager, who knocked his pen off his inkwell when she gave her name. He took so long to decide which room to assign her that she nearly demanded the name of a nearby boardinghouse. Only the surety that a blizzard would arrive that night and make the streets nigh-on impassable stopped her.

Finally, the fellow fumbled an immense black key into his hand and set off. The stairs' magnificence matched the foyer, with thick red carpeting, glossy wood, and glowing chandeliers flaring amid brightly polished brass. But the minute they stepped away from the stairs, the hallways darkened and the glossy wallpaper was replaced by thin paint.

"And here's your room, Miss Moreland," the manager eventually mumbled when he reached the hotel's far corner. He rattled his excuse for a key in the lock like a drunken drummer but finally managed to throw the door open. The solid pine panel swung wide until its casing creaked in protest.

He carried Charlotte's carpetbag inside without a second glance to see if the door's hinges had separated from the frame. Instead, he struck a match and lit the wall sconces, causing the gaslight to hiss like Cleopatra's asp in protest.

Charlotte studied the room with eyes made wary by too many Western boomtowns. Its cleanliness was as welcome as the stagecoach driver's liking for the hotel had been. Her grubstake was split up and hidden in multiple places so a robber couldn't take all of it. The poker circuit liked the place, too, since they'd recommended it for the tournament. That and its discount for lady poker players had made her break her previously inviolable rule never to attend a major tournament.

Even so, she was risking her money and her body. She'd make her own decision about whether or not to stay.

The gaslight's golden light spread cautiously over a bedroom tiny even by boardinghouse standards. A narrow iron frame was jammed against one wall to support a cheerless mattress. She could stand beside it in her bloomers without rapping her elbow on the wall. But could she twirl to check her bustle's fit? Not likely.

Two doors were somehow squeezed into the miniscule layout. Heavy velvet drapes framed the window like iron bars, while the neighboring building's raw timber loomed through the lace curtains. A narrow gap allowed a view out to the street where heavy clouds obscured the distant peaks.

"Hmm," Charlotte remarked noncommittally. How much would it cost for a larger room? Complete privacy was always hard to guarantee in a Western boomtown, especially within its sole hotel during a high-stakes tournament.

The manager shoved her carpetbag against the exterior wall. The gaily flowered wallpaper billowed and an ice-cold draft ripped through the room and across her toes.

Charlotte's smile tightened. Stage sets would be more trustworthy than this hotel's walls. Both were painted paper over flimsy pine boards. At least theaters paid actors to hide behind the partitions. In these mountains, greedy hotel managers demanded that desperate travelers pay them for the privilege of doing so. A conversation could be heard three doors away and a fist could punch through walls. A blizzard's howling gales could reduce the entire structure to firewood.

Perhaps she'd winter in California, after all, away from Colorado's heavy snows and any chance of being seen by somebody from Boston. It was only September, with no snow on the railroad routes yet. She took chances only with the cards, never with her life.

She donned her most appreciative expression, the one applauded by her deportment instructors.

"Sir," she began and fixed her gaze on the hotel manager. After all, he was the man best equipped to improve her accommodations.

"Well, well, Miss Moreland." The doorknob rattled against the wall and its frame squeaked. "What do you think of my fine hotel?" boomed a harsh Georgia voice.

Charlotte's skin flushed and she silently cursed the lapse,

a tell any beginning poker player could read. She couldn't afford any handicap, especially not when it bared the truth. Not anymore, not without anybody to back her.

She reluctantly turned to face Isaiah Johnson, the town's notorious mayor.

Chapter 2

He leaned against the door like a grizzly at summer's end, too thick and contented to move fast yet sporting the biggest, sharpest claws in the forest. He was dressed like a bear, too. Though he was garbed in a great tailor's finest efforts, his scarlet brocade vest displayed more tawdry self-indulgence than any dancing bear would sport.

His gaze would admirably suit a grizzly—a self-satisfied smirk of anticipation for the coming meal.

Her stomach flopped upward like a terrified salmon toward her throat. He couldn't possibly be her enemy, not when they'd first met only days ago in Leadville and exchanged fewer than a dozen words.

Behind her, she heard the manager's breathing quicken.

She sucked in more stale air through her gritted teeth.

"It's very beautiful and you must be proud The Silver King was built so quickly. Wasn't silver discovered less than a year ago, after gold was found?" She offered her best conversational red herring.

"Yes, ma'am, silver flowed right before my saddle-partner and I moved here." He was watching his manager closely, even though he addressed her. "Do you find your room acceptable?"

A chilly draft slithered past her neck and she rushed into a conversational platitude far too fast.

"Yes indeed, it's very lovely. I particularly admire the vibrant shade of red you found for the cabbage roses." A shade she'd never choose for her own dwelling.

"Thanks. Some fancy Atlanta company sent them up here." He glanced around the room, as if congratulating himself on every detail. "Since you're so happy"—the manager nodded vehemently—"guess I'd better be moving along to see how my other guests are settling in."

"Mr. Johnson!" Drat it, that came out more sharply than she would have liked.

The hotel manager froze in his tracks, inches away from her elbow.

"Yes, Miss Moreland?" Johnson's tone turned hostile. He shot the hotel manager a sharp glare and the much smaller fellow spread his hands wide, quickly disclaiming any knowledge.

"These quarters are elegantly decorated but not as"—she hesitated, then chose the most accurate, if not flattering, term—"private as I'd hoped for. May I please be transferred into another room?"

The hotel manager trembled.

"Miss Moreland, you do realize there is a big poker tournament being held here right now?"

"Yes, of course." What nonsense was he spouting? Dammit, she was entered in the tournament. "But I'd be happy to pay more."

"A lady of your *quality*"—for the first time, his voice dripped insolence—"can hardly be expected to share a room with strange men."

"Certainly not, sir!" She stared back at him, her spine rigid with centuries of blue-blooded Bostonian self-possession.

"I'm the owner of this hotel and I swear this is the only single room we have."

"It has two doors," she snapped back. "And no lock on the second door."

"Yes, you're sure right about that." Johnson's expression immediately transformed back into the lazy bear. "Since your objection's to that door, why don't you check it out?"

A strangled noise escaped from the hotel manager.

She shot a startled glance at the fellow but he wouldn't meet her eyes.

Johnson shifted slightly until his coat slid away from his hips and gunbelt. He raised an eyebrow.

The manager quivered again, then clutched his notebook close to his chest like a shield.

"I must check on the other guests." He brushed past Charlotte, so desperate to escape that he almost ran on tiptoes to avoid stepping on her skirts.

What on earth? Was Johnson so proud of this hotel that he didn't want anybody else showing off his pride and joy?

"The second door, Miss Moreland?" Johnson urged, his smile deepening into a gourmand's anticipation. "I'm sure you'll be greatly surprised by the wonders beyond."

A whisper ran over her skin but she shrugged it away.

"Certainly, sir." The sooner she refused the next room's unknown contents, the sooner she could escape this hole, which didn't even offer a chair to block any of its portals.

She wrenched open the interior door and strode through.

The room beyond was enormous compared to hers but dark as a goblin's cave. Thick red velvet covered every surface, like a crimson invitation to ruin. Frosted globes on the ceiling and walls cast flickering pools of light, which barely dispelled the shadows.

A big man, all tiny pig eyes above a starched shirt front and diamond studs stretched taut over an immense stomach, glanced up at her precipitous entrance. A slow smile spread over his face, displaying cracked yellow teeth. He set down his bottle of whiskey far too fast.

Charlotte skidded to a halt, her skin colder than any arctic draft could account for. *Oh damn, damn, damn.*

"Miss Moreland. I hadn't hoped to have the pleasure of seeing you again so soon." Jasper Simmons, Colorado's most powerful legislator, bowed to her mockingly. His reputation was worse than foul. Broken bones, even rape, were the least of the crimes laid at his door.

"Mr. Simmons." She gave him a polite smile that she hoped didn't resemble a grimace. She looped her bustle up behind her back where he couldn't see, and started to reverse her steps.

His lips curved in anticipation.

Her pace quickened. She'd barely escaped the last time they'd met, back in Denver. She'd had a bolt-hole then but where would she go here, if Simmons decided to push his luck?

"Thank you, Johnson, for bringing her to me so quickly." He nodded to the other man.

"My pleasure."

Charlotte froze in place, outrage stiffening her spine. The town's mayor knew of Simmons's depraved tastes? Would willingly assist him? She turned to confront the cur and fight for safety.

"Say the word if there's anything else you want." Johnson raised his hand to Simmons, who lifted his glass in an answering salute.

"You—you bastards!" Charlotte spluttered.

"You Northern bitch!" Johnson mocked. He laughed, every note rich with satisfaction. "Don't worry. Your adventure won't last long, only a few days. After that, if you're still alive, one of our local madams is willing to take you on as one of her girls."

"A common whore? Like hell." Outrage banished the chill from Charlotte's skin. Safety be damned. She'd die before she'd have anything to do with Simmons.

"You see? You'll do very well—you already have the language." Johnson clucked his tongue at her, joy dancing through his eyes.

Why did he want to see her destroyed? Did he hate her? Did it matter when the jaws were closing on the trap? She needed to save her life.

"Remember our bargain, Simmons." Johnson's voice was sharp and confident, as if he counted off markers on a poker table.

"Of course. You'll have your charter."

Charter? That sounded official and important enough for Johnson to put aside any morals he might have.

Dread crawled down Charlotte's spine. Could she reach the hallway without being caught? Probably not, but what did she have to lose?

Johnson slammed shut the other bedroom's door in her face before she could reach it.

She opened her mouth to scream.

"Miss Moreland." Simmons's fingers dug into her arms tighter than manacles.

She flinched then stilled. She would not give him the satisfaction of cringing, no matter how great the pain.

"How kind of you to allow me to renew our acquaintance," he crooned.

"A few words in a gambling saloon do not make you my friend." She squirmed and tried to yank herself away from him. His foul odor brushed the nape of her neck in a sickening combination of liquor, rank sweat, and cheap tobacco.

"You will be." He yanked her closer to him.

She ground her boot heel into the flimsy carpet to anchor herself. He wrenched her around again until she faced him. Agony shot through her shoulders.

Greed, slimy as his reputation, gleamed in his eyes. He stared at her avidly and his gaze stripped every inch of clothing from her. His hand lifted to peel back her jacket and she slapped him.

He backhanded her carelessly. She staggered and her eyes blurred for a moment. Blood's salty warmth trickled down her jaw. She brushed her fingers along her throat and crimson stained her knuckles.

How much harm had he done? How much more would he do?

"You're even prettier when you fight, little lady." He licked his lips. "You'll look real fine under me at the end."

She stared at him, even more horrified than before. Why would he want to rape *her*? Surely his money could purchase somebody willing.

He reached for her dress's neckline.

"I'll scream," she warned him through a throat grown tight with terror. "Somebody will help me."

"Do so and I'll enjoy listening." He skimmed his finger across the delicate lace and her pulse skidded. "Nobody will come."

"There are still some decent men left in Wolf Laurel," she assured him.

Surely there had to be somebody even in the wickedest town in Colorado. But the hotel manager must have known what was planned, since he'd assigned the rooms. Yet he'd run away when he knew she'd be coming in here and didn't warn her. She'd have to protect herself.

"Silly little pigeon." Simmons snickered. "Everybody here either works for Johnson or is terrified of him."

He slid two filthy fingers inside her neckline and started to pull it down.

Charlotte brought her knee up sharply in a move learned long ago at the North Boston Soldiers' Rest Home. Hard bone, only slightly muffled by cloth, slammed between Simmons's legs and into his privates.

He doubled over and shrieked like a woman.

Nobody responded.

The sick feeling in Charlotte's stomach intensified. She truly was alone.

She clenched her two hands together into a fist, then neatly clubbed her attacker on the back of his head. He collapsed onto the floor at her feet, with only the faintest stirring of his chest to indicate life.

Her stomach lurched hard into her throat and she clutched her palm over her mouth. No matter what she'd seen before, she'd never dealt violence to another individual. The feel of Simmons's hair, the sharpness of his skull dropping out from under her hand . . . The absolute limpness of his body in that first instant, like a fish tossed onto ice in a shop window . . .

Her stomach heaved again. A lifetime's training insisted that nobody should have to deal out such violence, no matter what the provocation. In Boston, the police would have answered her summons.

His previous victims would no doubt mourn his continued survival but she didn't have the time. Simmons had left other women with faces sliced into ribbons, or dying amid blood-soaked sheets. The hotel manager had run rather than help her. The town's mayor had forced her into Simmons's arms. She could only look to herself for help, no matter how ugly the deed.

Now she needed to escape. But where?

Another hotel? That wouldn't be far enough. Johnson was the mayor and he would probably find her, then snatch her away. This was the best hotel, the only one considered safe enough for a woman traveling alone. She didn't even have a recommendation for another one, only a boardinghouse "if she wanted to sit up all night with a gun."

She'd never gambled with her physical safety and this

was no time to start, when the penalty for a mistake was rape by Simmons. She had to leave town.

She needed to catch the last stagecoach out of Wolf Laurel before Johnson discovered what had happened.

The fastest, quietest way to reach the depot was to go from the gambling saloon in the Silver King's lower level, then through the Hair Trigger Palace to the stage depot across the street.

Unfortunately, that meant passing through the wickedest establishment in Colorado without being spotted by Johnson's best friend, who owned the place.

Charlotte closed her eyes and willed herself to stop shaking. Then she opened the door to her room, grabbed her carpetbag, and started running.

Chapter 3

Justin Talbot stepped out onto Wolf Laurel's main street from his own piece of heaven, Hair Trigger Palace. Last time he'd been out here, Ace Moreland had cut his dreams down faster than a shotgun blast.

A cold wind promptly investigated him and the first snowflakes drifted onto his broad-brimmed black hat. If he stayed outside very long, he'd need better boots to handle the freezing mud. Not that matters usually took long with the Aspen Kid.

"Aspen!" Justin called, careful to keep his voice well below a shout. Even so, pedestrians within earshot turned to glance at him, then slipped into the nearest building like cats finding their fireside before a rainstorm.

The smaller man slowly turned around in front of the stage depot. The black window shade smacked the *Closed* sign against the glass.

"Talbot," Aspen acknowledged. His hands dropped to his thighs and hovered inches away from his guns. Even from this distance, he reeked of expensive whiskey and cheap perfume. He should have stopped buying drinks after he'd lost his horse.

"Got a dealer lying flat on the floor who can't wake up. Care to explain that?" Justin asked.

"Nothing to talk about." The Aspen Kid shrugged, his

brilliant red neckerchief sliding like sunset over his dark blue shirt. "I took my winnings and left. If your dealer got in the way, that's his problem."

"Aspen." Justin's drawl deepened to a dark purr. At that note in his voice, the few remaining pedestrians scattered and all but ran for the nearest door.

"The last time I saw my dealer, he was dealing cards for your game. You must understand that I view any affront to one of my men as an insult to myself."

Aspen fluffed out his coat like a bantam cock parading his tail feathers but paid no heed to the sky overhead. The storm clouds already hid the eastern pass with its stage road into Wolf Laurel. Snow must be falling there, with more to the west where the skies were darker on the higher mountains.

"He was clumsy and didn't know how to handle my action," the careless newcomer insisted, his fingers twitching cloth into place over his leather gun belt and cartridge case.

"What do you mean?" Justin kept his hands in the open, where they couldn't provoke a nervous, drunken gambler into starting something irrevocable. Hours of daily practice had taught them exactly where his guns were. He didn't need to flex his fingers to prepare, like an Eastern dude aching to display his measly skill and too green to realize how much he tempted his enemies.

"I play for the highest stakes"—Justin doubted that, considering who'd sat down at the Hair Trigger's tables before Aspen—"and that dealer kept too much of it for the house. When I challenged him, his answers were unsatisfactory."

"Perhaps you should reconsider your last statement, sir." The fine notes of South Carolina aristocracy settled deeper into Justin's voice on the last syllable. Just like his father, damn it.

He eased forward to block the path to the livery stable and any hope of the stagecoach.

A new gust of wind raced past the Hair Trigger Palace's solid brick stability and sank its cold, dry claws into his cheeks. Justin automatically adjusted his stance for what it told him a bullet would have to traverse. He'd long since stopped arguing with fellow property holders about how they didn't protect themselves and their employees against fire and wind.

The Aspen Kid fell back before him but counterattacked verbally. "The bastard cheated!"

"Are you saying that my dealer, in my house, was dishonest?"

Bill, my best dealer who's lying on the floor covered in enough blood to paint a dozen Red Indians for war? Bill Tyler, the Methodist deacon who's married with three kids? Never.

Justin's fingertips ached for his Colt's triggers but he held them away.

"Yes!" Aspen's shout rang through the street and he glared at Justin.

"Then I am dishonest, since it was my house." Justin's voice was very soft. The wintry world was crystal-clear now, since it was composed of only the Kid's eyes and hands. Life would be much simpler if Aspen gave a different answer—but that would mean the fool admitting he'd been dishonorable.

"Apologize now, Aspen, or I'll run you out of Wolf Laurel like the lying dog you are." Justin kept his hands out in the open, an honest man's distance from his beloved Navy Colts. They were as reliable as the woman who'd given them to him almost fifteen years ago. His pulse was steady, even though the old familiar knot in his stomach ached like a cannonball.

Aspen hesitated, his eyes narrowed on his opponent.

A gust of wind brushed his coat against his leg and coins clanked musically in his pocket.

Jealousy blurred through the other man's eyes.

Justin eased his fingers closer to his hips, and his guns.

"Everybody knows Wolf Laurel's mayor only keeps the Palace around," Aspen said, his lip curled in a mocking snarl, "because it's the fastest way to make more money. And he don't care how he gets it—skimming it off the top of a crooked poker table makes greenbacks smell sweet as a silver mine. He's just as dishonest as his stinking partner."

The Aspen Kid's gun blazed forward from his holster, pointed straight at Justin's heart—just before the Southerner's Colt deliberately thundered into action.

Aspen choked and clapped his hand to his chest. Anger burned through his eyes.

A hot wind roared past Justin's left sleeve, but he ignored it and kept his gun at the ready.

Crimson seeped through the other man's fingers and Aspen glared at his opponent. Horror flashed in his eyes an instant before his knees sagged like broken straw. He fell face-down, in a crumpled heap as void of movement as a barren field.

Justin holstered his weapon, his stomach knotted into the same roiling octopus it always assumed after he killed a man. Mother's gift had saved him once again.

Now to clean up the mess and go back to what passed for life. Someday flowers would bloom in his life more often than gunfire and young ladies would take his arm instead of giving him the cut direct.

A woman barreled into his back, all running feet and acres of skirt twisting between his legs to trip him up. Feathers brushed the nape of his neck like spring's first blossoms.

He lost his balance and tumbled toward the ground. Only bull-wrestling skills that he'd learned rounding up wild cattle in the Pecos River bottoms saved them both from rolling through the street's frozen mud. As it was, he wound up cursing viciously, with an armful of unfamiliar female clasped to his chest and his knee thrust between hers.

She was tall, slender yet curved in all the right ways to make his skin hum in anticipation. Scents of lavender and Castile soap teased his brain. He quickly glanced down to survey his catch but a black velvet bonnet, fashionably trimmed with ribbons and feathers, allowed him no more than a glimpse of creamy skin and a stubborn jaw.

"Excuse me for disturbing you, sir!" A husky voice snatched his breath away, strong as a jab to his ribs.

He'd heard that voice once before, in Denver under a springtime moon, when every rich note had shredded his wits faster than the finest brandy. Even Merlin's beloved sorceress, released from those legendary ice caves, couldn't be as lovely. Since then, he'd chased news of her like a bloodhound quartering a barren field.

Justin's heartbeat skittered for the first time that day.

She slipped out of his suddenly lax grip but skidded, unable to find solid footing on the treacherous ground. He caught her again, careful not to hurt her arms.

"Unhand me, sir." Blue eyes, brighter than any hope of heaven, blazed into his and ungloved hands pushed at his shoulders. "I must catch the next stage."

She'd cut him down, right here, with an imperious look from those same eyes less than an hour earlier, as if he was a loathesome criminal. "Ace Moreland?"

Purest terror flashed across her beautiful face, to be quickly replaced by arrogance. If he hadn't been holding her and watching her closely, he'd never have seen the dread. She jerked her head in reluctant agreement.

What the hell was she doing on the street again? What was she running from? Couldn't be the Pinkerton's agents who some bastard back East had sent to sniff out her trail across the Rockies.

None of those buzzards roosted in Wolf Laurel. He could still smell them easily, after hunting them down during the War.

He leashed his hungers tighter than the buckles holding his guns to his belt and loosened his grip on her.

Damn it all to hell, blood was matted on the tips of her blond hair. Somebody would pay for that. In their own blood, once he found the bastard.

His pulse settled into a slow, steady, eager battle rhythm that his first cavalry commander would have applauded.

Townsfolk sprouted along the boardwalk to watch them, like winter wheat avidly seeking the false spring's sunlight. More trotted down the alleys in fools' ever-present search for entertainment.

Brooks, the town undertaker, threw a tarp over the Aspen Kid's remains, then scratched a few lines in his note-book, his small frame fading from sight behind a burst of falling snow. Far too many businessmen had profitably learned that anyone killed in the Hair Trigger Palace—or by Justin—received a proper burial at his expense.

Moreland's gaze searched his features and recognition burned bright as a Colt's muzzle blast. She sucked in a short, harsh breath. "Talbot."

His name on her lips sounded like a church bell in a cemetery. He hurried to lay down words to erase those echoes before she could spook and start running again.

"Justin Talbot, ma'am, very much at your service." He bowed formally to her, as his mother had taught him.

"Like hell you are." Bitter knowledge, mixed with dread, filled her words. But she curtsied and acknowledged him with a quick brush of her fingertips across his hand.

Praise the Lord, she'd accepted him this much.

A door opened and slammed shut behind them with a dull thud, not the solid *thwack!* of good wood greeting honest brick.

"Thank God, Talbot, I knew you'd catch the bitch for me." Johnson's nasal drawl ripped through the gathering crowd.

Moreland's mouth tightened to a thin, terrified line in a white face.

What the hell is going on?

Justin pulled her close against his hip, wrapped his arm around her, and turned to face his long-time saddle-partner.

She twitched against him and dropped an inch, clearly ready to duck underneath his grasp. He promptly sharpened his elbow around her like a vise and tugged her even tighter against him. A snowflake couldn't have passed between them.

She harrumphed under her breath.

"Afternoon, Johnson." He kept his voice civil and his grip snug on Moreland. "What brings you out in this weather?"

What the devil was that Georgia native doing outside in shirtsleeves? He loathed foul weather. For him to greet a snowstorm in anything other than a buffalo coat and beaver hat meant there was serious trouble afoot.

"Hand her over and I'll head back inside." The shorter but equally strong man crossed his arms over his fancy vest and stomped his feet in their thin dress boots. "She can apologize to Simmons up in his room."

Simmons? That slimy weasel, who's throttled more women than he has fingers to count them?

Ten years of riding with Johnson side by side, fighting for their lives back to back, insisted that his pal had to have a good reason for forcing a good woman into that brute's clutches. But he couldn't discuss it here and risk exposing his friend's devious tactics when half the town stood within earshot. Those gossipmongers had elected Johnson mayor with far less fuss than expected. Sure as two cups of cavalry punch could knock out a civilian, fewer bribes had changed hands than was customary during an election.

Nine-Fingers Isham, Johnson's favorite bouncer, appeared out of the shadows behind the mayor. He rocked back and forth slightly, his fingers ostentatiously shoving his coat away from his guns.

Damn. Johnson would be twice as ornery with that jail-bait to back him up.

Justin needed time to create a private chat between them and stop his old friend from ruining himself in front of his constituents.

"Don't think so, Johnson." Justin slowly, deliberately smoothed her beruffled mantle with his free hand and watched his old friend's eyes widen at the unusually possessive gesture.

She uttered a tiny squeak, which a chipmunk couldn't have heard from a foot away. Then she patted his fingers and leaned confidingly against him, as if he was the most welcome man in the world.

Good girl, she'd taken the hint, even though she was shaking like a leaf.

"She insulted my most important guest." The Confederate veteran's expression darkened with rage and he leaped off the boardwalk into the street. "Nothing's bigger than that."

A rude comment linking Simmons's reputation to Johnson floated past from somebody hidden deep in the crowd. The mayor's hands twitched closer toward his guns. He glared at his partner, not the rabble-rouser.

The crowd fell quieter, probably in anticipation of a showdown, the greedy cows.

A muscle throbbed in Justin's cheek. At least his so-called innocent would live to be haughty another day, if he did her fighting.

"Ace Moreland's here to see me." Justin's voice held

steady on the biggest lie he'd ever told his partner. No way in hell would he allow her to be hurt—or the Georgia veteran to be bushwhacked by hypocritical townsfolk.

He lifted her hand to his lips—and the sweet scent of lavender blurred his senses.

"Don't feed me that bullshit, Talbot." Johnson glared at him from only a few feet away, his hazel eyes narrowed until they were almost yellow with rage. "We work together, like we have for the past ten years to build an empire."

"Not in this." Justin kept his voice to the same harsh whisper his friend had used. "Not with a woman at stake."

"What's different about her?" His saddle partner's voice rose to a threatening growl. "You've never stayed with a lover for longer than a weekend, let alone flaunted one. Besides, Ace Moreland won't settle down with any man."

"Certainly not you." Moreland spoke for the first time, since Wolf Laurel's mayor had burst onto the street. She nestled closer to Justin until her feathered bonnet teased his jaw.

He knew damned well his face softened. Was it his fault he wanted to kiss her cheek and pull her closer?

"Mr. Talbot's invitation was irresistible." Her rich voice deepened into a husky invitation to sin, unlike her earlier, sharper tones. "I find myself anticipating every minute in his company."

She stroked Justin's hand with a cat's elegant, anticipatory sensuality. Slow, drugging heat stirred to life within his blood and moved to follow her fingers' every languid move.

"I don't believe either of you." Johnson was still vehement.

Everyone on the street had fallen silent in order to listen.

How could he prove a prior connection to Moreland?

"Go ahead and stick your head in the sand," Justin

drawled. "Miss Moreland and I will enjoy the music at the Hair Trigger Palace from my box."

"You'll take Ace Moreland up to the top floor?"

She jerked convulsively.

A smirk broke over Johnson's face and he slapped his thigh with a loud guffaw. "Pal, she will slap your face and bolt out of there faster than an overloaded mule breaking the plow's traces."

Justin clenched his jaw against a profane retort to stop the Georgian's ugly comments. Moreland saved him the difficulty.

She rubbed her cheek against his shoulder like a cat claiming a well-loved fireside.

"Mr. Talbot has promised me a most delightful show," she purred. "Shall we go, darling?"

Darling??? Oh yes, of course, she needed to use an endearment for her so-called lover, no matter what she truly thought of him.

She smiled up at him from under her bonnet. Blue ribbons fluttered across her mantle, as if fighting the wind. Hell, that bit of cloth wasn't worth a damn against a Colorado snowstorm, let alone a blizzard's beginnings.

"Sure. Afternoon, Johnson." He touched his hat to Johnson. It'd be easier to talk when they didn't have dozens of listeners eager to pass on gossip.

The other Confederate veteran nodded, equally curt, and stood aside. His eyes were dark and calculating, which put his temper in the certain-to-rise-again category.

Crap, now he looked like a stubborn pig. Justin bit back a sharp retort, out of courtesy to his lady.

Johnson snorted, flipped him a rude gesture, and stomped back into his hotel.

Pity they couldn't settle this here and now with their fists, as they would have ten years ago.

Moreland didn't wait for them, God bless her, but hurried toward the closest building. She slipped on the Hair Trigger's icy steps and Justin caught her in a single long stride. This time, her fingers clutched at his lapels and a whiff of her scent teased his nostrils.

Even more of his blood sprang to life despite the wind's bitter lash.

Lavender and Castile soap were clearly the Devil's handiwork.

He cursed, tossed her up into his arms—and greatly enjoyed her smothered shriek. She might slap his face in a few seconds, but he'd have this much to remember her by.

Then he shoved the Hair Trigger Palace's swinging doors open and carried her inside, with her carpetbag beating time against his leg.

Chapter 4

Thump, thump! The great doors swung shut behind them and sent a burst of cold air swirling through Charlotte's skirts. Wall sconces and heavy lanterns overhead flickered briefly, then burned sullenly once again to hint at ornate columns and dark green walls. In the distance, a long, broad shaft of light split the saloon's center to mark the stage. From there, a curvaceous soprano sang passionately of death-defying love in songs translated from Italy's latest operas.

Card tables were stuffed onto the Hair Trigger Palace's floor. Men crowded around them more intently than frogs ever studied dragonflies in a tropical jungle. Each side of the room below the balcony had its own bar. There an oil painting of a complacently nude female was surrounded by glittering rivers of glass bottles lit by dozens of candles. Skilled bartenders in crisp white shirts and dark vests served whiskey, bourbon, beer, and every drink known or imaginable to a constantly shifting throng.

The air was hot and greedy, heavy with anticipation for the upcoming sights.

She could have touched the balcony's underside from where Talbot held her against his chest.

She was trapped more completely than in Simmons's room. Damn, damn, damn, why had she simply let herself be carried off? Surely being a woman didn't have to limit her choices that much, did it? She could have done something else, the way a man would have.

No matter how much drier this was than the town out-side—which was hardly difficult with a storm about to begin—she was still inside the Hair Trigger Palace, the most dangerous concert saloon in Colorado's wickedest city. Even worse, Talbot, the best shootist in the Rockies, carried her, steady as her father's finest stallion.

She was cold to her bones, yet everywhere he touched, her treacherous flesh longed to be closer. Closer to the soft glide of a fine wool frock coat shifting to follow the strong male form underneath, closer to the unhurried breathing caressing her cheek, closer to the sensual aroma of bay rum rising from his skin to invite her touch. This was insanity.

She needed to escape, despite the unbidden warmth steal-ing into her from his proximity. She had to leave Wolf Lau-rel before the weather and Johnson combined to chain her to Simmons's bed, no matter what Talbot did.

"Put me down," Charlotte ordered and thumped his shoulder hard. She'd fought and survived before. She could do it again. Somehow.

"Try to look as if you adore me," Talbot whispered and let her slide far too slowly down his front. His profile glowed dark gold in the shadows under his hat, like a Greek hero amid Hades' fires.

The saloon's heat seeping into her toes was far less no-ticeable than the slow glide of woolen coat and silken vest across her skin, or the hard muscles in the shoulders and chest underneath. Protection and temptation incarnate.

No, and no, and no. She could not afford to lose her head over another attractive man. No amount of loneliness ex-cused her folly with that fast-talking gambler.

"You . . . you . . ." She glared at him, for once unable to find words.

A wickedly teasing laugh flashed through his eyes so quickly she almost missed it, before his countenance turned sober again. "My lovely Miss Moreland. I first glimpsed you in Denver at Ed West's saloon." He brushed a kiss across her knuckles.

The simple touch jolted into her heart.

Somebody coughed politely nearby and Charlotte blushed hotly, then immediately, silently cursed her own inexperience with flirtatious men. If only she was back at the poker table where she knew the rules and how to dampen the risks.

"Evening, Garland." Talbot drew out every syllable as if he was rolling out a welcome mat. He turned Charlotte with a dancer's grace to face the newcomer. "My dear, may I present you to Sam Garland, my right-hand man? Sam, this is Miss Moreland."

"A pleasure to meet you, Mr. Garland." She extended her hand to the big man, whose neat black frock coat equipped him to disappear into New York's Wall Street far better than into a mining town's howling mob.

"Pleasure is all mine, Miss Moreland." He shook her hand briefly, his grasp nicely calculated to protect her from a potentially crushing grip. Formalities satisfied, he clasped his hands and waited.

A passerby started to approach their circle too closely. Garland's calm visage immediately shifted into a furious glare. The miner held up his hand in apology and stumbled away, seconds before spilling his beer on Talbot. Garland sniffed in dismissal and settled back, his duty accomplished far more efficiently than Johnson's minion had done at the hotel.

"Miss Moreland and I will watch the show from upstairs," Talbot said.

"All the regular boxes are sold, sir." Garland frowned. "The poetry recital is a larger draw than expected."

"No, I meant my box. I don't need to hear Poe's *Raven* again, and my box has curtains, like the others on that floor."

At the top of the house, where the fancy women plied their wares. She'd never thought a single night's folly would dump her irredeemably into their class.

Charlotte kept her expression bland and unreadable, despite the urge to run screaming into the storm outside. Thank God for the discipline so painfully learned in Boston's finest finishing schools. It had proved useful in more than one mining town.

"Of course, sir." Garland carefully avoided looking directly at her. "Your box is ready, just the way it always is."

"Excellent. Please have Russell send up a pot of his special coffee."

Not liquor to numb her resistance?

"Certainly, sir," Garland agreed. "Anything else?"

"I don't want to have any trouble tonight."

"Sir?" Garland looked nonplussed, clearly startled by an unusual statement.

"If anyone's temper should be frayed by visitors—such as the mayor's staff—don't let them blow off steam in here." Talbot's voice was no less deadly for all its quiet.

He'd set his staff to guard against Johnson's men? For her?

Surprise, then delight, raced through Garland's eyes. But when he spoke, he was steady as a deacon making vows. "Whatever you say, boss. Hair Trigger Palace will be polite as a Boston dowager's front parlor."

"Thank you. Come along, my dear." Talbot urged her into a walk and she went willingly, after nodding goodbye to Garland. Her feet had thawed enough to obey her, although she couldn't have carried off a full-dress ball amid Boston's finest circles.

He led her up the main stairs to the second level, where well-dressed men and women leaned forward to watch the show from boxes the equal of any in London or Boston. There was less tobacco smoke here above the tables, and Charlotte could see the singer for the first time.

A man shoved his way into the center of the tables below and turned to look around. His scarred face was brutal under his bowler and Charlotte shivered when his gaze sliced across her and Talbot.

"Nine-Fingers Isham," her escort muttered and glanced down at her. "Johnson's man."

The intruder started to charge toward the stairs but Garland blocked his path. Isham tried to object but the Palace's man insisted on taking the newcomer over to the bar, close to two burly bartenders. A big tankard of beer appeared and Isham glared at it.

A moment later, he grasped the handle and leaned back to ostentatiously stare at a single, empty box high above. Garland took up his station beside him, equally polite, equally deadly.

Charlotte's hair lifted off the nape of her neck. If she moved an inch away from Talbot, she'd lose his protection and that of his men. God help her.

"Don't worry, Miss Moreland. He can only watch, as long as you're with me," Talbot said under his breath.

"Thank you," Charlotte replied, equally softly.

Talbot nodded in response to eager greetings from audience members and continued upward, still lightly holding her hand and carrying her carpetbag. They emerged into a much narrower, but equally clean, hallway. One side was painted in vibrant green, while the other offered a series of silk curtains in between gilded columns. Chinese lanterns swayed over narrow Oriental carpets. A man groaned happily from within one curtained box and a woman chuckled inside another.

Charlotte twitched her skirts away from the fluttering drapes, as if they might speed up the frissons gliding across her skin. Walking with Jeremiah Holbrook had never felt like this.

On the other hand, her escort took no notice—of either the goings-on in the boxes or the numerous bullet holes in the walls. He growled at a candle that had recently been shot in half and stopped to put the pieces back in the wall sconce.

"Does that happen often?" she ventured to ask.

"Nightly. We check on all of them frequently." He ground his heel hard into an ember until it vanished. "It's why I only use candles, not kerosene."

"You'd have had a fire." She couldn't keep the horror out of her voice. If it wasn't built of brick, such a conflagration would turn this building into a bonfire within a handful of minutes. And afterward the block and the town, unless the citizens turned lucky in the wind and their ability to pump water and deliver it. Even big cities like Chicago and Boston had burned to the ground within the past few years.

"That doesn't happen to what I care about, not if I can help it." He glanced at her, his expression as harsh as when he'd faced Johnson.

"It has before."

"Yes." His tone slammed the door on any additional questions. Not that she'd have inquired—she'd already gone further than Western manners deemed polite. Angering somebody who wielded guns so easily would be very unwise, no matter how ready he seemed to protect her.

He twitched open the curtain to the last box at the end and she preceded him inside.

It was a cozy nook, where the carpets were deep enough to block the floor's chill. A leather settee, large enough for two big men to sit on with a jewel-toned, velvet quilt tossed across its back, occupied the center. A small charcoal stove offered cheerful warmth from one corner, while a single polished brass spittoon hid in another for the obviously few guests who'd dare chew tobacco.

One man's comfort ruled here, not careless ribaldry like the floors below or brazen sensuality like the corridor outside. It hardly looked suitable for somebody who spent hours practicing with those heavy, heavy guns in his hands, either. This was graceful and elegant, like a showpiece created for somebody bred from generations of blue blood.

Charlotte was more confused—and more attracted—by her protector than ever.

He set her carpetbag down in the niche beside the proscenium arch above the stage.

"May I take your mantle?" he offered. "It must still be quite damp from the snow."

"Oh yes, of course." She shrugged it off, into his waiting hands. Faint wisps of steam drifted up from the fine wool to merge into the tobacco smoke from below where the opera singer was bowing to raucous applause.

He handed it outside, between the curtains.

"May I take your bonnet, too?"

She hesitated. It would be scandalous to uncover her head when she was so utterly at his mercy, especially when so many respectable women here wore their bonnets. And yet it was her sole bonnet. If she was to salvage its ribbons and feathers from their current bedraggled mess so she could leave town without appearing the fool, her headgear must be dried quickly.

Damn.

She bit her lip and unpinned the once-fashionable bit of millinery with almost military speed. Her hands were steadier when she untied its bow and handed it to him.

"My servants will see to it. They've restored far more damaged clothing." He shook the bonnet slightly, as if he could envision its former Parisian flair.

"May I see your cheek? If it's badly injured, I can send for a doctor—"

"No!"

"Are you sure?"

Her eyes met his in the drifting golden light. He looked predatory, like a hunting cat. "Who hurt you?"

"Why are you so eager to find out?" she parried, unsure of the look in his eyes.

"It would give me the best excuse to destroy the man who did it to you," he replied calmly.

Her jaw dropped. For the first time in three years, trust blossomed in the pit of her stomach. Perhaps she might not be alone and helpless any longer.

"It was Simmons," she said cautiously.

"That brute!" She didn't like Talbot's smile at all but it was comforting, too, mainly because his fury wasn't directed at her. "It'll take a little extra planning but I can dispose of him."

"Honestly, I'm just a little bruised." Suddenly, she didn't want her unusual protector injured. "I can move my mouth easily and . . ."

He lifted her chin gently to inspect her cheek under the hanging lantern. His lean, strong fingers were very disturbing, perhaps because she wanted them to linger.

"Besides, I don't think you can completely blame Mr. Simmons," she babbled on. "Johnson shoved me into his room."

"The mayor." Her escort's dark eyes flickered but his grip stayed protective.

"He gave me the hotel room beside Simmons. Showed me through the connecting door, which didn't lock, and . . ." She closed her eyes against the memories.

"What about the hotel manager?" Talbot's voice rasped in his throat.

"Ran away before then."

"Damn." The word was very soft. "I swear to you nothing like that will happen again," he said strongly. "You're right about the bruising. I can have a poultice fetched if you need it, but otherwise I suspect you mostly need a hot drink to take away the chill."

"What haven't you seen and done in here?" Charlotte whispered. While she'd spent an eternity in gambling saloons over the past three years, she'd never thought much about concert saloons, their far rarer brethren.

"I sell pleasure—but nothing illegal. I don't run a brothel and I'm not a pimp. Adults rent space from me to pursue entertainment of their choosing." He set her bonnet atop a coat tree. "Mining towns are frequented by hard men."

"And dangerous." As she knew all too well.

He draped the velvet quilt over her shoulders. "But they can be very profitable, if you're prepared."

In the distance, the singer curtsied once more and ran offstage. The audience rustled and glasses clinked more loudly. "Hurry up with that red-eye," somebody demanded.

There was a soft knock and a bartender appeared. Charlotte quickly took her place on the settee, determined to appear an experienced woman of the world no matter what her hammering pulse said.

Talbot offered her a cup of coffee, laced with cream and speckled with crimson and gold. She sniffed cautiously, then again far more happily. "What is it? It smells delightful."

"Coffee with chocolate and spices. It's a Mexican recipe." He sat down beside her with his own cup.

A very tall, cadaverously thin man strutted onto the stage and fingered his lapels.

"Yeehaw!" somebody yelled down below and a torrent of gunfire erupted into the ceiling.

Charlotte cringed. She could endure one or two shots, however close, but a fusillade sounded like a massacre.

"Gentlemen!" Talbot shouted over the railing. "The next

man to welcome our guest like that gets a taste of his own medicine."

Charlotte managed to crack open her eyes, amazed she hadn't dived under the settee. Where had she gained such confidence?

Talbot had a shotgun at his shoulder, as did Garland and every bartender.

There were a few apologetic coughs, then pistols disappeared back into holsters. The rowdier miners sat back down and the more cautious members of the audience emerged from under their seats or behind their boxes' paneling. The actor poked his head onto the stage from behind a sturdy column, like a wary tortoise investigating the early spring air. Polite applause greeted him this time and he sauntered forth more cautiously.

Silence fell when he reached the stage's center. Even the bartenders' usual clatter as they passed fresh drinks disappeared. The actor swept the crowded room with his pale eyes as if he could see through the darkness into everyone's soul.

" 'The Raven' by Edgar Allan Poe," he announced and a woman loosed a long, heartfelt sigh of anticipation.

Talbot shoved his shotgun under the settee. Only Charlotte's fast action kept her skirt from being pinned by it.

"Once upon a midnight dreary / While I pondered weak and weary," the actor intoned. His hands inscribed circles as if casting spells upon his enthralled audience.

"Do you want to listen or may I close the drapes?" Talbot asked softly. "I doubt you want to see Isham."

"Please shut them," Charlotte assured him. He sealed them carefully, then joined her on the settee. "Besides, I enjoy Shakespeare better or even Burns. Do you like Shakespeare?" she asked, desperate to make conversation in these very intimate confines.

"Very much. My mother used to read his sonnets and

plays to me." He took a sip of coffee, his lean length comfortably relaxed across the leather.

"His sonnets, too?" Charlotte blinked at him. She could believe that a woman would teach her son to cherish the plays, since those were commonly performed. But the sonnets were frippery bits of rhyming words, more often relegated to the feminine sphere.

"When to the sessions of sweet silent thought / I summon up remembrance of things past . . ."

Talbot's rich drawl, far more attractive than the actor's melodramatic tones, faded and he shrugged. "She was an Anson of Chillington and wanted her only child to enjoy English poetry."

"Chillington? Earl Chillington?" Charlotte came up onto her knees to look at her companion more closely.

"He's a second cousin, who received the house and title in England, while my mother inherited everything else."

"A fortune," guessed Charlotte, backed by generations of banking instincts.

"She brought it as dowry to her Southern marriage." He waved that off and swallowed more of his richly spiced drink, as if for solace. "The War wiped it out." He swirled his coffee for a moment before answering the question Charlotte hadn't asked. "My mother died only a year after the fighting started."

"I'm very sorry." Charlotte dared to put her hand over his. His expression carried such anguish, similar to her father's on the rare occasions when he mentioned her mother.

"It was better that way. The Low Country's climate was very hard on her and we still had enough property to keep her comfortable." Ancient pain snarled behind his gritted teeth before his fingers laced through hers.

"My mother was from Scotland," Charlotte offered and shifted so she could sit next to him. She could at least offer the simple comfort of her presence, even if he didn't want to say much about his mother. "Father made me memorize Mr. Burns's poetry in her memory."

"Of a' the airts the wind can blaw," Talbot began and cocked an eyebrow at her.

"I dearly like the west," Charlotte finished triumphantly.

"Here's to poetry, Ace." He lifted his cup to hers.

"Charlotte," she corrected him, the first time she'd freely given anybody her real name in three years.

A true smile warmed his eyes and broadened his mouth. It changed his face from a sculptor's masterpiece to a study in sensuality. "Justin," he offered in exchange.

"Justin," she agreed and clinked her cup against his. Maybe it wouldn't be too dangerous to take shelter from a blizzard at his side. At least if she could forget about his voice, scent, and body, it would be safe.

Chapter 5

"This is my private bedroom," announced Justin hours later and threw the door open.

Charlotte blinked at a tiny chamber, barely sufficient to hold the wrought iron bedstead, plinth with a basin of water, and straight-backed chair. "Are you sure we can both sleep in here? It's hard to believe you can fit in that bed."

"Normally I sleep at my own house, further up the mountain."

"Where it's quiet."

"Where I can practice gunplay in private," he corrected her.

She hiccupped a breath. She'd forgotten all too fast the true meaning of the pistols riding so easily at his hips.

"I only use this room to snatch a few hours' rest or if the weather's too foul to get home, like tonight."

A cold draft rustled her petticoats, emphasizing his point. She quickly stepped inside and he closed the door behind them, his lean body heating her back like a torch.

"You can undress behind the screen." He tilted his head toward the corner behind them. "After that, the bed's yours. I'll take the floor."

"You'll freeze!"

"Worried, Charlotte?" His white teeth flashed in a rare grin.

She flushed. "Of course. You've been very kind."

"Not my standard reputation," he said wryly. "But I've survived worse than a hard floor under a sturdy roof and I doubt you'd sleep a wink if I were anywhere near you."

She couldn't think of a single response. That she was afraid of his guns? That after an evening spent bantering poetry with him, she didn't know if she was more afraid of his lusts or her own?

She was only certain her single night with Holbrook hadn't equipped her to deal with a man like Justin Talbot.

He gently tucked a stray lock of hair behind her ear. "Go on now, get ready for bed. Everything will work out well."

"Thank you." She tucked herself into the remarkably ample space behind the gilded Japanese screen and started yanking open buttons on her jacket.

When this was over, she would make twice as much money as she'd planned before returning to Boston to lord it over her supercilious stepmother and stepsisters. She'd need the extra concentration and time at the poker tables to stop thinking about Justin Talbot.

Ike Johnson lowered his lantern, satisfied. Talbot was locked down tight inside Hair Trigger Palace with the bitch. Almost as important, the season's first storm hadn't shown any gaps around the Silver King's windows. Maybe this year would be better than the last.

"Where is she?" His salvation's huge frame blocked the hallway, like an avalanche closing off a road. "You promised I'd have her by now."

Shit. Ike's heartbeat hit triple time but none of his nervousness showed in his voice. "She's still with Talbot. You'll have her tomorrow."

"I'll lose an entire day of whipping her." Simmons blew out a disgruntled breath. "You'd better get her to me fast or you won't have your precious charter. Sweetwater can pay me more gold to become the county seat."

"Don't worry about it!" Ike rushed to give an alternate explanation for his outcry than panic. "I'd like to see her under the lash myself. A Northern girl from the same blood as the soldiers who destroyed my home—and an adulterous bitch at that."

"Yes, she deserves to pay. She's a rare treat, unlike whores or anything Sweetwater can offer." Simmons licked his lips and stretched meditatively against the ceiling beams. Their creaking was hidden by the storm howling outside.

"Tomorrow." She'd be destroyed and Talbot would be his friend again. They always made up after a fight.

Simmons's eyes met his, narrow and red in the lamplight. "Better be soon so I'll have full use of her before I leave. I must board the next stage to make my recommendation to the governor."

"You have my word." Ike tossed him a salute like the infantry captain he'd once been. Just a few more hours and he'd rule Wolf Laurel again, with Talbot at his back.

The snow hurled itself against the windows in a fusillade of icy darts. The trees outside beat their branches against each other in a series of thunderous cracks.

Charlotte moaned and pulled the quilt higher over her head. But nothing could stop the wind from howling or her father from yelling at her, again and again.

"How dare you betray yourself and your family by spending hours with such riffraff!" her father yelled at her. They stood in his library, where the books were a distant blur and the velvet curtains rustled unhappily in the drafts. Even the gilded ceiling, normally warm and close, seemed far away and forbidding.

"How dare you call them that?" She glared back at him

from an arm's length away. Her cheek was swollen and bleeding on the inside from where he'd hit her, the first time he'd ever done so. But she'd never allow an outrage to her friends. "You should be ashamed to insult such heroes."

She raised her hands, ready to fight, as Alex Pelham had taught her. Her stepmother and stepsisters' faces swam into focus from behind her father's shoulder, smirking like carnival masks. She ignored them in favor of the greater danger to her heart.

"Insult?" Her father's voice dropped to an icy needle. "You have ruined your reputation and the family's name— and you say I dealt an insult?"

"Absolutely." She folded her arms over her chest. Every inch of her eighteen-year-old frame vibrated with certainty. Anything she could do at the Soldiers' Home paled before the sacrifices those brave men had made for their country. Surely playing card games, even poker, for hours, was respectable when conducted under the head nurse's vigilant eye.

"Go to your room, you impertinent whelp. You will have bread and water until you learn respect for authority," her father snapped, tall and proud in his black broadcloth coat.

She marched out to a chorus of her stepmother and stepsisters' virulent whispers. They grew in volume as she climbed the stairs and the winds screamed louder among the trees. She could no longer hear the little voice in her head urging her to wait and explain everything to her father when they'd both calmed down.

The stairs lengthened and flattened, surrounded by taller and taller walls, until they became the road out of Boston.

She walked on and on, into the blizzard.

The storm howled again and the quilt tightened around her until she couldn't move her arms and legs. She thrashed wildly, fighting off the smothering blur.

"Hush, darling. Hush." A man's rich voice, velvet-edged and totally unlike her father's, pushed back the storm's ice.

"Help me." She reached out, her eyes still shut. She'd had this nightmare so many times.

Strong hands peeled the cloth away from the pillows and smoothed it over her limbs. He gently rolled it down from her face to lay it at the foot of the bed.

She blinked up at Justin. His deep-set eyes were alive with concern under the blizzard's white light.

"Are you okay, Charlotte?" he asked very gently.

She gulped.

"Sounds like no." He sat down on the edge of the bed, looking very different clad only in a nightshirt. "Do you want to talk about it?"

She shook her head violently. Talk about where she came from—or her own stubborn stupidity in not giving her father an explanation?

"That's okay with me, sugar. A person's past is their own business out here in the West."

She shivered. The big quilt was a long way away. So were the secrets of whatever forces had created Justin Talbot.

"Are you cold?" he asked quickly.

"You must be." She started to shiver. "Perhaps we could share the bed."

"Are you sure?" He cocked his head at her.

"Just for warmth?" she offered. Surely she could brazen out a single night with Justin Talbot. He hadn't shown any signs of interest in her. Even if he did, it wouldn't be the worst thing that could happen and she had her experience with Jeremiah to inform her.

"Very well." He joined her under the remaining covers in a sleek movement, graceful as a cat diving into its den. His torso was warm under the fine linen but his extremities made snow-covered rocks seem cozy.

His foot brushed Charlotte and she yelped in surprise.

"Sorry," he muttered and stiffened, taking himself away from her.

"No, please." She caught him by the shoulders and pressed herself closer. If she'd been bold enough to share a bed with him, she could be honest enough to share her limbs' warmth.

"Charlotte." He wrapped his arms around her and relaxed slightly, enough that their toes brushed against each other. "You are full of surprises. Thank you."

"You're welcome." She dared to rest her head on his shoulder, since he didn't seem to want to mention the erection that pressed against her thighs. Her breasts were warmer than the rest of her body, more than his proximity would account for.

She stirred restlessly but said nothing.

"Still upset by the nightmare?" Justin's voice was a rich, sensual thread in the darkness.

"Uh—yes, a little." Could she say she'd been picturing him more the dream's horrific denizens? Better not.

"Let's try distracting you a bit."

"With what?" she asked, honestly curious. There was no light to play a game by.

He kissed the top of her head.

"I, uh . . ." What would he expect her to do?

"Just cuddle, sugar, that's all." Something in his tone hinted at nighttime comforts that she'd never known before. "All you need to do is relax and think about poetry."

"Okay." She could do that. She settled more comfortably against him.

"What does this make you think of? 'That time of year thou mayst in me behold / When yellow leave, or none, or few . . .'" His drawl slowed to a velvet secret.

" 'Do hang / Upon those boughs which shake against the

cold.' " She chuckled softly and closed her eyes. She'd played this game before. "Shakespeare, Sonnet 73."

"Very good. Your turn."

"Hmm. 'When I consider every thing that grows / Holds in perfection but a moment . . .'"

"You know your Shakespeare." His arms shifted her to a closer, warmer position. The storm's dangers were very far away and his attractions so close. "Sonnet 15."

She dared to slip her fingers into the thick, raw silk of his hair. It glided over her knuckles, potent as a caress. Something stirred deep inside her and her pulse quickened.

"Perhaps you should try a different poet," she mumbled.

"So you can fall asleep while considering the options?" He brushed his lips along her temple.

"Yes, let's try that."

He was silent for a long time. His heart beat heavily against hers before he spoke again.

"I thought once how Theocritus had sung / Of the sweet years, the dear and wished for years . . .'"

"Elizabeth Barrett Browning, *Sonnets from the Portugese,* Sonnet 1," she purred.

"Congratulations," he rumbled.

"Mmhmm," she purred and shifted closer to savor his cherishing. His mouth drifted over her eyes and her cheeks, setting off sparks in her blood.

She stroked his head, echoing the shimmer in her body. He murmured approval and caressed her throat. His lean, strong fingers cupped her head with the same delicacy necessary for spring's first flowers, not a Colt's heavy frame.

Their mouths glided over each other and their lips met. Their kiss was leisurely, sensual, as if they had all the time in the world and the storm raging outside was their personal guardian. But that wasn't enough, not when every taste and texture sent need spiraling out of control. Justin delved deep until Charlotte could think of nothing but him, his mouth joined to hers, and his strong hands creating firebrands under her skin wherever he touched. Her breasts ached under her nightgown until every breath seemed an effort.

Justin lifted his head and she whimpered a protest.

"Patience, sugar, you'll enjoy this, too."

"Promise?"

He raked his teeth lightly over the tendons in her throat. A slug of purest lust jolted through her body and heated her pussy. Her eyes crossed. "Oh, dear Lord," she muttered.

He chuckled and did it again, nibbling on her until she writhed under him with her hands locked on his shoulders. His whipcord-lean body pinned her effortlessly, teasing her with the faint friction of linen trapped between his strong muscles and her sensitive, sweating skin.

She flung her head back and fought to speak against the hunger pulsing in her blood. "When do you plan to end this?"

"Darling, this is only the beginning." His drawl was very thick.

She shot him an incredulous look, then thumped her head back against the pillow.

"We haven't even started to explore the delights below your neck."

"What?" Holbrook had never gone below her throat.

Justin's hand cupped her breast and squeezed lightly. Charlotte arched into him and moaned. Dear Lord, her breasts were so agonizingly sensitive and he felt so wonderful.

"That's my sugar," Justin crooned and slipped his hand inside her nightgown. He caressed her again, plucking and teasing her nipple. Everything centered there—sensation, yearning, pulses of lust between her breast and her heart— and she sank her hands into his back to encourage him.

How could so much of herself have become such a giant, throbbing ache? Even when she was alone and played with herself, she'd never felt anything so intense. Oh, dear heaven, but she was wet.

And when he switched to her other breast but continued to tease the first, it was better still. "Oh, Justin, Justin."

"Sweet, sweet darling, you truly don't know what to do, do you?" he muttered somewhere near her ribcage. She ignored him in favor of rubbing herself over his leg. It wasn't enough for satisfaction but it allowed her hot, aching core some relief.

His big hand stroked the outside of her thigh. She sighed happily and her hips soon matched his rhythm. His fingers shifted to the inside of her leg and slipped higher, teasing and stroking. She tried to thrust down on him but he grunted disapproval. She stopped, disappointment burning hotter than her pulse.

"Good girl," he crooned. He shifted and suddenly his thigh was outside hers. His warm hand cupped her mound, heating it like sunshine on a winter garden. Even breathing was almost too much to bear when her hips wanted to hurl themselves into his grasp.

She fought for words to plead with. The bedding was long since banished.

"I, ah—oh, Justin!"

His fingers slid in between her legs and he fondled her. He teased her folds, playing with them as if furling and unfurling them was his greatest joy.

"Justin . . ." Charlotte helplessly opened herself completely to him. He rumbled praise and need burned brighter in her.

All that mattered now was feeling his hands and mouth on her, the soft kiss of his clothing when he shifted position over her, the honeyed incitement of his voice building the fire in her blood.

Her hips rocked closer and closer to him. The first blunt finger to enter her was all joy, while the second came with extra cream and teasing.

He thrust his fingers into her hard again and again and her pearl was so sensitive. The brink was so very close.

"More, please more," she sobbed and ground herself down on his hand.

He rubbed her clit hard and simultaneously nipped her shoulder.

Charlotte shrieked and tumbled into rapture, as if she hurled herself down the finest sledding run in the world. Ecstasy flashed through her and her body shook over and over around his hand.

She could barely manage to kiss his shoulder in thanks afterward before she dropped into a sound sleep, just as if she'd trudged home from a long day's sledding.

One eyebrow askew, Justin tucked the bedclothes around his oblivious—Lover? Protégé?

He was the man who'd put that sated look on her face, not her so-called lover, not the idiot who'd ruined her reputation and earned her the title of *adulteress*. No matter what had happened during those days—or hours?—it hadn't taught her body anything about the pleasure to be found with a man. Or perhaps even touched her heart.

She wouldn't forget Justin Talbot.

Somewhere deep inside, his heart shouted *Huzzah!* just as when he'd celebrated more than one cavalry victory during The War.

He had to protect her, for so long as the storm lasted and she was trapped here. But perhaps there'd be opportunities for fun too.

What else could he teach her? What more could they enjoy together? He could stamp himself on her so thoroughly she'd always think of him, no matter whom she was with.

She gave a contented little snore and her fingers curved over his arm. His cock twitched happily.

Justin promptly slid under the covers beside her, a smug grin lurking on his mouth.

Chapter 6

"Good afternoon." Justin nodded to the dozen men crowded into the Crystal Saloon's back room. Its abundance of leather armchairs, red wallpaper, mounted longhorns, and brass spittoons testified to its title of Unofficial Mayor's Office.

He'd dressed up a bit for this call, choosing his best black Stetson and the frockcoat a British tailor had deemed suitable for London's finest clubs. It also hid all his weapons.

"Greetings." Johnson lifted his drink in a polite salute. Nine-Fingers Isham came to attention behind him, quivering like a bulldog eager to fight.

The regulars gaped at Justin over their glasses of beer and whiskey and his eyes narrowed. Damn it, did they think yesterday's quarrel had broken up his partnership with Johnson? It would take more than a few harsh words to destroy ten years of friendship.

"Any other urgent business with the mayor, gentlemen, before next week's council meeting?" Justin swung the door back and forth through a small arc, as if he was playing with a hatchet.

The town councilmen shifted in their seats and glanced uneasily at each other. Drinks slammed down onto tables. Johnson froze with his glass halfway to his mouth, then finished swallowing.

"No? If not, I'm sure you're very busy men, who have many important things to attend to." Justin held the door wide and stood aside so Johnson's sycophants could depart. No audience needed if he was to hear the truth about what had happened between Charlotte, Johnson, and Simmons.

His saddle-partner shot him a hard glare, then rose to shake hands and make polite farewells.

Justin ignored the sideways looks directed at him. Most of Wolf Laurel's so-called *moneyed elite* still hoped to either bribe or intimidate him. Isham departed last, after a final, insolent scan of Justin's weapons.

Their mayor locked the door behind them. "You shouldn't have chased them out like that."

"Thought you'd be bored by their constant prattle about the poker tournament's profits." Justin swung a side chair around and straddled it. "That's in the bag now, since you collected the entry fees yesterday."

"Crap. How'd you know?" His old friend let out a rough bark of laughter and Justin joined in, glad to share a joke.

"Where's Moreland?" The question echoed like an officer's parade ground command. "I thought she'd join the tournament, since she paid the fee."

"No, she's at the Palace's standing poker game, down in the basement." Johnson's intensity made Justin's laughter fade into the same polite wariness he'd show a stranger.

Heavy footsteps moved away from the other side of the door.

Justin cursed the departing eavesdropper privately, then added a warning to his old friend. "She's more than holding her own against the regulars. Half my bouncers are down there enjoying the show and ready to protect her."

The only other genuine Confederate officer in Wolf Laurel looked him in the eye, then folded his lips and walked over to the sideboard. "What'll you have to drink?"

"The usual." There had to be something left of their friendship.

Johnson handed him a glass full of rye whiskey. "Here's to the blue-belly soldiers, without whose attempt to bushwhack you and steal your horse, we'd never have met."

"Here, here." They clinked glasses in their oldest of toasts and drank.

Christ, he hadn't much cared where he went or what he did that autumn when he returned from surrendering to the Yankees. Not after seeing his home's blackened rubble and sere fields, empty of life except vultures and shifting shadows.

He'd spent a few minutes at his father and brothers' graves in Charleston but shrugged off any condolences from their admirers. He had no need to remember bullies and demagogues, who'd spent years stealing their wives' money and whipping up rabble then hiding from the resultant fight. Even at eighteen, he'd been cynically amused that he was the only Talbot to go off to war.

His hand tightened on his glass and he drank again, to honor his English mother. She'd been his closest friend during childhood, even through his wildest escapades. In return, he'd tried to protect her from the world she loathed—where a wife had to make way for her husband's concubines in her house and live with bastards who resembled her husband far more than his legitimate children. Where chains and whippings and screams sounded through the landscape as often as the clink of tea cups settling on fine porcelain and violin music drifting out of the ballroom.

Justin had learned to be glad death had sent her to a better world. The only time he'd almost wished to join her was after he left her grave to head south and west. Surviving five years of war was easier than traveling that wasteland.

He cocked an eyebrow at his old friend.

"Ten years since you first saved my life back in Georgia."

Johnson's vitality had shaken him back to life and given him a new purpose.

"Done the same for any other scarecrow in a gray uniform." Johnson slid the bottle down the table toward Justin and opened another for himself. "You've returned the favor a dozen times since, in good times and bad."

"As have you. Remember that flood on the Rio Grande, back in the San Luis Valley? I thought we'd never get out."

"Or that brawl in Abilene." Johnson whistled. "I remember it every day when we practice gunplay together. An hour or two disappears mighty fast when measured against surviving fights like that."

Justin nodded agreement and took a small sip of whiskey. The bottle must have been a gift, since his friend normally preferred far better brands.

"How's the hotel business?"

"Couldn't be better." Johnson glanced at him in surprise. "Between it, my two saloons, and the dry goods store, I should make back my investment within two years."

Too damn slow for a mining town that was likely built on a glory hole and would disappear the moment the ore did.

"Hey, pardner, if you need a loan to tide you over—"

"No!" The word rang through the room, sharper than an ice saw.

Justin rocked back in surprise, then leaned his arms on the chair back to study his old pal. They'd shared cash through good times and bad before. What was the difference now?

"No," Johnson repeated more politely but his eyes were still angry and ashamed. "Some members of the town council gave me a loan months ago to cover everything I lost in the '73 Panic."

"But—"

"I was doing well before then, beating the damn Yankees

at their own moneygrubbing games. Taking back everything and more than they cost me when they burned my
farm." He laughed bitterly. "From now on, maybe I'll use
your tactics—kill them in their tracks wherever I can."

"Johnson, you know damn well that's not what I do!"

"You're fucking efficient at killing, Talbot, just like
everything else."

Shit, what did Johnson think he was?

Justin pulled his temper back and tried for sanity.

"You know there are too many Yankees to kill them all.
You can't turn a wave by yourself. You have to make peace
with it." The way he laid flowers at a church every year on
his mother's birthday, in honor of everyone he'd left behind
in South Carolina. Or drinking sherry every Christmas, in
hopes one day he'd be respectable enough to celebrate it
again with his mother's cousins at Chillington Castle. Keeping the present alive and building for the future was more
important than taking revenge for the past.

"I want to use the bastards like manure, Talbot. Spread
them like shit over my fields." Johnson splashed more
whiskey into his glass.

Justin went back to cash, his saddle-partner's favorite
subject.

"Everything you lost in the Great Panic? Look, you know
we've shared the shirts off our backs before. Let me give
you the money to cover that and you won't have to worry
about repaying strangers."

Johnson told him the amount.

Justin gaped at him. "That's enough to buy half of Denver."

"Certainly all of its saloons."

"I can still give you the cash." He'd have to sell—Christ,
what wouldn't he have to sell? But Johnson had been more
of a big brother to him than his long-dead blood kin had
ever bothered to be.

"No, I don't have to make payments on the loan until next year. Just shut up and listen to me, will you?"

Justin glared at him. Inside, he kept on calculating how to pay off his friend's debts.

"Talbot, you're always so damn conservative."

"Am not!" He slapped his thigh for emphasis.

"Are so—at least when it comes to making sure no fool can ruin your property."

Justin flung up his hand in agreement.

"We invested our money separately and I put mine with the fancy folks on Wall Street. Bragged, too, about how well it was doing—until the Panic hit. And every penny vanished."

Justin couldn't deny that. He was still glad he'd kept quiet back then, too.

"Didn't know what I was going to do until after we'd been here a few months." Johnson broke the awkward silence. "A delegation from the town council offered me the job of mayor with the loan to clear my mind. Said they wanted somebody who'd stick around for a while and I said yes."

"You never told me."

"Didn't think you'd like me making a deal that I could get out of just by watching the town melt into the hillside when the ore gave out."

"No, I wouldn't have." He'd have done his best to wring Johnson's neck.

"Yeah, sometimes that Palmetto Aristocracy upbringing gets in the way of your common sense."

Justin took another small sip of whiskey. Did the glass's jagged pattern reflect his old friend's true personality? "What did your new pals think I'd say to the deal?" he asked when he could trust his voice again.

"Why would they worry about that?" Johnson stared at him over a fresh drink. "We've always worked together. I do the talking and you help carry the deals out. You're more valuable than dudes like Isham because you frighten people better."

Shit. Justin closed his eyes. His reputation yawned before him, more appalling than an ice fall's thousand-foot drop.

"What about our talk of retiring someplace where guns are not necessities?" he asked, when he could trust his voice better.

"That silly daydream? I always told you that if you stuck with me, I'd build you an empire, not castles in the air." He raised his glass to an engraving of a Confederate veteran's shattered farmstead. Then he poured the golden liquor down his throat, his eyes shut in ecstasy.

Justin drummed his fingers for a moment, then shoved the decanter away. Neither memories of his childhood home's burned-out remains, nor alcohol, spurred him as much as today's problems. And honor.

"When will you hand the woman over?" Johnson caught the decanter easily and refilled his glass.

"I won't." Justin put down his glass, careful not to break the fragile crystal. Now they were getting down to this conversation's true meat. Just a little longer and he could ask what had happened when Charlotte met Simmons.

"I thought we just agreed that neither of us like big fights." Johnson's Georgia drawl grew thicker.

"We did. But she's a woman and I won't let Simmons have her." Shit, Simmons had hit her, and she hadn't even been with him five minutes.

"I don't understand you. It's not as if your morals are sunshine bright when it comes to bed partners."

Justin gritted his teeth and reminded himself to stay calm. He and Johnson never had the same tastes, which was why they didn't share the same whores. "All of my lovers were willing. Miss Moreland is a lady and wishes nothing to do with Simmons."

"It's only for a few days."

"She'd be lucky to stay alive. No."

He watched his friend rapidly swirl his drink in his glass until it resembled an abyss, rather than a lamp-lit cloud.

"Why are you doing this, Johnson?" Justin dropped his voice to a lower pitch, as if his old friend was a skittish horse to be coaxed through a winter pass. "Why are you pushing so hard to get Simmons's attention?"

"I told you—he can make Wolf Laurel the county seat."

"Yeah, half the council is parading for his attention. If it happens, hordes of miners will come here to register their claims and spend their money."

"They'll use my hotel—and visit your Hair Trigger Palace. We'll be rich. Even after mining dies out, loggers and ranchers will spend fortunes here."

"But Sweetwater is a better bet to become county seat. It's on the other side of the pass and it has better roads. The railroads already love it so its citizens have more money for bribes and chicanery in the legislature. How can you stand against it?"

"By giving Simmons the only bribe he can't find anywhere else." The veteran fighter's jaw set hard. "A beautiful white woman he can seduce—"

"Flog!" Justin pictured Charlotte's fragile white skin shattered and bleeding under the whip, while she screamed and screamed . . .

The other Southerner shrugged indifferently. "Doesn't matter. She's an adulteress who sleeps with married men."

"One man." Justin surged onto his feet. "Nobody knew he was married until his harridan of a wife arrived to drag him back to Cincinnati."

"So what?" Johnson matched him and glared at him from only a few feet away. "Moreland crossed the line and she's now a fallen woman. She doesn't deserve protection."

Justin's hands twitched over his guns and he fought to control his temper.

"If your sister," he said as coolly as possible, "was in the same predicament—"

The former infantry officer knocked him down with a hard right hook to the jaw.

Justin fell over the straight-backed chair, which slammed into the side table. Glasses and decanters rattled, and alcohol sloshed out.

Where the hell had that blow come from? Damn it, Johnson always got in the first strike.

He sprang back up onto his feet, more than willing to fight.

"My sister was never a Northern whore, lifting her skirts for married men!" his saddle partner roared.

Oh hell, he couldn't duel over a long-dead female's honor. He managed a curt bow. "My apologies."

"Accepted." Johnson's nod was even briefer. "You'd better leave now before I kill you."

If you can . . . Justin glared back at him. They'd never fought each other, not even in the wildest barroom brawls.

"Don't send Isham and the boys to fetch Miss Moreland, Johnson. Ten years of friendship won't stop me from shedding blood to defend her." Wolf Laurel's mayor wouldn't act against him but he'd damn sure send his bully boys to wreck anyone and everything else.

Justin closed the door as softly as he'd draw his knife from its sheath. Then he ran through the blizzard for the Hair Trigger Palace.

He'd long since stopped believing in any god merciful enough to keep eavesdroppers from doing the worst harm imaginable.

Chapter 7

Charlotte shook out her bustle and swiveled her hips one last time to make sure her skirts rustled well within the tiny powder room. It was always tricky to hide money within her crinoline's wire hoops. Placing coins and greenbacks inside small silk purses was easy, even if she had to be careful not to let anything clank. The difficulty came in balancing everything so that her wool skirts and petticoats still floated over the floor like an ocean wave. Lurching like drunken sailors would shout what lay underneath.

Today's take was good but not enough to overflow her other hiding places in her corset or jacket. Somehow the Palace's regulars had seemed more like friends than opponents, especially after Justin—no, Talbot—had introduced them to her by name. She'd competed for the joy of the game, rather than strip them of funds and speed her return to Boston.

It had felt so natural, just like waking up to the coffee he'd brought. No embarrassment, just conversation—and the growing sensation she needed to go somewhere else soon, lest she sink roots here.

Which she couldn't.

She scanned herself in the mirror over the washbasin and her mouth reluctantly slid into a smile. Justin would have to clean this room more often. The hallway outside, which ran between the poker parlor and the wine cellar, also offered bedrooms for rent to a few very expensive courtesans. It was a civilized space, painted green and decorated like a European hotel. One of their clients had used this latrine afterward to shave—messily.

She'd get to tease Justin, the king of cleanliness and forethought.

She gathered up her handbag containing her grubstake and sallied out, feeling much better about her prospects.

The moment she stepped into the hallway, a man's rough hand clamped over her mouth. He yanked her against his body, his other big paw manacled around her wrists, and started to drag her down the hallway. Nine-Fingers Isham matched strides with her abductor in a miasma of sweat and whiskey, his heavy Colt pointed toward the poker parlor.

Charlotte's escort, an older gentleman uncommonly good with both knives and jokes, lay crumpled and motionless just inside the bedroom door opposite. A thin trickle of crimson smeared his once-pleasant countenance. He'd been injured trying to help her, simply because a friend had asked him to.

Sheer rage flashed through her, first heating then chilling her thoughts. By God, she wasn't going to stand aside and wage her battles with words anymore, no matter what etiquette said about ladies' behavior.

She bit down on the filthy digit in her mouth. Her captor grunted, his thin mustache twitching like the rat he resembled, but he didn't release her. He was almost running toward the wine cellar and its stairway to the Hair Trigger Palace's back door.

She ground her teeth harder. This time, her captor's grip loosened slightly.

She scrabbled for purchase in the thin carpet and tried to pull away.

"God damn it," Nine-Fingers cursed, "keep the bitch quiet. Get the ether on her, fast."

"Charlotte?" Justin called from ahead. "Charlotte, where are you?"

Two men against one—and her as a hostage in the middle? What options would Justin have? None.

Charlotte closed her eyes and sank her teeth into her enemy with all her strength, the way her friends at the Soldiers' Home had attacked enemy battlements in the dead of winter.

He howled and she bit harder, traveling past reeking flesh and stinking blood. She needed to protect Justin so these brutes wouldn't shoot him over her head.

He screamed again and yanked his hand out of her mouth, then hurled her away from him. She slid down the fern wallpaper and landed, her skirts a crumpled mass, between the doors to the courtesans' bedrooms.

The lighting was better down here than on the floors above, good enough to see Justin poised at the foot of the narrow stairs with Colts drawn and murder in his eyes.

She could hear pounding from the hallway's other end.

"Put down your guns or we'll kill her." Nine-Fingers stirred her hem with his boot. His cohort shook blood off his finger and moved to his side.

Charlotte cautiously came up onto her knees. She needed a weapon in order to help.

"You'll never get out of here with her," Justin countered. "My men will kill you."

"Those big sturdy doors you're so fond of? We locked the one leading to the poker parlor. At this hour, nobody's looking for refills from the cellar so they won't use the back door." Nine-Fingers sniggered. "No, looks to me like it's two against one."

Oh, dear Lord, may this work . . .

Charlotte hurled her purse, with all of her grubstake's precious gold in it, at the rat's legs. It thudded into his boot and he jumped into the air. When he came back down, the long, corded handles wrapped around his ankles. He stumbled and fell onto the floor, cursing viciously as he fought to free himself.

Now Justin only faced one man's guns.

Nine-Fingers fired first, almost directly over her head. Justin's gun belched fire—and the brute crumpled onto the floor, his throat a crimson wreck. Thunder deafened her ears and black smoke filled the hall.

The rat-faced man's scarlet fingers grabbed for her out of the smoky haze, followed by his gun.

She screamed—and Justin fired again. The hand twitched, then fell back.

Justin pulled her up onto her feet and into his arms. Charlotte clung to him, trembling as if she'd never walk again. Her heart was beating faster than the winds still racing around the roof high above.

She'd encountered violent death before, since her arrival in the Colorado mining country. But this was somehow far worse than seeing another poker player die at the table across from her. This time, the danger had pointed directly at someone she cared deeply about, rather than a stranger.

Her protector pressed kisses to her hair. It took several moments before she realized he was shaking as much as she.

"Justin, darling, I'm fine."

"The blood?" He ran his thumb lightly across her lips. Her pulse turned hot, rather than cold with terror. "By everything's that holy, if a drop of it's yours, I will—"

"It's all his. I bit through his hand."

Justin continued to stare at her mouth. "Damn, but I was terrified."

"Justin." She wet her lips. Her hands twitched with the need to hold him. He had to stop looking at her like this.

"Charlotte." He kissed her ravenously and she answered him the same way, intent on reclaiming every bit of joy she'd so nearly lost. Holding him was like holding life itself—strength, heat, the headlong rush to share. Even the hot shaft rising between his legs promised ecstasy, rather than frustration and pain.

His tongue plunged between her lips, enticing her. She rose onto her toes to come closer. *More, please, more . . .*

A door slammed open behind them.

Justin whirled and placed himself between her and the intruders. An instant later, he relaxed and Charlotte dared to peek around him.

"Sorry for the interruption, boss." Garland touched his hat and tucked his shotgun back into its sling. "Thought you might need some help down here. Happy to see I was wrong."

"Glad you came."

"Sorry we didn't make it sooner." Garland's face flushed to a dull crimson. "Didn't expect trouble, not with—"

"The latrine being only two steps away from the poker parlor? And me taking such a ridiculously long time in there?" Charlotte came all the way around Justin to help protect Garland with an explanation for the attack.

Justin nodded curtly. "Isham must have come through the back door, then waited in one of the bedrooms. We'll do better next time."

"Damn right," Garland agreed. His expression said he expected rough words from his employer later. "We'll start by doubling the fire patrols. Johnson likes to watch things burn."

A muscle throbbed in Justin's cheek but he agreed.

Charlotte glanced up at him, then moved a little further away from the dead men littering the floor, victims of Johnson's greed.

Justin was fighting his best friend. God alone knew if he or anyone else would die.

Chapter 8

The conjurer bowed again, flourished his two very-much-alive rabbits, then left at a brisk trot. Guards sauntered onto the stage with pistols prominently displayed.

Last night's poetic sensation strolled out, still looking as if he hadn't eaten in a year. This time, the crowd cheered and clapped instead of shooting holes in Justin's new tin ceiling.

"Have you changed your mind about the actor?" He glanced at Charlotte. "The opera singer and cancan dancers follow him."

He rotated the bill of fare every evening for variety in order to attract a fresh audience to fill the Palace's non-stop hours. So far tonight, she'd enjoyed the trained dogs, a cornet soloist, and the conjurer.

"And listen to the audience shout 'Nevermore!' again, every time he cues them with 'Quoth the raven'?" She shook her head with an exaggerated shudder. "I thank you, no. I'd almost prefer to stare at more snowflakes."

Justin chuckled.

Outside, the air was clean and soft under a full moon and the storm's last snowfall. Here in his box at the Hair Trigger Palace, the air smelled of lavender and the faint, lingering wonder of her pleasure. The world beyond Wolf Laurel would reach them tomorrow and the stagecoach would arrive within a day or so afterward.

What would he do when she was gone? Survive. He needed to send her out of the mining town to get her away from its mayor's attacks.

His hand wasn't entirely steady when he pulled the drapes shut. Sitting down beside her felt too much like coming home.

"Thank you for saving my life this afternoon." She kissed her fingers and laid them against his cheek.

"I'm sorry you were abducted. If I'd had any idea that would happen, I'd never have left." He caught her hand and pulled her close.

"Of course you had to go alone. You needed to speak to your friend." She leaned confidingly against his chest, for all the world as if she still trusted him to look after her. "It was my fault those brutes had a chance to capture me. If I hadn't spent so long primping, they wouldn't have had time to arrange their ambush."

He hugged her lithe form a little nearer, thinking her precious as the first taste of spring. She murmured a little noise of agreement that lifted his soul.

The couple in the box next door were chanting Edgar Allan Poe's verses, together with the actor.

Justin forgot about them and the rest of the audience with the ease of long practice, and to protect his sanity. He'd memorized "The Raven" in childhood, long before he'd learned how well its performance filled concert saloons.

"You need to leave town soon," he told his darling.

"Can Johnson mount an attack again so quickly?"

"It's the only way to keep you safe." His heart lurched away from the thought. After so many years of fighting to save the man's life—and so much shared laughter—he couldn't simply take Johnson out as an obstacle and plant him in Boot Hill. Doing so would irredeemably stain his soul.

But Charlotte had brought joy and light into his life. He couldn't risk losing her now.

She hesitated, then nodded.

"I don't want anybody else to die on my behalf—and I don't want to destroy your friendship with him."

"It's already gone on his side."

"Are you sure? What about you? Can you forget ten years that quickly?"

He hesitated, then shook his head.

Her quick look of sympathy pierced his heart.

He cuddled her close, letting her pulse sing to his. More than anything else, he needed to know she was safe. Would he ever forget how helpless she'd looked crumpled on the floor at her kidnappers' feet? And then how neatly she'd hurled that missile to knock one off balance?

Where could he send her?

"You should go back to Boston, not stay on the poker circuit."

"That's impossible!"

"Why? Were you convicted of a crime?"

"No, but—"

"Then there's still a place for you there. You'd be safer beside the Atlantic Ocean than here in the Rockies, with Simmons offering a price on your head."

"My father said I was a slut."

"What the hell?" How could her parent be that deluded? Justin didn't know whether to plot a lecture or a drowning.

"My stepmother said all the time I spent at the Soldiers' Home, tending the war veterans, was actually loose conduct." Charlotte flushed.

The darling probably didn't know how to act immoral with a multitude of men. Her stepmother needed to be strangled.

"The jealous bitch! And he believed her?"

Charlotte nodded. "We had a dreadful fight and I stormed out. I haven't been back in three years."

"Did you ever offer an explanation?" He caught her hands.

"No, I was too angry."

Sounded like all the times he and his father had fought when he was eighteen.

"Since then, I've concentrated on making money." She looked up at him from under gold-tipped eyelashes, the same color as all the success she'd enjoyed. "I plan to return to Boston as a wealthy woman and make my stepmother and stepsisters jealous."

"Ah." Now that definitely sounded like the relationship between him and his half-brothers—nothing but vicious competition every inch of the way. Regrets for what could never be regained stirred within him.

"Honey, is your father still alive?" He kissed Charlotte's hands.

"Yes. I'd have seen his obituary if not."

Ah, the unconscious arrogance of class and fortune which expected to see their important announcements widely distributed.

Justin closed his eyes for a moment to push away ancient grief. The old days were gone. Like wintertime, they'd passed by to be replaced by the new ways. No man could stand in the path of change.

"Charlotte, you should make peace with him while you're both still alive. You need to make the most of the time you have together."

"No! Do you know what he said? Do you know how he insulted the brave soldiers who fought for this country?"

Justin's mouth twisted wryly. Was he about to defend blue bellies, the long-hated Union troopers who'd destroyed his world? Or could he finally live in peace with them, the way Lee had surrendered his sword at Appomattox?

"Darling, I'm sure if you speak gently to him, you can make him see reason, even about that." Good, he hadn't actually defended any blue bellies.

"But . . ." Her chin still jutted defiantly.

"Family is worth fighting for, at all costs, even if it means swallowing a little pride."

She tapped her fingers as if seeking a new argument.

"You know I lost my mother to The War. I lost everyone else, too—including my father, my two elder brothers and their families, even my cousins." His voice had turned soft, his drawl thicker than if he stood once again in Charleston. "I'd give anything to go back and have one more day with my father or brothers. Or sail down the Ashley River again and see Northwick Plantation rising fresh and clean from the gardens."

He halted. He'd said too much, far more than he'd told anyone. Even Johnson only knew he was a South Carolina veteran who'd lost everything to The War. The Georgia native preferred to dwell on his own lost farm and assume Justin's heart ached for the same simple reasons.

"Oh, Justin, I'm so sorry." Charlotte leaned up and kissed his cheek.

He turned his head and captured her sweet mouth. She tasted of youth and springtime, of hope for a civilized life in which battles were fought with words—and ladies' handbags!—not guns.

She kissed him back sweetly. Her tongue moved more confidently today than yesterday, as if she too hungered for his taste. Her slender fingers kneaded his shoulders like an eager little cat seeking warmth and pleasure.

He rumbled encouragement and ran his hands down her back. Dear God, but she was deliciously strong under that delicate frame. Damn her corset, he wanted to taste skin. Here and now, in a public place, not in a bedroom's respectable privacy.

He needed her acceptance of his wildness, of his speed with guns, which matched her own dangerous skill with cards.

The thought made his blood heat under his long black coat and starched shirt. He left her delectable mouth to nuzzle her sweet temples and eyelids. Tonight he could see all of her, unlike last night in his bedroom when she'd been a sorceress glimpsed under floating, icy shadows. Now he could savor the sweet flush that rose when he suckled her lip, and anticipate how she flung her head back to encourage his attentions to her neck.

Ah yes, her beautiful throat. Long, white, flexible as a swan. She uttered the most delicious little sighs, too. She made him groan until he had to kiss her there even more often, so their neighbors wouldn't hear him.

Her breasts rose against his chest, fast and urgent like her hot breath ruffling his hair. "You're wearing too many clothes," she whispered into his ear.

"So are you, even if you don't have a hat." He drew back slightly to fill his eyes with her beauty.

"Are you sure you want to do this? Someone might hear us."

"The curtains are closed. It's quiet." She pointed her chin in the air, defying him to contradict her.

"At the moment." He kissed the inside of her wrist. "Until I do this . . ." He glided his teeth over her delicate tendons and she moaned.

"Wretch." She blinked at him, her breasts rising and falling faster. "Have you done things like this before?"

"Frequently."

"Ooh!" Her eyes sparkled. "Secrets to learn another day."

She softly stroked his cheek and he leaned his head into the delicate caress.

"Such a close-cropped beard." she whispered. "It's very soft."

"The barber enjoys my regular patronage."

"I enjoy the results, even though they're not fashionable."
Her husky voice hinted at a shared conspiracy. Her slender
finger slipped inside his starched collar. "Do you shave here,
too? Your skin is so smooth—but your chest felt prickly
through your nightshirt."

"Good Lord, didn't that idiot Holbrook teach you anything?"

"We only had one night together. Besides, you're much
more enticing." Color burned in her cheeks and lust flared
in her eyes before she veiled them.

Justin's pulse leaped. Sweet Lord, had she finally, completely forgotten her initial mistrust of him? Maybe he did
stand a chance to win her.

"Well, now, I do feel the temperature rising in here." He
cupped her jaw and stroked the delicate pulse points at the
back of her head. Her hands moved restlessly over his chest
and arms, in the untutored, hungry pattern of an eager yet
uncertain woman. He smiled privately and began to unbut-
ton her jacket. He'd had a lifetime's training for this.

"Take off yours first." She caught his wrist. "I want to
feel more of you."

His eyes opened wide before he gave her a very predatory
grin. "As my lady commands."

Charlotte flushed but held her ground. She watched ea-
gerly as he rapidly stripped off his coat and hung it on the
coat tree. He turned to face her—and God help him, he
paused nervously. His cock was thick and tense against his
thigh.

Would she spook over his guns or his lust?

Her eyes darkened. "Take your vest off," she whispered
huskily.

His cock surged happily.

He removed the scrap of dark silk even faster than the
heavy broadcloth. But he hung his weapons belt with his

Navy Colts over the leather settee where they'd be within easy reach. Even if they frightened her, he had to protect her.

Now only fine linen hid his chest from her and his cock was shouting its eagerness to greet her.

She held out her hand to him.

"Nevermore!" shouted his damn customers, as if they were speaking about any future for him with Charlotte.

Even so, he kissed her again and her nails raked down his back as if she wanted to devour him. Slowly unbuttoning her fine wool jacket to further increase her excitement took an infinity of discipline.

Ah, but when he finally opened the dove grey cloth to bare her, it was like revealing a flower. Her breasts rose and fell rapidly above her chemise's ruffled lace and ribbon. Her sweet curves blossomed above a blue satin corset which disappeared into her skirt.

His fingers itched to yank it open, peel everything else off, and bury himself within her. Impossible, no matter what the fire hurling through his blood screamed.

Wild and decadent, just as he'd always dreamed.

He kissed her breasts and traced every delectable salty trail of sweat and lust trickling across them. She moaned and pulled his head closer.

He rumbled agreement and strummed her nipples with his fingers until they became sensitive, aching peaks. Damn it, he wanted her to feel that her corset was just as much a prison as his damn trousers were for his cock.

She slid down the settee to lie half under him, flushed and panting, utterly desirable. Lust jolted through his veins, from his lungs to his balls. His chest was hot and tight, and even his shirt's fine linen rasped his suddenly sensitive skin.

He tipped one of her breasts out of its silk and steel cage. She gasped but kneaded his shoulders more deeply, her hands now moving to the same steady beat as her writhing hips—and the blood pulsing in his cock.

"Hurry," she whispered. Her sorceress's voice was husky and irresistible.

It only took a moment for his hand to find its way under her skirts. She was wet, so wet, and her cream hot as the fires of life. She tightened her legs around his finger.

"More." Her eyes met his under their heavy lids. She ran her tongue over her lips before she could force the remaining words out. "Not just your fingers."

"Here? Are you sure?"

Her eyes had drifted shut again, but she nodded vehemently and clumsily tried to pull him closer.

Responsive as she was, what the hell would she be like with more experience? Was there anything she wouldn't do? Better finish this before his cock tried to find out. He'd already dreamed about fucking from behind.

He fumbled for a condom among the shotgun shells in the table drawer. He was only slightly more steady when he unbuttoned his fly and sheathed himself.

"Beautiful," Charlotte murmured and fondled his hip.

His heart stopped. All his blood rushed to the base of his spine, desperate to join her in the most primal manner possible.

An instant later, he knelt between her legs. Some faint vestiges of intelligence were thankful that this settee was damn sturdy and disinclined to creak.

He teased her and fondled her through the slit in her drawers until her pussy was ripe and wet and eager for him. He whispered to her about what he'd do with her pearl when they had more time, about how he'd eat her like the sweetest candy, and savor her juices like the greatest wine.

The scent of her musk rose around him, hot and sweet to match her lavender.

She slid her small hand down his belly and gently pumped his cock. "Justin."

That guttural growl . . .

Why the hell was he waiting?

He gathered her hips in his hands and lifted her onto his cock. By some miracle, probably lust, he entered easily. He tried to pause, to give her time to stretch. But the little sorceress grabbed his shoulders, arched her back, and drove herself straight down onto his cock. Her silky intimate hair tickled his thighs and her cotton drawers rustled across his trousers. Her little white teeth were a sharp crescent on her lower lip.

His heart leaped into his throat. His balls were tucked high and tight, somewhere halfway up his cock. If he moved, he'd blow into orgasm like a sixteen-year-old kid.

She took a deep breath—and lace rustled across her unfettered breasts. He tried to close his eyes.

She took another—and those unskilled, inside muscles of hers shifted around him into a new pattern. This time, he did close his eyes.

She took another, then rose up—and he prayed. He honestly didn't think anybody, even a gentleman, could let her go. She came down on him again with a happy sigh.

This time, he caught her by the waist and heaved himself upward to join her in the most primal stroke possible. She slammed herself back down on him—and climaxed on a long, rapturous sob.

The sound triggered his own rapture. He exploded into ecstasy as if an artillery barrage had erupted throughout his body. Long pulses drummed every last bit of seed down his spine, out of his balls, and into her. Stars burst behind his eyes and he shuddered over and over again.

He was vaguely glad afterward that the cancan's dancers and wild music had hidden any noise they'd made. Of course, if anybody commented, he'd live up to his reputation and show them how unhealthy it was to hurt her feelings.

He was also happy that Charlotte's complete relaxation allowed her to sleep in his arms without any uncomfortable questions or small talk.

Unfortunately, it also allowed him time to think about what he'd lose when she left.

He couldn't keep her here, since Johnson would be coming after her. The stubborn bastard would probably send her on to Simmons even if the brute had already left town.

He couldn't court her for marriage, at least not yet. While she was trapped here in Wolf Laurel, he was the only man who would protect her. If she said yes to his proposal, he'd never be sure she hadn't just been making the best of a bad situation. He didn't want that uncertainty hanging over their heads in the future.

Marriage. Love. Yes.

He smiled faintly. He wanted both. Hell of a time to figure that out about himself.

Charlotte needed to be courted like any properly brought-up young lady he'd introduce to his mother. Pulling that off would be harder than getting her out of town alive.

Ike Johnson kicked his safe's door shut behind him. Damn it, why did Talbot have to be right about how much promoting the poker tournament would cost? He'd lost money on the damn thing, especially after pampering the highfaluting players who were the so-called *main attractions*.

The floor creaked. Ike stiffened, then quickly smoothed on a hospitable smile.

"Evening, Seward." The damn town councilman weighed more than a two-horse hitch—and his mind moved faster than one. He ran the biggest bank in town and held Ike's loan.

"Evening, Johnson." He probably thought his flat Ohio accent sounded powerful. "Do you have the charter yet?"

"No, but I expect to have it before Simmons leaves." Ike ground his teeth. His father always said not to yell when stating the obvious but sometimes that was fucking hard. "If he gave it to us before he makes a thorough inspection, the rest of the committee might suspect something, even though his is the only vote that counts."

"True." Seward picked up an inkwell from Ike's desk and turned it around in his hand. "What will happen if he doesn't receive the right bribe?"

Ike stiffened. "He'll have it."

"Are you certain?"

"Completely." Ike spread his hands. He'd deliver the bitch if he had to burn down the Hair Trigger Palace to find her.

"If Wolf Laurel doesn't become the county seat, it's hard to see how you'll make the payments on your loan."

"There's no due date on the loan." Ike's throat was suddenly very dry.

The Northerner's narrow eyes stared at him like a wolf eyeing a scrawny deer. "No, the date is blank because the bank gets to fill it in."

"You conniving bastard."

"Not at all. You received an extremely advantageous deal." He tossed the inkwell into the air.

Red filmed Ike's vision but he beat it back. Seward had a partner here in town, plus another in Denver. Killing him would solve nothing.

"Who will you find to deliver the bribe to Simmons?" The banker replaced the inkwell on the table, clearly satisfied with the conversation. "Word on the street is that Nine-

Fingers' death has scared everybody else off. It'll cost four times as much or more to stage another attack on Talbot."

Shit. The only way he'd found anybody before was to use Nine-Fingers Isham. That piece of jailbait had owed him too much to even think about asking for money.

"You don't know everything I've got up my sleeve," Ike said gruffly. "The bribe will reach Simmons in time."

He'd grab the girl by himself. Talbot would never shoot him.

Chapter 9

"You should stay inside," Justin said again.

"I'm following you," Charlotte repeated for at least the third time in the last ten minutes. "Who would possibly try to kidnap me on a sunny morning? All we'll do is walk across the street to the telegraph office, check for news, and come back."

"If anything happens—" He didn't look happy. But who would dare attack them when Justin was carrying two Navy Colts at his belt, plus another at his back? Not to mention all those knives secreted in various intriguing places.

"I promise you, I'll duck." She gave him a hopeful smile, while Garland glared beside her. Unfortunately he hadn't redeemed his reputation in Justin's eyes after not preventing yesterday's attack. So he couldn't argue that he alone could protect her. She wouldn't refer to that, but she wasn't above ignoring him in favor of clinging to every possible minute with Justin.

"Very well."

They stepped out of the Hair Trigger Palace's front door and onto the boardwalk. Its roof had sheltered it from the worst snow and allowed Justin and Charlotte a brief pause to adjust their eyes to the morning's brilliant sunshine.

The last snow had fallen after midnight and the winds had died shortly thereafter. Brilliant sunshine turned the crisp, cold air into knife blades. Glistening spears of ice dangled from every roof. Gangs of men, paid by the saloons, had attacked the snowdrifts at first light. The alleys and streets were now hard-packed, slippery paths.

Saloons and shopkeepers had thrown open their establishments to welcome miners and townspeople. Pedestrians bustled along the boardwalk or picked their way cautiously across the street.

Simmons drank coffee and scratched his belly on the Silver King Hotel's front porch, next door to the Palace. His hot eyes tracked her like a rabid dog.

Charlotte followed Justin into the open, grateful for the sawdust somebody had spread to provide better footing.

"Talbot!" Johnson yelled from the Crystal Saloon two doors away.

Justin turned slowly and Charlotte kept pace.

"Good morning, mayor," Justin acknowledged, his response far more civil than the look on Johnson's face.

"I need to speak to your companion. She owes me her entry fee for the poker tournament."

"What? I never signed an agreement to play in that tournament."

"Everybody knows that's why you're here in Wolf Laurel."

People were disappearing into buildings like rats seeking their burrows.

"I won't pay you a nickel." Not for the privilege of nearly being kidnapped and raped.

His expression turned ugly and cold as a gallows. "Are you telling me you welsh on a debt?"

Shopkeepers now slammed shutters into place. A few men, including Simmons, moved onto the boardwalk steps leading onto the street where they could see better.

"Johnson, you know those are fighting words. Why are you trying to pick a duel with a woman?" Justin's rich drawl held all the civilized memories of a long-dead world.

"Because she's a cheat and a coward. Any man who protects her—"

"Johnson, we've been saddle-partners too long for me to listen to this nonsense."

"Talbot, for Christ's sake . . ."

"Miss Moreland and I are heading for the telegraph office, after which you're welcome to join us for coffee. You have been, and will always be my friend—not my enemy. Good day." Justin ostentatiously turned his back on the town's mayor and started walking again.

Charlotte tagged unhappily along behind him. Fine words from Justin, but what if Johnson placed money ahead of friendship? Somebody would have to take action.

"Why, you son of a bitch—"

Charlotte jumped at Justin's back and knocked him aside.

BAM!

The bullet blasted across her arm as if a fiery train had hit her and she fell down, skidding into a water trough.

BAM! BAM! Oh, dear Lord, Johnson was still shooting.

BOOM! Justin fired his Colt over her head.

A man screamed and somebody was running toward them.

Charlotte cautiously lifted her head. Her sleeve was scorched. Crimson started to blur its edges.

"Darling!" Justin dropped to his knees beside her. "Are you all right?"

"I think the bullet grazed my arm."

He started to examine it. His dark eyes met hers for a moment. "You saved my life."

"Of course."

Justin shook his head and compressed his lips even tighter. He was very white.

"Where's Johnson?" she asked.

"Dead. His last shot went wild and took out Simmons."

"They can share the same grave," she muttered.

Justin choked in unwilling laughter, then lifted her up. "Can you stand? We need to bandage this."

"Yes, of course." Her feet wobbled underneath her but everything was easier with his arm around her.

"Charlotte?" Another man forced his way through the ever increasing crowd.

The well-remembered voice made her head come up from Justin's shoulder. They turned back from the Hair Trigger Palace to face the newcomer.

"Charlotte, my dear?" Her filthy, bedraggled father swung down off his exhausted horse and leaped onto the boardwalk. Behind him, two sage mountain men in fringed leathers and buffalo skins folded their hands on their saddle horns and grinned proudly. He couldn't have arrived with more unusual attire and companions if Elijah's chariot of fire had deposited him. He'd lowered himself to perform this hunt on his own, rather than send Pinkerton's agents.

The shock was enough to deaden even her arm's increasing anguish.

"Father," Charlotte acknowledged cautiously. If he was about to demand she return to the same prison as before, overseen by her stepmother . . . "How did you get here?"

"My friends brought me to Wolf Laurel. I was afraid you'd slip through my fingers again so we rode through the night." He'd lost weight and his clothing was made for mining country, not Boston.

"Through the storm—for me?" She couldn't imagine how he'd traveled without his private railway car. "How did you find me?"

"A Denver gunsmith told me you'd come to Wolf Laurel." The Moreland patriarch cast a suspicious eye at Justin. "He warned me to hurry because he wasn't sure you'd stick around long."

"He loves you," whispered Justin in her ear.

"I came alone, since I'm now a divorced man."

She gaped at her father. The head of the Moreland family divorced? That scandal would match or possibly outweigh anything she'd done. "I'm not sure I believe you."

"I bought that woman off with ten thousand dollars and Putnam's old Beacon Hill townhouse, one of the few to survive the fire."

"The one with the gaudy ballroom and the huge dining room?"

"The same." A smile almost touched his lips.

"You didn't give her enough money to heat that enormous pile for more than a few years, once she buys clothes for her girls. They'll be paupers." Charlotte had never hoped to see such a perfect revenge on those harridans.

"Yes, I understand they sailed for Europe to hunt in fresh waters. But I care not. I've come to beg my darling daughter's forgiveness." Her father's eyes pleaded with hers. "I should have asked for your explanation, rather than believing shapeless lies and losing my temper."

"Oh, Papa!" Tears spilled down her cheeks. They'd always promised to be honest with each other and that lapse had hurt her the most. She reached out to him with her good arm and he kissed her cheek.

"Who is this fellow?" he asked sternly a moment later.

"The man who saved my life," Charlotte answered.

"Her suitor, with your blessing," Justin said simultaneously.

She stared at him. She'd never thought Justin would leave the West.

Then she began to smile. Perhaps she could have a future with him after all.

Boston, Christmas Sunday, 1875

Decked out in garlands of pine boughs and roses, the Moreland carriage turned the final corner to the family mansion on Beacon Hill. Inside, Charlotte held hands with her new husband.

The Boston church bells filled the sky with cascades of brilliant joy, as glittering bright as the skies. A stream of carriages like golden bonbons turned into the street behind them.

The crowd broke out in cheers, hailing a pageant brighter than anything in a concert saloon or variety house.

Scents of coffee and chocolate drifted from inside, as the Moreland servants carried hot drinks to the policemen guarding the street corners. Tempting aromas of hot cider and hot chestnuts wafted past, from the food provided to the crowds.

Liveried servants in burgundy and gold flung open the mansion's great double doors. Inside, Charlotte could glimpse garlands wrapped around the grand staircase and gilded angels dancing below the chandeliers. Red and gold ribbons transformed all the furniture into gigantic ornaments. Servants bustled between the kitchen and the drawing room, carrying even more edible delights for the banquet to come.

Their sleigh drew up before the great mansion and her father stepped out. He scanned the throng for a moment and an unaccustomed smile touched his harsh, patrician face. He bowed and waved to his fellow citizens, then stepped onto the crimson carpet leading into his home.

Justin handed Charlotte down from the carriage. She was swathed in furs and velvet against the cold, and sapphires glowed at her throat.

She leaned against him for a moment, to catch every bit of intimacy before they faced the throng inside. The crowd's cheers redoubled and Justin's smile lit his eyes.

It came more often now, on this side of the Mississippi.

She reluctantly waved at the people nearby but didn't take her eyes off her beloved husband.

"Are you truly happy here?" she asked, low enough that the grooms couldn't hear.

"Completely." His smile deepened. "I have everything my mother wanted for me, and more. Plus, the most glorious future imaginable in your arms."

His hand rested briefly on her waist where his child grew.

She blushed, then her grin blazed to match his. They hadn't mentioned that detail to her father yet.

"Come, my darling Ace, let's greet our guests."

She shivered happily at his use of their private nickname.

"The sooner we introduce my cousin, Earl Chillington, to everyone, the sooner we can depart on our honeymoon."

"I adore you, Mr. Talbot." She tucked her hand into his elbow, fully in accord with his grasp of the necessities. Life would be an eternal delight with him at her side.

To Match a Thief

MAGGIE
ROBINSON

Chapter 1

Jane Street, London, October 1820

Lucy Dellamar looked down with dismay at the diamond brooch in her hand.

It had happened again.

She hadn't meant to steal it, though it was clear she had, for why else would it be cutting into her palm? But there it had been, carelessly twinkling on the bedside table of her neighbor Victorina Castellano, where anyone might come upon it and pocket it. At least Lucy had not taken Victorina's matching earrings that were right beside it, although she probably should have. Sets were more valuable when kept together.

Botheration. No time for regrets about her light fingers and inadequate forethought. Lord Ferguson would be happy, and that's all that counted. It meant a roof over her head for another month at least, and perhaps a choicer cut of meat even if the cook had already quit. She would buy it and cook it herself.

Lucy was hungry right now. Thieving was hard work, though whoring was worse. It hadn't come to that—yet.

Even if she did live on Jane Street, 'Courtesan Court,' the most wicked street in Mayfair.

Lucy lived a total lie. Oh, too many 'ls' upon the tongue, but there it was. Six years ago, she had been plucked out of obscure quasi-poverty by Lord Percival Ferguson and offered a job she could not refuse.

There was no reason to say no. She had been a twenty-four-year-old spinster, deserted by her fiancé, a thief far more cunning than she ever aspired to be. For all she knew he was dead—there had not been a word from him in over seven years.

Lucy's new job was remarkably easy. Lord Ferguson had asked her to pretend to be his mistress, because it was expected that a man in his position in Society would keep one. She was in fact, one of a long line of women that poor Percy had kept over the last twenty years.

The earl swore he'd never touched a one of them aside from a gentle steer of an elbow, which she could easily believe, as he was having it on with her strapping young butler, Yates. Percy and Yates had been lovers for quite some time, and the Jane Street address had proven a convenient spot for their assignations. Everyone in the ton thought Lord Ferguson was visiting Lucy, when it was really Yates's bed he sought. Lord Ferguson could be himself in his little house, and if that meant borrowing Lucy's rouge pot and silk stockings, what was the harm, really?

But some months ago, Percy had lost most of his fortune through spectacularly unwise investments, and Lucy was very much afraid her days on Jane Street were numbered. The maid and the cook were gone, resulting in Lucy herself dusting and polishing the few bits of silver that were left and tying her own laces. She supposed it was only right that she begin to earn her keep, for really, the past six years had been a blissful blur of indolence and amusement. Percy had exquisite taste and had dressed her in everything he himself would want to wear—and did—so she had been turned out beautifully. Expensively. Totally a la mode. There had been nothing new—not so much as a plain-edged handkerchief for either of them—in seven months, and Lucy had resorted to selling a few of her older dresses to help pay for candles.

Percy's mother was pestering him to marry an heiress, which would never suit. He couldn't touch his Scottish estate or his London townhouse—they were entailed for the heirs he would have only with the most miraculous of miracles—but the Jane Street house would fetch a pretty penny. Everyone in the ton would forgive Lord Ferguson if he was forced to sell his love nest due to financial reversals. They would not forgive him if they caught him in Lucy's black lace peignoir, nor would the inevitable heiress his mother would force him to marry if she had her way.

Percy looked better in the peignoir than she did—black washed her out. She was too pale, her milk-white skin and red-gold hair better suited to pastels. Of course, a courtesan was expected to wear more vibrant colors, so she did, much to Percy's delight.

The clothes were an improvement over what she had been wearing the day Percy found her in her aunt's Edinburgh millinery shop. He had stepped in to get out of the rain, he'd said (but truly, he had been drawn by a lovely peacock-blue hat trimmed with matching feathers Lucy had set in the window fifteen minutes before). She wore a plain gray dress with a starched white apron, its pockets holding needles and her long-shafted scissors. When he'd offered her a job, she'd been so shocked she sat down and stabbed herself in the thigh.

Percy hadn't hired her because she was beautiful, although she was more than passably good-looking. She'd turned a head or two in her time, not that she wanted to remember *those* days. No. He said as soon as he looked into her light brown eyes—directly into them, because she was just his height—that he'd known she was just the girl for him. And when he glimpsed her enormous feet, he was in transports.

Lucy was very tall for a woman, and slender—flat-chested, if one wanted to be brutally honest. She and Percy were nearly identical in size, so she was able to fulfill his lifelong dream to deck himself out in the best women's clothing without arousing suspicion. Of course Lord Ferguson accompanied Lucy for her fittings at the finest London dressmakers' shops. Of course he fingered the fabrics, suggested the styles—he was paying the shot and knew what he liked to see his rather gargantuan mistress in.

Under Percy's tutelage, she had blossomed—the awkward ugly duckling had turned into a graceful, gliding swan, whose irregular height set her far apart from the ordinary. Lucy would be lying if she claimed she didn't like to play dress-up, and her current position had released her from the tedium of pleating velvet onto straw and sewing stuffed songbirds onto bonnets and listening to her aunt's continuous opprobrium. Her aunt now had to harangue some other girl, and pay her, too. Lucy had received very little for her efforts save the roof over her head and poor fare on her aunt's table. Percy had made her eat so she could order bigger clothes to fit him.

Her eating days were coming to an end. She could not keep stealing from the courtesans on 'Courtesan Court.' They already looked at her with distrust, and her invitations to the weekly amusements the girls hosted while they waited for their protectors had dried up. Stealing was *wrong*, even if the girls had more useless trifles than they needed at the moment. But someday their fabled beauty would fade—they'd grow stout and whiskery, and then all the diamond pins in the world could not replace their golden youth. A mistress had to make provisions for the future.

But so did Lucy. She was thirty years old, after all, already well past her prime even if she didn't look like an old hag—Percy's special skin potions had seen to that. She just had to find a better—legal—way to secure her future. She didn't fancy getting transported to the antipodean penal colony.

She might bump into someone she knew.

No, she would not think about *him* now. He'd done enough to ruin her dreams without taking over her waking hours too.

She fetched a hat—a quite pretty one she'd made herself, red ribbons and cherries to match her red pelisse, and went to see Mr. Peachtree with the pin tucked into her reticule. He was an honest, honorable broker who believed her lies and thought he was helping her to get free of the wicked Lord Ferguson. The fact that Lord Ferguson gave his mistress such odd gifts—mismatched teaspoons, jeweled snuffboxes, small *objets* that could easily be stuffed into pockets or down bodices—hadn't seemed to occur to him yet.

Lucy was *not* a thief, although she had been taught by the best. And he had stolen her heart and sent it back broken.

Chapter 2

No one who saw him now could ever guess precisely how primitive Sir Simon Keith's beginnings were. Thanks to Providence, his teeth were mercifully straight, his black hair clipped a la Brutus, his shirtpoints starched high, his cravat snow white, his jacket tailored to perfection—the list could go on and on with a plethora of commas. He was a veritable nonpareil, tall, dark and almost too handsome.

It was only when one noticed his long fingers, nails irrevocably grease-stained from years of manual labor in its truest sense, that one realized that Sir Simon had not been to the manor born. He'd been very good with his hands (whether with women or machinery or removing the odd watch from an unsuspecting cove's pocket) since he was a boy on the streets of Edinburgh. When he joined the army at the age of seventeen, under some duress if it be known— there was a price on his head and the local constable was keen on his trail—the military seemed preferable to prison. His superiors had soon discovered that whatever one put in front of Private Keith he could fix. When he put his mind to something, he could turn a bit of string and a scrap of metal into anything one would like. His mid-battle adjustments to a crate of useless but much-needed rifles earned him a rapid promotion, until he was taken out of the field altogether and put to work at a drafting board in the War Office. One thing led to another, and now Sir Simon owned his own foundry and a fistful of patents.

With peacetime cutting into his profits, he'd seen the way to convert his materiel to less deadly accoutrements and was now deep into the promulgation of a railway system that would stretch from one end of Britain to the other, using his own engines, of course. He had been knighted for his service to the Crown in squelching that fiend Napoleon, was unbearably rich and only thirty. Who knew what his future held?

It *should* hold a wife. Some nice, proper well-bred girl who would help him advance in Society. She needn't be rich—he had more money than he knew what to do with— but she'd have to have a pedigree to make up for the one he lacked. Simon supposed a girl like that would be rather dull in bed, but that was all right. He had an appointment this very afternoon to meet with Lord Percival Ferguson, a fellow Scot. The gentleman was a bit eccentric—the earl preferred to wear his kilt even in town—but Simon didn't mind. He'd heard old Percy was hard up and planned to sell his Jane Street house. Simon could set up a mistress there to escape from his boring future wife.

If Simon purchased a property on that sought-after street, he really would consider himself 'arrived.' Imagine, a boy from the Edinburgh slums keeping a high-class London courtesan. What would Lucy say?

Ah. Poor Lucy. His lost love. Dead and gone for years. Whilst he was out and about fighting and inventing for King and Country, she toiled like a slave for her wretched aunt. He'd come back for her too late. The aunt had chased him out of her hat shop with a fistful of hatpins and he'd lost himself in a pint or two for longer than he cared to remember.

He'd promised to return, and had, once the war was over and he had something to show for it. But she'd died six years ago, poor wee thing.

Well, 'wee' was not precisely correct. His Lucy was a Valkyrie, an Amazon among women. But she'd fit against him to perfection and he missed her every day.

Calf love it may have been, but it had stayed true. Simon had even taught himself to read and write to surprise her. He still had every one of her letters—all five of them—unopened of course, because at first he could not admit to being such an ignorant sod as to need someone read them to him. His old gran had sent them after he was safely established in his regiment, if "safe" meant not having his head shot off yet.

By the time he knew how to read, he couldn't bear to be reminded of what they had shared. Poor Luce must have given up hope on him, or counted on the Corsican monster to win.

But England had prevailed five years ago, in no small part due to Simon. And Simon would prevail too—buy Ferguson's house, acquire a mistress to put in it, find a wife. Have a few little Keiths—for that was his name now—although with his imposing height, they wouldn't stay little for long.

Lord Percival Ferguson looked ill at ease, and well he should. It was not just because he was wearing a fine suit of gentleman's evening clothes, either, although he had chosen a blindingly puce vest to add a bit of color. "All I'm asking you to do, my dear, is give the man a chance."

"How could you, Percy? You cannot sell me along with the house!" Lucy paced her sweet little sitting room, her long legs making short work of the distance. Pale copper braids flew behind her, striking her cheek when she turned.

"Lucy, darling, I'm not selling you. I thought to give you some security, chatting you up with Sir Simon. You and I have been good friends—the best of friends—for six years. I don't want to imagine you out in the cold."

And it *was* cold. October chill had set in. Winter would be upon them soon, and where would she go? "I suppose you'll want to keep my fur cloak, too! Damn it, Percy, you can't pass me off like a basket of dinner rolls."

"Just one meeting, love. If you don't like him, you don't need to stay. We can make some other arrangements. I can't give you very much in the way of any congé, though, you know. I'm beyond broke. But I sang your praises—"

"Lied, you mean!"

"Nonsense. I'm sure you'll be very skilled in the bedroom if you put your mind to it. There are books to help you, you know. That neighbor of yours writes them."

Lucy shot daggers at him at the idea of reading dirty books, even if she already had a time or two, so he changed his tack. "Sir Simon is handsome. Rich. If I didn't have a tendre for my Yates I'd be quite taken with him myself. And he's much taller than you, no easy feat. The man is an Atlas. I got a crick in my neck looking up at him, and we were sitting in chairs at my club."

Simon. The name alone was an ill omen. Just what she needed as a reminder of her past. Why couldn't the bluidy man be called Harold or Henry or George? "And he's a complete, utter stranger! Percy, you have gone too far."

He shrugged in apology. "That's what I do, my dear. I've never known my limits. Bane of my existence. Mama's, too."

Lucy did not wish to think of Percy's dragon of a mother. She held a hand against her flat chest, as if to keep her crumbling heart from bouncing out and shattering on the carpet. "This is intolerable. I'll have to go back to Edinburgh."

"You know your ghastly old aunt won't have you. She's told everybody you're dead. You'll scare the life out of the old neighborhood if you turn up. You're pale as a ghost as it is."

Lucy stopped her march to the wall. "To her I *am* dead. She thinks I'm a Fallen Woman."

Percy cleared his throat. "You *are* a Fallen Woman," he reminded her gently.

"I should never have told you about that boy! And anyway, I was practically a child. I didn't know any better."

"I know. You placed your fate in the hands of a handsome thief." Percy sighed and looked rather like a sympathetic basset hound, all mournful eyes and wobbly jowls.

Lucy and Percy really *were* friends, really almost like sisters, so to speak. They had confided nearly everything to each other over the years. He knew all about that bastard Simon Grant, or as much as she was willing to tell him, and she knew—well, she knew enough to blackmail Percy for the rest of his life if only he had any money. She flung herself down on the sofa, allowing her misery to swallow her up.

"Och! I'll nae be able to do it!" she said, sobbing into the sleeve of her sensible white night rail.

It was unusual for her to lapse into her Scots accent. Percy had drummed every conceivable ladylike lesson into her, and that included erasing the nature of her humble origins. She spoke English far better than Queen Caroline, and dressed more elegantly too.

"Oh, you're breaking my heart," said Percy, tearing a lace-edged handkerchief out of his pocket and sobbing next to her. "I wish I'd never listened to that dastardly scheme to import those mulberry trees and silkworms from China. But I could have cornered the silk market! Just think of the dresses we could have had."

Lucy hiccupped. "You couldn't have known the trees were diseased and the silkworms would become poisoned and die." That had just been one catastrophic business failure. She was too kind to bring up the others, but Percy did himself after he blew his nose.

"And that Nigerian prince took me in as well. All that money transferred to him, and he was nothing but the son of a goatherd. There isn't even a king in his country! Well," Percy said, flourishing his rather damp handkerchief, "I expect my luck is about to change. Steam engines, Lucy. That's the future. Sir Simon has assured me that to invest with him will bring me untold fortune."

"Percy! Don't tell me you've traded this house for shares in some fly-by-night enterprise! Again!" She smacked Percy on his hollow chest.

"No, no. Nothing like that. Sir Simon says—"

"I don't give a fig what the bluidy man says! It's cash you need, Percy, and a lot of it! How will you be able to pay our dressmaker?"

"We'll come to terms, never you fear. In six months I'll be rich as Croesus. But not," he said, wiping a tear from his watery brown eye, "in time to save you. It's all I can do to find Yates a job at Mama's."

Percy's mother lived at Ferguson House in Portman Square, which was of course Percy's and not his mama's at all. If it were up to Lucy, she'd send the witchy old countess back to Scotland and hope she got lost in a Highland snowdrift.

Percy brushed her tear-stained cheeks with a dry corner of his handkerchief. "Just try to like him, Lucy. That's all I ask. He's a wee bit rough around the edges—his knighthood's a recent thing—but he seems a gentleman. And he is very good-looking. He wants a place to entertain his investors, and Jane Street has cachet. Think of the dinner parties you can preside at as hostess."

"You sold the damned dining table, Percy," Lucy reminded him. Now she ate down in the kitchen or on a tray in her sitting room if she ate at all.

"It was a signed Sheraton—of course I did. You should wear the fern-green-striped gown with the cream Brussels lace when he comes to call. The emerald parure, even if they're paste. And you might want to pad your bosom until you sign your contract. After that, it's every man for himself. Caveat emptor, don't you know."

Lucy smacked him again, but her heart wasn't in it. What choice did she have? This Sir Simon might not even like her anyway, unless he wanted to borrow her clothes. She was not the usual run of mistress, especially since she hadn't bedded a man in thirteen years. She would always be too tall, too pale, too opinionated. Percy had done her no favors dragging her down here into this hotbed of sin. She could have happily gone blind stitching rosettes and ribbons to hats for the rest of her life, waiting to inherit her aunt's millinery shop.

All possibility of that was gone now.

Lucy wiped her nose on her sleeve, eschewing Percy's offer of the snot-ridden handkerchief. "When is he coming?" It had better not be tonight—Percy had found her with her hair in braids in bed with a good book—well, it was a very bad book, really, and that was the whole point—to tell her he'd given her away.

"He's going to call on you tomorrow morning. He says he wants to get a good look at you in daylight."

Lucy narrowed her eyes at Percy. If she didn't love the benighted man, she'd wish him to the devil. "Like a horse."

"Now, now, like a beautiful woman who needs no dim candlelight to shine. But—er—ahem—I would appreciate it if you didn't divulge the precise nature of our relationship when you speak to him."

"Of course I won't betray you! Haven't I been loyal for six years?"

He took her hand and kissed it, the only part of her body his lips had ever touched. "I know you wouldn't mean to, but he might ask unsettling questions." Percy was blushing. He had a great deal to blush about.

Lucy snatched her hand away. "Your reputation is safe with me. If your mother couldn't worm it out of me the horrible day she came to visit, I doubt this Sir Simon will rattle me. But I will keep my fur cloak, Percy. It's only fair. The red fox matches my hair."

Percy sighed. "Oh, all right. It's too hot to wear indoors anyway. But I expect Sir Simon will want to dress you in new clothes. Perhaps we can put my things in storage for happier days ahead."

Lucy did not think there would be happier days ahead for her. In all likelihood, she would have to make the role of courtesan she had played for the past half-dozen years come true. The tiny bit of virtue she still possessed as a thief and a liar was about to be tossed out onto the cobblestones of Jane Street. "I haven't agreed to become his mistress yet, Percy."

Percy grinned. "But you will. I believe he's perfect for you. I have a feeling about these things."

Lucy knew all about Percy's feelings, and wished she had never, ever put that peacock-blue hat in the window.

Chapter 3

After Percy went downstairs to celebrate the sale of his house with Yates, Lucy tossed and turned for hours, bunching up her tear-stained nightgown. In a fit of pique, she tore it off her head and tossed it on the floor. Now she was as naked as God made her. She supposed He'd known what He was doing, she thought doubtfully, but sometimes she wondered why He had not quite finished the job.

Around three o'clock, with the church bells bonging melodiously throughout Mayfair, Lucy stalked out of bed and headed for the whiskey she kept in her cupboard. This night—this morning, now—required strong drink to get through. Unfortunately she'd had to water down the 'water of life' to make it last, but it was better than nothing. Shoveling some coals on the fire, she sat naked, drank, and grimly surveyed her future.

She might seek employment with a milliner in town—she wasn't well-known like Harriet Wilson and her sisters and would not be recognized. Percy hadn't wanted to be seen everywhere with her except when he ordered their clothes at their private dressmaker's appointments—he wanted to keep a low profile and wear his corsets and clocked stockings in privacy. Of course the Janes—the other courtesans on Jane Street—would know she had spent six years of her life here, but they were famously discreet. If Sir Simon

Whoeverhewas didn't like her—and how could he, she thought, looking down in the flickering firelight at her long, angular body in disgust—she would have to make alternate plans.

She was *not* going to keep thieving.

She drank her glass, then poured another. The bells struck four. By five she'd run out of whiskey and coherent rumination, and crawled back in bed.

And that is where Sir Simon Keith found her at nine o'clock.

He knew he was unconscionably early, but he was a busy man. It was best to start the day as early as possible, because, while he had invented a great many things, he still hadn't figured out how to add hours to the clock. He'd rapped at the front door of the little house with no result.

But Lord Ferguson had given him a key, so he used it. A gust of wind blew leaves in on this bright October day, and he bent to pick them up and put them in his pocket. He may have been raised in a hovel, but he liked things neat now. The leaves joined the collection of roller bearings which kept his hands occupied when he wanted to think.

And this house was very neat, although not as furnished as he expected it to be. Empty squares on the tastefully papered parlor walls revealed where pictures used to hang. There was a sofa, one chair, an embroidered footstool. Double doors to a dining room led to three spindle-back chairs but no table. He examined the carpet—worn—and could see the impression where once the feet of a long table had rested. He pictured himself—after buying new furniture—having jolly parties with his mistress and men of industry who needed a light evening to be cajoled into investing in his enterprises.

She would be a clever girl, pretty, diamonds sparkling at her throat, sitting at the head of the table and charming the pants off the other gents. Not literally, though. Simon had standards, and he didn't like to share. Ferguson had said his mistress was exceptionally tall, and Simon liked a tall woman. He was such a big brute himself he'd always felt awkward covering some little dab of a girl. Lucy had been perfect for him, and he'd grown four inches and gained three stone since he ran away from her. Good food and plenty of it had that effect.

Simon sighed, running his finger along the banister. No, he didn't run away from *her*, but the circumstances. He'd be quarrying rock in Australia if he hadn't slipped away.

Or worse.

Where was everybody? The house was dead silent. He knew Ferguson was in dun territory, but surely there should be a maid somewhere for his mistress.

"Hallo!" he called at the bottom of the stairs, and waited.

Nothing. Maybe Miss Dellamar bunked it, not wishing to be transferred along with the deed to the Jane Street house. He could see her point. It was slightly distasteful, and he wasn't altogether certain he'd keep her on anyway, no matter how lovely Ferguson said she was.

But if they suited each other, it would save him the bother of finding a mistress. He'd been without a woman for too long. All work and no play had made Simon a very dull boy indeed. He was entitled now to a little fun.

Each Jane Street house was a little jewel box, holding a jewel of a woman. His prospective gem might not be at home, but there was no reason not to inspect the house. He'd visited an acquaintance for a gathering down the street a few doors down—there were only twelve houses in the cul-de-sac—and the floor plans were identical.

He climbed the carpeted treads. The first door at the top of the stairs led to a cozy sitting room. He entered, finding it filled with a good quantity of books piled haphazardly on rather homely furniture, the kind of stuff you might find in a country cottage, definitely not a brothel. Chintz and lace and what-not, feminine frippery. He was surprised there was no long-haired cat cluttering up the space. He picked up a book and read a few lines—bah, women's stuff, some rubbishy novel meant to turn your mind from your troubles. Ruined castles and anguished dukes. Sheer nonsense.

A half-finished straw capote—Simon was well-versed in ladies' hats—sat on a faceless form, strips of ribbon and hatmaker's tools laid neatly on a round table beside it. How quaint that Percy's mistress made her own hats, although judging from the form, her head must be enormous.

Good. He hoped she had brains. He wouldn't want to be saddled with some empty-headed female. He was too proud of his own efforts to educate himself, late as they had come. Simon wanted someone to discuss the changing world with him after he'd fucked her, someone to tell his dreams to. He'd heard Jane Street girls were not only beautiful but brainy, the crème de la crème of courtesans.

The door to the bedroom stood ajar, and Simon looked through the opening. *Blast.* He'd presumed everyone was out of the house. But there, on the middle of the mattress was Lord Ferguson's sylph-like mistress, Miss Dellamar—a Long Meg if he'd ever seen one. She slept—and snored—on her back, her face obscured by the corner of a pillow. Her covers and nightgown seemed to be crumpled on the floor, so he could look his fill with no obstruction to the rest of her.

Her skin was very white, as white as the sheets. She had no breasts to speak of, which did not bother him as much as it might have. His Lucy—well, there was no point in remembering what she'd looked like, but she had been small up top like this woman. Lord Ferguson's mistress had a thatch of bright strawberry-blonde hair at her apex, about the same color as the braids that splayed on the bed. Titian red, just like in the painter's portrait of Mary Magdalene, he reminded himself, now that he knew something about art. He supposed it was fitting that Miss Dellamar had hair like a Biblical prostitute.

Lucy's hair had been reddish too, but in their brief time together he'd never had the luxury of seeing it loose, falling down her back. In fact he'd never really seen her naked at all—just the odd few inches of skin as they hurriedly took their pleasure in one another in back streets and doorways in the dark.

The closest they'd come to a bed was in the back room of the hat shop when her aunt had the gout and was resting right upstairs. There had been an old stuffed chair—lemon yellow, it was, and he'd put Lucy on his lap. The look on her face had been comical until she realized what she could do. They'd been quiet with difficulty, and poor Luce was a nervous wreck thinking the old battleaxe would come limping downstairs any minute with every gasp she took.

Stolen moments for the boy who stole.

He could make all the noise he wanted now in this house—it was his, or would be in six days. Simon had the signed bill of sale in his pocket. Ferguson had wanted to give his mistress a chance to make other arrangements if Simon didn't like her, or vice versa. He wouldn't try to charm her if she took one look at him and shuddered. He was handsome enough—no one had complained—but he was one braw Scot, big enough to frighten away half the people he met.

Once he'd wanted to scare people into them giving him their valuables without a fight. Now he just wanted to get their money as investors, and it wouldn't do to have the ton think he was some unlettered savage.

If Miss Dellamar woke up right now, she'd probably toss the pillow at him and more besides. It wasn't very gentlemanly of him to stare at her nakedness when they hadn't even been introduced, even if she was a whore. He'd come back later.

Simon took one last look around the bedroom. An empty bottle of whiskey stood on a little table in front of the fireplace. Lord Ferguson had said nothing about his mistress being a tippler. If she was, she'd have to drink alone. After he learned of Lucy's death, Simon had lost himself for a bit. He couldn't bollix up all his business plans again. Clearheaded at all times, that's what he needed to be. And he had to admit looking at this woman's glorious body, his mind was becoming somewhat foggy.

Aye, he'd come back later. After noontime, when she'd slept off her drink and was dressed like a proper tart. He had plenty of things to keep him busy until then.

He reached in his pocket for the key so he could lock up and not leave her prey to someone who had less self-control than he had. His hand came upon a leaf, pale red the color of Miss Dellamar's hair.

It was a sign, he thought. What it meant he didn't know.

Chapter 4

Lucy awoke with a pounding headache. She was freezing, too, her coals being long cold. There was no maid to bring her hot chocolate or hot water or hot anything. Cross, she snatched up her night rail from the floor and shoved her head through the opening, then covered herself with her warmest woolen robe. Her hair was a horror of half-braided tangles, so she twisted it all up in a kerchief and tied it under her chin. She put on two pairs of thick socks for good measure. Percy would not approve of her ensemble, but damn Percy anyhow. At least she was warm, or would be.

"Yates! Percy!" she called as she descended the stairs.

When she got down to the kitchen, the stove was cold too, and there was no sign of the lovers in Yates's empty bedroom. Since the cook had decamped, young Yates had been splitting the cooking duties with her, and Lucy found a covered dish filled with apple tarts on the sideboard. She bit into one greedily as the clock chimed noon. Not enough cinnamon. But then, everything had been rationed here for months.

Lucy supposed this Sir Simon could supply her with plenty of cinnamon, and anything else she might want. Right now, all she wanted was to get warm. She tossed some coal into the stove and lit a match with the tinder box. Her hands were black, but she was too dispirited to wash with cold water. Huddling up against the fitful stove, she waited to defrost.

Thank heavens Sir Simon had not come calling. She was in no state to meet him, or anyone. Where were the men? It was not like Percy to rise early when he stayed the night, but she supposed it wasn't early anymore.

Lucy left the comfort of the stove and took a closer look at Yates's room. All signs of his personal affects were gone. *Blast.* Perhaps Percy was getting Yates settled at Portman Square. Yates would be under-butler during the day, and over-butler at night if Percy could conceal his activities from Countess Ferguson. Lucy had her doubts. The woman was a ferret and looked like one too.

Lucy really *was* alone. Percy had been so sure than she would suit Sir Simon he'd left with his lover. Lucy paced again, this time for warmth, sliding a bit on the tiled floor. She had knit the socks herself—one could only decorate so many bonnets in six years, even for two people. She really was quite domestic, she thought as she put the kettle on. By now she should have a husband and several children, but one was unlikely to meet husband material living with a cross-dressing earl as his faux mistress.

But she'd had her advantages and couldn't fault Percy for trying to shore up the Ferguson fortune. Life was expensive and fickle.

Lucy poked a nose outside the tradesman's door while she waited for the kettle to whistle. It was a lovely fall day—the sky was a brilliant blue, but there was a nip in the air which made her close the door in a hurry. There had been quite a few unpleasant transactions at the step the past couple of months—and at the front door too—which Yates had handled with his usual aplomb. He really was a very fine butler who never batted an eyelash when presented with an irate bill-collector or Percy in a ruffled scarlet ball-gown.

The clang of the knocker at the door above broke into her solitary reverie over her tea and second apple tart. *Blast.* If it was Victorina come for her brooch, she was too late. Lucy took another sip of tea and examined her painted nails. They were chipping, another sure sign of the destitution that was to follow if she did not accept Sir Simon's protection. If he offered it.

After three minutes of excessive banging, the ensuing silence was deafening. She waited another five minutes to make her way upstairs with a pitcher of warm water for her ablutions. A sponge bath was better than nothing.

Mindful of the sloshing water, it was not until she collided with the giant at her bedroom door that she realized her defenses had been breached. She shrieked and tossed the pitcher and its contents at her trespasser. The nerve of these dunning leeches to break into and enter her home for some trifling debt!

Well, perhaps not trifling. Percy, and she by association, really were up the River Tick.

"Lucy Dalhousie!"

For the longest minute she just stared at the giant, her brown eyes wide. She hadn't heard her own name in six years, and had been perfectly content to let Percy change it—what her parents had been thinking of she had no idea. Dellamar was so much more musical, so refined. When she found her voice, she croaked, "Simon *Grant?*"

"Sir Simon Keith now. The name Grant was too hot back then, so I enlisted in the army under my mother's maiden name. I—I thought you were dead. Your aunt said—well, it doesn't matter! I canna believe my eyes!" He was grinning rather idiotically, the babbling bounder, even as he drew out an expensive handkerchief and mopped the water away from his incredibly broad chest. "What are you doing here?"

"I l-live here."

"Are you Miss Dellamar's maid, then? I never pictured you in service, Luce. You were always such a fiery, spirited little thing."

Little? Lucy now knew the true meaning of tongue-tied. She believed hers was in a French knot. She unraveled the knot just slightly.

"*You* are Sir Simon? The Sir Simon Percy—I mean Lord Ferguson has sold his house to?"

"The very same! I've risen up in the world quite a bit, Lucy. I came to tell you five years ago, but that aunt of yours told me you'd passed away. Did you run off? No one could blame you—she was a wicked old bit-bat."

"I—" Lucy looked around the doorframe wildly. Tiny black spots floated in front of her eyes, quite distorting Simon's handsome face. His bright blue eyes—the color of the sky she'd just observed a short while ago—his firm jaw, his white smile—he was grinning at her like a looby!—his broad shoulders clad in dark blue superfine—she slid to the floor in a faint. It seemed like the right thing to do while she gathered her far-flung wits about her.

Simon was alive.

Not in prison.

He had come for her five years ago.

He was a knight.

Impossible.

He was looking to set up a mistress.

Her!

"Come now, lass! I know it's a shock, running into me like this." His laughter boomed. "And you did run into me, no mistake. I'm sorry I scared you, love. Wake up, now."

Lucy was not going to wake up. She wondered how long

she could lie on the floor with her head in Simon's lap before he called for a doctor.

He was loosening the belt on her robe, palming her forehead, pulling off the kerchief. Suddenly her head clunked on the floor.

"What's this?" he growled. "Lucy Dalhousie, your hair!"

Lucy cracked open one eye. The man was standing over her, twirling a leaf in his hand.

"Uhhh," she groaned. Her head truly did hurt, from the whiskey and the careless way Simon had stopped tending to her and dropped her.

That was just like him. Here today, gone tomorrow.

Gone for seven years with no word.

Staring at her as if she was a dead silkworm on a mulberry leaf.

She struggled to sit up. "I'm sorry my hair isn't tidier. I wasna expecting company, especially you after *thirteen* years."

"Surely Lord Ferguson told you I was coming." His tone was icy now, and that dazzling smile had disappeared.

Lucy lifted her chin. "I cannot recall."

"Oh, really? You cannot recall you had an appointment with the new man who was going to offer you another *carte blanche*?" His French accent was atrocious.

"Percy says a great deal of nonsense."

"Percy, is it? You are not the maid here, are you, Lucy? No wonder your aunt said you were dead. Och! The shame of it!"

Lucy sprang to her feet and punched Sir Simon *Keith* in the chest, the third time she'd hit a man in the same spot in less than twenty-four hours. "Don't you dare talk to me of shame! You were a thief! A liar! A seducer of innocents! I've only done what I had to do to survive."

"Fuck that fop? Really, Lucy, I would think you'd have

better taste than Lord Ferguson. There's something off about him."

Lucy bit her tongue and counted to ten. The nerve of him to accuse her of what she hadn't been doing after all he'd done and planned to do! "The only thing 'off' about him is his inability to make wise investments! And now he's given you this house in exchange for some pie-in-the-sky venture of yours. Did you tire of robbing people the old-fashioned way?"

"I am not a thief. Not anymore. I learned I could do something else with my hands besides pick pockets."

"Bully for you," Lucy grumbled. "I expect you'll want me to clear out at once. Get out of my way so I can pack."

He grabbed her arm. "Not so fast." He gazed down at her, his blue eyes assessing. Lucy really wished she was not wearing her lumpy socks on her feet. Or had coal dust on her hands. Or whiskey on her breath.

"Where will you go?"

"Oh, what do you care? You left me once. Now I'm leaving you."

He inched closer and Lucy stopped breathing. "Did you want to see me hang, Luce?"

"The world would no doubt be a much better place," she replied tartly.

"I trust Napoleon agrees with you."

"Napoleon! What does he have to do with all this?"

"I'll tell you about it some time. In bed."

Lucy stumbled backward. "I am not going to bed with you!"

"Just once. It might be nice to have you in an actual bed. For old times' sake."

"You are mad!"

Simon loomed over her. "A kiss then."

"I have not brushed my teeth!" She swept her tongue

over her teeth, dislodging a chunk of apple. She was not dressed for seduction. She did not smell like seduction. And if she knew anything about Simon Whateverhecalledhimselfnow, he would not settle for a single kiss. "Absolutely not! Unhand me, sirrah!"

"Och, you've been reading silly things, Luce. You sound like a heroine from a gothic novel."

"What would someone as ignorant as you know about books?" she asked spitefully.

"You'd be surprised, lass, verra surprised. I'm a changed man, I am."

"Hah," Lucy snorted. But she had no chance to say anything else, because Simon chose that moment to silence her with a kiss.

Not just any kiss.

A kiss that shook her down to her nubby socks.

His mouth captured hers. His lips were warm, dry, and his tongue tasted of spearmint. He wielded that tongue like a weapon designed to vanquish her and anyone else who got in the way of what he wanted. Any thought she had of denying him entrance evaporated—the searing heat of his hands at her shoulders held her in place. Flames licked from his fingertips down her spine to the emptiness between her legs.

Lucy forgot about brushing her teeth or washing or tidying her hair. She stood rooted in her doorway, standing on the wet carpet, her breasts pressed against his damp waistcoat as he kissed and kissed and kissed her.

There might be another word for it, but Lucy couldn't think. She could only *do*. She explored his mouth, shivering with cold and desire, her hands brushing against his tailored coat. He was so much bigger than he'd been—taller, heavier, stronger than the scrawny scarecrow boy she'd loved so. And his kiss was taller, heavier and stronger, too. He had been practicing.

Lucy found her courage and stomped on his boot with a wet-stockinged foot.

He pulled away, his face neatly arranged as if they'd done nothing more than shake hands. Lucy was sure her cheeks were on fire.

"You've improved some, I see," he drawled.

"I was thinking the same of you, you rat."

"I thought you were dead, Luce. What's your excuse? Fell for the first rich lord who came by? Or is Ferguson just the latest of many?"

Lucy was so furious she couldn't speak. And that was just as well. She'd promised Percy not to share his secret, and she had nothing to prove to Sir Simon Keith after what he'd put her through.

Revenge. She wanted it, a great, heaping portion of it. With cinnamon.

"Tell me, Simon, are you still a wanted man? I imagine the authorities in Edinburgh would like to get their hands on you, even after all these years, no matter what you call yourself now. You made fools out of all of them."

He scowled down at her, and for a moment Lucy felt a frisson of fear.

"What are you saying, Lucy?"

"I'll accept your *carte blanche*," she said, mispronouncing it as he had. "I'll live in this house and wear your clothes and entertain your friends and keep my mouth shut about your past. But you'll not have me in your bed again, Simon, for all the money in the world. I'll need some time to make other arrangements—three months should be sufficient." She lifted her chin again and stared him straight into his narrowed blue eyes.

"Three months. And I suppose you'll want money for your blackmail, too."

This plan was so new to her, she hadn't thought of that. "Of course."

He shook his head. "You've grown to be a miserable bitch just like your auntie, haven't you?"

"Quite." She turned her face so he wouldn't see her hurt.

Chapter 5

By God, she had bollocks. To think he'd keep a roof over her head without her getting under him. Or above him—he wasn't particular at this point. He shifted so she wouldn't see his cockstand. That kiss had been nothing like the hurried assaults they'd made on each other when they were kids.

Simon doubted seriously she meant to turn him in—the warrants out for his arrest must be tattered scraps by now. Surely the authorities had more to worry about than a skinny seventeen-year-old boy who stole to feed himself and his old gran over a dozen years ago.

He'd worked back then, too—anything he could get his hands on. Mended bridles at stables, hauled barrels of ale, ran errands for the local moneylender. One such 'errand' had been his undoing. He'd kept a little extra from the toff he'd had to persuade—not much, but enough to make his employer turn him in to the corrupt magistrate. And it hadn't helped when he'd had to tie a sweet little old lady to a chair on his last job.

Simon became expendable. His bad judgment meant he was running from both the law and his boss, even if the sweet little old lady hadn't pressed charges. He'd only been back to Scotland once—to find Lucy Dalhousie—for all the good it did him. England was his home now.

He was a new man—it was a new age with a new king, a time filled with the promise of industry, machinery, investment, invention. He had a different name, a different appearance. No one would connect the knighted, rich Sir Simon Keith with the impoverished boy he used to be.

Lucy had changed too. Oh, physically she still looked the same, all pale and slender, with her mermaid hair and bee-stung lips. Like a princess from a fairytale book or a medieval madonna. She used to be putty in his hands, a fact that had once thrilled his youthful pride. It seemed she had grown a backbone.

And she was a whore.

A badly dressed whore, in an old rumpled robe and ugly woolen stockings, with a smudge of soot on her nose. Percy Ferguson had truly fallen on bad times if this is how his mistress comported herself.

Simon imagined her in a copper bathtub, her hair unbound and floating on the surface of the water, her pink nipples hard peaks. He'd scrub the soot off and clean everywhere else personally and not mind a bit if she splashed him again.

Three months. Simon supposed he owed her that. It wasn't so long. But long enough for him to get her where he wanted her again.

And to get her out of his system.

He couldn't go on carrying a torch for a Jane Street courtesan.

"All right," he said. He wouldn't try to get her into his bed, but she'd said nothing about fucking anywhere else. It would be just like old times. He grinned.

She looked taken aback, her well-kissed lips wide open in surprise.

"I can't have you looking like that when we meet with my investors next week," Simon said, sweeping his eyes from her snarled hair and her wooly toes. "I hope Ferguson bought you some better clothes."

"I have an elegant wardrobe," she said haughtily. Damn but her chin kept lifting. Soon it would hit the ceiling.

"Good. I have an image to project. My mistress must be above reproach. And I'll need new furniture immediately. Good china. Silver. See to it and put it on my account. I'll write a letter of authorization for you." He went to the little desk in the corner, hoped the spindly chair wouldn't break under his weight, and began scratching away.

Again, she gawked at him. "You trust me to buy your furnishings?"

"Why not? You used to have aspirations to be a lady. Even when you had no money, you were nicely turned out."

He watched as the blush stole over her cheeks at his praise. But it was true. Lucy always had good taste. She'd chosen him, hadn't she?

"I'll get my secretary to secure a household staff. A butler, a cook, a footman and two maids should be sufficient for a property this size. Maybe a kitchen boy."

"That's more than we had before." He heard an odd gurgle behind him. "Wait a minute! Simon, you're writing!"

He raised a brow. "I told you I was a changed man, Luce. I read too, but not the nonsense you keep in your parlor. Romances—pah!" he said in disgust.

"Someone deserves a happy ending! There's little enough of that in the real world."

Finishing his letter, he signed his name with an embellishment below, much better than the 'X' of the past. He scattered sand on the paper and pushed it toward her.

"This should give you entrée into the best shops. And I want the best, Luce. Doona be mingy."

"I'll be a total spendthrift. I shall enjoy spending *your* money for a change."

She'd given him all her savings the last night he came to her, full of fear and promises. "I told you I'd pay you back those seventeen shillings, and I will."

"With interest, if you please."

"What a canny businesswoman you are. It's a pity I cannot employ you in my railroad scheme."

"I wouldn't work for you for all the tea in China."

"I prefer Indian, by the way. Please inform the cook. I'll give you a list of my favorites so that when I visit, I'll have what I want."

Her blushes had disappeared. "W-when you visit?"

"Did you think to be here all alone for the next three months, Luce?"

"I thought—you said you'd have parties for your business associates."

"Aye, that I will. But a man in my position is expected to have a mistress. I've got to keep up appearances. Visit this house regularly."

"Just like p-powerful men," she muttered. "They're all the same, leaving their wives and children behind, living a lie."

"I've no wife or children. Not yet. And you'll be happy to hear, I'm an honest dealer now. No shortcuts." He pulled another sheet of paper from her short stack. "I suppose we should put our agreement in writing. I can get my solicitor to do up something more formal, but this is between us."

Lucy folded her arms. She must be tired standing in the wet patch, as far away as she could get from him and still be in the room. "Write down I will have absolutely no sexual congress with you."

Simon bit the end of the pen. "Hm. Would that include kissing? I canna see the harm in kissing, and it will be expected by our guests that you show me some affection."

"I won't have you shoving your tongue down my throat!"

"I believe that was *your* tongue down *my* throat earlier."

She looked like she wanted to throw something. Simon hoped she wouldn't remember the pitcher by her feet.

"If I'm to spend all this money on your food and lodging for the next three months, plus pay you off at the end of it, we need to make compromises," he said reasonably. "I hardly think a little peck is going to pass for the lust I'm supposed to feel for my Jane Street mistress. Your breed is notorious, you know."

"I am not—" She snapped her lips shut.

"Yes, I know. You won't actually be my mistress. But we've got to make it look good. Real. I want to be the envy of every man I know."

"Then you'd better get yourself another woman. I'm hardly a great beauty."

Simon gazed across the room. His heart still skipped when he looked at her, even if she tried to scorch him with her scorn and looked like a washerwoman at present. "You'll do. For now. Perhaps I'll have better luck with my next mistress—find a wee biddable girl who'll look at me and thank her lucky stars."

Lucy snorted. He turned to the paper, wrote down a few brief, vague phrases and summoned her to the desk. "Here. Sign this. I'll let Lord Ferguson know I'm taking the house—and you—over."

She glided across the floor, stopping short of coming too close. She took the agreement from his outstretched hand and frowned. "Well, you may write, but I canna read it."

"Aye, that's why I keep a secretary. But this is too intimate an affair for him, wouldn't you agree?"

"I suppose." She snatched the pen from the desk and wrote her name. The document was worthless—neither one of them were who they said they were, but Simon was sure he didn't need a piece of paper to get where he wanted to be—inside his maddening, manipulative new mistress.

Chapter 6

Within two hours of Simon—*her* Simon!—taking his leave, the Jane Street house was invaded by a very superior Scots butler, a French maid, a French cook and a Cockney potboy fresh from Sir Simon's own townhouse. The footman and extra maid would not arrive until tomorrow, MacTavish told her in his soft burr; they had the day off. He had taken one look around Percy's house, clucked disapprovingly, and set everyone to work.

Lucy was grateful she had bathed and dressed to receive this swarm of people. Simon must have many more servants at home if he could spare all these for her. She had gotten used to having the house to herself these past months, with Percy and Yates occasionally coming up for air and a game of three-handed euchre. She was fairly certain she now had more servants than any other courtesan on the street, but nowhere for them to sit or sleep.

Folding Simon's letter in her reticule and taking the French maid Yvonne with her, Lucy went shopping and followed Simon's instructions, spending an enormous amount of his money. She noted she had become Miss Dalhousie again, if she deciphered Simon's bold chicken-scratching correctly, and she was apparently his cousin—his "cows" could not possibly be correct. It was apparent the shopkeepers could understand the intent of the letter even if they could not read the whole of it—it was amazing what the three words "Sir Simon Keith" did to light the gleam of avarice in their eyes. They fell over themselves to promise immediate delivery of bedding and paintings and furniture. Lucy didn't dither—she knew what she liked, and since she'd been instructed not to be mingy, she took that to heart.

By evening MacTavish had hung pictures back on the walls to cover the bare spots and Yvonne had put fresh linen on new beds in the attic. The French chef had taken over Yates's old room after producing a fabulous meal which still resonated on Lucy's palate. Lucy had tested every piece of new furniture downstairs, and now sat before her mirror, eyes half-closed as Yvonne brushed through her hair. It was lovely to feel the touch of someone, even if it was just her new maid.

Yvonne spoke very little English and Lucy spoke very little French, but they seemed to understand each other perfectly well. But when Simon turned up reflected in the mirror, standing at the doorway looking like the richest, most delicious dessert, Yvonne missed Lucy's panicked look and excused herself.

"I did not expect you this evening, Sir Simon," Lucy said, prim, as her heart beat erratically. She was grateful she was wearing a thick flannel nightgown buttoned up to her chin, none of Percy's sheer confections. Simon didn't need to see the pulse at her throat or her pointed nipples. She resolutely refused to face him, continuing to brush her hair without Yvonne's assistance, tangling it only a little.

"You've done remarkably well for one afternoon, Luce. The downstairs looks a treat." His image came closer to the dressing table until he was right behind her, bringing with him a clicking noise. Curious, Lucy looked into the mirror.

In one hand he had a set of small roller bearings, which he fitted on his fingertips as if they were rings. He seemed unaware of the nervous movement of his fingers, but watching him made Lucy dizzy. What would those fingers do next?

She tugged the brush through a knot. "I'm not done yet. The tradesmen's bills will be outrageous."

"As long as everything is in place for next Tuesday night. I've sent dinner invitations to my investors."

"You mean your marks," Lucy said, her lip curling quite contemptuously.

"Not at all. I told you I've gone straight. Your old protector Percy will be there as well. I hope that willna be too awkward for you."

Lucy wanted to give Percy a piece of her mind, but doing so in public would not be possible. "I'm sure I can behave myself. It's a wonder *you* doona feel uncomfortable with another man's leavings."

"Ferguson assured me you had a simple business arrangement. No one's feelings were engaged now, were they?"

"I've lived here six years. Percy and I began and parted as friends."

Simon lifted a slashing dark brow. "How quaint."

"Don't you believe men and women can be friends, Simon?"

"Don't be daft. Of course they canna. Men have a responsibility to the wider world and a woman's place is in the domestic sphere. They have nothing in common but the bedcovers."

Lucy picked up the abandoned hairbrush and ripped it through her hair again. "How ridiculous! You are a caveman!"

"I'm not saying men and women cannot converse intelligently together. I'm quite looking forward to our talks again—you always had something to say and I could only shut you up with a kiss. But a true friendship between a man and woman—impossible. Sex always gets in the way."

She remembered those kisses, damn it. And the most recent one.

Lucy couldn't very well tell him about Percy's lack of interest in her. But perhaps Simon was right—Percy was more like an addled big brother to her than a friend. Friends didn't sell one along with one's house.

"Well, doona worry. I don't intend to make friends with *you*."

"Aye, t'would be difficult. A man is not apt to harbor much affection for his blackmailer."

Lucy chewed a lip. She was regretting this arrangement already, but she needed time to get things settled for herself. No matter what Percy said, she was not putting all their clothes in storage. Some of them would fetch quite a bit, give her some seed money to escape Simon's clutches.

Nay, he was firmly in hers. 'T'was time the boot was on the other foot.

"Here. Let me."

Startled, Lucy watched as Simon took the brush from her hand and smoothed through her waves. His touch was not as light as Yvonne's. She imagined sparks of fire flicking through her hair as he swept from scalp to end. Sitting stiffly so as not to betray her reaction, she waited for him to finish.

But he did not. The brush came up again and again, massaging her head and flowing through her hair down her back so she could feel the soft boar bristles through the strands. Her eye flicked to the mirror where she could see Simon's look of concentration—he had wound the end of her hair now around his hand and held it, bringing it closer to his nose. He *sniffed*.

Lucy jerked away, but he didn't let go. "I am not a fellow dog, sir!"

"That's Sir Simon to you," he said, cheeky as ever. "I think we should get into the habit of you giving me the proper deference. It will be expected Tuesday."

"It's not Tuesday yet."

"Aye. Which is a good thing, for you've much to learn before then."

Lucy clamped down her tongue before she stuck it out at him. "I'm sure you'll find my deportment unexceptionable in company. Percy has already given me instructions on anything that might be suitable for moving about in Society." She'd had years of tea-pouring and frivolous conversations as Percy made her the bosom-bow he'd always wanted.

"Ah." Simon dropped her hair. "I've asked around. It seems Lord Ferguson kept his mistress very much to himself. Many had heard of you, but not a soul I talked to has ever seen the fabled Lucy Dellamar."

"Percy preferred quiet evenings at home. But you are mistaken. We often attended the musicales at Vauxhall Gardens." Of course they had both been masked, Percy wearing the most elaborate of their dresses. Yates trotted behind until he was called into the Dark Walk for a naughty thumb-at-the-nose to the ton while Lucy played scout.

"You like music, do you?"

Lucy did, so she nodded.

"Excellent. We'll go to the opera tomorrow."

She choked. "The opera? You? You are not serious!"

Simon slapped the hairbrush firmly back on her dressing table. "As you said, Luce, it's been thirteen years. We no longer know everything there is to know about each other. I've discovered I have quite an affinity for opera, Gluck in particular. There is a performance of his *Orfeo ed Euridice* tomorrow evening."

An affinity for opera? The boy she knew did not even know the word 'affinity.' "Really?" she asked, doubtful.

"Aye. The poor sod Orpheus mourning his wife reminded me of myself when I found out you were dead. I suppose your aunt did me a favor, then, making me susceptible to the arts."

Susceptible? Simon must have been sleeping with a dictionary all these years.

But with women too, most likely opera dancers. Why couldn't he find one of them to torture?

Nay, she was in a pickle of her own making. It was she who'd set the three-month rule. But three months of opera might broaden her horizons.

"Very well," she said, rising. "Do you have anything in particular you'd like me to wear for my public debut as your mistress?"

"Let's see what you have." Simon picked up a branch of candles and followed her into her dressing room, where a long row of cupboards held Percy's finery. Putting the candles down on a chest, Simon went through the clothes methodically in the dim light, shaking his head as he plucked up each one with his blackened fingernails. Lucy was glad to see there was at least one trace of the boy she knew in this immaculate stranger.

"None of this lot will do. Expect a box tomorrow afternoon."

"What do you mean? These things are perfectly acceptable! You needn't buy me new clothes, Simon."

"I should think you'd be glad to squeeze more coin out of me, Luce. Isn't that what mistresses do?"

"I'm not really your mistress."

Simon sighed. "Do you do nothing but argue?"

Lucy knew she was being difficult, but having Simon loom in her little dressing room made her uncomfortable for too many reasons she was unwilling to examine.

"I'm very tired, Simon. *Sir* Simon. It's been a long, harrowing day."

"You must want to get rid of me to dip into your drink."

"I don't drink!" Lucy said hotly, and then paused. How on earth did Simon know she had buried her troubles in a bottle last night? And drank every last drop, too.

"But before I leave you, I'll need to take some measurements to give to Madame Bernette tomorrow morning."

"Pardon?"

"Measurements, Luce. For the modiste. You're not the average woman." He looked down at her. "I see you come up to the knot of my neckcloth, so that helps, but what about the rest of you? Your arms and such. Here."

He snatched Lucy's arm and held it aloft, studying it as if it were the lost tablet of the Ten Commandments. He dropped it gently and took her shoulders in his warm hands, counting the inches between the span. And then—

Surely it was unnecessary for him to brush across her breasts like that to get to her waist. His thumbs seemed to take an eternity at her nipples as he patted his way down her body. Then they settled at her hips for a few seconds, while the rest of his fingers pressed against her bottom with intent, drawing her close to him.

"Simon!" she warned.

"Um," he said, his blue eyes dancing downward between them.

He could not see her huge feet from this angle, so what had attracted his attention so? Lucy followed his glance and saw the shadow of her pubic hair through her nightgown. All this time, she might have been naked in front of him!

When she looked up, her brown eyes met his blue ones.

They were dark, flinty, the eyes of a man who measured, took what he wanted and asked permission later.

It seemed he wanted a kiss. Another one. All right, she could do it. She closed her eyes and waited.

And then felt him set her back.

His mouth was a grim line. "I willna have you looking like a martyr when I kiss you, Luce."

"I—I wasn't thinking of you kissing me! I've got an eyelash in my eye."

"Oh? Which one?"

"The, uh, left."

He cupped her cheek and examined her furiously blinking eye. "Hold still. You're like a damn butterfly."

Lucy felt his breath on her face. She wished she could be repulsed, but it was spearminty again, clean. Gently he pulled down the skin at the corner of her eye and stared.

She rolled her eyes away. His were too bright, too knowing, and he still had the longest black eyelashes of anyone she'd ever seen.

"It's fair dark in here. I canna see a thing."

"Mayhap I am mistaken," she said.

"Mayhap ye are."

Her Scottish Simon was back, his brogue rough on his tongue. She lifted her face to his, her own tongue licking her lips in nervousness.

He calmed her with the quietest of kisses, a mere warm whisper, one hand still on her cheek and the other splayed flat on her back. She wanted him to push her hard against him, but there was still a maddening space between them.

Och! What was she thinking? It was one thing to kiss the rogue but quite another to rub against him like a cat. Lucy took a half-step backward, and their kiss was broken.

"I'll come for you tomorrow evening. Until then." He saluted her with one finger and walked out of the dressing room. Lucy stood rooted to the floor, the candles flickering in his wake.

"He could have taken a dress to give to Madame Bernette as a sample! There was no need of him to ever touch me!" she said to the empty room. Duped *again*. It would be the very last time.

Chapter 7

When the box from the dressmaker arrived in the middle of the afternoon, Lucy was tempted to throw it into the roaring fire her maid had set in her chamber. There was plenty of coal now to keep the chill of the fall day away, and Lucy had eaten so much at breakfast and luncheon she wondered if she would fit into whatever Simon had ordered for her.

But when she opened the pale pink-striped box, any thought she had of destruction was nipped in the bud. Within was a dress made of apricot-gold tissue, quite simple, almost Medieval in design. The sheer sleeves were long and ended in a gold-thread-embroidered point to her knuckles. Gloves would be impossible to wear with such a sleeve— what had Simon been thinking? One went to the opera in opera gloves! The neckline, also embroidered, cut across her shoulders and was low yet not disgraceful. Lucy had little to show anyway and was happy that would not be revealed.

The bodice fit her like a dream. Blushing, she remembered why. His strong hands had cupped her as they traced down to her waist, cupped her for far too long, as though Simon was a blind man trying to feel his way.

"Zis dress, she iz divine!" Juliette crowed as she helped Lucy into it. "*Regardez*! Ze matching slippers."

Indeed, under the folds of the dress at the bottom of the box were gold satin slippers, *gigantic* satin slippers. Lucy would look like hammered copper from head to toe. The fabric was nearly identical in color to her hair.

There was a letter beneath the shoes. Lucy recognized the bold yet illegible hand.

Wear your ham down tonight.

Sir Simon Keith

As if she didn't know his name, when all too well she did. Ham must be hair in Simon's dreadful handwriting, although she was tempted to visit the kitchen and make Simon's written wish come true. Imagine a rope of meat dangling from her waist. *That* would certainly cause talk.

Lucy swallowed. She had been hidden away here for most of six years. She moved about only Jane Street with any freedom at the courtesan teas and card parties the girls hosted to keep ennui at bay while they waited for their gentlemen. Lucy may as well have been a nun.

Tonight she would appear in public on Simon's arm. She'd read plenty of Percy's gossip rags over the years, and now knew who they meant when they occasionally mentioned "the brilliant and brawny industrialist Sir S—— K."

And she was afraid.

Percy had made her a pet project, so she knew which fork to lift. He'd taught her to stand tall and be proud of her height, calling her an 'original.' But she'd never had to acknowledge before the world that she was a whore.

And now she did.

Simon's whore.

Although she would not let the man anywhere near her again.

Who was she fooling? She'd be trapped in a carriage with him in a few hours. If she knew Simon, he wouldn't be satisfied sitting opposite and discussing the weather. Alone, most likely, in a darkened opera box. In this dress, she'd glow like a candle, inviting his caresses and kisses—it would be expected. She imagined hundreds of opera glasses trained upon them and shivered.

At least she had her fox-fur cloak to guard against the crisp October night and her own stupidity. She'd wrap herself up to her eyelashes and claim she was cold.

Simon had not expected Lucy to come downstairs in her cloak—he'd dreamed all day of seeing her float down the steps in the filmy dress he'd purchased for her. He'd been lucky—some other tall woman had fallen upon hard times and had been unable to pay for it. With a few minor adjustments, Madame Bernette had assured him it would be perfect for Lucy.

And now he couldn't see it.

And he needed to, because he wasn't quite finished dressing her.

"Good evening, Sir Simon," she said, her eyes cast down at her toes.

"I see you are ready. But I am not."

She raised a sculpted brow. He remembered his Lucy having wilder eyebrows he'd had to smooth over with a thumb.

"Take off those animal skins. It's a wonder a soft-hearted girl like you can bear to wear the results of such cruelty."

Lucy stroked the pelt protectively. "Foxes are predators, Sir Simon. If you like an egg with your breakfast, don't speak such nonsense to me."

"There's nothing wrong with good stout wool."

"And yet you leave the poor sheep naked and nicked. Nay, there's fault to be found in most anything man does."

"And women too."

"But not in such proportion, and not with Society's blessing. Did you not make your fortune designing weapons of destruction and death?"

Her barb hit home, and he felt his face flush.

"I saved many lives as well—English lives."

Lucy sniffed. "And you a good Scot."

Simon drew a breath, puffing his massive chest to even greater size. "We're not going to fight a war between us now, Luce. I can see I'd better be on my guard against your philosophical discourses."

She batted her rust-colored eyelashes at him. "And me a mere woman. It's a wonder I have a worthwhile idea in my head."

Simon was not interested in her ideas at present, just removing that monstrous red fur from her body. He stepped closer and unhooked it from under her chin, dropping it to a puddle at her feet.

Sweet Jesu. His throat dried.

Lucy glimmered in the hallway candlelight like a living flame. She had left her hair down, securing it back from her face with a twist of golden ribbon. Her pure oval face was untouched by any maquillage, her whiskey-colored eyes unblinking. The dress—Holy Mother of God—the dress was so perfect Simon wanted to tear it from her body. He allowed himself to touch a bare shoulder with one fingertip, and felt a sizzle right down to his groin.

"Very nice," he croaked.

"Thank you. The dress is lovely. Now that you've seen it, may be go? We wouldn't want to miss the chorus of nymphs and shepherds."

Simon was taken aback. "You know the story?"

"MacTavish does. It's not every butler that gets to accompany his master to the opera."

Simon knew he was a democrat to his toes—he treated all his employees, whether they were house servants or foundry workers, with the same courtesy as he would want to be treated himself. He was generous to a fault, but at least it meant there was no unrest in his foundry. The workers had no reason whatever to feel exploited. Simon had been on the receiving end of discrimination all his life—and it was still coming from the snooty peers whom he could buy and sell in one afternoon. That would change, and Lucy would help him.

"Mac is very fond of opera. There's no reason why cultural opportunities should be reserved for the rich."

"What a reformer you are! I quite agree, else two people like us would not be speaking of classical mythology and German composers to each other."

His mouth quirked. "We have come a long way, haven't we, Luce?"

"Not far enough. I shall be delighted to see the back of you in three months." She bent to retrieve her fur.

Did he believe her? He didn't want to. He wrestled the fur out of her hands and threw it over the banister. "Not yet. I have something else for you."

Simon reached into his pocket. She'd have to have a heart as cold as the stones not to appreciate this necklace. He held the gold strand of topaz and diamond flowers between his fingers to catch the light, with satisfactory result. Lucy's mouth opened, but no sound was expelled.

"Hold still." He walked behind her, sweeping her amber waves over a shoulder and fastened the catch. Her neck was so long and so white and his fingers trembled just a little. He was usually steady—the smallest gear or bearing gave him no trouble, but damn this catch was a vexing thing. He turned her to face him. The necklace settled just above her collarbone as he'd thought, the golden leaves connecting each dazzling cluster. The pulse leaped at her throat, and Simon was compelled to kiss it, brushing his chin against the hard jewels.

They were not the only thing that was hard, but Lucy was loose, pliant in his arms. In his experience, women liked furs and jewelry, and Lucy was no different. She'd turned into quite the adventuress, living on Jane Street and becoming the bought lover of a peer. He shouldn't blame her—her options had been limited by her gender. It wasn't as if she could design cannon and rifles to arm a nation.

He moved from her throat to the soft, smooth flesh under her chin, and nipped her where only he would see his mark. She flinched but was still silent, allowing him to continue his journey to her mouth. Her lips were naturally rosy and tasted of vanilla. Her eyes were closed, but not, he thought, in martyrdom. Her lashes fluttered and her cheeks pinked.

But if he kept watching her as he kissed her, his eyes might cross permanently. Instead, he concentrated on the task of making love to her lips, relying on touch and taste and scent. And hearing too—her breaths hitched, and a little moan traveled from her mouth to his.

Their tongues joined. There was nothing tentative about the kiss or the lust that was still shared between them. It was as if they were still fifteen, in the first flush of discovery. Simon had courted her for two years, if courting was the correct word for hurried couplings in convenient—and in-convenient—places.

Fifteen was half a lifetime ago for both of them. So much had changed, but not this. Simon did not want to go to his favorite opera. He wanted to haul Lucy upstairs and ravish her until neither of them could walk.

Her hand scrabbled at his chest. He'd never be able to tie his complicated neckcloth if she succeeded stripping him in the hallway. Unless she was trying to push him away, but he didn't think so. He gave a final, shuddering sweep inside her mouth, then kissed her on her nose.

"We'd better go."

Lucy's pupils were huge, black, almost obscuring the brown of her eyes. How often had Simon picked up a glass of whiskey and saluted his lost love?

"Um, yes."

She stood like a queen while he covered her shoulders with the dead foxes, counting the minutes until he could slip it from her and show her off, let the ton know that the mysterious Lucy Dellamar was *his* now.

And would be far longer than three months if he had any say about it at all.

Chapter 8

The music soared over the chatter in the theatre as Simon scowled into the darkness. How could these infidels titter and laugh as tragedy played out on stage? To think the ton thought *him* uncivilized—it was they who did not appreciate a work of such genius. Women dripping in too many diamonds and gentlemen—if they could be called that—more than half in their cups. The opera to them was another place to ogle scantily-clad women and tell ribald jokes. To flaunt their alleged wit before other vulgarians such as themselves. He had half a mind to yank Lucy up and leave—his evening was spoilt by the drunken young lords below who came to the opera to prevent anyone from being heard and seen except themselves. Christoph Gluck must be rolling over in his grave.

"Bluidy hell," Simon grumbled.

"I'm sorry, Simon," Lucy whispered. "Is it always like this?"

"Not always. Tonight is especially bad. Opera is appreciated on the Continent. Maybe I should take you there."

But now was not a propitious time to leave England, not with his financial future in the balance. But wouldn't it be fun to introduce Lucy to the wider world? Maybe someday.

He reached for her hand, reassured to find it was still rough in spots from working straw and stitching trim. Lucy's aunt had taught her well, and the hats Lucy had designed had been the talk of Edinburgh until she left six years ago. Everyone he had met when he went back home had told him how successful she'd been, not that her aunt let her keep the profits of her labor.

Simon still had to pinch himself that Lucy was sitting beside him and not lying in some graveyard. All this while she had been kept by Lord Percival Ferguson, still making hats, but for herself now.

She wasn't wearing one tonight. A hat would have covered the river of rippling hair he'd asked her to leave loose, and she had complied. He had never seen her look so magnificent—gilded, pale, aloof, her head raised as he guided her through the throngs in the lobby. People had parted as though for a queen, and an instant buzzing behind his back told him they were now talking of the woman with Sir Simon Keith. He'd waved off the few curious faces he knew, not wishing to introduce her. Keep her to himself.

It was an odd feeling. He had wanted to show her off, claim her, raise himself in Society just by owning a house on Jane Street and keeping a beautiful mistress in it. But now that he had what he wanted—more or less—he wanted to protect Lucy from the prying eyes and vicious tongues of the ton.

He had her to himself now in the dim opera box, so close he could smell her lilac perfume. She'd always loved lilacs—one spring he'd hacked off branches from a house on St. Andrew's Square and brought them to her. He'd robbed the garden more easily than the house, and was somewhat more pleased with Lucy's joy at her flowers than what his fence paid him for Lady Murray's jewels. He brought her hand to his lips and kissed her knuckles, then the soft mound of her palm.

The design of the dress assured her hands remained bare, and he had plans for each and every digit. His eyes never leaving the stage as Orfeo wept, he suckled each of Lucy's talented fingers—the fingers he would soon turn from hat-making to making him hard. Harder. Her hand trembled in his, so he knew he was making progress. He ran his tongue lightly from base to the tip of her polished fingernails. She tasted of lilac soap and salt—her hands were damp. She had been nervous.

Good. He wished to keep her off-balance, the better to topple her into a bed.

"Stop *licking* me," she hissed.

He paid no attention, circling his tongue in the center of her palm. Lucy shifted in her seat, reminding him there were other places to kiss. He was about to find out if she tasted as good as she looked.

Simon slid off his ruby-velvet padded chair to his knees.

"What are you doing? Are you ill?"

"Och, aye. Quite prostrate. There's only one thing that will cure me." He raised her skirts over her long legs so quickly she didn't have a chance to pull them down.

She slapped the top of his head. "Simon, you are mad! People will see!"

He looked up to her in the shadows. "No they won't. If anyone looks this way, they'll think I left the box for a moment. Sit back and enjoy yourself, Luce."

Her mouth hung open, then she rapped his head again. "You will not—I cannot—Simon!"

Good. Now she was quiet as a clam. He angled her hips in the chair for better reception. She was, mercifully, not wearing drawers, just sheer apricot stockings banded with butterfly garters. He left her legs alone this time and homed in to her center. Her nether hair tickled his nose as he dipped his tongue into her pink folds. He found her bud and sucked it swiftly into his mouth. Lucy shrieked at a conveniently loud time in the libretto, then sat rigid as he plied his skills.

Not quite lilac. But all Lucy.

Soon he made it impossible for her to sit still. She turned liquid beneath his hands and mouth, bucking under him until he worried he'd lose a tooth in her frenzy. What if he pulled her down to the floor with him, took her as poor Orpheus argued with the Furies for admission to the Underworld?

Simon wanted admission to Lucy's underworld in the very worst way.

He knew the instant she came apart, her juices bursting on his tongue. He gentled her until she came down from her transports, then pulled a handkerchief from his pocket.

"How dare you?" came the furious whisper above his head. He ducked quickly as her hand came down again.

"Fortuna favet audaci."

"*What?*"

"Fortune favors the brave, Luce. It's on my new crest." Simon blotted his mouth, almost reluctant to wipe away traces of Lucy's arousal. He'd paid good money for an escutcheon immortalizing his knighthood, for all it really meant—which was nothing.

Lucy mumbled something unintelligible while Simon adjusted himself in his knee breeches. He had another act to sit through and was uncertain if that would be possible without some relief. It was unlikely Lucy would help him, despite what he'd just done for her.

He bounced up and resumed his seat. Lucy was tugging frantically on her dress, removing her long white legs from Simon's sight. Simon noted the silk tissue had been sadly wrinkled during the past few minutes.

It hadn't taken Lucy long to break down, he thought, smug. He'd been so busy lately he'd given little thought to sexual exercise, but that would change, whatever Lucy said. He observed her profile as she stared at the stage, her lashes batting a mile a minute. He pretended to concentrate on the music, but was aware of her vibrating angrily in the next chair, her rather large foot twirling in time to the orchestra.

"Wait a minute! Orpheus is a woman!" Lucy said suddenly.

"Yes. The role is almost always performed by a woman. Unless it is sung by a castrato." He shuddered at the thought. Simon might like opera, but his devotion to it only went so far.

"How ridiculous. I want to go home."

"Use your imagination, Luce. Madame Olivetti is built like a munitions factory."

"I don't care how big she is—how can she be singing about her love for another woman?"

"Such things do occur, I assure you. Close your eyes and just listen to the music."

The vehemence of Lucy's glare was lost in the gloom. But she sat back, her fingernails scratching at the velvet on the chair arms. Simon blocked out the rudeness from the audience and lost himself from his cares until Lucy's huffs and puffs were impossible to ignore.

"All right," he sighed. "We'll leave. Stay here and I'll get the carriage brought round."

The evening had not turned out quite as he'd planned, but the night was still young. If he was sufficiently brave, who knew how it would end?

She couldn't blame the dark, or the mournful aria, especially now that she knew that Orpheus was a fat woman with a lyre. She had succumbed to Simon with such ease she wanted to bat herself over the head with her reticule. But he had surprised her, doing such a thing. He had never—well, she hadn't known a man could do that to a woman when she was young. She knew it now, of course—Percy's lessons had included many other things besides elocution and table manners. She had spent most of the last six years agog at all the new information, far from her aunt's narrow restrictions.

What Simon had done had felt wicked. And so very, very good. His tongue had been rough and hot and perfect. He'd known just where to swipe and swirl it. No doubt he'd had his head buried under skirts for years practicing. In opera boxes *and* out.

Lucy gathered up her fox cloak, although she was much too warm to put it on. The smoke from the limelight and the crush of the crowd could be felt even up here in Simon's private box. She was sure she looked a fright, although at least her hair hadn't fallen out of its pins because there had been no pins in it to begin with. She had shocked everyone wearing her hair down—she might as well have been wearing a sign that said 'Courtesan.'

Her fingers reached for the topaz flowers, wondering if Simon would expect his gift back when she left him. At one time she'd had a tidy little fortune salted away, but when Percy lost his money—threw his money away—she had contributed to their little household by whatever means she could. If she could worm money out of Simon, perhaps she could repay her neighbors for their missing teaspoons and jewelry.

Damn Percy anyway. After all she had done for him, he had not even come to check on her yesterday or today, just abandoned her to Sir Simon Keith. She would summon him tomorrow to tell him his plan had worked only too well.

She watched the stage as the hinges of Hades opened, feeling much like Orpheus. Then a warm hand rested on her shoulder. It was Hades himself.

"Are you ready, Luce, or have you changed your mind? The ballet dancers are coming up."

"And I'm sure you'd like to see their legs as they prance around, but we are leaving," she said tartly.

"Och, I've seen the legs I wanted to tonight." Simon grinned down at her, like a well-satisfied wolf.

"You won't be seeing them again!"

But Lucy was afraid her words were empty of bite, just as her head was empty of rational thought when Simon Grant was near. He may have changed his name, but he was still the same Simon and she was still the same stupid, stupid girl.

Chapter 9

Three months. Ninety days. Two-thousand, one-hundred and sixty hours, give or take a few minutes. Lucy was very good with numbers—she'd kept her aunt's books as well as surpassed the woman in creating the loveliest hats this side of Paris. Many a marquess's wife would insist on a springtime trip to Edinburgh to purchase Lucy's hats. In three months she might be able to set up a small business right here in London, if she could stay away from Simon.

Not likely. He sat opposite her in his expensive carriage, whistling as the horses clip-clopped to Jane Street. She snuggled into her fur, resentful of his good cheer.

Well, why shouldn't he be cheerful? He'd seen half an opera and half of her. But that would be all, she swore it.

MacTavish opened the green-glazed door before they could alight from the carriage. "Is anything amiss, Sir Simon? The opera cannot be over so soon."

"It is for us," Lucy said, sailing into the house with her nose high.

"Miss Dellamar does not share our love for Gluck, I'm afraid. Mac, would you be so kind as to open a bottle of port and bring it upstairs to Miss Dellamar's sitting room?"

Lucy turned on him. "You can't stay!"

"Now, Luce. I remember to the letter what my limits here

are. There's nothing in our agreement that says I can't have a drink with you upstairs any time I want."

"I don't drink!"

Simon raised a dark brow.

"I don't! Not very often." And when she did drink, it was good Scottish whiskey. "Mr. MacTavish, you may bring port for Sir Simon, but I'd just as soon have a glass of *uisge beatha*."

The butler didn't bat an eye. "Very good, Miss Dellamar."

"And send Miss Dellamar's maid off to bed, Mac. We'll have no need of her tonight." Simon unhooked her cape and tossed it to the butler, then extended an elbow for the trip upstairs.

"I suppose you think *you'll* undress me."

"Only if you ask," Simon said innocently.

"I'll never ask the likes of you to help me do anything!" Unfortunately in her anger, Lucy missed a step and Simon saved her from plummeting down the stairs.

"Lucy, Lucy. It is I who should be angry—I've been denied my rights in bed."

"You have no rights, you wretched man! We are not married." Lucy shook him off and threw herself down on a cozy chintz chair in her little parlor. The fire had been lit, and the room tidied. She didn't like that one bit. Tomorrow she'd speak to MacTavish to have the staff leave her things alone.

"But I am your protector for the next three months. It's not every man who would agree to keep a mistress and not make proper use of her."

"Proper *use*?" Lucy saw stars, felt her blood pound at her temple. Simon would give her an apoplexy before those three months were done.

Simon stretched his legs before him on the sofa, knocking the table askew. "You know what I mean. A mistress is supposed to be biddable. Flatter a fellow. See to his needs. You wouldn't even let me sit through my favorite opera."

Lucy straightened the table between them, not that it was a sufficient barrier. "No one is keeping you here, Sir Simon. Perhaps you should go back. Right now. They'll let an important man like you back in."

"No doubt. I invested in the production, for all the pleasure I got out of it. The audience would have enjoyed a troupe of trained monkeys just as well."

Lucy almost laughed, which would quite go against the animosity she was projecting. She was saved from herself by MacTavish, who carried a silver tray with two bottles, two glasses and a crystal bowl of shelled walnuts. He placed their refreshment on the table and left. To Lucy's surprise, Simon leaned forward and poured two glasses of whiskey.

"How can you do without Mr. MacTavish at your house?" Lucy asked, taking the glass from Simon. She glared at his dirty fingertips on principle.

"Oh, I've an under-butler, and an under-under butler. Mac's sons. One of them serves as my valet, too. They're glad to be out from under his thumb and are out-Mac-Tavishing him at every turn. The house is so damned proper now I'm afraid to drop my stockings on the floor."

Lucy did smile now. Once Simon had more holes than socks on his feet. He'd never known his parents, and his ancient grandmother had been too frail to fight his youthful follies.

Simon had been wild, and Lucy had been tame. They were doomed from the start.

She took a sip of whiskey and watched as Simon tossed a walnut up in the air and caught it between his teeth. He was like a blue-eyed lion, toying with his prey. Lucy did not want any part of her to wind up between his teeth again.

Although—what if she were to set more rules? Rules that only benefitted her? She might not allow him into her bed and into her, but what was stopping her from having Simon repeat his performance at the opera?

Lucy held the cards, or at least Simon thought she did. In truth, she could not imagine turning him into the authorities. And who would believe that rich Sir Simon Keith, industrialist *extraordinaire*, was once a scrawny Edinburgh thief? Simon had progressed even back then from pickpocket to cat burglar, so how natural it was for him to continuously rise and improve himself.

She's seen the looks he'd received tonight at the opera—looks of curiosity, envy and grudging respect. She'd always known he was smart, and far too skilled with his hands. Now it seemed she had his tongue to add to his attributes.

"I have an alteration to our agreement, Simon," Lucy said abruptly.

Simon put his drink down. "Oh?"

Lucy picked hers up and took an enormous swallow of Scotch courage. "Yes." And then she proceeded to tell him, stumbling over only a word or two.

Simon did the best to keep a straight face. His plan was working even more quickly than he'd hoped. To have Lucy dependent on him for her pleasure would be the first step into getting her to give him his. She blushed and stammered her way through the new rules and Simon nodded his head like an old sage considering their wisdom. When she was done, he leaned back on the flowery couch and pursed his lips. He pulled out a bearing from his watch pocket and stroked it absently.

"And you say I may touch you everywhere but you will not touch me?"

Lucy nodded.

"So, really, I'm to be your mistress and you're to be my master."

Her eyebrows knit. "That sounds very odd."

"Odd it is. Let me get this straight. I'm to feed and clothe you. Keep you in style at Jane Street for the next three months. Make love to you from head to toe—"

"Not really!"

"Your distinctions are negligible, Luce. Just because I'm not thrusting my cock in your quim doesn't make it any less satisfying for you. Be at your beck and call. Pay you off at the end of it—you haven't yet mentioned the sum of your extortion, by the way—just so you will not have me arrested for my boyhood indiscretions."

"They were a bit more than indiscretions. There was a price on your head."

"Do you plan on collecting it?"

Lucy gaped at him.

"Suppose I say no to all this. Are you prepared to tap the night watchman's shoulder and ask him to summon you a constable so he can take evidence?"

Lucy lifted her stubborn chin. "Aye. And don't forget my seventeen shillings. With interest."

Simon closed his eyes. She really was too beautiful when she was angry. "Very well. You've got me over a barrel, you do. I'm shaking in my boots."

"You don't believe me."

"I might not. But I can't take the chance, can I now, Luce? I've built up a nice new life for myself—I've got hundreds of people dependent upon me for their livelihoods. I can't change the face of England from a prison farm in Australia."

"They might hang you instead."

She said it with a great deal of enthusiasm. Aye, his Lucy was definitely angry at him. Damn it, he *had* come back for her. He couldn't help it if she'd gotten impatient and run off with that popinjay Ferguson.

"An excellent point, and I'm fond of my neck." He slipped the bearing back in his pocket and tugged at his neckcloth. There would not be much need to think tonight if he was lucky. "Well, I suppose I'd best begin these oner-ous duties, seeing to your comforts. You don't mind if I re-move my jacket and tie, do you?"

Lucy's mouth dropped open. "N-now? But you just—"

Simon grinned. "I did, didn't I? But it can't hurt you to do it again. I don't think anybody's ever died of too many orgasms. Well, perhaps a lecherous old man may have met his Maker a time or two, but you're still young yet, and in reasonably good health, I trust."

Lucy had no answer to that. She continued to stare at him as he unbuttoned his figured black satin waistcoat. When he reached the top button of his fine lawn shirt, she shot up off her chair.

"That's enough."

"I live to serve. What would you like me to do?"

He was fairly certain she mumbled "Go to the devil." He'd already been there and back—he could still hear the cannon and smell the sulfur.

"I need help with my dress."

"Certainly, my lady."

She was still as a marble statue as he twisted her gingery hair out of the way and attacked the row of golden thread and hooks. He'd always had nimble fingers, and in seconds the fabric gaped at her back. She wore a back-lacing demi-corset over a plain white shift and he loosened the strings without being asked. "Now what?"

She pivoted to face him. "Now you are to sit back down on the sofa and finish your whiskey. I will call when I'm ready for you."

So he was to be deprived of seeing her glorious naked body revealed, but he had his memory of yesterday morning. It was probably just as well he not see all of her tonight—he was already hideously uncomfortable in his nether regions.

Simon sipped his whiskey standing up, leaning an elbow on the marble mantel. The room was cozy, not like the lair of any courtesan he'd ever visited. There were no naughty inspirational pictures on the walls, or much in the way of valuable objets d'art. Sold, probably, to keep Ferguson afloat. The earl had been up to the tips of his ears in hopeless schemes—Simon would alter the man's luck before too long.

And then would Ferguson want his mistress back?

He couldn't have her.

Bluidy hell. Simon loved Lucy still, after all these years. He wasn't sure why—she was no longer the stars-in-her-eyes girl who permitted him liberties in the shadows. She was, come to think of it, a bit of a shrew, her tongue as sharp as her cheekbones.

But he couldn't marry her—she'd been Ferguson's mistress for six years. Any idea he had of assuring his children's place in Society would be shattered if he made a woman like Lucy his wife.

Double bluidy hell. Simon tossed the rest of his whiskey into the flames, where the flare was so bright he had to step back before he singed his silk stockings.

But no one had ever seen her.

Except for tonight—but he had not introduced her to a soul. She could have been his cousin come to town. She'd been around to the shops with a note that said just that, although it was not likely a country cousin would furnish a love nest on Jane Street for him. But Simon had the money enough to bribe the storekeepers. If Ferguson's silence could be bought—and Simon was sure it wouldn't take much as the man was fair desperate—Lucy might have a chance.

Triple bluidy hell. His investors' dinner here next week. He'd have to cancel it.

Simon's mind whirred like the gears to his inventions. He

might not have a formal education, but no one could say that Sir Simon Keith was not a canny Scot. If anyone could see a way to turn wicked Lucy Dellamar back into innocent Lucy Dalhousie, it was he.

However, first he had to gentle Lucy with his hands and tongue, a task that was altogether more simple.

Chapter 10

Lucy's hands shook as she tied the ribbon of her pale yellow robe. It had not been to Percy's taste—he was altogether into more flamboyant jewel-tones. She smoothed her hands down the silk and contemplated kicking herself for changing her arrangement with Simon.

But damn it. She'd been without so much as a peck on the cheek in thirteen years. She was almost half-dead already, if she was lucky enough to live to be a septuagenarian. Her prospects for marriage were dismal at best—how could she explain to a decent man that she'd lived on Jane Street for six years? *Everyone* had heard of Jane Street.

Six years ago she'd jumped at the chance to escape her aunt and her empty future. It was even more empty now. Lucy was a fool then, and a fool now.

But she would have something to remember on those cold future nights as she tacked silk flowers onto the crown of a hat and shooed away her cats. She'd have a cat right now, but Percy claimed they made him sneeze.

Percy. Her brows scrunched. *Simon*. They scrunched even more. Men were impossible, but a necessary evil.

Lucy fluffed up her pillows and her hair, swallowed her reservations and called Simon's name.

Her voice wavered, but he must have been listening closely. He walked through the connecting door in an instant, his dark hair gleaming like polished ebony in the candlelight.

His eyes were bright too, flicking over her form as she sat propped up on her bed.

"You're lovely, Luce."

"You don't have to talk at all—there's no point to your flattery."

"It's nae flattery. I mean it." His voice was pitched low, his Scottish burr fighting back from the English civilization he'd imposed upon it. She wanted to stick her fingers in her ears.

"Words are cheap. Get on with it."

Och, but she was bold as brass, when inside she felt like a puddle of oozy oatmeal. But it was rather fun to order Simon about. She had been much at his mercy when they were young, always waiting for a snatched kiss or a few minutes when she could simply *look* at him. He'd been beautiful in his way. But she had to admit he was far more beautiful now—he'd grown into his height, filled out. His body rippled with muscle as he walked across the room toward her.

However, she'd never ask him to remove his clothes. That would be too much temptation. Lucy might lose her head and forget that she was in charge here.

"What is it you want, Luce?"

She didn't know. She shrugged. "You'll think of something appropriate."

"It'll nae be *appropriate*," he said, grinning like a wolf. He'd always had good teeth for a poor boy. Lucy was particular about teeth. Soon these teeth might be skimming down her skin, taking a wee nip here, a wee nip there—

"What was that, Luce? I didn't quite hear."

She must have let out a groan. She could barely think for the buzzing in her head. "N-nothing. Perhaps you can start by kissing me. That would be pleasant."

"Aye. Pleasant. And how do you want me, Luce? Sitting next to you on the bed, or lying down?"

"Sitting is fine."

He reached out and put a finger on her mouth. "So you'll be wanting a kiss on these lips here then, not the other ones."

He looked so terribly proud and pleased with himself for bringing up that wicked thing he'd done at the opera. She whacked his hand away. "To start."

"Your wish is my command, my lady, else I'll find myself in the bowels of a prison ship. I hear there are rats and very bad men aboard. 'T'would be a waste of my talents to be transported." He scratched his shadowed chin—his beard was coming in dark at this late hour. "I'm not sure King George would let me go."

Lucy sat up straight, forgetting all about kissing. "You know the new king?"

"Sure and I do. Who do you supposed knighted me? I'd met him several times before, o'course, when I—och, never you mind. You wouldn't understand."

"I'm not stupid!"

"Nae, you're sharp as a tack, but you're not an engineer, are you? I did some things for the Crown during the war—and after too—that are complicated. I should have asked for a pardon then." He took a step backward. "Who knows, perhaps it's not too late now."

Lucy's heart stilled. The evening was not turning out quite as she hoped. She should be in Simon's arms and he should be kissing her senseless, not that she had much sense to begin with. "You'd admit your guilt? Let people know who Sir Simon Keith really is?"

"Aye. Then people from my past could hold nothing over my head. And let me keep it."

Lucy was appalled—if he confessed he'd have no reason

to stay here and do what she wanted. Do what she *needed*.
"You'd be ruined."

"Aye, that I would. All my pretentions to fit into Society
would be shown to be the foolish dreams of a gutter thief.
Ah, well. It was too much to hope for that I could get away
with it all forever."

"No, Simon! You've worked too hard, come too far."
She swallowed. "Never mind about the kissing. You don't
have to do anything you don't want to." She looked down
at her hands, so white against the yellow of her robe, and
sighed. "You should know I couldn't clap you in jail. I was
wrong to try to blackmail you. I thought I needed time to
get settled—and teach you a lesson, too—but I'll be fine.
Better than fine. Just give me a day to pack and I'll be out of
your hair and you can get a new mistress."

Simon sat down on the bed, shifting her into him. He put
his arm around her. "Those are the most words you've said
to me in two days."

"I said quite a lot to you in my head."

He brushed her cheek with a fingertip. "I'll bet. You
never were a shy one."

"But I was. I was bold only with you, and look where
that got me."

The stubble of his cheek tickled her forehead. "I'm sorry
you felt you had no choice but to become Ferguson's mistress."

"I—" She couldn't say anything. She'd promised Percy.

She needed to talk to Percy—explain to him that Sir
Simon Keith was *her* Simon, come back as if from the dead.
Percy was a romantic—surely he'd release her from her
promise, or possibly even explain things to Simon himself.
He didn't have to go into every excruciating detail—and he
owed her something, since she'd resorted to thieving for
him.

"But it's all water under the bridge, Luce. We can't change

the past now, can we? We wouldn't be the people we are today without it."

This philosophical Simon was a stranger to her, but the comfort of being in his arms was familiar. She snuggled in closer, grateful that he'd shed the layers of clothing a gentleman—even if he was a pretend gentleman—wore.

"I'd like to kiss you anyway, blackmail or no," he whispered. "Will you let me, Luce? Will you be my mistress tonight?"

Why not? She would leave tomorrow—today, now, from the hands of the little china clock at her bedside. One night with Simon might not make up for thirteen years without, but it was the best she could do.

"All right." She'd save being sorry for later.

She couldn't miss the flash of smug triumph on his face. *Damn.* Lucy hadn't put up much of a fight. She had folded from her blackmail scheme at the first sign that he was willing to throw his life away and confess to his sins, and had agreed to sleep with him despite the harm to her heart.

But Simon would never have been so stupid as to tell the king or anyone else—more likely he would have stuffed Lucy bound and gagged in a closet like he did to poor Lady Murray when she came home to discover him rifling through her jewel box. Lady Murray had testified that the young man had been remarkably gentle and courteous as he had done so—nevertheless, it was considered kidnapping, even if Simon had seated her on a padded chair in her own closet, with her gouty foot up on a footstool.

Simon fumbled with the ribbons of her peignoir.

"I've changed my mind."

His fingers stopped tugging. "Pardon?"

"A lady is entitled to change her mind." Lucy wiggled out of Simon's arms. She was immediately chilled.

"I dinna understand."

There was no smugness on his face now, just a few wrinkles on his brow and a petulant lip. He was the picture of adorable confusion, but she vowed not to succumb to that puppy-dog look.

"I misspoke. I don't want to be your mistress. Or any man's mistress."

"You're coming a bit late to that conclusion, aren't you, Luce?"

Lucy clutched her hands into fists before she slapped him. But now that she had two fists good and ready, why not? She punched him on his stubbled chin. Not hard. But hard enough.

"Oy! What's that for, now? I'm not laying a hand on you, you daft wench."

She scrambled off the bed. "You're right, Simon. I *am* daft. To think I almost—well, never mind. I'll thank you to leave now. I'll be out first thing in the morning. Percy wants all the dresses, so I won't have much to pack."

Simon rubbed his chin, looking wounded, as if such a hulking man could really be injured by anything smaller than a large-bore cannon. Then he shook his head, a dark curl flopping over his left eyebrow. "Nay. I'll not leave. We have an agreement. In writing."

Lucy swallowed back a shriek. It would do no good to work herself up anymore—she was already feeling an uncomfortable pulse at her neck. "Very well. Sleep with your agreement. *I'm* going to go sleep on the sofa in the upstairs parlor. Good night."

She made it halfway through the door before she was trapped in Simon's arms again.

"Let me go!"

His breath was warm on her cheek. "Never."

She could feel the pounding of his heart against her chest. "You let me go before. Why do you want me now when I don't want you?"

He looked down at her, his blue eyes feral. "Don't you, lass?"

He was insufferable.

He was right.

What was it about this thoughtless brute that made her lose her wits? She was practically elderly now—she should know better. She *did* know better.

One night with Simon might lead to two—or more—and then she really would be losing her pasted-over virtue. He'd soon tire of her.

He'd marry.

And then where would she be?

"*Please* let me go."

"I canna. Ye fit perfect, Luce. Can ye nae feel it?"

Oh, she felt it. She felt *everything*. His erection pressed into her belly, his fingers stroking her back and playing with her unbound hair, his lips against her temple. He sounded now like the boy she had loved, who had sweet-talked her until she'd gorged and sickened on his honeyed words. Tears spilled down her cheeks.

"Och, Luce, dinna ye cry." He brushed the tears away, then kissed their traces. Lifting her mouth to his, she tasted her salt and his mint. She allowed him to delve into a deeper kiss, for how could she not? She could stand in the doorway forever kissing him, as long as he held her up.

But it seemed Simon had other ideas. He scooped her up as if she weighed nothing and carried her back to the bed, where he laid her down as if she were a fragile egg. But that was his last gentle maneuver, for his hands tore at her clothing and his mouth feasted on her newly exposed skin. He nipped her throat and worked his way down her chest, thumbing her nipples to diamond-hard peaks. Somehow he made her feel full and womanly, cupping one breast in his large warm hand as he suckled and swirled at the other.

Lucy felt a tug to her womb as his tongue worked his new magic.

For it was new—her Simon had not the expertise that Sir Simon possessed, nor had he had the luxury of making love to her in a soft feather bed all those years ago. The combination of his skill and her comfort—and discomfort, too, for how could she combat the scorching heat that washed over her?—made her sink deeper into the mattress in confusion, torn between purely receiving and reaching out to him.

Lucy ached in places that had been neglected too long, most especially her heart, which threaded and jumped as if being squeezed. She might die any minute, but please not before he finished with her. Before they finished with each other.

Her body was waking, each brush of his fingers and lips sparking against her skin. It was no longer enough to lie passively as he swept her up in sin. She needed to feel his skin, too. Somehow she emerged from her dazed languor to pull up Simon's shirt. Lucy wanted to touch his chest as he was touching hers, but with a growl he captured her hand and thrust it lower. His cock was enormous, stiff, straining to be relieved of the constraint of fabric. She obliged, fingers trembling at his falls.

His cock was hot and velvety in her hand. It, like the rest of him, seemed to have grown from what she recalled. But she couldn't see for herself, as Simon's shaggy dark head obstructed her vision. So she went on sensation alone, thumbing the raised vein from root to tip. It jerked in response and Simon's tongue twinned with it in a desperate thrust around her nipple. Lucy fitted her hand around his cock and drew it up, then down in the dimly-remembered dance they'd perfected in their snatched moments. She had not lost the knack—Simon expressed satisfyingly anguished sounds as she glided slowly around his member. His hand abandoned a breast and sought her center, replicating what he'd done in the theatre, using a thumb instead of a tongue to press against her pubic bone. A few short, hard strokes and she was crumbling again, fragmenting, shattering, breaking apart and grateful for every scattered shard.

Her breathless cries didn't stop him. Simon had said something about too many orgasms. She had lost count already and she was as good with numbers as he was good with his hands. As Simon continued the onslaught, Lucy quite forgot to touch him, so witless was she.

But he soon remedied that, easing his fingers away. Before Lucy could come down from her heights to miss him, he settled himself over her and inched inside her.

She was tight. It was slow going, but he was patient, his shadowed face a study in concentration. He was too beautiful to look at, so she turned her head. His arms corded at her sides, muscled and entirely masculine, his hands splayed near her shoulders. His blackened fingernails fascinated her—he was so clean everywhere else. The nails were clipped short and buffed—by a MacTavish, no doubt, if Simon sat still long enough. He seemed like a tightly-coiled spring, bursting with energy and industry. It was only at the opera he'd been physically quiet, mesmerized by that outrageous woman who played Orpheus. Lucy supposed after Percy she should be used to people switching genders, but she was still not entirely comfortable with the idea. The thought of it all would send her strict aunt into a state of permanent vapors.

Lucy chided herself for thinking of her aunt at a time like this, when Simon was doing his damnedest to connect himself to her. But perhaps she should distract herself—not think about how perfect he felt as he entered her and withdrew, how hard and hot he was, how—oh! that twisty thing he still did that touched her just where she needed most to be touched—how liquid and loose she felt as she lay under him, like a pond that still rippled from a rock being tossed in.

But Lucy felt the ocean coming, crashing waves and lunar pull, and thoughts of aunts and opera dissolved in the storm that was Simon, his face in exquisite agony—she had to look up now—his blue eyes beseeching. There was perfect understanding between them. No barrier. No hesitation. No regret.

"Yes," she whispered. Yes and yes and yes. He swept down to kiss her when he came, an uncontrolled kiss and clash of teeth and tongue that took her along with him. Her hips rose to meet the last deep thrust and she wrapped her long legs around him, drawing him in and keeping him safe.

They shuddered together, damp, disheveled, exultant. Simon still kissed her, moving his lips from hers to her nose, her eyelids, her forehead. She felt like a child blessed at church.

Lucy had wondered all those years ago what this would be like—to love Simon in a proper bed, to not be afraid of discovery, to allow him to spill within her. They had been remarkably careful as youngsters, not wanting to bring another poor baby into the world. If she fell pregnant after tonight, she expected Simon would see to it that she and the child were provided for.

A child would be a miracle—she'd not allowed herself to think along those lines for years, watching her youth vanish along with her reputation.

Simon's baby. Lucy envisioned a dark-haired busy boy whose pockets would be filled with clockworks and coils of wire.

Och, she was a sentimental fool, dreaming of a future that was not to be. This was just one night—it meant nothing. Would lead to nothing, and shouldn't. What would she do with a child, bringing it up alone? Simon thought she was a whore, would probably take the child from her. Even if she told him the truth, he was not apt to believe her. What woman who lived on Jane Street for six years could be innocent?

Lucy shut her eyes, smoothing a cheek on Simon's shoulder, the scent of his skin as familiar to her as her own reflection. Some things never changed. She'd fallen victim to him again but she couldn't blame him. Lucy had been hungry for a man's touch for too long. The fact that Simon seemed to be the only man who made her heart stutter was not his fault.

She should say something to him as he held her tight, but she didn't trust herself to speak. He was equally reticent, the only sound in the room the steady hiss and hum of burning coals in the fireplace. They lay entwined until Lucy's heart slowed and the sweat chilled her skin.

Simon noticed her shiver and hugged her. "Are you cold, Luce?"

She nodded. He reached for the edge of the blanket and wrapped it around them, but it was still not enough to warm the ice within. She would have to leave tomorrow—today. Where would she go? She hadn't a friend left in the world except Percy.

Percy. Perhaps he'd take her on his staff. She could be his secret lady's maid. A hopeless chortle erupted.

"What's so funny, Luce? Dinna tell me you find this pickle funny."

Lucy pulled away. "This pickle?"

"Aye. I'll not be fighting you tooth and nail every time I take you to bed. We need to set some ground rules. I'm that fond of my chin."

Lucy was too. Right now it was dusted with the beginnings of his dark beard and he looked like a delicious pirate. "Just because—" Lucy swallowed. "This was a one-off, Simon. I still plan to leave."

His lips quirked. "This meant nothing to you? You needn't lie to me, Luce. I know women. I know you. You were every bit as engaged as I."

"Are you expecting me to sing your praises? You'll have a long wait. I've had better."

Lie, lie, lie. It was the only thing that would free her.

Simon didn't seem in the least perturbed. He stroked her flushed cheek with a fingertip. "Perhaps you can teach me a trick or two from your repertoire. I'm always interested in learning new things, especially if they add to my pleasure. If I could teach myself to read, I don't doubt you could teach me to fuck you with greater finesse."

Finesse. He *had* been reading the dictionary. The look on his face told her he didn't think it was possible for him to improve his amatory skill, and he was right, damn him.

"You are revolting." She wriggled in his arms but he wouldn't let her go.

"I hear the courtesans on Jane Street are unsurpassed in the sexual arts. So, what's your first lesson? I'm an eager pupil."

She resolutely shut her eyes. "I'm tired, Simon. I want to go to sleep."

"All right."

Lucy waited for him to let her go, but she was still clamped in his arms. She poked his chest. "Go home, Simon."

"Nay. I'm perfectly comfortable right where I am."

"Well, I am not! I can't sleep with you here, all over me. I can't breathe."

"You seem to have enough breath to yell at me. Hush now." He kissed the top of her head.

Unbelievable! She writhed a bit, but it was clear Simon would not give way. Lucy would just have to hope he forgot to hold her once he fell asleep.

But it was dawn before he disentangled himself from her, and that was only so he could stoke the fire and kiss her body awake in warmth.

Chapter 11

There was much an important man like Sir Simon Keith had on his plate this day, but at the moment he could not recall a single appointment or obligation. In fact, he really never wanted to leave the bed again to do anything but make love to Lucy, now that the chill had been driven from the room. The fire roared merrily, the October sun streamed in between the chintz curtains, and his mistress lay dazed and dazzled in a patch of light. Her hair was the color of the fine copper wire he used in his electrical experiments, a lovely rose-gold. He wrapped a strand around his finger, almost feeling its own current to his heart.

They'd shared a connection years ago, when she was coltish and shy but the most beautiful girl he knew. Lucy was beautiful still—in her own particular, out-of-the-ordinary way. Or would be if she weren't scowling at him, her bronzy eyebrows beetling. Had she already forgotten what he'd done to her this morning? Twice.

At some point he'd have to devote a portion of his brain to rescuing Lucy from this life of debauchery and make her his wife. For there was not a question in his mind after last night and this morning that he wanted to marry her. The idea of her sleeping—and not sleeping—beside him filled him with intense, obstinate desire.

Simon didn't care how many men she'd slept with. He'd been her first, by God, and he would be her last. If having Lucy meant giving up his tenuous hold on London Society, well then, so what? He'd still have his money and his ideas. He could work from anywhere. Wouldn't it be restful if he spent more time at his Cotswold estate? The fresh air would put roses in Lucy's cheeks, and the country was a better place to raise children anyhow.

Simon's blurry vision of domestic bliss was interrupted by a sharp elbow to his ribs. "Get off me."

Simon raised an eyebrow. "What's the magic word?"

"Now," Lucy ground out.

He glanced at the china clock. She had a point. If he stayed here much longer his secretary and the MacTavish boys would not forgive him.

He nuzzled her long white neck. "I'll leave after breakfast."

Lucy whuffed her disapproval through flaring nostrils. "Surely it's too late for breakfast."

"That may be, but I'm hungry nonetheless and my staff will have food warming for us. Shall we eat here or go downstairs?"

She sat up, nearly breaking his nose. "Eat in *bed*?" She sounded fair horrified. What kind of imbecile was Percy Ferguson that he didn't eat in bed with his mistress? There were any number of things that could be done with a pot of strawberry jam.

"Never tell me your maid doesn't bring you a pot of chocolate to your bedside."

"*Your* maid does. But I sit in my upstairs parlor with it and read the news sheets. I'm not a lazy slugabed. I have things to do."

Odd. He thought mistresses lolled about until their protectors came each night. "What are all these things?"

"I read. I still make all my own hats. The girls on the street have their entertainments. Card parties and such."

"It sounds like a grueling schedule."

"You may mock me, but it's not as though we women have as many choices as you men. You belong to some silly club, don't you? I expect you read and play cards there, too."

"Not often. But I've got to be where the important men are."

"The *rich* men, you mean."

Simon laughed. "You make being rich sound like a crime. Perhaps you missed your century. You should have been born French fifty years ago."

"I don't want anyone to part with their head. Only you," she muttered.

"Luce, tell me you've not enjoyed being Ferguson's mistress all these years, here in the lap of luxury. It may have been a little lean these past few months, but you had a nice long ride while it lasted."

Damn it. There came her fist again. He ducked just in time. "Be reasonable, woman! Can you honestly tell me you'd rather be hunched over making hats in your aunt's backroom, lucky to get a few farthings when she thought to pay you? I know I wouldn't want to go back on the streets, cadging for my crusts of bread."

"You could have found a steady job."

"I was willing to do honest work, but there was so little of it." And he *had* done all he could, legal or illegal, to keep his old gran in medicine and food. It still grieved him that his soldier's pay was not enough to keep her alive longer. He'd sent every bit of it home.

"You're still a thief. You're robbing me of my time."

Simon laughed. "And what is so pressing today that you must leap out of bed?"

"Have you forgotten? I'm leaving. I need to pack."

Simon felt a deep stirring of anger. He'd gone long enough without what he needed in life. Lucy was *not* going to leave just when he'd found her again.

"The devil you say. I forbid it."

"You forbid it? That makes me even more determined." She squirmed in his arms, rubbing up against him in a delightfully vexing way.

"We have an agreement. In writing."

"And who can read it with your dreadful penmanship? I signed it under duress. With a false name. You couldn't possibly hold me to it."

"I can hold you to anything." To emphasize his point, he squashed her to him. All of him. She made him randy as Pan, bless her. Lately he'd been reading up on Greek mythology to pass the time. Terrible, violent stuff. Those gods were capricious, they were. "And the duress was strictly on my end. You were, I believe, blackmailing me."

"And you've broken our bargain! You are in my bed!"

"In *my* bed. I own every stick of furniture in this place."

"But you don't own me."

Simon sighed and relaxed his grip. "Aye. That I do not. You are your own woman, Lucy Dalhousie."

She punched him in the shoulder feebly. "Stop calling me that! It's a ridiculous name."

He could change that. If he could change Lucy's mind about leaving. What she needed was a proper wooing. With strawberry jam.

"Be sensible, Luce. You have nowhere to go now, do you? What harm can befall you by staying on Jane Street a wee bit longer?"

"I wish I'd never come here," she mumbled into his chest. Her breaths tickled a bit. So she *was* sorry she'd lived a life of sin. That was a start to getting her back on the straight and narrow. How strange that a lad such as he had turned out more respectable than she. Lucy had been one long lecture in the past, when he wasn't kissing her to shut her up.

What an excellent idea. He lifted her stubborn chin and swept his tongue against the seam of her lips. She didn't make it easy for him, but she didn't draw back. He toyed with the corner of her mouth, lifting it to a lopsided smile, then skimmed his way to the other side.

Simon felt tentative fingertips exploring his jaw. He didn't want to burn her delicate white skin with his beard, so he flipped her on top of him, giving her more control. He was rewarded with her opening mouth and the silken warmth of her long body. By all the saints, he never wanted to stand up again. Possibly couldn't. He thumbed her pale nipples until they pebbled beneath his touch, wishing he could kiss her there as well as her soft, sweet mouth. Wishing he could kiss her everywhere all at once. Devour her with kisses. Every sharp angle. Every gentle curve. Taste her from tip to toe and make her come again and again.

He opened his eyes to see Lucy's closed, her gilt eyelashes fanning the blue flesh beneath her eyes. She had not slept well, then. He had not let her. It had been impossible not to take her at dawn as she drowsed in his arms, and then again just a scant half-hour ago, when she was wide awake and prickly. But he'd smoothed her the best way he knew how. She was temptation incarnate, and he was as starved for her as he'd been as a callow youth.

Without breaking the kiss, he lifted her hips and impaled her on his cock. She shuddered around him, liquid and lush. She slid up as he raised her, came down as he sank into her, so deep they were one being. How could she think of leaving?

Was her responsiveness just an act? His Lucy had never been a good liar. But many years had passed since she'd fibbed unconvincingly to her aunt and snuck out with him.

She was a famous courtesan now, a woman Lord Ferguson bragged about throughout London. Did she kiss Percy like this, so hungry and angry? Did that fop ever cause that flush to her cheeks and the hammering pulse at her throat? It was torture for Simon to think of her with anyone else, for all that he'd been no saint himself.

But there would be no other woman. No woman but Lucy. All he had to do was make her see their future the way he did. He was a persuasive fellow—he'd managed to wangle his way all the way up to the king. One mere commoner should be no problem.

Ha. There was nothing common about her. He thrust up one final time, his seed spilling where it was meant to be. Lucy was his. For the next three months. For a lifetime.

She struggled out of his arms and flopped on her back, her heated body fragrant with lilac scent. "You canna keep doing this, Simon."

He held back his chuckle. He was rather proud of his performance, not that he was about to take all the credit. "Doing what?"

Lucy waved a limp arm. "This. I canna be your mistress. 'T'isn't right."

" 'T'was right for me, Luce. No more nonsense, now. It's only for three months. Then you'll have your money and go your own way." *Over his dead body.*

Lucy's chin jutted skyward. Simon was beginning to dislike the ambition of that chin. But she said nothing, just huffed a little and pulled up the covers to rob him of seeing her beauty.

He sat up. "I suppose I should leave you then. I have things to do, too."

"What, no breakfast in bed?" she asked, her tone sarcastic.

"Not today. But tomorrow. Definitely."

He was rewarded with another huff. Simon got up and

went to the pile of neatly folded clothing and dressed without the benefit of a valet. Today he'd have fresh sets of clothing sent around so he wouldn't be seen in yesterday's dirt and opera attire again. But so what if he was spotted unshaven and in evening wear in the daylight? That would only add to his reputation.

It was Lucy's reputation that concerned him. He hoped she wouldn't wander all over town claiming to be his mistress.

Not likely. She did not seem completely won over to the idea, but he had to make sure.

"You are not to leave the house today. I'll instruct Mac-Tavish to see to it."

Lucy flashed him an incredulous look. "I am to be kept prisoner here?"

"It's a pretty prison, Luce. We'll discuss my plans for you when I return tonight."

"I won't be here!"

"Aye, you will, if Mac has to tether you to the bed."

"You bluidy bastard!"

Simon grinned. "Tis true my mum wasn't married when she had me. Everybody knows that."

Lucy gave a strangled cry and hurled a pillow. Simon deftly stepped out of its path and into his shoes.

"You canna keep me here against my will!"

She was sitting up now, blankets dropped, chest heaving. Lucy's nipples were raspberry-hued and looked as if they'd taste even sweeter. If he kept staring he was never going to get any work done. He fiddled with his gold cufflinks.

"As I said, we'll talk tonight. Have a nice day, Luce."

Simon shut the door behind him. The thuds and shattering of objects and rather violent oaths were somewhat muted as he descended the stairs.

MacTavish awaited him, looking understandably nervous. "Good morning, Mac. Please see to it that Miss Dellamar is confined to the house today. She's in a bit of a temper, so do whatever you think is necessary."

The butler paled. "Is she not amenable to this arrangement, Sir Simon?"

"Don't worry. She will be."

Mac opened the front door for him, and Simon took a deep breath of Jane Street air. The other eleven houses were quiet, their mistresses probably sleeping the day away. Maybe Lucy would nap too, if she wasn't too cross. Simon wanted her awake tonight, however. He was going to do more than talk to her.

Chapter 12

MacTavish had raised a silvery butler-brow but sent the footman to Percy's house with Lucy's desperate message. If she was not allowed to go out of the house—as if she were a criminal—well, she thought ruefully, she supposed she *was* a criminal what with the pilfering she'd done, just uncaught—then Percy would have to come to her. Simon had said nothing about her receiving visitors. By the time he got around to forbidding them too, she would be gone.

Percy would help her. He'd have to. And she wouldn't have MacTavish or anyone else spying on her when she talked to him. She sat now in her little back garden, wrapped in her necessary fox fur against the fall chill. She hoped MacTavish didn't notice that all the back gardens were connected by doors set into the brick walls. Most of the doors were unlocked, so the courtesans could visit each other when the spirit moved them. More than a bit of gossip was passed or a cup of sugar borrowed—one never knew when one needed a good weep, an extra French letter or bottle of champagne.

But Lucy's neighbors had locked their garden-wall doors, fearing Lucy's light fingers. Smart girls. Lucy was sorry for all the thefts, she truly was. If she ever had a way to make it up to her neighbors, she would do so.

She tapped her foot on the brick path. She felt the cold of the marble bench on her bottom even with the barrier of fur. What was keeping Percy anyway? She had been most explicit.

Her impatience was stilled by the site of Lord Ferguson stepping from the dining room French door. It was obvious he'd taken considerable care in his toilette—his shirtpoints were so high they might poke an eye out if he wasn't careful. He was wrapped in a Ferguson plaid great coat, its predominant color royal purple. Oh dear. The man really was not subtle at all in his preferences.

"Lucy, my love, whatever is the matter? I came as soon as I could. Your note sounded quite dire."

She grimaced. "Dire indeed, Percy, and it is all your fault."

Percy swept his many capes behind him and sat down. "Whatever do you mean, love? What has happened?"

"Sir Simon Keith has happened, Percy."

"Ah, your gallant Scottish knight."

"Not mine!" Lucy snapped. "I don't want him. He's keeping me a prisoner in this house, even worse than you did."

"Now, buttercup. You were never my prisoner, just my mystery. We ventured out now and again." Percy reached for her hands, but she jumped off the bench and began to pace on the short brick path between the browning shrubbery. She was not about to succumb to his excuses or his boyish charm.

"Listen to me, Percy. Sir Simon is not who you think he is. He is *my* Simon."

"I thought you just said he wasn't yours," Percy said, frowning.

"He's not! I mean he is the Simon I knew when I was a girl."

"The *thief*?" Percy asked, his plucked eyebrows rising to his receding hairline.

"The very same. And worse than ever. You have to help me escape."

"Where will you go? You know I cannot bring you to Mama's. She's met you."

Lucy shivered. She remembered the occasion well. She'd rather pitch herself down an extremely tall cliff than live with Countess Ferguson. "I don't know. It doesn't matter. I want you to go next door to Victorina Castellano's and ask her to unlock the garden gate for me. I can get out that way."

Percy rubbed his chin. "The Spanish Spitfire? I thought you were not on good terms with her. Why should she help you?"

"Of course we are not on good terms! I've robbed her blind—for you, you ridiculous man—and she suspects me. Tell her I've changed my ways. Tell her I'll pay her back. Eventually."

"I don't know, Lucy. I shouldn't want to jeopardize my investment in Keith's consortium. He's bound to find out I assisted you. Can't you stay and just make the best of things?"

Lucy broke a fallen branch in half, not sure whether it was Simon's or Percy's neck she was snapping in her imagination. "Percy, you are a lily-livered coward."

"I'm a *poor* lily-livered coward. You of all people know that. You stole for me, Lucy, and I shan't forget that. Ever. It shames me, it truly does. But helping you run off from Jane Street, with no place to go, no money—why, I would be doing you a dreadful disservice. You can't just fly off into the mist like this. You need a plan."

"I don't have time for a plan," Lucy said crossly, sitting back down. "Will you at least take a note to Victorina?"

"I—I suppose I could. She wears the most marvelous mantillas."

Lucy rolled her eyes heavenward and was rewarded with a piece of ash falling from a neighbor's chimney. "Bluidy hell." She stuck a finger under her lid and rooted around.

"Don't rub it in!" Percy fished a lace-edged handkerchief out of his pocket and dabbed at the corner of her eye. "Now, Lucy, such language. What of our lady lessons?"

"I doona give a rat's arse about our lady lessons. Ouch."

"Hold still, I've almost got it. There. Good as new, although your eyeball's quite pink. You should go inside and rest."

"Doona change the subject, Percy. I'll go inside, but only to write to Victorina. Will you take the letter to her?"

Percy nodded. "If you can wait a day or two to leave, I'll see if I can't sell something to give you a little going-away gift."

Lucy squinted at him with her one good eye. "I thought you sold everything of value already."

Percy colored. "There may be something I overlooked. Yates can help me."

"All right. But the day after tomorrow is my absolute deadline. I shall simply die if I have to put up with Simon for longer than that."

"Is he no' a braw, strapping laddie?" Percy asked, mimicking her accent.

"He's *too* braw and strapping. You would faint dead away if you saw his ballocks."

"Lucy! Your language." Percy looked more titillated than disapproving. Lucy was not about to share what she had done with Simon, however. It was all too mortifying how easily she had fallen under his spell again.

"Let's go inside to write the note. You can go straight to

Victorina's and then come back to tell me what she says. If it's no, I'll ask Sophie Rydell on the other side."

"I shall try to be as persuasive as possible. I'll make her my bosom-bow."

"Just don't ask if you can see her closet," Lucy grumbled.

Lucy resumed her pacing, this time in her upstairs sitting room. She would miss this space—it had taken her six years to make it cozy and comfortable. She'd sewn the slipcovers and collected the books and arranged every stick of furniture to suit herself. It was her little kingdom—well, queendom might be more appropriate, as Percy had shared many afternoons and evenings here with her while he waited for Yates to finish up his various duties. Lucy had lost count of the number of hats she'd made or the pages she'd cut from romance novels and poetry books in six years of keeping loneliness at bay.

Percy had been good company when he was there, but Lucy had never really warmed up to the other women on the street. Their innate elegance had been intimidating, making her feel even more unlovely and awkward than she had as a girl in Edinburgh. Plus she had been afraid that somehow the true nature of her relationship with her benefactor would be revealed. Lucy certainly could not hold up her end of the conversation when the Janes compared notes and positions. Her dim recollection of adolescent sex with Simon was entirely inadequate.

After the bedroom—and opera—activity of the last few days, she had more of a base of knowledge to discuss from now. But since her thieving, the girls shunned her, and rightfully so. One day she'd make it up to them, even if she had to supply them with a lifetime of new bonnets.

Which reminded her. While she waited for Percy to return, she could work on the straw capote. The hat was intended for him anyway. How and where he'd wear it was no longer of concern to her, but braiding trim for it would keep her busy. If Victorina refused to help her, Lucy would simply send Percy to her other neighbor. Sophie was so high in the instep she could pass as a duchess, though a very naughty one. Sophie might be cooperative—she would be delighted to see the back of her. Lucy had never quite fit in, her Edinburgh edges roughing up the Jane Street silk.

Lucy unrolled some red velvet cording from its spool in her sewing box and snipped it into three lengths. It was soothing to cross the strands over and under, and before she knew it, she had a nice, tight braid. She fixed it to the edge of the brim with tiny, even stitches. The color would bring out the ruddiness of Percy's cheeks.

She heard the front door slam below—Percy had never been subtle—and waited for him to come upstairs. Instead she heard an altercation below, with MacTavish taking umbrage that Percy had let himself in, as always. Lucy tossed the hat aside and popped her head over the banister.

"It's all right, MacTavish. Lord Ferguson is used to making himself at home here."

The butler sniffed. "Most irregular, Miss Dellamar. I shall have to report this to Sir Simon. Your key, please." He held out a long, work-worn hand.

"My key?" Percy asked, his voice rising.

"Your key, my lord. Miss Dellamar is no longer in your—er, employ. It is one thing to visit at calling hours, ringing the bell and awaiting admittance like a gentleman. Sir Simon would not be best pleased that you have access to this establishment at any hour of the day. Or night," MacTavish said darkly.

"Are you implying I'm not a gentleman?" Percy was now

as red as the braid on his new hat. The color on his cheeks clashed with his purple and green plaid cape.

"I am doing nothing of the kind, my lord," MacTavish said, unperturbed. His hand remained outstretched. "You are indeed a peer of the realm, the—the flower of English manhood. But it is my understanding that Sir Simon wishes Miss Dellamar to be protected in her home."

"Protected!" cried Lucy. "Locked up, more like! Percy is my oldest friend, MacTavish, and he may come and go as he wishes. As *I* wish."

"I'm afraid Sir Simon's instructions preempt your wishes, Miss Dellamar. The key, Lord Ferguson."

"Devil take it!" Percy mumbled, but handed it over to the implacable butler.

"Come upstairs, Percy."

"Miss Dellamar, if I may be so bold—"

"No, you may not, not that I can stop you." Lucy gritted her teeth in frustration.

"It is improper for you to entertain a gentleman upstairs in your boudoir."

"I am not *entertaining* Lord Ferguson. We are simply talking. We are friends. We talked in the garden. Now we are going to talk upstairs."

"I'm afraid I'll have to report that to Sir Simon as well."

"Report away!" Lucy snapped. "Station yourself outside the door so you can eavesdrop!" That was the last thing she needed, but if necessary she and Percy could write notes to each other. She could read *his* handwriting.

The butler's neck stiffened. "I never eavesdrop, Miss Dellamar. I know my place."

"Hmph. Are you coming?" she called down to Percy irritably. This was becoming like a Romeo and Juliet farce with exceptionally star-crossed lovers.

"Yes, Lucy, but I can't stay long."

"May I take your cape, Lord Ferguson?"

Percy struggled with the silver clasp. MacTavish clearly intimidated him—he was indeed a lily-livered coward. Lucy turned on her heel and went back into her sitting room. She had half a mind not to give Percy his hat.

He finally entered, blushing.

"Well? What happened? You were gone long enough!"

Percy removed a speck of lint from his sleeve. "Do you suppose MacTavish suspects? That bit about the flower of English manhood was a bit much. And an insult. I'm as Scottish as he is!"

"Bugger the damn butler! Stick to the subject, Percy!"

Percy pulled out his handkerchief and gingerly blotted his brow. He hated arguments of any kind, and the scene with MacTavish had discomposed him. But Lucy was not going to let him off the hook. "Out with it!"

"Your Senorita Castellano is a very vivacious young lady. She insisted I have a drop of wine, and one thing led to another." He slipped the handkerchief back into his pocket, and Lucy saw a wisp of black lace.

"Oh, God, Percy. What's that in your pocket?"

Percy covered the bulge in his waistcoat. "I didn't steal it. She gave it to me."

Lucy covered her face. The image of Percy prancing around in a black mantilla was disconcerting.

"Don't worry—I told her it was for Mama. She doesn't suspect our little arrangement was not what it seemed. Vicky listened quite carefully to your predicament—sympathetic little soul, she is, all liquid dark eyes and mournful mouth. If Mama had not made me give up painting, I should have liked—"

"Enough about your mama! What did—Vicky, is it?—

say?" Lucy was rather put out. She'd never been asked to call Victorina by her diminutive.

"She's agreed to open the door in the wall. She would have done so at once, so taken was she by the tale of the brutish Sir Simon keeping you here against your will."

"He's not—I'm not—never mind."

"The door will be opened at noon, and she'll be ready to escort you through her domicile. She's sleeping in, what with her protector expected later tonight." Percy's fingers crept into his pocket. It was obvious he could not wait to get home and cover himself with lace.

"Noon. Noon is fine." Lucy began to pace again. "Can you get me money by then, Percy? As much as you can?" If Victorina was walking her through the house, there would be no opportunity for Lucy to filch anything else from her. It wouldn't be sporting anyway.

Percy straightened his shoulders. "I'll try, buttercup. I'll try. I'll send Yates around first thing in the morning. What will you do? Where will you go?"

"I don't know. Anywhere but here."

Percy shook his head, looking a bit mournful himself. "I feel responsible for you, Lucy. Is this really what you want—running away from a man who can keep you in style?"

"Sir Simon's style is vastly overrated." A lie, from beginning to end, but she had to get away while she still had a shred of independence. A few more nights in Simon's arms or wherever he put her was bound to lead to insanity.

"He's rich as Croesus, Lucy. Are you sure you cannot come to terms with him, especially if he is, as you suggest, a very fine figure of a man?"

"I'm positive." She picked up the capote and stabbed it with a needle. "I'll have this finished for you before I go."

Percy reached across the table and stilled her hand. "I don't care about the hat. I care about you."

"Then bring me money. Steal from your mama if you must."

Percy turned parchment-white, but he nodded in solemn acceptance. "For you, my dear, I might even consider it."

Chapter 13

Simon had had a hellish day. He'd spent the afternoon and evening holding the hand of a reluctant investor who could not see the benefit of sinking his fortune into a passenger railway system. Hauling coal and iron he could understand—inanimate objects could not complain over rough terrain and belching smoke. No civilized persons would consent to being loaded aboard a train like cattle, and so he had said. Over and over. Simon had plied the man with drink and a rich dinner, but had failed to part him with his money. Add to that this morning's fight with Lucy and the worrisome news MacTavish gave him as he crossed the threshold, and Simon was in sore need of comfort.

And not apt to receive any from his mistress, who was still, apparently, carrying on with Lord Percival Ferguson.

Faugh. What had Lucy ever seen in the earl?

The answer was distressingly obvious. Even though Ferguson had lost the money he had lured Lucy with, she still had feelings for him. According to MacTavish, she'd embraced him in the garden and let him wipe her tears away—tears of misery that she was forced to be with Simon now, no doubt. Then she'd taken the man up to her cozy sitting room and closed the door. Who knew if they'd slipped into the bedroom through the connecting door? MacTavish had timed the earl's visit, and perhaps its brevity was a function of Lucy's skill or Ferguson's lack thereof.

Damn it all to hell and back. Simon was jealous—jealous of the flamboyantly-dressed dandy. Percy the Peacock. Simon's own clothes were good quality, the first stare of fashion, but they were conservative—a man of his background could not afford to risk impropriety. He wondered if Lucy would like him better if he wore a scarlet waistcoat and too many watch fobs.

Six years was a long time to be one man's mistress. Some of the men Simon knew picked up and discarded women with alarming alacrity. He had to give Percy credit—the man knew how very special Lucy was.

Could Ferguson *love* Lucy? Worse, could Lucy love him back?

Och. There was no point to fash himself. Lucy belonged to him now. He would make her see reason and marry him. He would ask her. Tonight. There was no point in waiting—they'd waited thirteen years.

Of course, he had asked her once before, although Simon could not recall his precise words. It had been assumed by both of them that they would wed once their financial circumstances improved. He seemed to recall that Lucy had wanted him to stop stealing first, and he would have—he just never had the opportunity to quit until he ran away into the arms of the army. Now he had more money than he knew what to do with, although not quite enough to finance his ambitious railway project on his own. He didn't want to beggar himself again, either. As a frugal Scot, he had money tucked away for a rainy day. For a snowy one, too.

Aye. He'd propose. He should have brought a bouquet of flowers. Or a ring. Simon pictured Lucy tossing either item at him—she was so snappish when he wasn't fucking her.

That's how he'd do it! Get her wet and hot beneath him, bring her to the brink, then whisper in her ear. She'd scream yes before she knew what she was saying.

With a growl of satisfaction at a problem solved, Simon began to unwind his neckcloth as he mounted the stairs to Lucy's bedroom. He wouldn't jump on her right away at this late hour, although God knows he longed to. Nay, he'd woo her a little. Wake her slowly with feathery kisses along her swan-like white neck. Warm the gentle swell of her breast in the palm of his hand. Circle a tender pink nipple with his tongue.

With every step he stiffened, aching for Lucy in a way he couldn't explain. Simon was not a poetic man by nature, much better with his hands than his words. But Lucy—her flaming hair and alabaster skin and brandy-colored eyes—unlocked something within his humble heart.

He paused at the sitting-room door. The room was in darkness, but a flickering light beneath the connecting door told him Lucy was still awake. He moved quietly, trying not to bump into the odd collection of furniture Lucy had crammed into the space. He almost made it when he tripped over a stack of books piled next to a crewel-work chair. He reached for purchase, but the chair toppled right along with Simon. He landed awkwardly on his chin and his cock and heard the unmistakable crack of breaking bone.

Damn him for a clumsy oaf—once he'd been like a cat in the dark, climbing trellises and trees, nimble and stealthy. Now, if he wasn't mistaken, he had snapped his left wrist because Holy Mother of God and all his Saints the pain was excruciating.

Lucy flung the door open. "What are you doing on the floor?"

Simon swept the blood from his tongue. "Inspecting the carpet."

"Well, get up and let's get this over with. I'm tired."

"What an enticing invitation to your bed. Just what a man wants to hear." Perhaps he wouldn't propose tonight after all. He rolled onto his back, the corner of one book biting into his shoulder blade. "Lucy, would you please ring for MacTavish?"

"What for? From the smell of you, you've had enough brandy. No wonder you're falling on your face."

"It was the damned books," Simon ground out. "I am not drunk."

"Ha. I suppose you're going to tell me it was only a business dinner."

"It *was* only a business dinner. I admit I had a brandy. One."

Now he wished he'd had more. Simon closed his eyes, willing the spiraling stars away. He heard Lucy take a long sniff, and couldn't resist looking up at her to see her lovely nose twitch. She had some nerve being so judgmental when she was dead drunk that first morning he found her in bed.

"Lucy, I'm sorry if the smell of my breath offends you, but you must get MacTavish. I believe I've broken my wrist." Simon's stomach flipped and he wondered if he was going to puke on the carpet. He devoutly hoped not.

"What?" She stepped closer and bent over, a long braid dangling above Simon's face. "Your chin is bleeding!"

"My tongue, too." He hoped his cock was in one piece. "I landed funny. Broke my—dignity."

"Devil take it! Let me see your wrist."

Simon realized he had been squeezing it with his right hand. Good thing it was only the left, although he was ambidextrous. He'd made his fortune with his hands, and damn him if he was out of commission for any length of time.

Lucy was on her knees now, a lovely sight, backlit from

the firelight of her bedroom. She was all copper wire and porcelain, her eyes narrowing as she examined him without touching. "Does it hurt?"

Simon considered telling the truth. But he was a man, and men did not complain of pain. "I'll be all right."

"Of course you will! It's only a broken bone. Maybe just sprained."

He wanted to tell her there was nothing 'only' or 'sprained' about it, but held his bloody tongue.

Lucy bit her lip in concentration. "It doesn't look right."

"Aye, that's what I'm telling you. Fetch MacTavish."

"Don't you trust me to splint it?"

Simon considered. Lucy would probably love to torture him as she wrapped his wrist, wiggling and waggling it until he'd want her to cut his hand off. On the whole he thought he'd rather have MacTavish. Or a doctor. Or, if it came to it, a priest. The priest could marry them and then give him extreme unction.

Lord, but he was being missish. It was, as Lucy said, 'only' a broken bone. He was nowhere near to dying, just wishing he was.

"MacTavish has experience with this kind of thing. He raised two boys."

"Yes, boys are known to be daredevils. I remember *you*."

"I'll not be scaling any walls tonight. Please, Luce, get MacTavish."

It was all he could do to screw his eyes up and not cry. The pain was shooting to his elbow now, like sharp shards of glass pricking up under his skin. He'd escaped injury in the war—he'd been hustled off the battlefield once his superiors recognized he had a brain to go with his brawn, and had lived a relatively charmed life. One broken wrist was not going to get the better of him.

"Don't move."

As if he could. He watched the flounce of Lucy's nightgown flutter around the doorjamb. He wished he'd asked her to remove the book out from under him before she left.

What rot. He didn't have to lie there like a beached whale on wool carpet. Simon struggled to sit up, the room spinning unhelpfully. He looked down at his cuff, suddenly much tighter than it had been. Clumsily he unfastened the small knot of gold that pierced the linen of his shirt and tossed it aside. His hand was swelling and turning red. Blast.

Lucy returned with MacTavish in tow, holding a leather satchel. The butler had donned his nightwear after delivering the bad news about Lord Ferguson, and he had apparently stuffed his nightcap into the pocket of his dressing gown. The tassel flicked forward as he bent to Simon.

"What have ye done now, lad?"

"You needn't make it sound like finding me on my arse is a regular occurrence. Miss Dellamar will think I'm a bull in a china shop."

"Hush. Can you move your fingers?"

Simon gritted his teeth and tried. The shards of glass united into one giant pane of pain.

"I see not. Aye, it's likely broken. Miss Dellamar, if you will be so kind as to step out of the room?"

Lucy looked very pale above him, like an angel, or what Simon thought an angel should look like. He wasn't really anxious to go to heaven anytime soon and find out for sure. He had plenty of time left on earth to atone for his faults, and the first order of business was to make Lucille Elaine Dalhousie his bride, even if she'd been sinful enough for both of them. He'd speak to God, explain. Build the Old Fellow an engine if words wouldn't work. Good Lord, he was losing his mind and was very much afraid he was about to lose his expensive dinner.

His future wife twisted her braid between nervous white fingers. "Will he be all right?"

"I'll see to it. Dinna fash yourself."

Simon watched her swallow, her long neck a lovely thing. She should have diamonds around her throat, bright stars that proved his love for her. He would see to it tomorrow—not stolen jewels, but a set from Rundell, Bridge and Rundell. If the firm was good enough for Prinny—King George IV now—Simon supposed he could find something that suited his Lucy.

"Don't worry about me, Luce. I'll be fine. It's only my left hand, after all."

After a moment's hesitation, Lucy slipped from the room. "A chamber pot, Mac. Or a vase. Anything will do."

"That's the way of it then."

For an older man, MacTavish stepped lively and supplied Simon with an empty receptacle into which he promptly vomited. "Sorry. Tried to keep it in."

MacTavish nodded, pitching the vile contents down into the garden through a hastily opened window. "Trying to look the hero for your lady. If you ask me, you'll use this mishap to your advantage."

"I'm not asking you," Simon said, wiping his mouth on his coat sleeve. "What do you mean?"

"Anyone with an eye in his head can see you're head-over-heels for the woman. And women like to play nurse. Let her take care of you and you'll work your way into her heart."

"It's only a snapped wrist, Mac. It's not a mortal wound."

MacTavish knelt beside him, rummaging through the satchel for a splint. "Aye, I know it. You'll soon be good as new. But think, man, you won't be able to button up your own breeches."

"You know I can do anything, even one-handed. And Jamie can help me if I have a spot of trouble."

"Why use my useless son when you have a lovely lady with a soft heart?" MacTavish wrapped a length of linen tight around Simon's hand, criss-crossing the fabric around his thumb. "I'll brew up some willow-bark tea for the pain. You certainly can't go home tonight in your condition. Let's get you undressed and put to bed," the butler said, fashioning a sling from another length of linen from his bottomless bag. "We'll put this on you tomorrow. I'll tell Miss Dellamar you're half off your head from a complicated break and can't be moved."

"Damn it, Mac. My feet still work. She'll think me a weakling."

The butler winked. "Aye. There's nothing a woman likes more for a while but to be in charge."

Simon shook his head in exasperation and got to his feet with some assistance. "This is like some bad melodrama. Next you'll suggest I cough up some blood." He crossed into the bedroom. Wherever Lucy had gone, she was not hovering in here.

"That could be arranged. Not real blood, mind, but some substitute. Pity raspberry season is passed."

"You are a diabolical man." Simon stood as MacTavish efficiently stripped the clothes from his body without too many jolts to his arm.

"Aye, and you pay me too well for me to be anything else. How are the boys doing anyhow?"

"Jamie is on his way to being as stiff-necked as you," Simon said as he stepped out of his smallclothes. "Hamish puts too much starch in my cravats, but he means well."

MacTavish pursed his lips in disapproval. "I'll speak to him. There's no need of that."

"Oh, leave him alone. You have me to bully."

"Not I. That will be Miss Dellamar's job. And you don't have to thank me when she falls into your arms. Well, I suppose I should say arm." MacTavish gave him an uncustomary leer and Simon knew he was done for.

Chapter 14

MacTavish's face was grave when he finally entered the downstairs parlor. Lucy had done her usual pacing, hampered now by the influx of furniture she had purchased for Simon. She'd banged her knee and finally sat down on a new chair before the butler had to bandage *her* up.

"Well?"

"Sir Simon is in a great deal of pain. It's a verra nasty break, Miss Dellamar, I won't lie to you."

"Should we fetch a doctor?"

The butler straightened to his imposing height. "I think not. No one should have anything to say about the job I did putting him to rights. He'll be out of commission for quite a while, however. I think it best he stay right here instead of returning home."

"Here? *All night*?"

"And for the next several days. I think it best. We can't have Sir Simon bouncing about in a carriage or walking home when anyone might knock him to the ground."

"This is Mayfair," Lucy reminded him.

"Aye, and I've heard of the troubles, even on this street, for all it's so fancy. Kidnappings and assaults, etcetera. And what about that woman who shot her husband at his mistress's house?"

"Simon is not going to get shot. Not yet," muttered Lucy. "I don't have a gun."

"Neverthless, I'm going to give him something for the excruciating pain, and he won't be fit to travel. He might even be delirious. You will assist me with him, won't you, Miss Dellamar? A man my age can't be expected to be running up and down the stairs at all hours."

"What about the footman? Or the maids?"

"Ah, I meant to tell you. There's been a death in the family. I've given them all the week off."

This was news to Lucy. Calvin, the footman, had been busy flirting with Mary, the extra maid, last time she saw them, and Yvonne was French. None of them seemed at all mournful, or in any way related. She stared hard at MacTavish, who stared back, daring her to question him.

"Can't you get your boys to come?"

He shook his head. "Ham-handed, the both of them. A sore trial to me, I can tell you. And anyway, a woman's touch is a healing balm for a man in agony. Sir Simon's recovery will depend on you. I trust you care enough to help the poor soul."

That was the problem. Lucy cared too much.

"And he'll be blue-deviled. A man like Sir Simon—why, his hands are his fortune. He'll be imagining he'll never get the feeling back and then what will he have to live for?"

Lucy knew what Simon had done and could do with his hands. In her mind's eye, she saw the roller bearings twirling around his fingertips. Saw his fingers keeping perfect time to music at the opera. Saw his brown hand easing down her body, leaving a trail of sensual fire in its wake.

"How long must he stay?"

"We'll have to watch for swelling and returning strength. Keep him quiet and pleasantly occupied. I don't mean to alarm you, but a splinter of bone could travel right through his blood to his heart and kill him."

Lucy had never heard of such a thing and so she said. But MacTavish was adamant—Simon needed to rest and recuperate upstairs in her bed, and she was somehow the key to his health.

Stuff and nonsense. She was leaving at noon tomorrow whether Simon needed her or not. Her arrangements were made. He had the money to hire a troop of doctors to care for him. Nursemaids, too, women who would not look down at his rumpled brow and feel a pang of longing.

Lucy marched up the stairs, grumpy already at the thought of sleeping on her chintz sofa. She certainly would not crawl into bed with the invalid. If MacTavish was so concerned about Simon walking down the street bumping into someone, lying next to Lucy would not be a good thing. She was always restless at night, rolling around and wrapping the covers up over her ears like a mummy. Except, of course, when she tossed everything on the floor. No, Simon would not have a peaceful night beside her.

A branch of candles had been lit in her little parlor, and the door to the bedroom stood wide. Lucy bent to scoop up the troublesome books that Simon had tripped over. So much for self-improvement, not they improved anything but the author's bank account. Lucy had a sweet tooth for the shocking novels of her neighbor Lady Christie. She placed them on the table with her hat form and unfolded the worn quilt that had been draped on the back of the sofa. She was just plumping a pillow when she heard unearthly groans.

"Urrgh. Aargh."

Sighing, Lucy entered the bedroom. "MacTavish will be up shortly with a draught for you."

"Urrr." Simon turned to her, his eyes sliding to the corner of the room. "Where are you, Luce? I canna see."

"I'm right here! Did you hit your head when you fell?"

"Aye. I've got an awful headache." He closed his eyes. "Everything hurts, as a matter of fact. Touch me, Luce. Touch me anywhere so I can feel your softness." His voice was raspy, as though he was suffering from the croup.

Lucy slapped a hand on his forehead. "No fever. I'm tired, Simon. We both need our rest. I'll just be in the other room, only a shout away."

Simon's blue eyes snapped opened. "Nay! Come lie with me. I need you."

Lucy wrapped her arms around her, shoving her hands inside her lace sleeves, else she might touch him again. He did look so very pitiful now, like a puppy whose paw had been crushed. "I'm sure you do not. MacTavish says you are not to be disturbed. He's mixing up something so you can sleep. Is the pain very bad?"

"He didn't mean you, Luce. I don't mind if you fuss over me."

"I don't fuss—I know nothing of nursing." She faked a yawn, keeping her hands firmly inside her sleeves. Let him see her back teeth—she prided herself on her good oral hygiene. "Good night, Simon."

"Wait!" Simon pushed himself up quickly, obviously forgetting both arms did not work. His lips whitened, but there was none of the earlier groaning. He really did look in dire straits now, unmistakably in distress.

"Lie back down, you silly man!"

"Only if you stay." He eased himself back on the pillows and flopped his bandaged wrist across his chest. His inky hair was damp on his brow, and Lucy fought the urge to brush it back. "Please."

She was spared a retort with MacTavish's entrance. He presented a glass with grayish liquid on a silver salver to Simon, who gulped it quickly.

"What's in it?" Lucy asked.

"This and that. The master should sleep in a little while, but he'll need watching until he does. It's all apt to get worse before it gets better."

From Lucy's experience, that was what life was all about, wasn't it? Grudgingly she sat at the side of the bed, as far away from Simon as she could get without falling on the floor herself.

"Come closer, Luce," Simon croaked once MacTavish had left. "I can't see you."

She sprang up. "I'll light some candles." There were plenty of them now, not tallow but wax. A wickedly wasteful amount, really.

"Nay! The dark is fine. Better for my headache," he said quickly.

"Your head will be fine soon." She wished MacTavish had given *her* something to drink to knock her out, to make her sleep for a hundred years. But then she'd miss her rescue.

How many more hours under Simon's thumb? Well, his bandaged wrist. She looked at the spinning clock at her bedside. Half a day more of servitude, minus the hours Simon would sleep. He'd be unconscious shortly. She could do this—she had to.

He patted the bed with his good hand. Reluctant, she resumed her position on the edge, wishing she had a bit more padding on her bottom to make this vigil comfortable.

"So, what did *you* do today, Lucy?"

"Nothing much. Finished a hat."

"Mac told me you had a visitor."

He would, the snitch. "Only Percy."

"Lord Ferguson? What was he doing here?"

"Oh, why aren't you asleep already instead of conducting an inquisition?" Lucy asked in irritation.

"Perhaps because I'm concerned about your associations in my house."

"It was Percy's house first. And he—forgot something."

The blue steel of Simon's eyes pierced her in the darkened room. Remarkable what you could see even when you didn't want to.

"Indeed. And what was that?"

"A—a hat for his mama. He's a very dutiful son."

"A hat. A pity he forgot again to take it with him."

"What do you mean?"

"Mac said nothing about hats. Or hat boxes. Unless Lord Ferguson secreted it under that ridiculous cape he wore. I've seen it, you know. The man canna dress to save his life."

Lucy was inclined to agree, but felt obligated to defend her friend. "His tastes are unusual, I admit." *You should see him in peach and puce silk.*

"What attracted you to him, Luce?"

His voice wasn't weak or breathless now, but clear as the midnight bells that reverberated outside. She shrugged. "His money, Simon. Isn't that what all whores are after?"

"You're not a whore! Or you weren't when I left."

"People change. I was tired of living in Edinburgh. Tired of my aunt. Tired of waiting for you. When Percy turned up, I snatched my opportunity."

Simon pulled himself up on the bank of pillows. "I did come back, Lucy. When I'd made something of myself."

I would have taken you unmade. "Too late. Let's not re-hash the past. There's nothing we can change, and nothing that I'd want to."

Oh, lie lie lie, and lie some more. If Lucy had her way, she'd be living in some snug thatched cottage with half a dozen children and Simon by her side. He could be a farm laborer or a farrier, it would not matter. Just a simple, honest life with a simple, honest man—was that too much to ask for?

Apparently it was. There was no thatch on Jane Street. And the fiendishly rich, fiendishly handsome and fiendishly inconvenient Sir Simon Keith was in her bed, with no plans to get out anytime soon.

The room was quiet save for the gentle rumble and hiss of the fireplace. Lucy wondered if he'd finally fallen asleep when Simon cleared his throat. "I'd change things."

"Would you choose to be less rich?"

"Don't be foolish. We both know the pain of poverty. With my money now I have a chance to help others get out of it."

"Like Percy," Lucy said dryly.

"He's the least of my projects. And if things go well, he will be rich again. Then what will you do?"

Lucy looked at him through the gray gloom of the room. Simon did not look one bit sleepy, and she wondered what MacTavish had put in his drink. "What do you mean?"

"Will you go back to him? Lucy, God help you, are you in love with the man?"

He sounded so wounded, so anguished, so absolutely stupid that she choked back her laughter. "In *love* with Percy? Of course not. I'm not in love with anyone."

"No one? Could you ever fall in love again?"

Here was her chance to hurt him and ensure her escape.

But she couldn't do it. Couldn't say the words that would end this pickle, as he'd called it.

"Who knows what tomorrow will bring?" she asked, her voice falsely bright. "Now, Simon, you must excuse me. We're both tired, and you'll do your injury no good by fighting with me all night."

His hand shot out and grabbed her arm. "It's not fighting I want to do, Luce."

She could feel his every fingerprint through the worn batiste of her nightgown, hot little circles sending sinful signals directly to her heart. No, not heart. Her lustful brain, perhaps. Certainly the juncture between her thighs. *Oh, Simon.*

She must have said his name aloud because he was draw-ing her to him. The man didn't need two hands for what he planned. Lucy remembered the old yellow chair in her aunt's shop, and how she bounced up and down on him like a shameless jack-in-the-box. Jill-in-the-box. Oh, why was she parsing words when his warm mouth was on hers, tast-ing of brandy and herbs? When his fingers skittered down her throat and plunged beneath her suddenly unbuttoned night rail? When her nipple peaked into his palm and the wetness seeped between her legs? When his tongue and hers danced the most delicious waltz?

What did she know of waltzes? She had watched Percy and Yates but had never mastered the steps herself. She was-n't the type of girl who would ever be asked to waltz at Al-macks.

Girl. She wasn't a girl, but a woman, past her prime even if she was flying awfully close to the sun now, feeling re-markably impervious to time's mutations. Simon had cer-tainly gotten better with age—who was to say that she had not also? He seemed perfectly satisfied to break their kiss and tug her nightgown over her head. Unravel her braids, angle her hip and thrust her down his cockstand. Efficient. Effortless. All one-handed. He was a wonder.

And then any coherent reflection on Simon's prowess with his hand, his lips, and his cock pretty much flew out of her head as she skirted the sun, then burned in its mass.

Chapter 15

Lucy lay on top of him like a smooth liquid rug, scorching, wet heaven. He was still buried inside her, his cock twitching every time her inner muscles contracted in aftershock. Even his broken wrist felt better. "You've got to marry me," he gasped.

Her head rose from his chest. "I beg your pardon?"

That did not come out quite right. He was an ass—a happy ass right now though, he had to admit. Beyond happy. Ecstatic. He'd have to go to a dictionary to find alternatives to the banal happy. He'd meant to ask her differently, perhaps a bit earlier in their encounter, when her head was thrown back, her mouth quirked in a mysterious smile, her eyelashes flicking.

"Will you do me the honor of marrying me, Lucy?"

Suddenly a whoosh of air streaked over his naked body and Lucy was clear across the room, leaving his cock quite forlorn.

"*What?*"

"MacTavish thought I should trick you by staying here to take care of me, but I don't want that. I want you with me because you want to be. I don't care what you've done. Or not done. We can go somewhere quiet where no one knows your sordid past and live the kind of lives we always dreamed of. Except I've got money now. You wouldn't have to live in some mean little thatched hovel with half-a-dozen brats. You're probably too ol—I mean, we'll welcome whatever the good Lord sends us, boy or girl, but it doesn't matter that it might be just the two of us. I can leave my money to charity."

Lucy's lovely mouth was a flat line. When she wiggled that line, Simon knew he had put a foot wrong. Possibly an entire leg and then some. "You think I'm *old*? You're three months older than I!"

"But I'm a man, lass."

"And I'm just an old hag, is that it? I've wasted half my life on you, Simon Grant, and I'll nae waste the rest of it!" She began marching around the room, her expression fierce. He was reminded of a print he'd seen of Boudicca some-where, only Lucy had no shield to cover her magnificent white body.

" 'Twouldn't be a waste, love. I'll give you everything you could ever want. Jewels. Furs if you must have them, al-though to take a poor wee creature's skin seems heartless." He hurried on. "You can even have that fop Ferguson visit now and again, as long as you promise to keep your vows. I'm a tolerant man, but I willna share my wife with that bluidy fool."

Lucy stopped her pacing. "You'd let Percy visit?"

Simon felt his heart break just a little, but he nodded his head. "We've all made mistakes. My greatest was not com-ing to you sooner. I wanted it all to be perfect, Luce, and then I thought you were dead. Now talk about a waste—all my efforts to improve myself for you, and you were gone."

She blurred before him. Must be the effects of Mac's po-tion. He was finally losing what few wits he had, and his eyesight, too.

"Simon," Lucy said softly, "are you crying?"

"Don't be daft. It's—it's just my wrist. The pain."

"You love me!"

"Aye, of course I do, you silly wench. Why would I ask you to marry me?"

"Even though I'm an infamous courtesan. Even though I'm old."

She sounded unnaturally happy. Perhaps she was the one losing her wits.

He nodded solemnly. "Aye, Luce. Even with your tawdry past, I want your future."

Then she laughed like a loon, fair startling Simon out of what was beginning to be a drug-induced stupor. There was something wrong with his eyes, too. Thank heavens the drink hadn't acted so quickly he'd been deprived of learning Lucy's luscious body again.

To his delight, she returned to the bed, placing herself precisely where she'd been before, every sweet inch of flesh covering his. As if they were a smooth-edged puzzle, pieces nesting together. A perfect fit, just as it should be. Her lips tickled his chest, and he brought up his good arm to hold her fast. He was more comfortable than he'd been in over a decade, even with his wrist throbbing like a piston steam engine.

"Ah av somting to tell oo."

"What's that, love? I canna hear you."

She lifted her head, and Simon's vision cleared. Lucy's eyes were bright with her own tears, and her lips quivered. "I have something to tell you, Simon."

He kissed her quiet. "You needn't tell me anything, Luce. I don't care about anything but tonight and all the tomorrows we'll have. Go to sleep. I'll get a special license. You'll be Lady Keith before you know it."

Lucy settled into him. "Mrs. Grant." That was all she said until the morning came.

Victorina Castellano stretched like a silky black cat beneath her bedcovers. The sun seemed particularly bright this afternoon once she removed her red velvet sleeping mask.

This afternoon! She observed the clock next to her bed, which she sometimes looked at while Lord Brighton was doing whatever it was that he was doing. Each time the minute-hand moved she felt obligated to say something encouraging, or at least he thought she was. The man knew no Spanish, so Vicky was able to play her small joke.

It was just past noon. She was supposed to unlock the garden door for that thief Lucy Dellamar. Vicky slipped out of bed, threw on a quilted robe and opened the little French door to her balcony. From this vantage point she could see into her neighbor's yard, and there was no shivering, penitent Lucy to be found next door. She would wait until Lucy made her exit, then go downstairs after a suitable interval.

Vicky waited. She was good at waiting. But after a quarter of an hour during which she brushed her hair and teeth, there was still no Lucy. *Maldita sea!* Lucy was more trouble than she was worth. But that *bonito* Lord Ferguson said she was being kept a prisoner by Sir Simon Keith. Vicky had met Sir Simon at a little party on Jane Street, and she did not think being his prisoner was such a bad thing at all. Those *ojos azules,* just the color of the sky this afternoon. He was *muy alto, oscuro y hermoso.* Rich as sin, too. Lord Brighton did not hold a candle to him.

Perhaps Lucy had changed her mind. If she had a brain in her red head, which Vicky had to admit she did, for the woman was very clever at stealing from all the Janes these past months. But perhaps now that she was being kept by Sir Simon, her light fingers would find something else to do.

Vicky called for her breakfast and enjoyed it in her usual leisurely way until her conscience pricked her. Inconvenient things, consciences. Vicky thought she had left it behind in Madrid, but no such luck. What if Lucy was lying at the bottom of her stairs, her neck broken? What if Sir Simon had locked her in a cupboard? There were so many possible 'what-ifs.'

She didn't go next door herself, of course—she had not yet put on her face. But her maid returned with the shocking news that Lucy and Sir Simon Keith had eloped to Scotland this very morning.

Madre de Dios! Some girls had all the luck, undeserved as it was. But Vicky's pique was somewhat assuaged by the very large bank draft Sir Simon had left for her, with a similar checque for each of the Janes that Lucy had stolen from. *Una conclusión feliz* for all, she supposed, if money could buy happiness.

Well, British bank notes were better than nothing. Vicky would go shopping—perhaps to find a pretty new hat. A new hat made one feel new again. She had always been jealous of Lucy's, most especially because Lucy would never share where she purchased them. The thief had told a silly story that she made them all herself.

A Knack for Trouble

MIA
MARLOWE

They say it takes a village to raise a child. Sometimes that's true of stories as well. I'd like to thank the ones who helped raise up "A Knack for Trouble."

First, my incredible editor, Alicia Condon, who invited me to join the Improper Gentlemen anthology. Her encouragement means everything.

I'd be lost without the support of my tireless agent, Natasha Kern. She frees me from worrying about business so that I can wallow in the joy of making things up!

Big thank-you hugs to my critique partner, Ashlyn Chase; my friend and trusted beta reader, Marcy Weinbeck; all the readers of my blog, www.miamarlowe.com/blog, who offered suggestions for naming my hero, and especially Alfke de Haas, the Dutch reader who came up with Danaher for Aidan's last name.

And lastly, dear reader, I'd like to thank you. When you read my story, you bring your imagination along for the ride to give my characters life. Without you, it's just ink on a page.

Happy Reading.

Chapter 1

We are such stuff as dreams are made on.
—SHAKESPEARE, *The Tempest*

1827, Royal Navy Docks, Bermuda

The soles of half a dozen Hessians slapped on the stone seawall overhead. Aidan Danaher peered up from the man-sized drain he'd scuttled through and extended the fingers of his right hand toward the nearest guard. As soon as he loosed a suggestion the guard raised a spyglass to scan the waves for the moonlit sail Aidan planted in his mind. In another moment the rest of the guards at Royal Dock followed suit. Unheeded, Aidan loped across the open exercise grounds and up the hill to the Commissioner's house.

The return trip would be dicier, since the *Knack* worked best when used sparingly. He'd worry about that when the time came.

Scaling the masonry and iron of the commissioner's house was simple. He knew where every finger- and toehold was. He'd helped build the damned thing, after all, and cursed every stone of it.

But not this night.

Aidan ducked from the wide second-floor veranda into the tall open window, leaving the balmy Bermudan night behind. The commissioner's thick-walled house was kissed by a soft breeze, a far cry from the airless convict ship tied up at the wharf that had been Aidan's home for the past two years.

Rosalinde waited in the shadows, as she had promised. Now she stepped into the shaft of moonlight pooling on the hardwood floor of her bedroom. Her chestnut hair flowed over her virginal nightshift like a wanton mantle. Her bare toes peeped from beneath her lacy hem, curling with nervousness.

"We must be quiet," she whispered, her eyes flaring wide in the silver light.

Fear, to be sure. But he also read so much trust in them it made his chest ache. "Aye, lass. Quiet as ever we can."

Aidan caught both her fidgety hands and brought them to his lips. Her skin smelled faintly of lavender, rose and jasmine blossoms he'd seen her tending earlier that day.

He wasn't keen on the idea of being strung up by His Majesty's Royal Navy for this night's work. But when he looked down at her wide eyes and trembling mouth, he decided she'd be worth it. She was everything fine in his world, standing before him on her little bare feet.

Aidan bent to kiss her, tasting her lips with gentleness, careful not to spook her. For months, they'd danced around this moment. As elected leader of the Irish convicts who were building the public works at Royal Dock, he'd been ushered in weekly to see the commissioner, Rosalinde's father, to air grievances or suggest improvements that would speed the work.

Commissioner Burke had warmed to him, thanks to the *Knack.* When Rosalinde needed a groom for her new Thoroughbred gelding, Aidan was taken off the grueling chain gang hauling limestone and put to work in the stables.

He had as easy a way with horseflesh as he did with people, so it was a simple matter to convince Rosalinde he could help her refine her dressage technique. She never realized the wicked beast's princely manners were due more to Aidan's *Knack* than her improved riding skills.

They'd talked of ordinary things, as if she were not his jailer's daughter. She'd made him feel human again. Once she realized the Irish had poets' hearts, she even read to him from her precious book of Shakespeare sonnets while he filed her gelding's hooves.

He'd stolen a kiss from Rose within a few days. In a few weeks, she allowed him to caress her breasts through her stiff riding habit. They drove each other mad by inches, a little more daring each day. Always in danger of discovery, always with only moments to savor their sweet wickedness.

This night was her idea. If Aidan was to teach her forbidden things, they needed more privacy than a stable provided. But a lady might change her mind at the last moment.

Loudly.

Her lips were sweet. Her tongue curled around his when he slipped it between them. When her tongue followed his back into his mouth, he suckled it for a moment, the heady victory shooting straight to his groin.

Rosalinde might be inexperienced, but she was going to give as good as she got.

He meant to see she received only good.

"Ye're like satin," he whispered, stroking her skin from her jaw, down her throat and around the scooped neckline of her nightshift. "No, like silk."

"And how would a convict know what silk feels like?" she asked, her eyes teasing.

"I wasna always as ye see me now, ye know." The less said about how he'd come to be transported there, the better. So he followed his fingertips' path with his mouth to distract her, skimming over her warm skin. Her nipples stood out like a pair of padded buttons beneath the thin muslin.

He cupped a breast and her breath hissed in sharply over fine white teeth. It was one thing to brush her softness with the back of his hand through layers of boning, undergarments and her riding habit. Quite another to have only thin muslin separating them. Her eyelids fluttered closed as she caught her lower lip between her teeth.

He wondered how much of this bedazzled night was due to the *Knack* and how much to the heated attraction they'd both felt the first time they'd clapped eyes on each other. He hadn't meant to use his gift on her for this, but he couldn't be sure he hadn't without being aware of it. The *Knack* came as naturally as breathing to him.

He had to wonder how many virgins would invite the likes of him into their bedchambers without that extra unseen nudge.

When she tugged the bow at her neckline and parted the muslin to reveal as luscious a pair of breasts as ever a man could want, he decided he didn't care if the *Knack* was to blame. He'd take what his gift brought him.

He feasted on her. There was no missish stiffness from his Rose. Her little sounds of arousal, her hands twining his hair made his whole body throb as she arched into him. He kissed and suckled and nipped till she swayed on her feet.

Aidan scooped her up and carried her to the waiting bed. As soon as he laid her down she was up again, her knees sinking into the thick feather tick. Her kisses burned with urgency. Her hands worked the buttons down the front of his threadbare shirt. One popped off and rolled across the Bermudan cedar floor.

"Patience, lass," he said. "We've time." He'd have to remember to retrieve it later, but when she began pressing wet kisses to his chest, the button fled to a small corner of his mind.

He helped her jerk off his shirt and began to work the hooks at his hips to drop the front of his trousers.

"No, I'll do it," she said.

He let his arms hang at his sides, content to let her explore. "Never let it be said I deny ye anything, lass."

She smiled shyly up at him, a devastating dimple kissing her cheek. He longed to climb inside that sweet imperfection and never come out. Then her fingertips traced the fine line of dark hair that started as a thin strip at his navel and spread once her hand disappeared into the waist of his trousers. All thought of dimples fled.

He nuzzled her neck while she fondled his abdomen, careful to avoid the part of him that throbbed for her touch.

"I love your belly," she said, her knuckle finally grazing his aching cock.

"That's not me belly, love," he said with a wicked grin.

Her eyes flared, and then her usually mild brows pinched together. "I know we agreed ye'll not . . . I mean . . . you said there are ways . . ."

His grin faded. "Ye know ye can trust me, aye? Nothing we share this night will do ye lasting harm."

Much as he wanted to make the two-backed beast with Rosalinde, he wasn't the sort to ruin a girl.

"But this is your first time to lie with a man," he said, lowering his mouth to her neck. He longed to bite down on that warm flesh and leave a love-mark on her white throat, but she didn't need any physical evidence of their time together. She shivered, despite his warm breath feathering along her jaw and tickling her earlobe. "So I must warn ye. Ye'll always remember me."

Her lips twitched in a smile. "Then you'd better make sure it's a good memory."

He straightened and looked down at her, a smile slowly spreading over his face. "Aye, lassie. Ye have me word."

He bent and claimed her mouth as she stroked him, exploring his length with tentative glancing caresses. He bridled himself. It had been so long since he'd sheathed himself in a woman's wetness.

If she wasn't a virgin . . .

A vivid image seared across his mind. He imagined himself rucking up her nightshift. He plunged his hand in to cup her sex. In his mind's eye, she was so wet, his finger slid along her cleft with ease, all slickery and slippery and hot and aching.

Then in reality, she grasped his hand and pressed his palm over her privities. Her intimate moisture soaked through the thin fabric as she arched herself against his fingers. She made a noise of impatience in the back of her throat.

Had he *Sent* her that image of a lover's touch? Was she only responding to a suggestion accidentally delivered by means of his gift?

Rosalinde made another noise of distress and broke off their kiss. Then she tugged her nightshift over her head, wrapped her arms around him and fastened her lips to his as if her life depended on it.

Her soft breasts pressed against his work-hardened chest. He reached between them to finger her sex. Just as he'd imagined, she was wet and swollen. Her little spot had risen, begging for him to stroke it. His mouth found her breasts again. He nipped her and she cried out in aching joy.

"Hush, lass," he said. "Else ye'll have my head in a noose."

Rosalinde blinked at him and clamped her lip shut. He was still holding her hot little mound. She throbbed into his hand.

Lasses were kept in such ignorance of their own power. He'd show her now what her body could do. He stroked her slowly, drawing out the torment. When her eyes rolled back, he invaded her, slipping a finger into her tightness.

She spread her legs to give him room. He circled her sensitive spot, teasing and petting her into a stiff little peak.

He rolled a nipple between his thumb and forefinger while the other hand was still busy playing a lover's game with her mound. He tongued her mouth, a rough parody of what he ached to do with his cock in her tight little channel. She groaned with need.

He planted fevered kisses on her neck, her jaw, the corner of her mouth, her closed eyelids. "Make that noise again and I'll spread your legs and rut ye blind."

"Do you promise?" she said with a gasp.

They flopped onto the mattress in a tangle of arms and legs, kissing and stroking. His hips were between her thighs. He was poised at her entrance. The head eased in a finger width before Aidan caught himself.

"Oh, don't stop," she whimpered, wiggling down on him. "I'm so . . . empty."

Pressure rose in his shaft and his ballocks drew into a snug mound. He'd fill her all right.

She rocked her hips, grinding against him.

He panted with the effort of not plunging into her. The pleasure of wanting was a knife's edge from pain. He'd never needed anyone so.

"Rosalinde, lass, 'tis a thing once done, canna be undone." But even as he whispered the words, his mind churned furiously. He saw himself riding her with long hard strokes. Then he'd prop her knees over his shoulders and plough into her over and over and if they broke down the bed, so be it. He'd go to the gallows with a smile on his face if only he could rut her senseless now.

Her eyes glazed over and her mouth went passion-slack. "Yes. That. I want you to."

Does she somehow see what I want to do to her?

"Do it," she ordered as if she'd heard his thought. "Aidan, I need you so."

He drew a shuddering breath and lowered himself to kiss her.

He'd had the best of intentions. He was only going to pleasure her, to show her how her body worked. Then she melted under him and he was powerless to deny her.

She throbbed, a deep, low drumbeat between her legs and his balls clenched in tandem. Blood surged hotly, tramping out a rhythmic tattoo in his head, like a hundred shackled men marching in lockstep. In another moment, they'd break free and run riot through his brain.

With teeth clenched to control himself, he eased in, stopping only at the barrier of her purity. He raised himself on his elbows to look down at her.

Her face was taut with need.

"You can stop the ache," she said, tight-lipped. "Don't make me beg."

The lass was in dire straits. How could he say no?

Especially when his body was clamoring for relief so loudly, his brain couldn't get a word of restraint in edgewise. He hadn't intended their tryst to spiral out of control like this. He'd never lost command of himself before.

She rocked her hips against him in a wordless plea and he covered her mouth to muffle her cry before he plunged in, shredding her, filling her.

Ruining her.

All his good intentions . . .

Welcome to the road to hell, me boy-o.

Chapter 2

What a piece of work is a man!
—SHAKESPEARE, *Hamlet*

1830, London

"My stars! Isn't he the cheeky fellow?" Lady Chudderley's thin-lipped mouth screwed into a moue of distaste as she raised her lorgnette to eye someone across the crowded room. "I never dreamed he'd actually come."

"Who do you mean, auntie?" The party had turned into such a successful rout, Rosalinde Burke was pinned in the corner next to her great-aunt. They were stuck between a sideboard, groaning under the weight of finger sandwiches and petit fours, and the French doors leading out to the Palm Room. She peered in the same general direction as her great-aunt, but couldn't identify the source of Lady Chudderley's consternation.

The old woman fanned herself with such vigor, the ostrich plume in her turban did a fair imitation of a charmed cobra as it bobbed above her head.

"I had no intention of inviting him, I assure you, but at the Gainsborough exhibition last week, he was so . . . engaging, I found the words tumbling from my mouth before I thought better of them." Lady Chudderley stopped fanning and her lips turned up in the ghost of a strangely girlish smile. Then she gave herself a stern shake and resumed flailing the air. "Honestly, one would think he'd have the decency to stand me up, since anyone with half a brain would know he wasn't truly welcome in Polite Society."

"Who?"

"Why, Lord Stonemere, of course." She slapped the fan shut to punctuate her words. "He's over there beside Lady Longbotham. Oh, I do hope he . . ."

Rosalinde knew Lady Chudderley was still speaking. Indeed, when was she not? But her voice faded away as if Rose had dropped suddenly into a very deep well. She swallowed hard.

Broad shoulders. Lean hips. It looked like . . .

The man turned his dark head as if he sensed the weight of her eyes on him and met her gaze. She forgot to breathe. He still had the same raw-boned Celtic features, the same wild masculine beauty. And she was still utterly undone by the mere sight of him.

Aidan Danaher.

She'd heard of the infamous Lord Stonemere. She had no idea he and the man who still troubled her dreams and caused her to wake with a blush of wicked pleasure were one and the same.

Rosalinde clutched the side of her plum organdy skirt, and then released it guiltily before her great-aunt could scold her for wrinkling her gown.

"Who . . . did you say he was?"

"Stonemere," Lady Chudderley repeated. "The barony was near to reverting to another branch of Stonemeres, but then the family solicitor turned up the heir. The title came down through his mother, you see. Most irregular, but as it happens, she was a baroness in her own right. Then she abandoned the estate to marry an Irishman of all things. While she left a property, she couldn't leave her title. The English side of the family is most perturbed over this development, as you can well imagine. An Irish baron in Wiltshire."

Lady Chudderley clucked her tongue against her teeth and shuddered in distaste.

As if being Irish is the worst of Aidan's sins, Rosalinde thought ruefully.

Then her great-aunt sighed. "But one must admit, he's a devilishly handsome fellow."

"Devilishly," she repeated, partly because she was incapable of independent thought at the moment and partly because the description seemed particularly apt. The devil in question was headed straight for her. Against his deeply tanned skin, his smile was blinding, as if light glowed from inside him. It hurt to look at him, but Rosalinde couldn't tear her gaze away.

Aidan bent in an elegant bow to her great-aunt, lingering correctly over the old lady's be-ringed fingers. He inclined his head and took Rosalinde's hand with the proper cool detachment as Lady Chudderley rambled through a totally unnecessary introduction. Then he rubbed the pad of his thumb around one of Rosalinde's knuckles, most improperly, when her aunt's attention was diverted for a moment.

Heat crept up her neck and spread across her cheeks. Her body needed no reminder of this scoundrel. As promised, she remembered him all too well.

"Oh, child," her great-aunt said with alarm when she glanced at Rosalinde. "You're positively flushed. Have you a fever?"

"No, but—"

"Perhaps a change of air, Miss Burke. Shall I be having the pleasure of dancing with you?" Aidan suggested as the strains of a string quartet in the adjacent chamber warbled over the din of multiple conversations in the packed room. The thick workman's brogue Rosalinde remembered was now merely a cultured lilt. "Lady Chudderley's excellent repast has crowded this hall past bearing. There'll be more space to breathe on the dance floor, I'm thinking. If you'll excuse us, my lady." He slanted a devastating smile toward his hostess and offered his arm to Rosalinde, daring her to take it.

Rosalinde's traitorous great-aunt giggled like a pudding-headed debutant, completely forgetting how inconvenient she'd found Aidan's presence only moments ago.

"By all means, enjoy yourselves," Lady Chudderley said.

"But I don't wish to leave you alone, auntie," she protested.

"Pish-tosh, child. No one is alone in this press. I declare, if this isn't the best turnout of the Season." She waved them away, fan and ostrich plume aflutter in perfect rhythm, and began to waddle toward Lady Longbotham.

"Come, Miss Burke." Aidan led Rosalinde through the crowd that parted like the Red Sea before Moses.

The string quartet in the next room finished a lively jig with a flourish. Her great-aunt had ordered all the furnishings in the music room removed to provide space for dancing. Only a few chairs and settees ringed the chamber where doting mother hens could keep watchful eyes on their chicks while the stylized motions of courtship were acted out on the dance floor.

No one's eyes were on Rosalinde. Except Aidan's deep green ones.

A thousand questions danced on her tongue but none of them would bear the possibility of being overheard. She rested her gloved hand lightly on him, but even so she was acutely aware of every speck of the man. His body heat radiated through her palm, up her arm, and then settled to roil furiously in her belly. He led her to the center of the dance floor a heartbeat before the first violinist's next up-bow and the quartet broke into a slow waltz.

Without a word, Aidan took one of her hands, settled his other at her waist, and began twirling her around the room with the natural grace of a dancing master. But his frown would have been more at home on the headmaster of a particularly strict public school.

"Ye didn't say goodbye," he said softly.

"I believe quite enough passed between us without adding the farce of a farewell," she whispered between barely moving lips.

Besides, she wasn't given a chance to see Aidan again. After her tattletale maid found his missing button under Rosalinde's bureau, she presented the incriminating evidence to the commissioner. When Rose refused to name the man who'd been in her bedchamber, her father sent her back to England on the next available packet. She'd been under her great-aunt's careful scrutiny ever since.

"You didn't keep your promise," Rosalinde countered, since the music was now loud enough to cover their conversation.

He was only going to school her in the pleasures of the body, not mark her for life. He'd managed to control himself well enough not to get her with child, but her maidenhead was thoroughly lost to that night of insanity on the island.

His eyes darkened, a shaded glen where the unwary might meet a bad end. "Nothing happened that ye didn't wish at the time. Most ardently, as I recall, or am I mistaken?"

Her cheeks heated afresh. How dare he remind her how he'd reduced her to pleading. She'd been an innocent, ignorant of the powerful urges they were playing with. He, on the other hand, knew full well what he was doing every step of the way.

"When a lady begs so prettily, how can a gentleman refuse?"

"You're no gentleman and we both know it."

"On the contrary, I'm every inch a gentleman. Born to it, don't ye know?" he said with a lazy smile. "Did I not tell ye when first we met, I wasna always as ye found me then?"

The brogue was back, thick and sensual, roughening his voice and sending a shiver of longing over her. The man could make love with words alone, letting his rumbling bass touch the deep places in her nothing else could reach.

Every inch a gentleman. For a blink, she was back in Bermuda, stretched out on her feather tick. Their bodies sweat-slick in the moonlight with the long, thick length of him pounding in and out of her. The emptiness finally filled. It was almost too glorious to bear.

Then when she could abide the hot sweetness no longer, her soul had back-flipped into itself and she unraveled under him. Shuddering and convulsing, she'd been more than naked before Aidan Danaher. He'd tasted her bared spirit as well as her bared flesh.

Rosalinde gave herself a silent reproof. This was not the time or the place to indulge such memories, but her body continued to riot in his presence, including a resumption of that blasted empty ache. She suspected if she excused herself and fled to the lady's retiring room, she'd find her crotch damp with wanting.

"I expect ye've questions regarding this turn-about of my fortunes. Me mum always had an air about her when I was young, ye see," Aidan said. "I always fancied her a great lady. As it happened, she was."

"So now you're a baron," Rosalinde said, trying to keep her voice even. "Is that why you were released from Royal Dock?"

"It is indeed. When Mum died, the lawyers figured out I was next in line for Stonemere and I was pardoned. Seems no one wanted a member of the Upper Crust, even one who didn't know he was, shackled like a common murderer."

His practiced smile faded. "Might give the salt of the earth the notion that there's not tuppence worth of difference between a duke and a ditch-digger. We can't have that, can we?"

She'd never asked why he was imprisoned when she fell under his spell like a besotted fool. It hadn't seemed important at the time, but now her breath caught at the word 'murderer.' "Were you guilty?"

His eyes glinted wickedly. "Sure and we're all guilty of something, aren't we, darlin'?"

He didn't pull her closer than propriety allowed, but she felt suddenly naked before him again. This man knew all her secrets, while she'd known none of his. She would not be pulled in by his easy charm this time. She lifted her chin in determination.

"Don't ye be fretting, lass. I'm not the sort to kiss and tell."

If only kissing were all there was to it. Even that would be bad enough—certainly grounds to force a marriage any day. Though Aidan had a title now, he didn't meet her great-aunt's requirement that she wed a respectable, well-connected gentleman. Rosalinde shuddered to think what kind of connections an Irish ex-convict might have.

"Obviously, I have no idea what *sort* you are, Lord Stonemere, but I'm no longer the naïve girl I was when we first met."

She'd been eighteen when Aidan climbed through her window. Old enough to know better. She often wondered what madness prompted her to indulge in that sensual odyssey with him. She blamed it on the bright Bermuda moon. Or the heavy air drugged with night-blooming flowers and pounding surf.

Or the smell of leather and warm horseflesh and Aidan's distinct masculine scent.

"I can only see ye've grown lovelier, Rose," he said, then leaned forward to whisper. "The hollows beneath your cheekbones still make me ache to kiss them."

She looked away from him lest she fall into his eyes. "You will not speak to me so familiarly, sir."

"My apologies. Ye're right, o' course. And I can see ye're no longer . . . naïve." His gaze swept her bodice apprecia-tively. When she scowled at him, he grinned back. "Don't fuss, Rose. I'm agreeing with ye . . . in a totally unconven-tional way."

"I prefer convention."

"I've me doubts about that."

"Did you ask me to dance so you could insult me?"

He frowned. "Of course not. What I meant was ye've blossomed just as I expected ye would," he said as they dipped in time to the Strauss tune. The pressure of his hand on her waist threatened to send her mind wandering back to that other wicked time, when his work-rough palms steadied her hips while he claimed her entirely. "I notice ye're still unmarried."

"That is none of your business," she said testily. Through her great-aunt's finagling, she'd been engaged to a perfectly acceptable young man shortly after she returned to England. Rosalinde cried off six weeks before the wedding, much to Lady Chudderley's dismay. Not because she couldn't bear to tell him she wasn't the virgin he expected, but because she couldn't bear the thought of letting him do the lovely secret things Aidan had done with her.

"The word about town is that you've an understanding with Viscount Musgrave," Aidan said casually as he led her through a graceful underarm turn.

She sighed. He didn't need to know so much about her life, when it was obvious she still knew very little about his. How did a man fall from heir to a British title to a shackled prisoner on Royal Dock? Even if he hadn't known he'd had a privileged birth at the time, his mother should have. And she ought to have used her influence then.

"Do tell me if ye've set a date," Aidan said. "They're laying odds on it at White's, ye see, and the purse is too fat to ignore."

"No, we haven't set a date." She jerked her gaze away from his knowing grin and tried to keep her eyes focused on a point north of his right shoulder. The room spun so, she was forced to give up and look back at him. "He hasn't actually proposed, if you must know."

Not for lack of her great-aunt's trying. Lady Chudderley was determined to make the match. She so badly wanted Rosalinde to set her cap for the viscount, she had sweetened the deal by promising to settle an astounding sum on her father the day Rosalinde wed Musgrave. It was high time the family made inroads back into the well-connected nobility, and Musgrave was related to nearly every peer in the realm by some degree of consanguinity.

Since Lady Chudderley had no direct descendants, unless Rosalinde married well, the Burkes would be relegated to the status of merchants and tradesmen when her great-aunt passed on. Since the commissioner's *investments*, her father's pet name for his gambling debts, had taken a disastrous turn of late, Rosalinde felt honor-bound to try to meet the old lady's terms for his sake.

Besides, she owed her father something after the way he'd spirited her home in order to protect her good name.

"Nothing set in stone between ye and Musgrave, then. Good," Aidan said. "That leaves hope for me."

Rosalinde snorted. It wasn't terribly genteel, but Aidan brought out unladylike urges in her of all sorts. "Whatever gives you the idea that I'd welcome your attention, sir?"

"Past experience."

She stiffened in his arms. He might have a title now, but as far as she was concerned, he was still an Irish convict.

One who'd been convicted of murder, no less. And she knew to her sorrow that he couldn't be trusted.

If only he wasn't so devilishly handsome . . .

She gave herself a mental shake. She'd made a mistake in the past, but surely she wouldn't make a cake of herself over the man's fine face and form now.

"I advise you not to address your attention to me, my lord, unless you enjoy spending your time to no profit," she said with exaggerated formality. "The man I wed will be a *proper* gentleman."

"Ah, lass. Ye'd be wasted on a proper gentleman and ye know it," Aidan said, then he leaned in to whisper to her. "A proper gentleman only beds his wife to get an heir. His mistress has all the fun while his wife faces the uncertainties of childbed. I ask ye now, where's the justice in that?"

She looked pointedly away from him as they continued to waltz. "If you cannot keep from being indelicate, I must ask you to refrain from speaking for the duration of this dance."

"Sometimes the truth is indelicate," Aidan said.

"You want the truth? Very well. At the risk of being indelicate, I confess I cannot bear the sight of you."

She pulled free of his palm on her waist. Without relinquishing her hand, he twirled her back into his arms as if her steps away were part of the dance.

"Indelicacy is one thing. A lie is another." He shook his head in reproof. "Never dabble in a game of *poque*, lassie. Ye can't bluff. Your face is an open book. Ye can bear me well enough and we both know it."

She stopped dancing and cast her eyes down at the tips of his shiny boots. "Release me this instant," she said through clenched teeth. "Or I will cause such a scene, they'll hear it all the way to Bermuda. And that's no bluff."

"Good," Aidan said with a laugh. "Sounds like just what this party needs."

"Pardon me." Another male voice jerked Rosalinde's gaze up. "May I cut in, Stonemere? I desire the honor of dancing with Miss Burke, if the lady has no objections, of course."

It was Viscount Musgrave, tapping Aidan's shoulder. His expression was calm and unruffled and as proper as tea with the vicar. Dear Edwin was the perfect antidote to this rogue who plagued her with improper thoughts of all sorts. Rosalinde could have thrown her arms around the viscount and kissed him right on the lips.

Of course, that wasn't a very proper thought either.

Botheration! One dance with Aidan Danaher had undone years of studied self-control. At least Lord Musgrave was coming to her rescue, like a white knight. She stepped out of the circle of Aidan's arms.

"The honor is mine, Lord Musgrave." Rosalinde smiled brightly as she dipped a shallow curtsey of farewell to Aidan. "Good evening, Lord Stonemere."

"It *was* a good evening. Whether it continues so remains to be seen," he said sourly; then he recovered his manners and sent her a polite smile. "I thank ye kindly for the dance, Miss Burke." He gave a curt nod to the viscount.

Viscount Musgrave took her into the correct dancing position and they tilted away from Aidan to the final lilting strains of the waltz.

"Oh, my, that was far too short. Seems I mistimed my request," Edwin said when the final chord faded.

His eyes were the color of the surf off Brighton on a high summer day. With his fair hair and square-jawed good looks, Rosalinde normally found Edwin Farrell Sotheby-Finch, Lord Musgrave, to be exceedingly fair to look upon. Unfortunately, a certain Irish scoundrel was playing havoc with her sense of manly beauty at the moment.

"Might I have the honor of another dance?" Edwin asked.

Rosalinde caught sight of Aidan over Edwin's shoulder and yanked her gaze back to the viscount's earnest face. "Of course, my lord. I should be delighted."

She certainly should be. Lord Musgrave was considered no end of a catch. A single dance with him was enough to set most maidenly stomachs aflutter. Instead her belly fizzed as if someone had loosed a jar of lantern beetles in it.

"And I'd be delighted if I could convince you to call me by my Christian name," Edwin said.

"If it were appropriate for me to do so, rest assured, I would, Lord Musgrave." Even though she thought of him as Edwin, the name had never passed her lips.

Formality was a small shield, but it was all she had to protect herself from a man's designs. Not that she suspected Lord Musgrave of any ulterior motives.

Rather, she held herself in suspicion. If she'd insisted on calling Aidan 'Mr. Danaher' instead of agreeing to go along with his easy informality while they worked together in the stables, surely she'd never have allowed him to kiss her. Or touch her. Or invite him to sneak into her bedchamber by moonlight to show her why her belly knotted at the sight of him.

"I hope it will become entirely appropriate for you to call me Edwin very soon," Viscount Musgrave said and then launched into a description of his doings in the House of Lords.

From the corner of her eye, she saw Aidan mouthing a message to her. She forced herself to attend to what the viscount was saying as they waited for the start of the next tune, but she could muster little interest in the poor condition of drains in the city or the bill Lord Musgrave was shepherding through the House of Lords in order to rectify the situation.

The music began, a stately quadrille this time. She and the viscount formed up with another three couples to complete the intricate turns and steps. Each time she looked up, Aidan was there, his lips forming the same words. With each pass, she managed to decipher another word. Rosalinde lost her footing and stumbled when his meaning became clear.

"Leave your window open."

Of all the insufferable cheek. The man must think her mad. She'd do no such ridiculous thing. It would mean ruin this time for certain.

Besides, she liked nice men, men who counted it a favor if she called them by their Christian names, men who worried over the state of drains and danced with their cool, dry hands lightly holding hers in perfect correctness.

But, God help her, some wicked, ungovernable part of her heart wanted to lift her window sash when she retired to her chamber that evening.

To see if Aidan Danaher would climb through it.

Chapter 3

The play's the thing
Wherein I'll catch the conscience of the King.
—SHAKESPEARE, *Hamlet*

Aidan watched Rosalinde through the intricate turns of the quadrille. Pleasant as it was to see her move with grace around the room, it was not so pleasant to see her do it in the company of another man. Each time she glanced his way, he silently repeated his request for her to leave her window open. After she missed a step, turned the wrong direction and nearly plowed into Lady Cowper, Aidan was satisfied his message had been received.

Now if she'll only do it, he thought with a long sigh.

He resisted the temptation to use the *Knack* on her. Once he was in her chamber, it would be a simple thing to be found with the lady *in flagrante delicto* and settle the whole question with a quick marriage to hush up the scandal.

He was a baron with means now. Once the initial furor died down, Polite Society would come to the conclusion that he wasn't such a bad bargain for her. He was looking forward to spending a good deal of time and money convincing her of that as well.

But if he used the *Knack* to gain entrance to her bedchamber, how would he ever know if it was he she fancied or if she'd been compelled by his gift to welcome him to her bed?

Love was freely given or it was not love.

Aidan was determined to have nothing less from Rosalinde Burke. In the darkness of his incarceration, she'd been the one spot of blazing color. Her kindness and generous spirit had kept him from growing bitter over the injustice of his situation. One night with her convinced him of the existence of a merciful God.

But Aidan didn't intend to show her any mercy. Short of *knacking* her, he'd make her love him or at least remember that once she had loved him. Surely that never really went away.

He stopped at the arched doorway leading into the room set aside for gaming and looked back at her. Rosalinde smiled up at her dancing partner and a red haze settled over Aidan's vision.

Viscount Musgrave wasn't a bad sort. Lord knows, it might have been easier if he was. They'd even been friends years ago during the short time Aidan and his brother came to live with their English cousins. Edwin was thoroughly decent, a stickler for good form and fair play.

Aidan could more than hold his own with cutthroats and thieves. Against an upright, proper gentleman, he wasn't quite sure how to proceed.

He'd charmed Rosalinde once. He only hoped he'd be able to do it again. In case she didn't lift the sash of her window to him, it was time to set plans for his alternate goal in train. He intended to clear his name.

Aidan steeled himself to abandon her to the dance floor with Viscount Musgrave and made his way to the gaming room. Six or seven tables had been set up around the long hall. Whist, euchre, loo, any type of game of chance a man might favor was in full swing. There was even a hazard table, the dice clicking merrily, in one corner. Aidan's cousin, George Stonemere, raked in the bones and gave them a shake. Judging from the hard set of his mouth, the dice had not been kind to him.

"If Lady Chudderley ever tires of being a meddlesome

busybody, she might set up for gaming hell proprietress in earnest," Aidan murmured.

At the *poque* table at the far end of the room, Rosalinde's father hunched over a dwindling stack of chips. The regretful expression on his heavily jowled face reminded Aidan of a dog who'd just pissed the rug.

After shadowing Mr. Burke on a trek through a number of gaming establishments one night, Aidan knew the man was in debt. In fact, he'd made it a point to quietly buy up the lion's share of Mr. Burke's vowels from his creditors, to keep Rosalinde's father from being hounded for repayment. The former commissioner had no idea Aidan Danaher held his IOUs, a princely sum. He suspected that despite his recent elevation to rank and privilege, Mr. Burke still considered Aidan little more than the Irish convict who used to muck out his stables and spit-shine his boots. When Rosalinde's father saw him, his face brightened with calculation and he motioned for Aidan to join them.

"Don't know why it is, Stonemere, but I seem to have better luck with the cards when you're playing too," Mr. Burke said expansively.

"Perhaps because it's always good luck to have a player with poorer luck at the table," Aidan said with a self-deprecating chuckle as he pulled up a chair. The play was fast and furious. He made sure Mr. Burke raked in the next three pots.

He and the commissioner had made their public peace months ago, when they first ran into each other on English soil.

"Knew you couldn't have been guilty," the commissioner had said gruffly. "Glad to see an injustice overturned."

Aidan had merely smiled. Mr. Burke knew Aidan had confessed to the crime of which he was accused, but because he now had a milord before his name, somehow that fact was conveniently forgotten. In public, at least. A man with a title might do anything with impunity, it seemed.

Aidan's mother must truly have loved his bounder of a father for her to have given up such power to follow him to a piss-poor potato farm in Ireland. Or maybe the old devil had used the *Knack* on her. Aidan was never quite sure how matters stood between the two of them. She was every inch a lady of quality and his father was as rough as they came.

"Such a man is a trial to the soul," his mother would say, but the smile that tugged at the corners of her sweet mouth also said such a man was wildly exciting.

Wildly exciting or not, his father didn't provide Aidan and his younger brother Liam with a stable home. The family moved from shire to shire, his da taking work where he could get it. When things got too hard, his mother had packed Aidan and Liam off to live with their English cousins in Wiltshire. After growing up wild as thistles in Ireland, transplanting them to Stonehaven was a disaster on all counts.

Two players tossed down their hands and excused themselves, clearly disgusted at the former commissioner's continued string of good luck.

"I see there's room for another player."

Aidan looked up to find his cousin George standing by an open chair.

Good. He hadn't even had to use the *Knack* to lure him to the table. Aidan didn't want to dissipate its power should he need it later, but he'd have done it if George hadn't moved to the *poque* table soon. He wanted to make sure George was in on the final hand. Without speaking, Aidan waved his cousin to a vacant chair. He didn't want to chance George hearing the slightest hint of excitement in his voice over this development.

"I, too, would like to play." Viscount Musgrave appeared suddenly, squeezing through the crowd.

Aidan frowned. Even though Musgrave had been visiting Stonehaven when the murder occurred, he didn't suspect the viscount and didn't need him around in order to further his scheme to clear his name.

Especially since Rosalinde was still hanging on the man's arm, all flushed and lightly winded from her exertions on the dance floor. A couple of curls at her temples had loosened and now dangled past her chin. The effect was too soft, too sensual for fashion. *Undone.* The light sheen on her cheeks reminded Aidan of how delectable she looked after a good hard swive, her skin glistening, spent with pleasurable effort.

Aidan tamped down his body's reaction to her. He needed to focus his energy elsewhere now. On his cousin George, mostly.

"There you are, Father," Rosalinde said as she hurried around to Mr. Burke's side. Aidan stood to acknowledge her presence, as all the men did, but she didn't spare him a glance. "Aunt is looking for you."

"Well, if Lady Chudderley comes here, she'll find me, gel," her father said. "My luck's running too high to leave the table just now."

"True enough," Aidan said with what he hoped was a hangdog expression. "Your father's about to turn out me pockets."

In truth, it had been a good trick to lose to him. Mr. Burke was an abominable player, but Aidan needed him to win. It was the only way to make his plan work.

"By all means, sit down, Lord Musgrave," Rosalinde's father insisted. "But don't feel badly if I beat you too." He turned his head toward his daughter. "Tell her ladyship I'll attend her after I relieve Lord Stonemere of the rest of his chips."

"Shouldn't take long at the rate ye're going," Aidan said amiably as the dealer started flicking cards at each of them.

Rosalinde made no move to deliver her father's message, instead taking up a position from which she could scowl at Mr. Burke most conveniently when he wasn't looking. Aidan decided it was preferable to have her here after all, so there'd be no confusion later about what happened.

Viscount Musgrave settled beside Aidan. "I must say, I wouldn't have figured you for a man who didn't mind losing."

"Cards are nothing," Aidan said, shooting Rosalinde a quick glance. She refused to meet his gaze. "But there are some things it would pain me a great deal to lose."

"I daresay prison taught my cousin patience in losing," George said artlessly.

Someone's breath hissed in surprise. It was one thing to be aware of a gentleman's unsavory past, quite another to throw it in his face.

"It taught me many things, but mostly that a man makes his own luck when it comes to the important things in life," Aidan said, breaking the uneasy silence. He glanced at the cards he'd been dealt. *Too good.* He tossed them, face-side-down into the center of the table, bowing out of a winning hand. "Certainly didn't improve me luck at cards though," he said with a laugh.

The next hand was better for his purposes. It was far worse. Aidan could hardly have had a weaker start, but he made a cautious bid.

"Want another drubbing, do you?" Mr. Burke said and matched his bet.

The viscount and cousin George were both in. Aidan raised his stakes, with less caution this time.

"I believe he may have the cards this hand," Lord Musgrave said as the bidding went around the table. "But I'll back my own."

When one of his opponents showed signs of flagging, Aidan *Sent* him a strong silent suggestion and they all continued to bid. Finally, Aidan shoved his remaining chips into the center of the table.

"I can buy that pot, you know," Mr. Burke said.

"But ye're too much the gentleman to do that. Allow me to sweeten it further, if ye will." Aidan leaned forward and caught the eyes of every player around the table. "My lake is teeming with trout. The woods in Wiltshire are full of gamebirds and trophy bucks. To my wager, I'll add a fortnight for all of ye as guests on my country estate. I'll show ye such sport, ye'll talk of it for the rest of your lives."

"Fur, fins, and feathers, eh? Some men prefer other quarry," George said with a wink. "Will there be women?"

"Of course. Bring your families as well. Perhaps your mother and sister would enjoy a country outing, Musgrave." Aidan turned to the viscount, purposely misunderstanding his cousin. He needed this to be a respectable house party, not a rakehell's orgy. Though if all went well, he'd have his own private carouse with Rosalinde.

Viscount Musgrave eyed Aidan thoughtfully for a moment. "It's been years since I visited Stonehaven. Very well, I'll take that bet."

"And I," Mr. Burke agreed, slapping down the appropriate wager.

George squinted at Aidan. "I wouldn't mind staying at the family seat again, though I warn you, this may turn into a more expensive wager than you intend."

Aidan let his lip twitch, hoping George would take it for a tell that he was bluffing.

"Let's see your cards, cousin." George pushed a stack of chips forward.

Aidan slumped his shoulders and tossed his pitiful hand into the center of the table. "Looks like ye gentlemen have sniffed out me bluff. I lose."

*   *   *

"But he didn't lose, Father," Rosalinde complained after the last guest straggled away from Lady Chudderley's party. "He's getting exactly what he wants. Lord Stonemere knows we'd decline a direct invitation to his home. Anyone in Society would."

"The girl's right, Loromer," Lady Chudderley chimed in. She gloried in browbeating Rosalinde's father whenever she could. Heaven had blessed her with no sons of her own to reprove, so her only nephew had to do. "And now Lord Stonemere's managed to trick you and the viscount and his poor cousin into a fortnight in his company."

"And our families. Don't forget that." Mr. Burke's face flushed red with irritation. "If you don't like the gentleman, why in blazes did you invite him here in the first place?"

"That's neither here nor there. Joining in a house party implies a far closer relationship than a chance invitation to attend a large rout." Lady Chudderley pursed her lips as if she'd swallowed a bite of herring that had turned. "Besides, it's never a question of whether one likes someone or not. Spending time in another's company is first and foremost about whether the association is a proper one."

"Then why invite him to your soiree if he's not fit company?" Mr. Burke's point was small, but it was the only one he had in the argument, so he worried it like a terrier after a rat.

Rosalinde knew perfectly well why her great-aunt had invited Aidan. He'd charmed her, as neatly as the serpent had deceived Eve in the garden. He'd charmed her great-aunt because it was what he did as easily as breathing.

But Rosalinde was determined not to succumb to that charm again.

"The fact is you've obligated this family to an unwholesome outing. For a fortnight, no less." Her great-aunt shook a bony finger at her father. "And I'd like to know what you intend to do about it."

"I intend," Father said testily, "to shoot a brace of pheasant and catch a stringer of trout. And the two of you will accompany me and, damn it all, we'll have a jolly time of it too, and that's that."

Lady Chudderley made a 'tsking' sound. "Mind your language, Loromer."

"Bother my language." He ran a hand over his thinning hair. "Hang it all, I don't see that there's a way around it. We have to go. If a man has debts of honor, it's incumbent on his creditors to allow him to make his markers good."

"Debts of honor, eh? There's a fanciful term for gambling losses," Lady Chudderley said, one gray brow arched. "Well, at least you've turned the conversation to a subject with which you're well acquainted."

Rosalinde rolled her eyes heavenward and made good her escape. Once her father and great-aunt began wrangling about his gambling debts, the argument might continue for hours.

When she reached her chamber, she found her maid Katie nodding on a chair near the fireplace. The door latch clicked behind her and the girl roused with far more cheer than the late hour warranted.

"There y'are, miss." Katie hopped up and skittered over to help Rosalinde out of the plum gown. "Was it a nice party? Did you have a loverly time, then? Me and Gus, we heard the music from downstairs and took a few turns of our own in the scullery. Right sprightly we was too. You wouldn't think it to look on him, what with him being such a big strapping fellow, but my Gus is fair light on his feet."

The restful thing about having Katie as her maid was that Rosalinde was rarely required to add anything to a conversation with her. Katie was perfectly capable of keeping up both sides with no apparent effort.

"Will you be wanting me to brush out your hair?" Katie asked after she stowed the gown in its place and helped Rosalinde out of her corset and petticoats and into her lacy nightshift. "My Gus loves to brush my hair."

"No, I'll manage," Rosalinde said, before Katie could launch into a description of the other things her Gus loved. The little maid had married the tall, well-favored footman last March and to hear Katie talk, one would think marital bliss hadn't been invented before they tied the knot. Rosalinde's body was already achy and restless, already keyed up enough without a whispered recital of her maid's bedtime activities. "Go on, Kate. I've kept you up late enough as it is."

"Aren't you kind?" Katie said, stifling a yawn as she shuffled to the door. "G'night then, miss."

Rosalinde pulled out the pins holding her coiffure in place and shook her hair loose with one hand. Then she began brushing the long strands, working out the worst of the tangles with her fingers.

She glanced toward the window.

Since she was on the upper story of her great-aunt's townhome, and her property backed onto St. James Park, it was unlikely anyone could see in to spy on her. But she turned down the gas lamp, just in case. She usually sneaked a bit of Shakespeare before bed, but after the way Aidan had stirred up her belly, she didn't think she could bear any more *Romeo and Juliet* this night, lest the dull ache of emptiness never let her sleep.

"Leave your window open." She could almost hear Aidan's voice in her mind.

As if she was fool enough to do that again. What sort of round-heeled ninny did he take her for?

She wandered to the window, still stroking her hair absently. The Season was nearly over and many families were preparing to leave the growing heat of London for the coolness of their country homes. Her bedchamber was certainly warm enough to justify opening the window a crack in hope of a breath of breeze. By day, London was becoming a sweltering miasma of unhealthy smells. When the stars came out, they seemed to chase away the worst of the stale fug.

"Just for a bit of cool night," she murmured as she un-locked the casement and pushed up the sash. Besides, it was a good thirty feet to the garden below. No harm in opening the window a bit.

She leaned out and surveyed the neatly trimmed hedges and immaculate flowerbeds, awash in shades of gray. The patter of the garden fountain floated up to her. Rosalinde made out the cobbled footpath snaking through the small space, the vine-covered arbor and the settee near the roses. From this angle, no one could hide from her gaze.

Aidan was nowhere to be seen.

"What did you expect?" she grumbled to herself as she straightened and paced away from the window.

He had no intention of coming to her. Aidan might have shinnied up the exterior of the commissioner's house, but her great-aunt's smooth-walled townhome offered no finger- or toeholds to a midnight climber.

Was it a test of some sort? Was he watching from the deeper shadows somewhere simply to see if she'd open the window at his bidding?

She reached to close it, but as she did, a rope dropped from above and dangled before her. As she watched, open-mouthed, Aidan climbed down the rope, hand-over-hand, one leg hitched around the cord, until he was level with her sill. He cocked his head and shot her a wicked grin.

"Well, lass," he whispered. "Ye'll have to step back a bit if ye intend to invite me in."

Chapter 4

Oh, wilt thou leave me so unsatisfied?
—SHAKESPEARE, *Romeo and Juliet*

She planted her fists on the sill and leaned out till she was nearly nose-to-nose with him. "I'm not inviting you in."

"D'ye think your reputation will be better served by me hanging outside your window where anyone might see me?" He turned a half circle, but stuck out his foot to stop the rotation so he remained facing her. The muscles in his upper arms strained the seams of his shirt with their rock-hard bulges.

"Since when are you concerned for my reputation?" she hissed.

"Everything about ye concerns me, lass." He let go of the rope with one hand so he could tuck an errant lock of hair behind her ear. "Ye should know that by now."

She caught herself leaning into his touch and jerked back with a snort, knocking her crown on the window sash. She rubbed her head with one hand and reached to close the window with the other. "Go away."

Aidan grasped the sash, refusing to let her close it. "Not until we've had a chance to talk and I hardly think this is the place for it."

"Really? Then might I suggest that civilized people send round their cards to announce their intent to visit and then come calling during their hostess's 'at home' hours. It sounds like lunacy, I know, but people make it work."

"I didn't figure you for anything so dull, Rose," he said. "Do you really want me to do that so we can sit in Lady Chudderley's parlor and talk about the weather and you can serve me cucumbers on stale bread?"

"No, so I can arrange not to be at home when you come."

"Are ye trying to tell me ye don't want to see me?"

"Very good, Aidan," she said dryly. "That wasn't such a long walk, was it?"

Aidan shook his head. "Then why did ye open your window at all?"

She had no answer. Even to herself, the idea of washing the stuffiness of her room with the unwholesome air of London seemed thin.

"I'll tell ye why." He grasped the window sill more firmly and pulled himself close. "We've unfinished business, we two. And neither of us will rest until it's settled. If ye don't let me in this night, ye know I'll only be back on the morrow."

Rosalinde stepped away from the window, her heart thumping out a brisk tattoo. This wasn't some magical night on an island. This was London. She'd be ruined, thoroughly and completely, if he was caught with her here, but she knew he'd give her no peace unless she allowed it. "Come in then, but for pity's sake, be quiet."

I'm going to hell, she told herself as he swung his long legs through the opening. His trousers molded to his muscular thighs and his open-collared shirt revealed enough of his chest to make hers flutter.

Practically naked, so far as Polite Society was concerned. A gentleman never appeared before a lady in his shirtsleeves unless the lady was his wife. But then, except for an accident of birth, Aidan Danaher was not really a gentleman. No true gentleman sported such a well-muscled chest. Only a man who'd toiled and sweated in the baking sun developed such disturbing attributes, and a simple shirt did nothing to hide them.

Of course, she was in her nightshift, so Rosalinde supposed it might be argued she was no lady at the moment.

"Rose, sweetheart," he whispered and started to draw her into an embrace, but she straight-armed him and skittered out of reach.

"You said you wanted to talk to me, so talk," she said warily.

"I also said we had unfinished business." His eyes glinted in the dimness, feral and unpredictable. "I've wanted ye from the moment I first clapped eyes on ye. Can ye deny ye want me, lass?"

"I want to keep my reputation more."

She had to say that. It was the only way to keep from succumbing to him again. If she let him kiss her, let him touch her, she might burst into flames. She might do that yet if he didn't stop shooting her such smoldering looks. It was time to change the subject.

"How did you come to be waiting on our roof?"

"Not your roof exactly. More like your garret. Your neighbors in the next townhouse have already left for Dover for the summer."

He sat down and toed off his boots and Rosalinde almost chided him for it till she realized he'd travel across the hardwood more softly unshod. A shoe, more or less, did nothing to make their situation more acceptable.

"Did ye know all the homes on this block have a common attic?" he asked.

"I shudder to ask how *you* know it."

"Well, prison does lend itself to low associations and a good bit of intelligence can be had for a price. Once I discovered the neighbor's house was empty, it was a simple thing to jimmy the lock and slip in the back. When I reached the attic, I only had to count my steps till I figured I was over your townhome. There's a garret window almost exactly above yours. I kept watch till I saw your window open and ye leaning out to have a look about."

"And you were that sure I'd do it?"

"Ye can't blame a man for hoping, can ye?" He smiled and shrugged. She would have loved to pummel the smug look off his face, except that he was so deucedly handsome, she couldn't bring herself to raise a hand to him.

Lady Chudderley certainly wouldn't show such restraint if she caught him here. She'd seen her great-aunt ruin an ivory fan drumming it on a man's chest for far less an offense. For tuppence, Rosalinde was tempted to call for her.

Then Aidan's smile faded and he eyed her with the intensity of a cat before a mouse hole.

"What's so important you risked your neck and my reputation to speak to me about it?" Rosalinde asked.

"I want to know how much ye've heard about the crime I was convicted of," he said.

"Almost nothing. Until this night, I didn't know it was murder."

Looking at him now, sitting in untamed stillness, she could believe him capable of it. This was far beyond simply being unacceptable in Polite Society. Aidan Danaher was *unsafe.*

He studied her hearth rug. "They say I killed a lass, an upstairs maid at Stonehaven. Folk say I met her in the grotto behind the manor house, throttled her and left her for dead. Her name was Peg Bass."

Rosalinde swallowed hard. "Did you do it?"

"I confessed."

A chill swept over her.

"While ye're at Stonehaven, ye'll hear more of it, I'm

sure." A sad smile tugged at his sensual mouth. "Londoners haven't had the full sordid tale yet and it's too dainty a dish for gossips to resist."

"That's assuming we'll come to your house party."

"Ye have to. The wager saw to that." The smug grin was back. "It would be exceeding bad form for your da not to allow me to pay back my debt of honor."

"Seems you have everything figured out."

"All except you." He rose, silent as a cat in his stocking feet, and walked toward her. "I've come to ask ye to trust me. Ye must believe me when I tell ye not everything is as it seems."

She stifled a nervous laugh. Why hadn't she let the fact that he was a convicted criminal matter to her before this? On the island, he was simply the fellow in the stable who made her insides squirm with pleasure each time she caught sight of him and her heart skip whenever he smiled at her.

"You want me to trust you," she said. "It's a little late for that."

"I know. It seems a lot to ask after what happened, but by all that's holy, I swear, I truly meant ye no lasting harm."

There was nothing holy about it. A confessed murderer, right there in her bedchamber. If she screamed, would anyone come in time? "Is that what you told Peg Bass?"

He sighed. "I suppose I deserve that."

"No, what you deserve is to finish out your sentence at Royal Dock."

"Probably. Ye're right about the heart of the matter. Justice has not been served to Peg Bass." He paced toward the window as if he was about to leave, then he rounded on her. "Viscount Musgrave is all wrong for ye. Tell me ye don't really intend to marry him."

She blinked at him in surprise. Aidan confessed to murder, and then denigrated her choice of beaus. The man's impudence knew no bounds.

"I can't imagine why a girl wouldn't want to marry the viscount," she said. "He's well-spoken, well-connected, has more than two coins to rub together and he's not at all hard to look upon. There's not a thing wrong with Edwin."

"Oh, it's Edwin, is it?"

"And so it should be. We've been friends for a while now and—oh, why am I explaining myself to you?"

"Mayhap ye're trying to convince yerself?" He moved toward her.

"I wouldn't take much convincing where Viscount Musgrave is concerned." She stepped back a pace. "He's a fine man, with an upright character and a sense of 'oughtness' and . . . well, he's everything you're not."

"Aye, he's a regular paragon, is Viscount Musgrave." He caught up one of her hands and traced circles over the pulse point at her wrist while he was speaking. Pleasure sparked over her skin. She knew she should tug her hand free, but what he was doing to her felt so wickedly good, she couldn't bring herself to move.

"Answer me this then," Aidan said, his green eyes questioning. "Would you open your window for Edwin?"

"He's too much a gentleman to ask."

Aidan chuckled softly. "Or perhaps not man enough."

She tugged her hand away to slap him, but Aidan stopped her with a tight grip on her wrist.

Rosalinde sucked a breath in over her teeth. Everything about the man was wrong, but her body didn't seem to realize it. Her breasts ached, nipples tight, longing for him to hold them. Her skin was on high alert, waiting for his caress. His masculine scent flooded her nostrils. She was feeling so much, she couldn't think clearly.

Aidan swung her around and pinned her against the wall

with his body. His hardness against her belly made the low throb begin in earnest. He released her wrist and brushed her lips with his.

"Ah, lass, I want ye so much. More than me next breath," Aidan whispered. "But I'll not ask ye to give yourself to me. I've come to show ye I can be trusted."

The roughness of his cheek scraped across hers, a pleasing burn. "And how do you intend to do that?"

"To pleasure ye without taking, to give without expecting ye to return aught." His gaze held her in place even more surely than his hard strong body. "If ye allow it."

He feathered kisses along her jaw. How did he imagine she could form a coherent thought, much less give consent, while he beguiled her senses so?

" 'Tis what I meant to do on the island, but . . . I hardly know what happened that night." His dark brows drew together and he looked genuinely puzzled. "If I didn't know better, I'd say ye witched me."

"What a strange manner of courtship you have, Aidan Danaher. Most women resent being called a witch."

"Only the ones who don't have the power to bind a man with just a glance." He kissed her temples and closed eyelids.

She shivered, but not from cold. The man's heat radiated through her whole body. "And I've bound you?"

"I'm helpless before ye, Rose." His hand found her breast and caressed her through the thin muslin. "But I'm glad ye own this for what it is—a courtship."

"Not a very proper one," she said breathlessly. He was doing such wicked things to her nipple with his thumb and forefinger, it was hard to draw a deep lungful.

"No, I'll grant ye that. I wouldn't know proper if it bit me on the arse." His grin was sin incarnate. "Something I'd love to do to ye, by the by."

Her bum tingled at the scandalous thought.

"But my aim is the same as the good viscount's. I want ye, Rosalinde. I want ye to be mine entire. In that respect, Musgrave and I are alike."

"No, you're not at all the same," she said, aware that he was pulling up her hem, but the ache between her legs wouldn't let her complain of it. "Edwin is approaching me correctly, in full view of Society. And he's offering an honorable union . . . well, my great-aunt assures me he will once he gets around to it. He's giving all the right signals, she says. But all you're offering is . . ."

His fingertips swept up her bare thigh and dallied in the curls between her legs. She was unable to finish her thought.

"Bliss?" he suggested.

"Sin," she countered before her eyes rolled back. He'd found that blessed little spot that shot pleasure through her and started stroking it. Need made her legs tremble.

"And delicious sin it is too, to be sure," he admitted before he covered her mouth with his.

When she'd sailed home from Bermuda, she'd walked the decks as often as it was allowed. Watching the endless ocean stretch out on all sides of her, she wondered what it would be like to be cast adrift in such a boundless, wild space. Now, she thought she had an inkling.

She was drowning in this man, going down for the third time. He washed over her, robbing her of the will to resist. He bid her follow him to the deeps. He promised rapture. He'd take her there.

But would she ever return?

If ye allow it, he'd said. She pushed against his chest with all her might. "Do you mean it, Aidan?"

"Probably," he said with a lazy smile. "What are ye talking of, Rose?"

His head dipped down and he suckled her nipple through her nightshift. Need zinged from her breast to her womb.

"Are you truly bound before me?" She managed to force the words out. Her insides coiled as his fingers continued to stroke her most sensitive spot.

"Aye, lassie, I stay or go at your bidding." He dropped to his knees before her and pressed open-mouthed kisses on her sex.

The whole world went soft and liquid. Her legs turned rubbery. She remained upright only by pressing herself against the wall and, by dumb luck, reaching over head to catch hold of the gas sconce.

She'd thought his hand was an instrument of vice. What he was doing with his tongue should be outlawed. No woman could ever gainsay a man who enslaved her with this brand of bliss.

This went beyond ruination. He'd own her, body and soul, after this.

Without being aware of it, she was softly chanting his name.

"Aye, lass, ye've the right of it. Call my name and I'll always come to ye. Awake or dreaming, I'll climb through your window and bear ye away. Ye're mine."

"No," she whispered. She belonged to herself. He'd already claimed her maidenhead. She couldn't give this piece of her soul to a man she couldn't trust, who tricked and beguiled her at every step. "No, Aidan."

He stopped.

Her body screamed for him to continue, but in the brief respite, sanity rushed back into her head. She looked down at him, past the damp spots on her nightshift where her breasts showed through the material as if it were fine gauze, past the crumpled hem, to his dark, tousled head. He met her gaze.

"I can't . . . let you . . ." she said between gasps.

She couldn't bear the sight of his wickedly handsome face, his lips wet with her moisture, for another moment. She covered her eyes with both hands.

"Go away, Aidan. Please go away."

The only sound in the room was his rough breathing. She was holding hers. If he didn't obey her, she'd never have the strength to say it again. She would let this man ravage her and she would wallow in it, knowing herself for a weakling and him for a womanizing cur who preyed on such weaklings.

Then a minor miracle occurred.

Her hem dropped and the nightshift billowed around her bare ankles.

When she removed her hands and opened her eyes, Aidan was standing before her, his face unreadable.

"At your word," he said simply and kissed her. Even though it was as chaste as kiss as she could imagine, she tasted herself, all musk and salt, on his lips. Then he turned and strode to the chair where he'd abandoned his boots. Mouth set in a hard line, he tugged them on. Then he went to the window, pausing to look back at her.

"I want ye so bad, I—" He stopped himself and drew a deep breath. "But I want your trust more. The only reason I go now is so ye'll know ye can rely on me, Rose. Will ye remember it in the days to come?"

She nodded. She would never forget it. He'd kept his word. Her body still clamored for his touch, but her heart hoped for so much more.

"I'll remember."

A wry smile twitched his lips. "Then I guess ye'll open your window to me again some night."

"Perhaps."

He groaned. "When a lass says 'no' or 'aye,' at least a man knows where he stands. 'Perhaps' fills a man with hope and dashes it at once. Sure and you're trying to kill me, Rose."

Then he slipped out the window and climbed up the rope. Rosalinde waited until he pulled the line up after him before she lowered the sash very gently.

"No, Aidan. I'm trying not to love you," she said softly. "But I'm afraid I do."

Chapter 5

All that glisters is not gold.
—Shakespeare,
The Merchant of Venice

"B'gad, look at the size of the place!" Rosalinde's father leaned out the coach window to get a better view of Stonehaven. They'd taken the train as far as Swindon, where they were met by the baron's factor, who ushered them into a sumptuous brougham.

"'Is Lordship wasn't expecting guests to bring servants," the man had said gruffly.

"If he's unable to accommodate a few domestics, perhaps we ought not presume upon Lord Stonemere's hospitality," Lady Chudderley said with a sniff.

"No, no, I expect it'll be all right," he allowed, and let Gus help him load their baggage into the boot. Then Katie and Gus had squeezed onto the driver's seat with him.

Lady Chudderley complained of the ruts and potholes as they wound through the White Horse country till the sun cast long shadows over the green meadows. Rosalinde found the journey full of rustic charm.

Stonehaven, however, was anything but rustic. They caught their first glimpse of the manor from a distance on the tree-lined drive, a shining stone edifice surrounded by rolling hills. Little white dots—"Sheep," her father said— kept the grounds neatly trimmed. Standing an impressive four stories high, the pale marble façade was painted rose by the fading light, its architecture pure Georgian, graced with dentils and Palladian windows.

"No wonder the English Stonemeres were so keen to keep it in their side of the family," Lady Chudderley said. "I've seen poorer-looking marquisates."

"Don't let the outside fool you," her father said. "Lots of fellows with titles are land-rich, but cash-poor. The baron may not have a pot to piss in."

"Loromer!"

"Ahem! My apologies. That's what comes of spending too much time with military types," Rosalinde's father said.

She rolled her eyes. His speech had always been salty, long before he took the position at Royal Dock.

"What I mean to say is, Lord Stonemere may be a good deal lighter in the pockets than he appears," he said.

"Perhaps you should ask him," Rosalinde said as they pulled up to the entry. "Unless I'm mistaken, here he comes."

Streaking across the sea of green, a man on a bay horse loped toward them, scattering a flock of sheep in their path. As they neared a gate, instead of stopping to open it, the horse and rider gathered themselves and sailed over the top of it, landing without breaking stride.

Rosalinde's breath caught at the perfect union of man and horse. It took her back to the first time she'd seen Aidan astride. His mastery in the saddle was the first thing that made her see him as a man, not just the convict who worked in the stable.

"Excellent seat," Lady Chudderley said approvingly. "The man's a veritable centaur. He may not be respectable, but Lord Stonemere does possess a few admirable qualities."

More than a few, Rosalinde amended silently. He'd shown himself trustworthy.

Aidan reined the gelding to a stop near their carriage, but didn't dismount. The horse tossed its head, restive and eager for another run. A butler in formal attire and a housekeeper in a starched white apron appeared on the doorstep to receive the new arrivals.

"Greetings. Welcome to Stonehaven," Aidan said from atop his steed as his servant handed Rosalinde and her great-aunt from the carriage.

Gus hopped down and saw to their baggage. Katie half-whispered urgent commands on how best to accomplish the task, as if her lumbering husband were incapable of unloading a boot without her supervision.

"The rest of the party has already arrived. Phipps will see ye to your chambers. I believe Mrs. Fitzgerald makes it her mission in life to show guests over the place. She's proud enough of it, ye'd think she built it with her own capable hands." He tossed the sturdy housekeeper a teasing wink. "But if ye'd care to refresh yourselves first, be sure to let her know ye'll take her tour later."

Her father and great-aunt thanked their host and headed for the tall double doors, but Rosalinde pulled off one of her gloves to stroke the gelding's velvety nose. Ears perked forward, the horse whickered softly.

What she really wanted was to be invited up to sit on the crupper behind Aidan and fly hell-for-leather across the heath on the back of this fine beast. Her arms ached to wrap around Aidan, her breasts pressed against his back. And if her skirts rode up as they flew across the ground, so be it.

A hot flush burned her cheeks when she met Aidan's quizzical gaze.

What was it about him that always brought out the most improper urges?

"We're about to lose the light now. Would ye be wanting to ride tomorrow before breakfast?" Aidan asked. "I've a

Thoroughbred mare that would do well for ye, I'm thinking."

"Only if she can give this big devil a merry chase," Rosalinde said with a laugh.

"I suspect she can, lass," Aidan said. "We'll give it a go on the morrow then. See you at supper."

He turned the gelding's head aside and nudged him into a trot, then a canter and lastly a full-out gallop over the grassy heath. Rosalinde watched until they disappeared into a fold of the rolling land, then she followed her father and great-aunt into the expansive manor.

Despite her complaints over the discomforts of their journey, Lady Chudderley was too curious about Stonehaven Manor to retire meekly to her room without a tour, so Mrs. Fitzgerald showed them over the grand house. They followed the stout Scotswoman through rooms filled with Flemish tapestries and suits of armor, past long gilt-framed portraits of barons and baronesses gone by. The barony was an old one, the first Baron Stonemere being created shortly after William the Conqueror swept over the land and changed it forever.

Of course, this manor house was much newer, only fifty or so years old, but there was a ruin of the old tower at the far end of the garden beyond the row of trees.

"Should any of ye wish to chance a ramble through the briars, that is," Mrs. Fitzgerald cautioned.

"There's a maze and a grotto too, I'm told," Mr. Burke said.

The housekeeper's lips pursed in censure and she shot Rosalinde's father a chilly glance. "Aye, the curious among ye will be wanting to see that, no doubt. 'Tis where that poor girl was found. His Lordship has ordered that all his guests be given free rein over the estate, so none can stop ye, if ye wish to go there. And to your left, sir, would be the conservatory."

Mrs. Fitzgerald ushered them into an immense glass and wrought-iron space, filled with exotic plants and more orchids than Rosalinde had even seen. The air was heavy with the moist breath of green growing things. She closed her eyes and inhaled the heady floral scent. Her great-aunt's Palm Room was but a pale, tame imitation of balmier climes. This wild profusion of life transported Rosalinde back to Bermuda with its abundance of hibiscus and rhododendron.

Back to the madness of her first dalliance with Aidan.

When she opened her eyes, there he was, standing by a gardener's shelf in the far corner, pottering with an orchid.

"I thought Aid—Lord Stonemere—was riding," Rosalinde said. He'd changed into a shoddy pair of trousers and donned a work smock. "How did he get here so quickly?"

Then when the man turned and looked at them full on, she realized it wasn't Aidan, though the resemblance was striking.

"That's His Lordship's brother, Liam," Mrs. Fitzgerald said in a half-whisper, then raised her voice. "Sorry to have disturbed you, Master Liam. These are some of the baron's guests."

"Then they are my guests too," he said slowly, walking toward them. "Do they like orchids?"

"Yes, very much," Rosalinde said. Aidan had never mentioned having a brother. Now that he was closer, she realized the similarity between Aidan and his brother ended with their coloring and bone structure. Liam's darting gaze never met hers and she knew without being told that there was something a bit off about him.

"They aren't really flowers, you know. They look like flowers, but it's only a disguise," Liam said, his voice strangely flat. "Orchids are parasites. That means they kill their hosts."

Her lips twitched in a nervous smile. "They're very beautiful all the same."

"Yes," he said, studying the tips of his own boots. "But they aren't good, are they? Not really, I mean, if they kill what helps them. Still, I like orchids."

Mrs. Fitzgerald introduced Rosalinde and her family to Liam and then tried to shepherd them out the door.

"Don't think I won't remember you," Liam said. "I remember everyone I meet."

"That's good," Rosalinde said as she trailed the others out. "I'll remember you too, Mr. Danaher."

"Miss Burke."

She stopped and turned to face him. "Yes?"

"Will you call me Liam?" His dark brows rose hopefully as he worried a corner of his smock, wringing it in his big hands.

She hadn't honored the same request from the viscount, but Edwin hadn't seemed to need her to use his Christian name as much as Liam obviously did. "If you call me Rosalinde."

His face split in a wide grin and he cast her a quick shy glance. "Rosalinde," he repeated.

"Good day, Liam."

"Oh," he called after her. "Just so you know. Whatever you hear, I'm not an orchid."

A shiver swept over her as she rejoined her family. *Not an orchid.* It was an odd thing to say, but odd didn't begin to describe Aidan's brother.

"Ah, here's Mr. Phipps come to collect ye, now," Mrs. Fitzgerald said.

The butler escorted them to their rooms. Lady Chudderley and Rosalinde's father were given chambers on the first floor, one curving staircase up from ground level. Contrary to her father's assertion, it appeared Aidan wasn't the least light in the pockets. The rooms were furnished with an eye to both opulence and comfort.

Rosalinde's room was on the second floor. When Phipps opened the door for her, she found Katie already there finishing the last of the unpacking.

"Now this is a proper turnout," Katie said after Phipps bowed and left. She arranged Rosalinde's gowns in the spacious wardrobe to make certain they wouldn't wrinkle. "A room fit for a duchess, and no mistake."

The chamber was very fine, even more sumptuous than the ones given to her father and great-aunt, but Rosalinde feared, being so high in the house, there was no chance Aidan would climb in her window any time soon.

As if a lady would even think such an improper thing, she lectured herself.

"What about you and Gus?" Rosalinde asked. "Have you been given suitable quarters?"

"If you call the room of a dead girl suitable," Katie said with a shrug. "They put us up in that Peg Bass's old chamber. Won't no one else sleep there. Nice enough, I suppose, for the likes of us, but I tell ye, miss, I'd not sleep a wink there either without my big Gus by my side."

"Peg Bass, the girl who was murdered."

"Aye, that's the one," Katie said as she pummeled the bed pillows into the desired fluffiness. "That be some dark doings there. Her neck wrung like a chicken, they say."

Rosalinde's insides squirmed. Aidan couldn't have done such a thing.

Could he?

She ran a fingertip along the carved post of her bed. "How do the servants here feel about serving the man who confessed to killing her?"

Katie frowned. "That's just the perplexing thing, miss. They don't seem to mind a bit. Nary a one had aught to say against His Lordship. In fact, I got the strangest feeling they're actually proud to serve him."

Rosalinde smiled at that. The staff of Stonehaven was too well-trained to be as familiar with the family as Rosalinde allowed Katie to be, but servants knew everything that went on in a great house. Rosalinde was sure they talked amongst themselves about the family they served. Who was a better judge of a man's character than the ones who cared for his daily needs?

"All of 'em seem happy to be here except the new upstairs maid," Katie added, tilting her nose into the air and giving her head a shake. "Lily Wade. She's a puzzlement, that one. Claims to come from Cheapside, but acts like she's too good to empty a chamber pot. Hasn't been here long, though. Maybe a week. She's not much of a maid, the bootblack boy says, but she's a looker and no mistake."

"Peg Bass was the upstairs maid too, wasn't she?"

"Aye, and by all accounts, a fair piece of muslin she was. Quite fetching, they say." Katie straightened the counterpane and smoothed the elegant damask. "Just like Lily Wade. Cook says Lily's far too free with the time she spends in the Master's chamber for her tastes. She says Lily stays a lot longer than it takes to turn down a bed of an evening, if ye take my meaning."

Rosalinde's belly spiraled downward. It was an open secret that men of privilege sometimes dallied with their help, but she hadn't expected it of Aidan. Not even after the lurid tale of Peg Bass. "That's enough, Katie."

"Oh, right. Begging your pardon, miss. Gossip is a prayer to the devil, me old mam used to say. Pay it no heed. If that'll be all, miss, I'd best see to Lady Chudderley." Katie headed to the door, stopped and turned back. "It may not be my place to say so, but if I may be so bold, I hope ye'll turn your eye toward Viscount Musgrave while we bide

here. Lord Stonemere is quite a takin' fellow, very handsome to be sure, but the viscount—he's quality, he is.
Through and through."

"That'll be all, Katie," Rosalinde said through clenched
teeth.

The maid bobbed a curtsey and left.

Rosalinde sank down on the foot of the bed.

Aidan wanted her to trust him. Part of her wanted to, but
now that Katie had raised the specter of it, a darker part of
her heart imagined him tangled up with the good-looking
upstairs maid, Lily Wade.

Not everything is as it seems, he'd said. But that wasn't
exactly a repudiation of his guilt, was it? Everything she
knew about Aidan was shadowed with half-truths and con-
jecture. She couldn't look at him without being swamped by
a fluttering pulse and shortness of breath. How could she
think clearly while her body ran riot?

She pulled her precious book of Shakespeare from her
small satchel and thumbed through the dog-eared pages.
Everything was so much simpler in his plays. It was easy to
mark the villains and cheer the heroes when you knew immediately who they were.

Truth was so evident in a playhouse.

What if the part that wasn't true in her real life was the
bit about being able to trust Aidan Danaher?

Chapter 6

The fault, dear Brutus, lies not in our stars,
But in ourselves if we are underlings.
—SHAKESPEARE, *Julius Caesar*

The white soup would've done credit to a duke's table. The duck and braised lamb were a triumph. Now the liveried servants were bringing out a treacle folly festooned with berries, a dish worthy of some Eastern potentate's decadent salon. The first bite melted on George Stonemere's tongue, but once it slid down his gullet, it galled his belly.

By rights, this ought to have been *his* feast. He shot a quick glare toward his cousin Aidan at the head of the long table. There he was, the Irish upstart, laughing and conversing with the viscountess and her lovely daughter, as if he'd been to the manor born.

George sighed.

"Is the treacle not to your liking?" Rosalinde Burke murmured at his side. "I confess I find it delicious."

"Oh, the food's fine," George said, quickly mastering his expression. It wouldn't do to show his resentment openly. "And I must commend my cousin on the seating arrangement of his guests. I'm delighted by your company."

"Thank you, sir," she said, but her gaze darted toward the head of the table as well. "The baron does seem to know how to entertain in high style."

"Indeed." George swirled the excellent claret in the gold-rimmed goblet and downed the last of it in one long gulp. "But then Stonehaven is designed with this sort of gathering in mind. And loftier ones, as well. It has sheltered both statesmen and kings."

"You have been here often?

"I grew up here." In fact, before it was learned that Aidan had not died in prison as everyone believed, George was about to be named conservator of the estate. No one could expect that half-wit Liam to function as the baron, even if he'd inherit the title.

And after a decent amount of time, who knew? Accidents happened all the time, especially to one as easily distracted as Liam. The title might very well have swung back to George's side of the family.

But Aidan's return changed all that.

"In fact," George said, grimacing at the irony, "I was born in the very chamber my cousin is so *graciously* allowing me to use for this fortnight."

"Then you knew Ai—his lordship—as a boy?"

"I knew him as a young hellion," George said. No point in mincing words if he wanted to turn opinion against the man. "He came here when he was about fifteen. In truth, I held out no hope of his ever managing in Polite Society after the upbringing he'd had. As the twig is bent and all that."

George sneaked another glance at his cousin. Judging from the crimson flush on Lady Sophia's face, Aidan was doing quite well with Polite Society. The chit couldn't take her eyes off him.

"So that's his game," he murmured.

"I beg your pardon?" Miss Burke said.

"I was just thinking what a charming couple my cousin and Lady Sophia make," George said between clenched teeth. "He could do far worse than to ally himself with Viscount Musgrave's sister. A smart match, that."

Rosalinde Burke's lips went white as chalk.

So the wind blows in that quarter as well. George had never seen why his cousin should so ensnare the imagination of every female who crossed his path, but Aidan invariably did.

"You know, it occurs to me, Miss Burke," George said. "Your father was the commissioner in Bermuda. If you were there as well, and I believe I heard somewhere that you were, you and my cousin might have met during his unfortunate incarceration."

She gave him a thin-lipped smile. "The island is not as small as you might imagine, sir. However, since his lordship was the elected representative of the Irish prisoners there, I believe he may have come to the house to meet with my father from time to time."

She flicked her gaze toward Aidan and George read a fleeting glint of despair. Then a wall seemed to rise up behind her lovely eyes when she looked back at George.

"However, since your cousin was pardoned, I wonder that you mention his unsavory past with such regularity," she said with primness. "Especially when the Crown considers itself satisfied with his innocence."

George stifled a snort when she defended Aidan. So the lucky bastard had gotten to her. Well, when the barn door has been left open once, the mare is more likely to go wandering again. Only this time, with any luck, he'd be the one to ride her instead of his damned cousin.

"A pardon doesn't signify innocence, you know," George said. Why did no one ever seem to remember that Aidan had *confessed* to the crime? "But I fear I've offended you without intending to. Let us not quarrel, since I predict we'll be great friends by the end of this gathering. I believe everyone is dropping formalities for now. In fact, I'm certain I heard Lady Sophia call my cousin by his Christian name before the fish course arrived. Won't you please call me George?"

Rosalinde choked on her bite of treacle and covered her mouth with her hand for a moment.

"Are you quite well?" he asked with solicitude. That settled it. If she was chafing for want of Aidan, she'd be ripe for his taking.

She dabbed her lips with her linen napkin and took a sip of claret. "I'm fine . . . George."

"I'm vastly relieved."

He also figured he was halfway up her skirt. A woman scorned was always ready to exact her revenge on the one who'd spurned her by swiving a willing substitute silly. George would be delighted to aid her in that cause.

"You know, whenever there are house parties, inevitably the guests are all called upon to entertain in some fashion." And a handful of entertainment she'd make too, but for now George would concentrate on the public frivolities. Then, with any luck, the private ones would take their course. "I've been told I have a remarkably true tenor, so I'd be happy to take a song request from you later, if you like. What special talent will you regale us with, dear Rosalinde?"

He could think of several skills he'd enjoy teaching her later. She had a delicate pointed tongue and such lovely pouting lips. His cock stiffened at the thought of those lips wrapped around it. Some women could relax their throat muscles with a bit of practice. He wondered how much of him she could take in.

A few tendrils had escaped Rosalinde's chignon. George imagined fisting her heavy hair, forcing her to her knees and pulling her head back.

A few well-placed smacks and a woman can always do more than she thinks.

George pulled his napkin from his neck and draped it over his lap lest she see how she was affecting him. No need to spook her.

"I don't play the pianoforte and I fear my singing voice will never be compared to a flute," she said as her fork chased her dessert around her plate. She seemed to have lost interest in the treacle, for she never raised it to her mouth. "But I have been told my recitations of Shakespeare are very fine."

"Ah! *Shall I compare thee to a summer's day?*" he said.

When her eyes lit up, he saw his way in. The girl only wanted a bit of wooing. Time to bone up on the Bard and he'd be in Rosalinde Burke's bed quicker than Romeo shagged Juliet.

But when she looked back at his cousin with a wistful smile tugging her lips, he realized he might need more help than Shakespeare could give him. Of course, some of Shakespeare's heroes put paid to their rivals in short order. MacBeth. Cassius. They certainly knew how to *screw their courage to the sticking point.*

Or maybe he should take a page from Iago, and drive his cousin wild with envy and mistrust. It could work, provided Aidan cared a fig for Miss Burke.

George smiled and signaled for the wine steward to refill his goblet. This party was shaping up to be a good idea after all.

The parlor game was still in full swing, but Rosalinde was so sick of "The Minister's Cat" she feared she might cough up a hairball. Or maybe it wasn't the game itself. Maybe it was the fawning way Lady Sophia directed all her clever little repartees to Aidan. Rose was so distracted by him whenever it was her turn to add something original to the nonsense that she could only stammer the most banal offerings.

She excused herself and pushed through the tall doors of the solarium and out onto a long Italianate veranda overlooking the garden. When a breeze rose, the sweet scent of heliotrope rushed past her nostrils. The moon had newly risen, three-quarters full so the garden spread out in shadows below her. It was no fussy French confection. This was an English riot with blooms spilling everywhere, only trimmed enough to bare a silver-pebbled path among the dense growth.

She glanced back toward the manor, but no one had followed her. Disappointment fizzled in her chest. Surely Aidan could have managed a moment away from his other guests.

If he cared enough to notice she was even gone.

Beyond the garden, the maze squatted malignantly in the deeper darkness, its hedges sheared down to man-height instead of being left to grow entirely wild. In the center, a low mound rose.

The grotto.

Rosalinde leaned on the granite balustrade and squinted at it. A light emanated from the center of the maze, as if someone had left a lantern burning inside the hollowed earth.

"Well, it appears you've located the infamous grotto," a masculine voice sounded behind her.

She turned to find Edwin walking toward her. Tall and powerful in his green jacket and buff trousers, he moved with masculine grace. When the man approached, he was a sight to set feminine hearts aflutter.

Why does he not ruffle mine in the slightest?

By rights, he should. The viscount was her great-aunt's choice for her. Even her maid urged her to encourage him, for pity's sake. She tried to summon a flicker of attraction, a swirl of some sensation worthy of the charm Edwin exuded, but she could feel nothing but polite interest in the man. At least his topic of conversation was one she could warm to.

"You speak as if you know something of the grotto's history," she said.

He came and leaned his forearms on the balustrade beside her. The masculine scent of citrusy bergamot and spicy sandalwood swirled around him. "I should. I was here that summer."

"Oh." She didn't need to ask which summer. The murder of the upstairs maid was evidently uppermost in everyone's mind. "So you knew the baron before."

"Yes, but he wasn't the baron then. I don't think Aidan even knew he was likely to be," Edwin said. "He and Liam had been here three or four years. While it was obvious Liam would never make a scholar, Aidan showed surprising quickness. He and I were supposed to go to Oxford together that fall, so our families thought it might be good for us to become acquainted ahead of time."

"His cousin George was here that summer too, I believe."

Edwin turned to look at her, his face half-shadowed, half-silvered by moonlight. "Now there's the one who had expectations. George always thought this would be his. He had no idea there was anyone in his path until Aidan and his brother were sent back here."

"So George had an interest in seeing Aidan removed," she reasoned. Rosalinde hated the thought that she'd just had supper next to a man who could murder a poor serving girl, but the alternative was that Aidan might have done it. "You don't suppose George—"

"Aidan confessed," Edwin reminded her. "Someone else was suspected at the time, but when Aidan came forward, that was that."

"Who else was suspected?"

He brought his fingertips to his brow and shook his head. "It escapes me now. That summer was such a muddle for us all. Most of all for George, who thought he'd be the beneficiary of the whole sordid scandal."

Edwin straightened and stared at the grotto. "No one reckoned on a pardon since Aidan didn't press the issue of his inheritance at the trial. At the time, he only seemed interested in seeing the matter closed as quickly as possible. But it appears his mother had a few friends at court who were willing to work on her behalf, even after she made such a disastrous choice."

"By that, you mean abandoning an estate to marry a man she obviously loved."

"Is there any other way to see it? If she'd wed an Englishman, her sons would have grown up here instead of in Ireland."

"You have something against the Irish?"

"No, not at all. But you must admit, they aren't like us, are they?"

Insular, pretentious prigs, you mean? almost escaped from her lips, but she bit back the retort. She'd learn more from Edwin if she kept him talking than if she insulted him. Her chest ached at the thought of Aidan being responsible for Peg Bass's death. There had to be another explanation.

"I think I know what you mean," she said. "There's something a bit wild about the Celts. *Fey*, I think Aidan would call it."

A touch of magic. A force of nature. Sometimes if she half-closed her eyes, she thought she saw it draped over him like a gossamer mantle.

That otherworldly quality was one of the things that drew her to him. That and his natural good-humor.

Aidan was a convicted felon, but he laughed more than any man of her acquaintance. He'd worked with his hands without complaint, when all the time he was really a gentleman. When he was pardoned, she imagined he thought it a grand joke.

Back in Bermuda, when she watched him curry the horses with his big strong hands, all she could do was imagine what those work-rough palms would feel like smoothed over her skin.

"I consider myself his friend, you understand, but 'wild'

is precisely the word I'd use for Aidan," Edwin said as he covered one of her hands with his.

It happened so unexpectedly, she didn't have time to evade his capture of her hand. His palm was cool and dry. Her great-aunt would be enraptured by this new development, but all it did for Rosalinde was make her fingers feel curiously clammy.

"I wish we all hadn't fallen into that game of *poque* with Aidan at Lady Chudderley's," he said. "Then none of us would have to be here."

"From someone who claims to be his friend, that doesn't sound terribly friendly."

"Perhaps because more than friendship sways me now. I hope you'll be cautious around him, Rosalinde," Edwin said. "I'd hate for you to be hurt."

"Why would Aidan hurt me?"

"Oh, he wouldn't do it intentionally," Edwin said. "He's not the sort you'd think would harm a woman. In fact, I'm fully prepared to believe the whole sordid business with that maid was somehow accidental. But I also believe Aidan is dangerous. More so now than ever."

"Why?"

"Because when a man has killed and gotten away with it, he has no boundaries. No 'thus far and no farther,' if you will," Edwin said in a stolid upright tone that would have done credit to a Methodist preacher. "A man without limits is always dangerous."

A shiver raked her spine.

Edwin brought her hand to his lips and pressed a kiss on it. Her great-aunt would be in a near paroxysm of joy, but Rosalinde couldn't raise so much as a flutter in her chest.

"I'd protect you from him," Edwin said. "If you give me leave to do so."

"And who will protect her from you?" came a voice from the shadows.

It sounded like Aidan, so Rosalinde turned, but his brother stepped into the full moonlight instead.

"Liam, what are you about, skulking there in the dark?" Edwin asked.

"I never skulk. Skulk means to hide and I wasn't hiding. I'm just easy to overlook. You always said so, Edwin."

The viscount made a low noise of irritation in the back of his throat. "What are you doing out here then?"

"I was lighting the lamp in the grotto," Liam said. "I always light the lamp for Peg Bass. Someone has to. How else will she see to get home?"

"Why haven't you joined the party?" Edwin demanded.

"I don't like parlor games. I like orchids. I'll go to the conservatory." Liam started toward the house. "You should go in too. Before she comes."

"Before who comes, Liam?" Rosalinde asked.

He turned and slanted her a quick look that seemed to suggest she was the daft one. "Peg Bass, o' course. I'd go in now if I was you." He walked on for a bit, then turned back, glancing in Rosalinde's direction, but not meeting her gaze. "Sometimes when Peg comes, she's angry. You wouldn't like her then."

Chapter 7

I am afeared,
Being in night, this is all but a dream,
Too flattering sweet to be substantial.
—SHAKESPEARE, *Romeo and Juliet*

The last door had been latched a good quarter of an hour earlier. Aidan waited until the house was so quiet he could hear the creak of the oak tree outside his window before he lifted the candle from the sconce that opened the secret panel in one wall of his suite. A narrow passageway yawned before him, but he didn't hesitate. Rosalinde's chamber waited at the end of the hidden corridor.

He wished he'd been able to warn her of his coming. There was always the chance that she'd be startled and scream when the wall opened to admit him to her room. Unfortunately, there hadn't been any opportunity for private speech with her all evening.

As host, he'd had to circulate among all his guests. Each time he'd tried to snatch a moment with her, Viscount Musgrave or his cousin George hovered nearby.

He thought the evening would never end.

The passageway stopped and he peered through the thin slit in the wall. Her room was dark, so he saw nothing. A breath of air soughed through the crack and his candle flame wavered.

She must be abed. If she'd been awake, he'd have tried speaking to her through the thin false wall to warn her of his presence, but now he'd simply have to chance it.

He pressed the release and a wall panel rolled back on

hidden hinges, far enough for him to ease into the room. Fortunately, the mechanical system was in excellent repair and the operation silent as an owl's flight. Aidan pinched off the candle flame and peered around.

Rosalinde wasn't in bed. She was framed by the open window, gazing out over his garden. Moonlight silvered her and rendered her nightshift nearly transparent. Her unbound hair flowed to the middle of her back, but her long legs and tapered waist were silhouetted in a magical glow beneath the thin muslin.

His very own faery princess. She ought to have been winged. Even without them, the way she strained toward the open window convinced Aidan she half-believed she could fly if only she tried hard enough.

She sighed.

Please God, let that sigh be for me.

"Lass," he whispered as he moved further into her room.

She made a little squeak and whirled to face him.

"Don't be afraid," he said in a half-voice. " 'Tis only me."

"Only me, he says," she muttered as she took several steps toward him, her shoulders slumping with relief. Then she stopped herself and glared at him with cold fury. "How dare you risk my reputation by sneaking into my room like this? Anyone might have seen you in the hall."

"No, they mightn't," he said, pointing to the gape in the wall. "I had you placed in this room especially because of the secret passage. No one knows I've come and no one will mark when I leave."

"I'll mark it right now," she said archly. "I'm sorry, my lord, but you seem to have stumbled into the wrong chamber. Unless I'm mistaken, the viscount's sister is across the hall."

"What would I want with the viscount's sister?"

"The same thing you wanted with me, I'll wager. You were certainly doing your best to charm her all evening."

Now that he was closer, he noticed that her cheeks glistened damply in the silver light. A stab of guilt lanced him. Surely she hadn't been weeping. "I was simply tending to the needs of all my guests, Rose."

"Lady Sophia seemed particularly receptive to your tending."

Aidan shook his head. "I didn't single her out for attention."

The *Knack* was a blessing and curse sometimes. When he set himself to be appealing and agreeable to all, invariably there were a few mixed signals.

"Well, she was certainly hanging on your every word and draped herself over your arm every time I turned around." She started to move away from him.

"Rose, don't you understand the purpose of this house party at all?" He grasped her shoulders to make her stay with him.

"You've made it obvious. You invited me here to torment me while you woo another." She balled one fist and pounded his chest a few times, gaining steam with each blow. "Even the viscount's mother gave you several soft-headed looks this night. She's still a handsome woman. No doubt, she'd be up for a romp should you wish to climb through *her* window."

"Are ye daft? No, lass, ye've missed my plan entire." He caught her hand to keep her from pummeling him, uncurled her fist and planted a kiss in the center of her palm. Her fingers remained scrunched for another heartbeat or two, but then she relaxed and gentled under his touch. He laced his fingers through hers to ensure that she wouldn't run off or start beating him again.

"Do ye think I don't know what folk say about me?" he

asked. "This fortnight I hope to change Society's opinion of me for good."

"Rubbish. No one else's opinion matters so to you."

"Well, ye've the right of it there. Your opinion is the only one that really counts," he said softly. "But I know what the world thinks matters to ye, so I would have them think better of me for your sake."

"A most convenient philosophy. And original to boot." She turned her face away. "A killer who cares what others think of him."

He grasped her chin and forced her to look at him. "Do ye believe me guilty?"

"Have you told me otherwise?"

He released her. She had him there, but the only reason he'd confessed in the first place was to protect someone else. What good would it do if he denied the confession later? The whole trouble might start up again.

"Search your feelings, lass," he said. "What does your heart tell you on the matter?"

She met his eyes then, her soft gaze penetrating to the last wrinkle of his soul. He'd never been more tempted to *knack* someone in his entire life. One simple suggestion would do it and she'd believe him as spotless as the vicar's sheets, no matter what anyone told her later.

But either she trusted him or she didn't. He couldn't use his gift this time. He didn't dare breathe.

"My heart says it doesn't know the whole story," she finally said. "And I want to know, but I'm afraid to know at the same time."

"Why?"

"Because I love you, Aidan Danaher," she said, pulling away from him and flinging herself face down on the bed. Her shoulders shook with emotion. "God help me, but I do."

Aidan moved to join her, stretching out full length beside

her so he could stroke her back. Fierce joy made his chest ache. He could scarce believe his luck. Trust *and* love in one star-kissed night.

And without using the *Knack* at all.

Then he realized with dismay that she was weeping. "Easy, Rose. Ye don't have to cry."

"Yes, I do." She continued to blubber into her pillow. "It's the height of folly for a woman to declare herself first. You'll despise me for being weak and soft-headed and—"

"Love is never weak or soft-headed. It lifts us out of the mud and puts us on the same footing as the angels. Loving you saved me, lass."

"But I can't seem to help it," she went on as if she'd not heard him.

Alarm bells jangled along his nerves. Had he compelled her to love him without realizing it? "Why d'ye say that? D'ye feel at all odd?"

Sometimes the people he *knacked* complained of a slight, sudden headache at the time, a chill on their limbs and a memory lapse later.

"Odd doesn't begin to describe it." She sat up and glared at him accusingly. "I can't even look at you without my heart threatening to leap out of my chest."

He smiled. No one had ever complained of that after he *knacked* them. He ran his palm over her crown and smoothed down her rumpled hair. "Your head doesn't hurt, then?"

"No," she said with a little shiver.

"Are ye cold?" He traced a fingertip along the lacy neckline of her nightshift. Her mouth parted softly and her eyes went darker.

"No, if anything I'm far too warm," she admitted with another shiver that he now recognized as delight in his touch. "Though most folk would say I'm definitely not thinking clearly."

He leaned forward to kiss the corner of her mouth, right at the juncture of smooth skin and moist intimacy. "I like the way ye're thinkin, lass."

"Because it works to your purpose."

He feathered a row of kisses along her cheekbone. "And what purpose would that be?"

Her face turned to follow his lips, tracking him like a sunflower tilts toward the sun. "You obviously mean to seduce me."

He brushed her lips with his, a tease. "Is it working?"

"Um . . ." She caught his bottom lip and suckled it for a moment. "Yes," she said in a long exhale, then sat up straight. "No. Wait. What was that you said about loving me?"

So she had heard him.

He cupped her cheeks in both his hands. "Aye, lass, I love ye. And it saved me, Rose, in ways ye can't conceive." He kissed her closed eyelids. "Prison takes more than the prime of a man's years. It eats away at his soul. But even after ye left, when I thought I'd never see ye again in this life, I had something prison couldn't touch. I had you." He ran the pad of his thumb over her lips. "Or at least, the memory of you."

Her lips twitched in a smile.

"Sometimes one shining moment is all a man ever has, but I had a whole string of Rosalindes in me head. You on the back of that wicked Thoroughbred, putting him through his paces. Walking through Royal Docks with your arms full of flowers for the house." His hand wrapped around the back of her neck and drew her forehead to touch his. "Lying beneath me, all gasping and spent after ye came so sweetly. Did ye not think of me after?"

Her lips turned upward in an impish smile. "From time to time."

"Did ye, love?"

"Only every night."

Then she leaned forward and kissed him. Hard.

If we only kiss, we've been a bit improper, but no worse than if we were alone in an alcove sneaking a kiss at a ball somewhere, Rosalinde reasoned. Their kiss deepened, an undiscovered country, soft and wet as an autumn evening with the promise of a crackling fire later. His tongue invaded and she gave it a suckling welcome.

Aidan laid her back down and stretched out beside her on the bed, kicking off his boots and dropping them by her bedside.

Lying beside a man is improper, she admitted to herself, *but it's not as if he's on top of . . .*

He settled over her, his hard groin pressed on her belly. His iron-hard length rocked on her in a slow knock.

Well, at least we're both still dressed.

He rose up and pulled his shirt off over his head. She couldn't keep from smoothing her palms over his chest. His nipples hardened under her touch.

I suppose it's less improper for him to be shirtless than if I were the one who's undressed, she decided.

Rosalinde continued to stroke his broad shoulders and down his arms. Muscles rippled under his smooth flesh and he cast off as much heat as a fire.

"I want to learn every inch of your skin by heart," she said, planting a kiss at the juncture of his shoulder and neck.

"A pleasant prospect." He chuckled and raised himself on his arms to peer down at her. "Why?"

"So I know where I am with you. So I can close my eyes"—she suited her actions to her words—"and say to myself, 'Yes, that's the little scar on his shoulder.' " She fingered the slightly raised weal of skin and then planted a kiss on the spot. Then her fingers drifted lower past his navel, slipping beneath his waistband which seemed unusually loose. "Or I can think 'Oh, there. That's his lovely flat belly and . . .' "

Her hand met his shaft, hard as granite encased in smooth warm skin. She grasped him at the base and her eyes flared open.

"Once again, that's not me belly, love," Aidan said with a laugh.

While her eyes had been closed, he must have undone the buttons at his hips and peeled back his trousers.

Most improper. She ought to feel indignant at the liberties he'd taken, but the way she was running her hands over him, cupping and fondling his ballocks, she supposed she was taking a few herself.

But as long as I'm still wearing my nightshift.

He reached down and smoothed her hem up her shins, over her thighs and before she knew it, he'd pulled her shift off, turning the long prim sleeves inside out in his haste to be done with it. Then he tossed the nightshift to the floor and grinned down at her.

"Oh, it's a sight, ye are, lass." Then he shucked out of his trousers and pulled off his socks.

They were both in the glorious altogether. His gaze swept over her as if he were a starving man and she the last bun on the tray, but she didn't feel the slightest urge to cover herself. She felt no need to restrain herself from looking her fill either.

Aidan was beautiful in all his parts—hard, strong, soft, vulnerable. He was both needy and giving, bereft and bountiful.

"*All that's best in dark and bright,*" she whispered. Good and bad. Praiseworthy and shameful. It didn't matter. She loved all of him.

"I suppose that's more of your ruddy Shakespeare," he said hoarsely, his face taut with hunger.

"No, that was Lord Byron, not that it matters particularly. It just seemed to fit," she said softly. "But I don't suppose you came here for poetry or intend to woo me properly."

"No, lass. I came to make love to ye. Most improperly."

"Well, then," she said with a shuddering sigh as she looped her arms around his neck. "You'd best get to it.

Chapter 8

Love is a smoke made with the fume of sighs,
Being purged, a fire sparkling in lovers' eyes
Being vexed, a sea nourished with lovers' tears.
What is it else? A madness most discreet,
A choking gall and a preserving sweet.
—SHAKESPEARE, *Romeo and Juliet*

Aidan settled his hips between her splayed legs, propping his upper body on his elbows, and looked down at her. He ached to plunge in, but he had to be certain this time. He'd taken her without meaning to that first night on the island and then later she'd sent him away when he'd been determined only to pleasure her.

Her lips parted softly and her chin began to quiver.

"Why have you stopped?" she asked.

"Because I don't think I'll be able to in a moment and I want you to be sure this time."

Her teeth glinted in a melting smile. "I'm sure, Aidan. I won't send you away."

He brushed his lips across her brow and then dropped a kiss on the tip of her nose. Her belly quivered in a small giggle.

The urge to swive her senseless was still just as strong, but suddenly he was in no hurry. She wasn't going to send him away. He could love this woman with toe-curling slowness.

He wanted to savor her, to taste her, to mark every inch of her skin with his lips and claim her entire.

He rolled off her.

"Where are you going?"

"I'm only after looking at ye, Rose." He gave her a long perusal, from the crown of her head to her lovely feet.

They were delicate and well-formed with high arches. Her small toes were topped with neat square nails, smoothly filed. He moved down and raised first her right foot, then the left, to his lips for a kiss on the joint between her big toe and its nearest neighbor. Each time, he was treated to a long view up her legs to the shadowy realm between them.

His cock urged him to more than looking, but he restrained himself from claiming her sex, then and there. He'd drive her to helpless need first. He ran a hand along her shin, over her knee and up her inner thigh.

She tensed.

"Whisht, lass. Trust me."

She nodded and closed her eyes, letting him spread her legs a bit further. He teased her intimate folds with glancing touches and circled her sensitive spot till she writhed in aching fury. He could finish her now, but he held back.

He wanted to hear her beg. He stilled his hand.

"Aidan," she moaned. "What are you doing to me?"

His balls ached in pleasurable torment at her obvious distress. "Ye're not the only one in need, Rose, but believe me, the wait will be worth it."

She shot him a disbelieving glance. "You promise?"

"On my honor as a gentleman."

"Ha."

He leaned over her and kissed her roughly. "Then will ye accept my word as a scoundrel?"

She loosed a silvery laugh and then quickly covered her mouth at the outburst. She needn't have worried. Stonehaven was built "hell for stout," his da would've said, with walls thick enough to keep its residents' deepest secrets.

"At least the pledge of a scoundrel would make it a believable promise," she whispered.

"Then ye have my word as a veritable prince of rogues," he said as he eased his shoulders between her knees to spread her wide. He delivered a string of kisses up the inside of her leg. "Now lie still. If ye can."

The skin of her inner thigh was soft and sweet. Her scent bloomed afresh each time his lips drew nearer to her sex, all musky and warm. He pressed open-mouthed kisses on her, running his tongue into her intimate cleft.

She made a helpless little sound of need.

He raised his head to peer at her. Rosalinde's dark hair was spread out over her pillow in an undulating fan around her head. She'd draped a forearm over her eyes. A way to shield herself from him, he supposed. Before this night was through, he'd batter down every wall she raised between them.

Her mouth was slack and her breaths came short and quick. Her breasts rose and fell, the taut nipples straining upward.

Her slightly rounded belly quivered. Her legs were splayed in abandon. Her dark curls glistened wetly at him, beckoning him to dive into them.

He parted the soft lips of her sex to revel in the pink secret world of her. The inner folds and slick crevices, the tight little raised spot that throbbed for his touch, the snug channel that would be his ultimate goal. When his thumb passed over her, she quivered and clenched all the small muscles in her groin so the lips of her sex pursed in a parody of a wet kiss.

He'd never imagined anything so erotic in his life.

He tongued her and she raised herself into his mouth. He suckled the little spot, swirling his tongue over it.

The sounds of longing she made went straight to his cock. Pressure rose in the shaft. If he kept at this, he'd end up spilling his seed on her sheets.

He moved up her body, ignoring her sigh of frustration, leaving a trail of nibbling kisses along her ribs.

He ran his tongue along the crease beneath each breast. She rocked her pelvis against him and he throbbed in needy agony.

He laid his head between her breasts and heard her heart galloping beneath his ear. Her growing want flamed his. He drew a deep breath. The goal was to make *her* beg for him, not for him to succumb to the need to take her in a greedy heartbeat.

Once he reduced her to pleading, *then* he could take her.

For now, he forced himself to run through the plans he'd set in motion—anything to delay his body's reaction to Rose.

Staging the grotto, setting the trap, waiting to catch Peg Bass's real killer. He felt steady enough to move on to her breasts. They were smooth and warm and topped with tight peaks. He nuzzled them, running his open mouth around her areolas, teasing her with his nearness. *Ready the magistrate, nipple the culprit—damn, I mean 'nab the culprit.'*

"Aidan, please," she moaned, arching her back and thrusting her breasts upward.

He forgot all about his other plans and closed his lips over one nipple while he massaged the other with his thumb and forefinger.

Her hands ran over his head and down his back, grasping his buttocks. She rubbed herself against him.

He raised up to look at her. "Ye're supposed to lie still."

"I'm supposed to try."

His face stretched in a wide smile. "Well, then lass, the time has come. Ye only had to ask."

He bent his head and claimed her mouth in a deep kiss. Everything else fled from Rosalinde's mind. The world was seared away in his fiery kiss and her whole life sizzled down to the wonder of his mouth on hers and his skin gliding smoothly against her skin.

She reached between them to stroke his hard shaft and fondle his balls. He growled with pleasure and a thrill of power surged over her. He brought her to her knees with such ease.

How lovely it would be to make him plead. But the ache between her legs throbbed with a vengeance. Mayhap she'd play at tormenting the man with pleasure after her own need was stilled.

Then Aidan rolled, pulling her on top of him.

"Now, love," he said, folding his hands beneath his head. "Mount your steed at your pleasure and ride him as you will."

She sat up abruptly, surprised. "You want me to . . ."

"I want you to take me in to suit yourself," Aidan said, grasping her hips and positioning her so she was sitting on his groin.

Rosalinde's face crumpled in confusion. "But what if I do it wrong?"

"Impossible." He sat up and wrapped his arms around her. "I love you, lass. This is play time for us, a time for our hearts to knit together and find ways to share delight. Only in your case, ye don't have to fret. Everything about ye delights me. Between you and me, there is no wrong."

She bit her lower lip in anticipation. "Very well. Lie back, my lord," she said, giving him a playful push against his chest. "I'm going for a ride."

The moon dipped below the horizon, darkening the chamber, but the woman astraddle Aidan's groin seemed to glow like a being aflame. Lust boiled through his veins. For a moment, he imagined tossing her off, dragging her to her knees and mounting her from behind, but he held himself back.

He'd given her the reins. He couldn't jerk them away without losing the trust he'd gained.

Rosalinde was a quick learner and lost no time repaying him for the way he'd tormented her. She rubbed herself along his shaft. He writhed beneath her, desperate for her to take him in, equally as desperate not to beg her to.

"Now?" The word escaped his lips.

She leaned down and kissed him, raking his chest with her taut nipples. "Not yet."

She slid down onto his thighs. His cock strained upward and his balls drew into a snug mound. The wiry hairs on his scrotum stood at attention. She traced the centerline between his balls with a fingernail, leaving a line of abrasion on the sensitive skin.

His breath hissed over his teeth. A drop of seed formed on his tip, a milk-blue pearl.

He half-sat up and reached for her, but she straight-armed him.

"Not yet, I said." She pushed his hand away gently. "You promised to lie still until I give you leave to move. Remember?"

"Aye, lass," he said through clenched teeth as he settled back into the mattress. "My word is good."

"I should hope so. If a woman can't trust the word of the prince of rogues, what's the world coming to?" She moved up and settled her naked rump on his groin, clearly pleased with herself.

His balls tightened. The tip of him protruded between her legs. She'd obviously been paying attention when he stroked her most sensitive spot, for she'd discovered the bit of rough skin beneath the head of his cock and massaged it with her thumb. He broke out in a sweat, biting his lip to keep from spilling his seed onto his own belly. She leaned forward and kissed him hard.

The need to be inside her was excruciating.

"What will you do if I give you permission to move?" she asked.

"I'll . . . ah . . . I . . ." He was incoherent with need. "I'll . . ."

Wet and slick, she slid over the length of him, coating him with her arousal. "Move, Aidan."

He raised his hips to meet her. She teased him with her soft wet entrance but didn't let him slip in.

She arched her spine and let her head fall back, thrusting her breasts forward. His jaw went slack with desire.

Aidan ran his hands up her thighs and spread the lips of her sex. He thumbed her most sensitive spot.

She groaned. She tossed her head and leaned back, supporting herself with her hands propped on his thighs to give him better access to her. Her muscles stiffened. Then her entire body bucked with the force of her release. A long, jagged "oh" escaped from her lips as her insides contracted. Her breasts quivered with each fresh wave.

Finally she raised her head and looked down at him in open-mouthed wonder.

He grimaced, satisfied that he'd brought her to such a spectacular release. His aching erection made a true smile impossible.

"Now?" he asked.

"Yes, now."

She took him in hand and guided him in. Rosalinde moved slowly, obviously reveling in the power of engulfing him, consuming him. Her insides molded around him like a wet fist.

He touched her as she moved and she started tilting her pelvis into him.

Clever girl. She'd already learned she could control the

pressure on her sensitive spot. Judging from her shortness of breath, she was racing toward the pinnacle again.

Her first spasm began.

Aidan went off like a Roman candle inside her until he was utterly spent. Her inner walls clenched once more and then she collapsed on his chest, boneless as a sleeping cat.

He stroked her hair, inhaling its soft floral smell. Glad she'd made no move to separate from him. Her breathing slowed. He felt her cheek twitch in a smile against his breastbone.

She was happy. Warmth flooded his chest. Pleasing Rosalinde Burke was the finest thing he could aspire to in all his living life.

"I love ye, lass," he whispered, but she made no answer. Then very softly, there came a small, ladylike snore. He pressed a kiss on her tousled crown and wondered how long he could remain inside her.

The way he felt right now, a lifetime would be too short.

Rosalinde woke later to find Aidan easing out of the bed.

"Where are you going?" Aware of her nakedness as she sat up, she bunched the sheets around herself. Aidan made no attempt to cover his glorious body as he stooped to gather his discarded clothing.

"It'll be dawn in a couple hours," he said, leaning one knee on the mattress to kiss her. "Surely ye're not wishing for your maid to discover me under your sheets."

"No," she said, not entirely sure it wouldn't be a good idea to put a simple, if scandalous, end to their improper courtship. They'd marry in haste and the rest of the world could go chase itself. "I suppose not."

He cupped her cheek. "I'd almost rather stay than keep breathin', but I'd have ye proud when ye become my wife."

Her heart swelled. He was right. She'd almost forgotten

her duty to marry well so her great-aunt would bequeath her unentailed property and a decent sum to her poor father. Lady Chudderley was just vindictive and controlling enough to slight him in her will if Rosalinde thwarted her wishes. In order for Aidan to meet Lady Chudderley's requirements that her betrothed be a proper gentleman with the right connections, they couldn't very well be embroiled in a disgraceful start.

"Never fear. I'll be proud when I become your wife." She kissed him and despite his protestations, he climbed back into the bed with her, rolling across the crumpled linens in a tangle of arms and legs.

Then he swore softly. "No more, love. I must go."

She sighed in frustration as he dragged himself away and gathered up the rest of his garments, heading toward the secret panel. He was still naked and his cock stiff when he turned to look at her one last time.

"What a stubborn man you are," she said, eyeing him pointedly. She let the sheet fall to bare her breasts. "You know you want to stay."

He groaned with need. "Sure and ye're trying to kill me, Rose."

"No, only to love you."

"I know it doesn't seem so, but right now, leaving is the best way for me to love you. But meet me in the stable at dawn, aye?"

Only a couple hours away. She nodded and he disappeared into the darkness. The wall whirred shut behind him.

She sank back into the feather pillows, but her body was too keyed up to allow for sleep. She supposed she ought to don her nightshift so Katie wouldn't suspect anything out of the ordinary.

Then she noticed a dark shape on the floor.

She rose from bed. All her joints felt loose and achy, but

it was the good ache of having been well loved. She stooped to discover one of Aidan's stockings next to her discarded nightshift. She quickly pulled the shift over her head and tried to find the secret entrance in the wall.

"Bother!" she muttered after she ran her fingers over the place where Aidan had magically appeared without finding a way to open it. Evidently the lord of Stonehaven only wanted a secret entrance between his chamber and his lady's if he was the one who controlled access to it.

After the debacle with Aidan's button in Bermuda, she shuddered to think what might happen if the man's stocking were discovered in her chamber here. She padded to the door and peered into the hall, hoping to skitter to Aidan's room and back without being seen.

Rosalinde opened her door a crack. The swish of kid soles on hardwood made her stop. She put an eye to the slit in the door and saw a woman in a maid's mobcap and apron moving furtively down the hall. Buxom and bold, she fit Katie's description of Lily Wade, the upstairs maid.

Lily stopped and scratched on one of the doors. Someone opened to her and she slipped into the chamber, silent as a wraith.

But in that slice of a moment, Rosalinde saw the face of the man who opened the door clearly.

All the air whooshed out of her body in a single rush. Shakily, Rosalinde pulled her door closed and sank to her knees beside it because she no longer had the strength to remain upright.

How could she have been so stupid? So gullible as to believe protestations of love from the admitted prince of rogues. She was never going to read another sonnet as long as she lived. Poetry and iambic pentameter had obviously turned her brain to pudding.

The chamber Lily had entered in the middle of the night without so much as a "by your leave" belonged to Aidan.

Chapter 9

I will roar you as gently as any sucking dove; I will roar
you, as 'twere any nightingale.
—SHAKESPEARE, *A Midsummer Night's Dream*

Songbirds put the finishing flourish on their pre-dawn
hymn to the sun. They'd escaped the night terrors of the
fox and owl, and the eastern sky wavered in shades of pearl.
It was worth singing about.

Aidan knew exactly how they felt as he crunched across
the graveled exercise yard toward the stable. When he'd
emerged from Royal Dock with his health and sanity intact,
he'd thanked God. Then he swore he'd discover who really
should have taken berth on that prison ship. He owed Peg
Bass that much.

He was close to knowing. He felt it in his bones. In the
green morning air. In the heady joy of Rosalinde's love.

He hoped to choose a suitable mount for her and have it
saddled and ready before she appeared.

He found his groom already up and mucking out the stables.

"Where is Balor?" Aidan asked when he noticed the
empty stall. Named for a Celtic god with a venomous eye,
the beast was only a small step up from Beelzebub himself.
Balor was a looker, sleek and black, and in all that horse's
vice-ridden life, Aidan was the only one who'd ridden him
successfully. He suspected the *Knack* deserved most of the
credit.

The groom sprang to attention and tugged his forelock.

"Miss Burke's riding 'im, m'lord. Picked him out herself, she did. Ye must admit 'e's a prime bit o' horseflesh."

"And you saddled him for her?" The wee fool. Didn't she realize her equestrian skills weren't up to this challenge? Not without Aidan to *Knack* the beast for her. And even then, with Balor, it didn't always work.

"I didn't want to, but she insisted." The man twisted his cap in nervous hands. "Beggin' your pardon, your lordship, but you told me I should honor the requests of your guests. I thought ye'd be along direct like, so I saddled Camlan for ye."

Aidan swung onto the back of his preferred mount. Camlan, a big bay, was less wily than Balor, but he was deeper-chested and willing and would run himself to death if Aidan demanded it. "Did you see which way she went?"

"She asked the way to the ruin."

Aidan swore with vehemence and Camlan leaped forward, barreling across the exercise yard and into the open meadow beyond, hooves digging into the black turf. The ruin of the old tower was overgrown with tangled brambles and blackthorn. If Rosalinde's mount threw her on one of the narrow game trails in the wood surrounding the ruin, she could be seriously injured.

He caught sight of her dashing across the meadow ahead of him. When a hedgerow rose before her, she took the jump in a glorious bound and landed safely without Balor breaking his headlong stride.

When Aidan and Camlan sailed over the same hedgerow, she glanced back. But instead of slowing to allow him to join her, she leaned forward over her horse's head and urged him to more speed. Aidan gained on her over the uneven ground, but he held his breath lest her mount step into a coney hole and send her flying.

When she turned Balor's head into the wood, he called out to her to stop. She ignored him.

He dogged her into the dense overgrowth, ducking under low hanging branches and dodging whippy tendrils of woody vines. When the weathered gray stone of the tower rose before her, Balor reared, screaming his wicked head off.

Rosalinde dropped the reins and clutched the gelding's black mane. Aidan rushed forward and snatched the dangling lines.

"Down, ye big bastard!" Aidan bellowed and splayed his fingers toward the beast, sending the full power of the *Knack* roiling toward the horse. Balor dropped his front hooves to the ground in a heartbeat and stood still, quivering but compliant.

"Give me those reins," Rose demanded.

"Well, now, if ye want them so badly, perhaps ye shouldn't have dropped them. Are ye trying to damage yourself?"

"Why should I do that when you're so very willing to do it for me?" She narrowed her eyes. If she'd been a cat, she would have hissed at him. "Leave me alone."

She unhooked her knee from the sidesaddle and slid off Balor's back without waiting for his help. He dismounted, looped both horses' reins around a hawthorn trunk and followed her into the tower ruin.

"What's wrong?"

"What's wrong, he says." She lifted her hands in a gesture of frustration as she stomped through the overgrown grass amid moss-covered walls pocked with arrow loops. "I suppose you expect me to be grateful you managed to drag yourself away from your bed so you could keep our dawn assignation. Honestly, Aidan, I don't know where you find the stamina. Katie said that woman looked the sort who could wear a man slick and I quite agree."

"Who are you talking about?"

She rounded on him. "Lily Wade."

"Oh," he said slowly.

"Yes, oh. I know men expect to keep light-o-loves, but by God, what woman would put up with one under the same roof? Or did you think me too besotted to notice?"

"Ye're mistaken, love. My dealings with Lily Wade are nothing of the sort. She's merely performing a service for me." He reached out and grasped her arm. "And not the one ye think."

She yanked her arm away. "Believe me, you don't want to know what I think."

He grabbed her and pinned her between his body and the stone wall. She struggled, but he didn't release her.

"Will ye stand still so I can explain?"

She stopped trying to jerk away from him, but just to be on the safe side, he pressed his body against hers. A man was never kicked by a horse if he walked close behind its rump. He'd only feel the hooves if he gave the animal room to maneuver. He didn't dare give Rose any space at all or he suspected she'd put a knee to his groin. She finally stilled when she realized she couldn't wiggle free, but turned her head to the side to avoid his gaze.

"Lily Wade is not a serving girl," he explained. "She's an actress."

"Oh, that makes it so much better. And just what service is it this actress *performs* for you?"

"It could compromise matters for me to say."

"I'll bet."

"Rose, ye must understand. I don't want to involve you because the less you know, the safer you'll be."

She shot him a venomous glare. "You mean the safer *you'll* be. And whether I like it or not, it seems I'm already involved."

He sighed. "She's helping me discover who really killed Peg Bass. Last night, she came to my room to report that she'd done as I asked and set the trap for the real killer."

Her features softened. "Why did you confess to the murder in the first place?"

"They arrested Liam for it," he said, easing his hold on her somewhat. "He'd never have survived prison."

Her brows knit together as she digested this bit of news. "Are you sure he didn't do it?"

"Sure as I'm holding you. Liam is odd, I'll grant ye, but he's not at all violent. They arrested him because he used to leave orchids for Peg Bass and moon about over her a bit. She was always kind to him, but that was as far as it went. He'd never have hurt her."

"He lights a lamp for her in the grotto every night," Rose said. "Doesn't that sound as if he has a guilty conscience?"

"He says she was afraid of the dark and Mrs. Fitzgerald backs his story. The girl never ventured up the back stairs without a candle."

"You're sure it wasn't one of the servants who killed her?"

He shook his head. "Do you really think the worthy Mrs. Fitz wouldn't know if they did? The only thing she was sure of at the time was that the poor girl was gone with child by someone who wouldn't or couldn't do right by her. If it was one of the servants, there'd have been a shotgun wedding. She'd have seen to it."

"Then if it wasn't Liam," her eyes widened as she followed the thread of logic, "then it was someone else who was here that summer."

"Aye, lass," he said. "And I mean to discover who."

Aidan's eyes were impossibly green as he gazed down at her, lit from behind with a wild spark of determination. Then something changed and they darkened as his pupils expanded. Rosalinde felt the subtle shift of desire in the contact between them and her body responded. His mouth descended to hers even as she stretched up to meet him.

He was delicious. Warm. Unbearably male. She gave herself over to him and he took her. His kiss alone was enough to start the low throb of need in her belly. She groaned into his mouth.

Before she knew what he was about, he'd lifted her skirt and found the slit in her pantalets. She was swollen and achy and so sensitive, her insides contracted in greeting at his first touch. Her mind might harbor doubts, but her body knew this man and welcomed him.

She worked the buttons to free the hard bulge in his drop-front trousers. He lifted her thigh and hitched her leg over his hip.

Then he released her mouth and gazed down at her as he entered her in a single slow thrust, his thick length filling her so deeply she was forced to stand on tiptoe.

"You're mine, Rose. Mine alone." Then he was caught in the heat of rut and thrust into her repeatedly.

"Harder," she urged between clenched teeth.

She didn't have to tell him twice. They moved together, grinding against each other as if they wanted to climb into each other's skin.

The secret part of her began to coil. She was so close. Desperation made tears cling to her lashes.

Only a little more . . . only a little . . .

Then she convulsed in his arms, her whole body shuddering over the force of her release. He stopped pumping and thrust into her deeply. A hoarse cry tore from his throat and his seed shot into her in hot pulses.

Rosalinde had no way to gauge how long they sagged against each other with her back against the cool, lichen-covered stone. She was only aware of their hearts falling into a steady rhythm and their breathing coming together as one. Aidan finally slid out of her and smoothed down her skirt.

"Seems I let me cock lead me a merry chase." He slanted

her a crooked grin. "I shouldn't have taken ye in such a desolate spot. I'm sorry, lass."

"Don't you dare be sorry," she said fiercely. "Do you think it matters to me one jot where we are so long as we're together? And if you'll recall, I'm the one who led you here on a merry chase."

A smile stretched across his handsome face as he tucked in his shirt and refastened his trousers. "Aye, lass. So ye did. Only next time, don't be trying it on that big demon Balor." He leaned down and gave her a quick kiss on the neck. "I'm awfully fond of your sweet body just as it is."

"Agreed." The horse's power had scared her more than she wanted to admit. "But now that we're here, I don't suppose there's any harm in snooping around, is there?"

"Nary a bit. In fact, I've been meaning to come have a look-about." He strode into the next empty room, sending a covey of quail scurrying through the underbrush. The tower rose around them, the open sky vaulting above its gray walls. "When Mrs. Fitzgerald showed me the secret passage between the master's chamber and some of the others, it gave me pause. What's to say that's not something used time out of mind here at Stonehaven? There might be a connection between this old ruin and the grotto, I'm thinkin'."

Rosalinde followed. "Why would that be important?"

"If there was, it would untie a knot I've been puzzling over. Might be how the killer got away without being found in the maze." He walked around a sapling growing up in what used to be a long hall in the ancient keep. "There."

He pointed to a dark portal in the gray stone. The English oak was rotted away, but heavy iron hinges still jutted from the stonework.

Aidan stepped into the doorway and looked down. "Might be it."

Rosalinde peered around him. A set of stone steps led

downward. To the dungeon, perhaps? The scent of damp and rot and ancient misery rose to meet her nostrils. "If we're going down there, we'll need a torch."

"And some kind soul's left us one, darlin'." A pitch-daubed stick was thrust into an iron ring in the wall. Aidan lit the torch with a phosphorus match and started down the stairs. "Careful. They're uneven and a little slick in spots."

He reached behind him to take her hand as they descended. The stairs ended in a long, man-height corridor stretching away into the blackness. The torch chased away the tunnel's clinging dark and Aidan swept aside the long dangling cobwebs.

"How long has this keep been abandoned?" she asked.

"A couple hundred years or so."

"Then that torch shouldn't still have been here." The other wood about the place was gone or nearly rotted away.

"And if nobody's been about the place for even a hundred years, there aren't near enough cobwebs," he said.

Rosalinde thought there were quite enough for her taste, but refrained from saying so. Clearly, Aidan was onto something. Someone had passed through this subterranean passage within at least the last few years.

Which would correspond with the time of the upstairs maid's death.

In one place, the abandoned passage had partially collapsed. Plant roots tickled down from the ceiling, but they managed to squeeze themselves around the obstruction and continue on.

The tunnel dead-ended into a cunning contraption of pulleys and levers that appeared to wedge an opening in seemingly solid stone. To Rosalinde's relief, the old system still worked, though the grating of stone on stone strafed so loudly, she was sure someone would hear it in the main house.

Then another sound came from behind them, a long,

keening wail. It was the cry of a soul in extremis. The torch guttered and then flared. Rosalinde clutched Aidan's arm.

" 'Tis only the wind," Aidan said. "Now that we've opened this side, the passage acts like a long whistle."

Rosalinde wasn't so sure. Then she remembered Liam saying he lit the lamp in the grotto for Peg Bass and that sometimes, she was angry when she came. Perhaps Aidan's brother had heard the same disturbing sound and colored it with his own imagination.

Aidan stomped on a slightly raised stone, triggering the complete opening of the exit. They stepped into the low-ceilinged chamber of the grotto. Its curved walls were pocked with shells and brightly colored stones. Shafts of daylight fingered through openings to the outside. The ceiling was frescoed with bacchanalian scenes, nymphs and satyrs in varying degrees of undress.

"Oh, it's *A Midsummer Night's Dream*," Rosalinde said as she recognized Titania and Oberon, the Queen and King of the Fairies, and their court jester, Puck, cavorting on the sloping walls and ceiling. Perhaps she would keep reading Shakespeare, after all. "And look. There's poor Bottom with an ass's head."

"The grotto's not easy to find, owing to the maze being a complicated one," Aidan said. "But I expect these frescoes provided a bit of an incentive for randy fellows to keep trying."

"Women would find it fanciful. Or would claim to," she added with a sly smile. The lascivious artwork with bared breasts and rampant satyrs made her belly tighten a bit. It was easy to see the place as a trysting spot for lovers. Less easy to imagine it as the scene of a grisly murder.

"Where . . . was she found?" Rosalinde asked.

Aidan led the way past a sludge-clogged fountain and out into the bright morning. "Here. Right at the entrance to the grotto. Still warm, she was, when Liam found her. And when the servants came running to see why he was cater-wauling so, they met no one else in the maze."

"So that's why your brother was accused." Rosalinde slipped her hand into Aidan's, taking comfort from its warmth and strength.

"And in the confusion, the real killer disappeared out the secret way." Aidan narrowed his eyes and did a slow turn, taking in the spot.

Rosalinde realized he was visualizing the scene, imagining the last moments of the poor girl's life, when the one she looked to help her deal with the child growing in her belly had only helped her to the next world instead.

"And we'll have to return that way, too, love." Aidan extended a hand to her.

"Must we?" Damp, dark places were low on Rosalinde's list of happy spots.

"We rode toward the woods this fine morning. I could send a groom after the horses, but if we're discovered walking out of the maze bold as brass, the killer might figure out that someone else knows about his back door."

"You're right," she admitted.

"I'm right, ye say. Best we mark this day down then. Good to know it does happen on occasion."

"Only on occasion." She took his hand and led the way back into the grotto. "Don't let it go to your head."

Chapter 10

Was ever woman in this humour woo'd?
Was ever woman in this humour won?
—SHAKESPEARE, *King Richard III*

The next day, while the men fished, Rosalinde talked the women into tackling the maze. By the time they discovered the secret to the convoluted pathways and reached the grotto, Rosalinde's great-aunt declared herself completely done in. Not even the ghoulish prospect of visiting a murder site would budge Lady Chudderley into the shady interior of the grotto to rest. So they all trooped back to the main house, being treated to a litany of woe about her great-aunt's bunions as they went.

But Rosalinde made a mental map of the twisted lanes and blind alleys. When she returned to her chamber later, she drew out the path that led to the center of the maze on a piece of foolscap and stashed it among her folio of poorly executed watercolors.

After that, the women's days were spent playing cards or reading aloud while the men rattled about the grounds shooting at every hapless hind that wandered into their path. Rosalinde suggested archery or lawn bowling, but her great-aunt vetoed such "sweaty pursuits."

Evenings were dedicated to parlor games and impromptu recitals. Lady Sophia never missed an opportunity to try to ingratiate herself with Aidan by gushing over sentimental Irish poetry. If Rosalinde was forced to listen to the viscount's sister play *The Last Rose of Summer* on the piano forte one more time, she wouldn't be responsible if she boxed the woman's ears.

She badgered Aidan mercilessly whenever they could snatch a moment alone, but he wouldn't tell her how he planned to expose the true killer. He would only confirm the trap was being set, but would give her no details on how or where, or even whom, he suspected. It was maddening to think that someone she dined with was a cold-blooded killer.

After all Aidan's insistence that she trust him, it was infuriating that he didn't trust her. Baiting someone who'd already done murder was a game of brinksmanship, at best. She couldn't bear the thought of Aidan in danger or the idea of being helpless to do a thing about it. For tuppence, she'd plead illness and beg her father to return the family to London.

But when she looked across the music room at Aidan, his dark head lit by the soft amber gaslight, she knew she wouldn't leave. Not if it meant she couldn't snatch a glance at him whenever she wished.

And when the approach of nightfall meant he'd come through her wall and love her to exhaustion.

This evening, Viscount Musgrave was seated next to Lady Chudderley on the window seat. For most of his sister's little concert, Rosalinde's great-aunt provided a buzzing, whispered accompaniment directed at Edwin. He didn't respond in kind, but from the corner of her eye, Rosalinde caught him nodding in agreement from time to time.

When Lady Sophia finished a tortured bit of Schubert, Edwin stood and walked over to Rosalinde while the rest of the party clapped politely.

"It's a fine soft night. I've been told his lordship has a lovely patch of night-blooming jasmine." Edwin extended a hand to her. "Will you do me the honor of a turn about the garden, Rosalinde?"

Her gaze darted around the room. Sophia had latched onto Aidan's arm and was persuading him to sit beside her on the bench for her encore.

"Your sister isn't finished playing."

Edwin smiled and leaned down to whisper, "But I'm finished listening. I saw you stifle a yawn during that last piece. You're no music lover either."

Rosalinde could see no way to decline gracefully when he put it like that. She accepted his arm and let him lead her out the open French doors and into Aidan's riot of a garden.

"How do you like country life?" Edwin asked as the pebbled path crunched under their feet.

"I like it well enough," she said. "If I'm allowed to enjoy it."

Beyond her morning rides on a sturdy, pleasant mare instead of Balor, Rosalinde felt trapped inside with the other women. It was virtually the same as being in London, but with the benefit of an occasional breeze.

"If you were the mistress of your own place, that would doubtless change. Fresh air is good for a body. Children especially," Edwin said.

"Doubtless." It was difficult to disagree with conventional wisdom.

"Fengrave Hall, my own country house, is smaller than this, of course, but it's also much closer to London. It means that even when the House of Lords is in session, I can easily travel home for a few days each week," he said, as if that should matter to her.

"It sounds convenient." Honestly, if he wanted conversation, he ought to hit upon a subject open to debate. It was almost as if he proposed that everyone enjoyed good weather and dared her to dispute it.

"Truth to tell, it's a bit shabby at present," he admitted. "But I believe I've a remedy for that." He stopped walking and dropped suddenly to one knee before her. "Fengrave

Hall is in want of a mistress and I'm in want of a wife, Rosalinde. You have impressed me in recent days as one who could admirably fill both posts. Will you do me the honor of becoming my bride?"

She blinked hard. Even though her great-aunt had been pre-occupying him all evening, she hadn't suspected what was truly happening. Everyone knew Lady Chudderley had the means to make Rosalinde a great heiress, in coin if not in title. Evidently, her great-aunt had finally named a figure that got the viscount's attention.

"Edwin, I don't know what to say." She tried to gently tug away her hand, but he clasped it tighter and pressed a wet kiss on it. "This is a bit of a surprise."

"Yes, I know. For me too." He looked a bit chagrined by his kneeling posture. Edwin was always mindful of his dignity and soiling the knees of his trousers was wholly out of character. So were his next words. "But when Cupid cocks his bow, a man must . . . follow so."

Male laughter rose from behind them.

"Whisht, would ye listen to that? If ye want my advice, Musgrave—" Aidan came toward them—"a man who has no poet in his soul ought to at least stick to quoting the masters instead of mangling his own verse."

Edwin scrambled to his feet and glared at Aidan over Rosalinde's shoulder. "This is a private conversation, Stonemere."

"In my private garden," Aidan said. "Have ye found the jasmine yet?"

"No, but that's neither here nor there." A small muscle ticked under Edwin's left eye and his lips were set in a hard line.

"Ye mean to say ye didn't really have the flora in mind when ye spirited Rosalinde out here?" Aidan said with a charming smile. "And ye so almighty proper all the time, Edwin. 'Tis shocked, I am."

"Now see here—" Edwin began, the hackles on his neck visibly rising. His hands balled into fists and one arm drew back to deliver a blow.

"No, *ye* see." Aidan raised a splay-fingered hand toward Edwin and the viscount froze in place. "Ye must go back into the house now."

The fire went out of Edwin's eyes and a vague smile lifted his mouth. He turned to Rosalinde as if nothing had happened. "I must go in now, my dear. His lordship will show you the jasmine. Consider what I said, will you?"

She merely nodded because she didn't think she could force any words out her astonished mouth. Once his footsteps retreated beyond earshot, she turned to Aidan. "What was that about?"

"Oh, ye've just got yerself another beau, love. Nothing to trouble your pretty head about." He offered her his arm and started leading her along the path. "I really can't blame the poor blighter. Ye'll let him down easy, aye?"

"No, I mean, what was this?" She thrust her hand forward, fingers spread as she'd seen Aidan do.

"Oh, I had to *knack* him. He was about to start something he couldn't finish and I'd hate to have to knock a guest on his backside in front of a woman he's embarrassed himself before already."

His dismissive attitude toward his rival danced on her nerves, but she let that go for now. "You had to '*knack*' him?"

"I suppose ye haven't ever heard of the *Knack* on this most civilized of islands, have ye?" Aidan said. "And to be fair, 'tis not well known beyond certain circles on the Emerald Isle either. 'Tis a trick I inherited from me da. If I need someone to do a simple thing, I . . . *think* it to him and off he goes."

Rosalinde huffed out a surprised breath. "How does that work?"

"In truth, I don't know. Me da used to say the family could trace its blood back to the Old Ones, to the Tuatha de Danaan, back to a time when a simple man had more magic in his little finger than there is in the whole of the country now." Aidan stopped and looked back toward the house, a frown creasing his brow. "I wish I hadn't had to do it to your beau. My gift loses potency with repetition. I'll not be able to *knack* him again for another day or so, I'd expect."

Rosalinde swallowed this new information. "So you . . . *knack* people with regularity, do you?"

"Not as often as ye might think."

"Have you ever *knacked* me?"

He stopped and dropped a kiss on her forehead. "No, but ye've tempted me sore once or twice."

The more she learned about Aidan, the more a stranger he seemed. They walked on in silence toward the growing sweetness that signaled the jasmine was near.

"Why did you say Edwin had embarrassed himself before me?"

"He asked ye to marry him, aye?"

"Yes."

"Well, did ye tell *him* yes?"

"No."

"Then I'd say he was properly shamed."

At least Edwin had troubled to ask her formally. Now that she thought back on the matter, Aidan hadn't truly asked. He'd more or less informed her she'd be his wife after loving the will to resist right out of her.

What was that, if not wickedly close to being *knacked*?

"I didn't have time to give Edwin an answer, if you must know."

Aidan chuckled. "Are ye after seeing if I'm the jealous type?"

Rosalinde pulled her hand from the sheltered crook of his arm and stomped ahead of him on the path toward the four-foot clump of jasmine sprawling near a stone settee. The small waxy flowers were not much to see by moonlight, but their scent was so heady and sweet, it made her slightly dizzy.

"Rose, don't be like that." He came up behind her and slipped his arms around her waist.

"Or what?" She wiggled away from him. "You'll *knack* me?"

"No, lass. There'd be no point. If ye don't love me willingly, ye don't love me."

"And if you don't trust me, how can you love me?"

"I trust ye. Didn't ye see how little I minded Edwin? I know you're mine."

"No, I mean about your plans." She crossed her arms over her chest. "You won't tell me how you intend to trap the real killer."

"For your own good. Ye've no need to know."

"I'm an adult. Why don't you let me be the judge of what I need to know?"

"Rose, now see—"

"No, you see." She raised her hand in a parody of his *knack* gesture. "Either you tell me what I want to know right now, or I'll march right back into that house and tell Edwin I accept his suit in front of God and everybody."

"Ye wouldn't."

"Watch me."

When he did nothing for a few heartbeats, she wheeled and set off.

"It's the match my family wants in any case," she muttered. "Why shouldn't I?"

Aidan grasped her shoulders and whipped her around to face him. "Because ye don't love him."

"Love often has little to do with marriage on this most civilized of islands, or hadn't you noticed?"

"Rose—"

"Now, Aidan. Tell me now or I'm gone."

"All right, but ye must keep clear of it." He led her back to the settee beside the jasmine. "I won't be coming to your chamber this night. Lily Wade is turning the beds down as we speak. And she's leaving the same note on several of them."

"What sort of note?"

"Read it for yourself." He pulled a scrap of paper from his pocket and handed it to her.

The moonlight was bright enough to read the script scrawling across the page.

She was my cousin. I know what you did and I can prove it. Meet me at midnight to discuss terms. You know where.

It was signed *Lily Wade.*

" 'Tis vague enough I think only the killer will understand it." Aidan took the note back, refolded it and shoved it in his pocket. "He'll have to respond if only to discover what sort of proof she has and what she wants for her silence. Lily will wait before the grotto and I'll wait hidden inside, and we'll see who comes."

Rosalinde shivered. A cornered man could be driven to desperate acts. "It sounds dangerous."

"So was prison." He shrugged. "But if I'm to remove the taint from my name and claim ye before all with our heads high, it's a risk I must take."

It still wasn't a proper proposal of marriage, but Aidan was willing to hazard far more than the knees of his trousers to have her. That counted for something.

She still turned her face away when he tipped her chin up so he could kiss her.

"Someone might look out and see," she said. "And a kiss in the garden is as good as a betrothal when the world catches you at it. Then you'd have to marry me, regardless of how we might have to hold our heads."

"I'm not worried about that." He stroked her cheek with

his fingertips, feather-light. "But I greatly fear if I once start kissing ye, I won't be able to stop. Wonder what your great-aunt would say if she found us stretched out on this settee with your skirts hiked up around your waist."

Her belly warmed at the thought. "She wouldn't say a thing. She'd have an apoplectic fit on the spot."

"We can't have that," Aidan said as he rose and offered his arm. "A dead houseguest will ruin a host's reputation for years."

She chuckled at his nonsense as he led her back toward the main house.

"But once ye're well and truly mine, I give ye fair warning, Rose. I intend to have ye in every chamber of the house and behind every bush in the garden if I have to fit the staff with blindfolds to do it!"

Her body throbbed at the thought of a good bone-jarring swive with Aidan by the jasmine some night. "That's a bold ambition, my lord," she teased.

"Nay, lass." His eyes glinted with lust as they rejoined the others in the house. "A promise."

Chapter 11

I am a tainted wether of the flock,
Meetest for death: the weakest kind of fruit
Drops earliest to the ground.
　　—SHAKESPEARE, *The Merchant of Venice*

Aidan retired early and as good guests should, everyone else followed his lead. Rosalinde was a bit surprised not to find Katie waiting for her in her chamber. She tugged the bellpull by her bedside and started taking down her hair herself.

Her window had been left open, so she wandered toward it. She noted for the first time that there was a grape arbor at the far end of the garden. If Aidan lifted her hem there beneath the fat leaves and curling vines, would anyone be able to see from the house? Or if he slipped completely under her broad skirt, would anyone even be the wiser if they stumbled upon them?

The memory of his mouth on her sex made her belly clench.

Lord, she was becoming such a wanton. Now that her thoughts were bent in that direction, every place she looked presented unique sensual opportunities. She imagined coupling with Aidan under every shade tree, on the library's venerable desk, in the cramped butler's pantry, a hand clamped over her mouth to stifle her moans of pleasure. The cascading sensual images that scrolled across her mind's eye distracted her almost completely from the risky scheme Aidan was about to embark upon.

Probably why the man brought it up, she thought with a grimace.

A lamp winked on in the distant grotto. Liam had made his ghoulish rounds. Then Rosalinde saw someone tramping through the garden toward the maze, a long cape wrapped about his form.

Aidan. She'd know his determined stride anywhere. Of course, he'd want to be in place long before the killer crept out to meet the upstairs maid.

Katie still hadn't come, so she tugged the bellpull again. It was a good quarter-hour before her maid arrived, breathless and frazzled.

"Beggin' yer pardon, miss," Katie said. "But I couldn't get here a pinch faster what with us being so shorthanded and all."

"Shorthanded? How can that be?" Rosalinde gave Katie her back and the maid made short work of helping her out of her gown. "His lordship has an abundance of servants."

"Yes, but not an abundance of upstairs maids. Well, he wouldn't have need of any, would he, him not havin' a wife and all? That's why he hired one special for his guests, Mrs. F. says. But now that Lily Wade is long gone."

"Gone?"

"Sure as I'm standing here. Right after she came back from turning down the beds, she gave Mrs. Fitzgerald her notice with immediate effect. 'I've changed my mind,' she says, all hoity-toity-like. 'No amount of money is worth this.' " Katie lifted a pinkie and sashayed a few steps. "As if she already didn't do the least amount of work for the best of pay. I ask ye, did ye ever?"

Was this part of Aidan's plan as well?

"And she's gone, you say?"

"Saw her head down the drive with my own eyes, fast as shank's mare would carry her. Wouldn't wait till his lordship could be notified. Had to start walkin' and wouldn't nothing turn her." Katie shook her head as she helped Rosalinde into her nightshift. "Even with her leaving like that, I expect the baron woulda seen she had a ride to town to speed her on her way. He seems the kindly sort, don't he? Lily Wade's got herself a ten-mile walk in the dark or I'm mistook. But in the meantime, who's stuck with helping the viscountess and her daughter on top of me own work? Though it do seem strange the viscountess wouldn't bring her own lady's maid, don't it? Thought them titled folk all had the chinks. Well, mayhap not." Katie grasped Rosalinde's hair and started plaiting it for sleep, none too gently. "I hope that Lily Wade steps in some horse apples along the road and ruins her fancy little slippers, so I do."

Rosalinde extricated herself from Katie's heavy-handedness. "I'll take care of my own hair."

"Aren't y' kind?" Katie cast her a broad smile. "That's all to the good because I expect Lady Chudderley is ringing me bell off. If there's nothing else then, miss?"

"No. Good night, Katie."

As soon as the door latched behind her, Rosalinde turned down the gas lamp and scurried back to the window. In a few hours it would be midnight. What would happen when the killer arrived at the grotto and there was no Lily waiting outside to lure him in?

Her decision made, she went to the wardrobe and pulled out her simplest gown, one she could don by herself. Then she lugged a chair over to the window so she could watch the moon slip behind scudding clouds and mark anyone else who made a trek from the house to the grotto.

When midnight drew near, 'Lily Wade' would arrive before the grotto. As planned.

Aidan positioned himself in the deep shadows of the grotto, out of the yellowish circle of Liam's lamplight, so he could see the spot where the secret back exit was located.

Thanks to one of the many airshafts bored through the sloping walls, he also had a decent view to the place where the maze emptied into the grotto. Whichever way the killer came, he'd be ready.

He wasn't keen on firearms, but he and Liam had supplemented the family stewpot often enough as children using bows and arrows. A man with an arrow notched on the string would stop an unarmed one. He didn't think the killer would trouble to bear a pistol.

After all, he hadn't used anything but his bare hands to dispatch poor Peg Bass. Why would he try anything else now?

The rustle of footsteps on pea gravel raised his head. A small cloaked figure emerged from the maze.

Lily, as expected. He'd have to give her a substantial bonus for this night's work. Maybe even finance that play she was hoping to land the lead in. Her acting had been flawless so far. Now if she could only exact a confession from whoever came to meet her as Aidan had coached her.

She peered toward the grotto, as if trying to see where he was hidden, her hood clutched close to her face. Then she turned back and faced the gap in the hedges of the maze, her weight shifting from one foot to the other.

That nervous sway was a little out of character. Lily was a cool one, the sister of one of his cellmates in Bermuda. She was getting a bit long in the tooth to continue lifting her skirts for a living and hoped to make a splash on the stage before her looks deserted her completely. She didn't seem the type to be so antsy now.

Didn't she realize he wouldn't let anything happen to her?

Aidan cocked his ear for approaching footsteps, but only heard the scritching of insects, small nocturnal claws seeking their burrows and an occasional owl.

Then he heard something else. A muffled curse. Someone

was working their way through the maze, but had taken a wrong turn and run into a dead end. Lily must have heard it too, for she stopped swaying and stood dead still.

A man came out of the maze and walked toward her. Moonlight struck his face brightly enough for Aidan to recognize him.

"Hello, cousin," he whispered and drew an arrow from his quiver.

"All right," George said. "Your note got me here. I assume it's something to do with that Peg Bass. What do you know about it?"

Rosalinde swallowed hard. The way they were positioned, she was reasonably sure her face was in shadow. Now if she could only imitate Lily Wade as well as Katie did.

"I know me cousin Peg was far gone with your child," she said, altering her voice to match Katie's version of the uppity maid.

"Not mine," George said. "She wasn't my type. Not that I haven't tumbled my share of lady's maids, you understand, but I never touched your cousin."

"I've me doubts, gov."

"Oh, Peg Bass was pretty enough, but a bit too fleshy for my taste." He smiled and cocked a brow at her. "I like my women more on the willowy side. Like you, Lily."

She stepped backward toward the grotto. "Ye didn't have to kill her. All ye had to do was give her money. She knew ye wouldn't marry her."

"Again. You have the wrong fellow," George said. "Besides, you and I both know once the blunt starts flowing in cases like that, it never stops."

"I know ye stood by and let yer cousin take the blame for her murder."

"Aidan confessed. I saw no reason to doubt him."

"Even when you knew the truth."

George propped his fists at his waist. "The truth is, I'm here to find out what the hell *did* happen. If it wasn't Aidan, then who was it? Don't tell me he played the martyr to protect his chuckle-headed brother."

George's face scrunched in a frown that gave his words the ring of truth. He hadn't killed the upstairs maid and he was upset to learn his cousin Aidan might actually be innocent.

The wind kicked up and threw her hood back, baring her dark hair. Lily's blonde was so pale, it would appear white by moonlight.

"Wait a moment. You aren't Lily." As he started toward her, she turned and fled toward the grotto.

"The wee fool," Aidan murmured. What on earth had possessed Rose to masquerade as the upstairs maid? But he didn't have time to puzzle over it. A long, hollow keening started behind him and he heard the rasp of stone on stone.

Viscount Musgrave stepped through the secret back door to the grotto as Rose skidded in through the front.

"Rosalinde, what are you doing here?" Edwin asked, aghast.

Her jaw dropped and Aidan could almost see the connections forming in her head. Only the killer would know about the back door and think to surprise Lily Wade by using it.

"It was you, Edwin," she said as George jogged up behind her. "You killed that poor girl."

"Nonsense." Edwin stepped toward her. "My dear, you're overwrought with the moonlight and that beastly howling wind. You don't know what you're saying."

"I say, what's all this?" George peered around her, eyeing the yawning opening in the grotto's seemingly solid back wall. "Where's that tunnel lead?"

"It connects to the old tower," Aidan said, stepping out of the shadows with his bow raised. "Rosalinde and I discovered it while we were riding last week. But you knew it was there years ago, didn't you, Edwin? And you used the back way out the night Peg Bass died to avoid being caught in the maze."

"You can't prove it."

"Only the killer would have used it this night."

Edwin glared at him for a moment, then in a movement so quick Aidan wouldn't have thought him capable of it, he lunged for Rosalinde and pulled her in front of him. She screamed and struggled to free herself, but he held her fast.

"Let her go!" Aidan bellowed.

"No." Edwin pinned her arms to her sides and grasped her chin. "Drop your bow. Or I'll break her neck, Aidan, so help me God, I will."

The whites showed all the way around Rose's eyes. Aidan dropped the bow and arrow, sending them clattering to the cobbles.

"Why, Edwin?" Rose managed to croak.

"Because Peg Bass wasn't just a light-skirt chambermaid. She was a grasping, scheming bitch," he snarled. "And I was supposed to marry Lady Ellen Banbury."

Aidan recognized the name as one of the greatest heiresses in the country. There'd been rumors of an impending betrothal before he and Edwin prepared to leave for Oxford but nothing had ever come of it.

"My father was drawing up the final agreement, but the little bitch ruined the match for me." He spat out the words. "When Peg Bass turned up round-bellied, I broke it off with her and wouldn't pay a farthing for her little bastard. I ask you. How could I know it was even mine with a girl like that?"

"You still didn't have to kill her," George said.

"Yes, I did. She stole my signet ring, the filthy little thief, and she sent it to Lady Ellen by post with all the details of my . . . preferences." He shook with rage. "As if I'd have treated Lady Ellen like some worthless dollymop."

Edwin grabbed one of Rosalinde's breasts and gave it a hard squeeze. She cried out in pain, but his other hand at her throat kept her from struggling. Aidan's vision hazed over with red.

"Stay where you are, Aidan. I mean it." Edwin's eyes danced with madness, then his face went eerily calm. "Honestly, how could Peg expect me to let her get away with that?"

"Let Rosalinde go," Aidan said quietly, wishing with all his heart he hadn't *knacked* the man in his garden earlier that evening. If ever there was a time to be blessed by his gift it was now, but if he lifted his hand to Edwin, he knew no power would issue forth. He'd squandered it out of jealousy and the viscount would be impervious to the *Knack* until tomorrow at least. "You don't want to hurt her."

Edwin smiled. "No, I don't, because she's my ticket out of here." Then he tightened his grip on her neck. Gasping, she clawed at his hand, but he was too strong for her. "But I will if you try to stop me."

Then he pulled Rosalinde into the secret entrance behind him and stomped the paver that slid the stone closed.

Chapter 12

If we shadows have offended,
Think but this, and all is mended,
That you have but slumber'd here
While these visions did appear.
—SHAKESPEARE,
    A Midsummer Night's Dream

"Edwin, stop!" Rosalinde shouted as he hauled her through the subterranean pathway. Edwin extended the torch before him, but blocked so much of the light with his broad shoulders, darkness sucked at her heels as she scrambled after him. His grip manacled her wrist and once when she lost her footing, he dragged her across the uneven stones. "Please, stop."

"When we get to Gretna Green, we'll stop," he snarled.

Gretna Green? Surely he didn't imagine he could smooth this over with an elopement. She found her feet and scrambled back upright, still forced to lope along after him. "I won't marry you, Edwin."

"Yes, you will. Or you'll be ruined. Besides, your great-aunt has already agreed to a more than generous dowry."

"She'll rescind it when I tell her the truth."

He rounded on her and brought her nose to nose with him. "You won't do that. A wife cannot testify against her husband." His eyes glittered wildly. "Cross me and I'll sell you to a brothel in Cheapside. You'll die chained to a bed, but not nearly as soon as you'd wish."

The thought of her debasement seemed to rouse him, for he clamped her body to his, twisting her arm behind her painfully. Then he shoved her back, still keeping his grip on her wrist.

"You're trying to tempt me, you little minx. Trying to slow me down." His lips curved in a terrifying smile. "I'll make you pay for that later. Discipline. That's the ticket, my love. You'll like it, I promise."

"Edwin, think for a moment. Aidan and George both know what happened. You can't escape. If you surrender willingly, perhaps you can . . ." She didn't know what the authorities would do to him. Since he was a viscount, prison was unlikely, but Bedlam was a real possibility. He was clearly mad.

"No one will believe Aidan or George," he said, as if to reassure himself. "They both have too many reasons to lie."

Her belly lurched. His madness had a twisted kind of logic.

All she could think to do was slow him down. She kicked off a slipper and began to hobble. "Oh, please stop. I lost a shoe."

He stopped and flashed the torch around, illuminating the tunnel behind them.

"I don't see it. We need to go back a bit," she said, trying to pull him back down the corridor. He jerked her up short.

"I'll buy you new ones in Scotland." Edwin bent double and threw her over his shoulder. Then he gave her bum a vicious whack that vibrated up her spine and made her teeth rattle. "Try something else, my pet, and I'll wring your neck and leave you to rot in the dark."

"Fetch some help, George," Aidan shouted as he scooped up the bow and arrow and started running back through the maze. "We'll catch them at the old tower."

"It's too far. You'll never make it," George called after him.

Aidan poured on more speed as he sprinted for the stable.

All the horses startled when he burst through the doors, stamping and snorting their displeasure.

His groom stumbled out of his room at the back dressed in only his drawers. "What the—shall I saddle Camlan for ye, gov? By gum, he's gone."

"Even if he was here, there's no time for a saddle." Aidan threw open Balor's stall, grasped a handful of his black mane and swung himself onto the demon's back. He extended his hand toward the horse's head and sent every drop of the *Knack* he possessed. "Now fly, you big bastard."

The gelding's eyes rolled as the Celtic magic settled over him like a shimmering mantle. Then he leaped forward and shot out of the stable as if the cry of the Banshee rang in his ears and the hounds of Hell nipped his heels.

Pound. Pound. Pound. Balor's hooves dug into the turf and propelled them across the meadow in time with Aidan's shuddering breaths. If Edwin hurt Rose . . .

Aidan leaned over Balor's neck, crooning curses and urging him to more speed. The gelding sailed over the hedgerow and Aidan could have sworn the hooves never quite settled back to earth. They skimmed the surface of the ground, fast as Aidan's desperately beating heart.

Carrying her forced Edwin to slow down. And when they reached the point in the tunnel that was partially collapsed, he had to put her down. By then, he'd reverted to his usual courtly, tightly controlled self.

"You'll enjoy Scotland, I should think. Lovely countryside," he said as he led her around the obstruction of stone and detritus. "If it wasn't full of Scots, it would be heaven on earth."

"My mother was Scottish," she said stiffly.

"Well, no one's perfect," he said as he hoisted her back over his shoulder as if she were a sack of meal. "In a way, it means we start this marriage on a more even footing. We both have things to overlook in each other. You don't hold Peg Bass against me and I won't hold your Scottish mother against you." Then he laughed uproariously and she knew the madman was back.

The sound reverberated along the corridor, sending a shower of stone sloughing from the low ceiling. He picked up his pace, grunting with effort as he scaled the uneven stone steps that led to the tower ruins.

When he reached the top, he set her down. Aidan's gelding, Camlan, was hobbled near the entrance, his welcoming whicker strangely comforting.

"I wasn't expecting to need two horses, so we'll have to share, sweeting."

"Not likely, Musgrave," Aidan's voice came from the dark. "Ye may have gotten away with murder, but ye'll not add horse thievery or abduction to your list of sins."

Edwin yanked Rosalinde in front of his body again. In the deep shadows and spatters of moonlight, she made out the form of a dark horse and a man astride, arrow nocked, like an avenging angel.

"Back away, Stonemere, or I'll kill her."

"Last chance, Edwin." Aidan's voice was strangely calm.

"No!"

The arrow whirred past Rosalind's crown and struck Viscount Musgrave squarely in the right eye. His grip turned to whey and she leaped away from him. He sank to his knees and then fell forward, dead before his forehead smacked the stone pavers.

Her whole body shook in delayed tremors, but Aidan was suddenly there, enfolding her in his arms. Sobbing with relief, she sagged into his strength.

"Don't look, love," he urged. "It's over now and he'll never harm anyone again."

Her insides shook. Another person was dead at Stonehaven and Aidan was right in the thick of things. Depending on the view the magistrate took of these dark matters, Edwin could still harm them.

He could harm them very badly.

Three months later

Autumn frost kissed the English countryside and a riot of color burst forth, a final dance of glory before the coming bleak winter. Lady Chudderley braved the cool air for a turn around Lord Stonemere's garden and found her great-niece under the dry brown leaves of the grape arbor. Marriage obviously agreed with her, for her cheeks were ruddier than the weather warranted.

Lady Chudderley stopped her afternoon constitutional to chat with Rosalinde, whose broad skirts were spread around her on the stone bench. She seemed to be contemplating the dentils ridging the tall manor house, so Lady Chudderley took a moment to study the imposing edifice as well.

"A magnificent home. I must congratulate you, child. Even though he seemed unconventional at the outset, Lord Stonemere has proved to be, in every instance, the very sort of well-connected gentleman I required you to wed."

"I'm sure Father is . . . gratified that you are pleased."

"And well he should be!" True to her word, Lady Chudderley had bequeathed all her unentailed property and a goodly sum to her only nephew. Loromer Burke was set for the rest of his indulgent life. Rosalinde had refused the dowry she'd offered, since her new husband had no need of the funds. Lady Chudderley was mildly annoyed at that. It was difficult to control those over whom one wielded no monetary power.

"In the end, I suppose we must thank your husband's cousin George." She narrowed her eyes at her great niece, wondering at her distracted expression. Ordinarily, Rosalinde would never remain seated while her elder stood.

Honestly, one would think the girl would have the goodness to slide over and offer an old woman a seat!

"After all," Lady Chudderly went on, "George had the most to gain if Lord Stonemere found himself in difficulty with the law again."

Rosalinde smiled and drew a shuddering breath. "Yes, but fortunately George backed Aidan's account of the viscount's confession to Peg Bass's murder at every point."

Lady Chudderley frowned at her great-niece. "Dear me, you're flushed, child. Are you quite all right?"

Rosalinde's lips twitched.

Was the girl panting a little? It certainly wasn't a warm day.

"I'm . . . fine," she said. "I believe Mrs. Fitz has tea laid on the terrace. I'll join you later."

"You're not coming?"

"Not . . . yet." Rosalinde sputtered as if she'd choked on something. "Soon, auntie. I'll come soon."

"Hmph. Well, if you see that scamp of a husband of yours tell him I'd like him to join us for tea, too. The pair of you have been married a month now and come to think of it, this is the first time I've managed to catch you alone. It's simply not the done thing to be so besotted with one's spouse. All this mooning about is . . . well, most improper."

Lady Chudderley turned back to the garden path and headed toward the terrace, vaguely disconcerted by the exchange. There was something afoot, but she couldn't quite put her finger on it.

"She's gone," Rosalinde whispered.

Beneath her broad skirt, Aidan's mouth found the slit in her pantalets again and resumed his sensual rhythm. She closed her eyes. He'd tormented her with his wicked fingers while her aunt stood not three feet away, bringing her so near to a jerking release, she feared she'd explode. The man was beyond incorrigible.

Thank God.

Her insides coiled and then snapped, her climax shuddering through her in pounding waves. Aidan placed a final kiss on the lips of her sex and climbed out from under her skirt.

He sat down next to her, a smug smile on his handsome face. "Well, is Lady Chudderley right? Are ye besotted with your husband, madam?"

Rosalinde sighed. "I'm afraid so. Most improperly besotted."

"Good," he said. "It'll be my pleasure to keep you that way."

She smiled up at him. "And now we must do something about your pleasure, sir."

"Before tea?" His green eyes glinted with wicked delight.

"If we're quick about it. Come." She stood and offered him her hand.

"Where are we bound?"

"The library," she said as she led him past the jasmine and into a side door. "I've been wondering if that desk is as sturdy as it looks."

Aidan chuckled. "Seems I've corrupted you thoroughly."

"That you have, my love," she said as he swung her into a snug embrace. "And may I never repent."

"Not sorry ye didn't wed a proper fellow?"

"You said it yourself. I'd have been wasted on one." She kissed him, nipping at his bottom lip. "Besides, who'd ever want a proper fellow when she can have an improper gentleman?"

If you enjoyed this book, try Mary Wine's latest,
MY FAIR HIGHLANDER,
out now!

"Tell me you did not tell the barbarian Scot that he could court me."

Jemma Ramsden was a beautiful woman, even when her lips were pinched into a frown. She glared at her brother, uncaring of the fact that most of the men in England wouldn't have dared to use the same tone with Curan Ramsden, Lord Ryppon.

Jemma didn't appreciate the way her brother held his silence. He was brooding, deciding just how much to tell her. She had seen such before, watched her brother hold command of the border property that was his by royal decree with his iron-strong personality. Knights waited on his words and that made her impatient.

"Well, I will not have it."

"Then what will you have, Sister?" Curan kept his voice controlled, which doubled her frustration with him. It was not right that he could find the topic so mild when it was something that meant so much to her.

But that was a man for you. They controlled the world and didn't quibble over the fact that women often had to bend beneath their whims.

Curan watched her, his eyes narrowing. "Your temper is misplaced, Jemma."

"I would expect you to think so. Men do not have to suffer having their futures decided without any concern for their wishes as women do."

Her brother's eyes narrowed. She drew in her breath because it was a truth that she was being shrewish. She was well past the age for marriage and many would accuse her brother of being remiss in his duty if he did not arrange a match for her. Such was being said of her father for certain.

Curan pointed at the chair behind her. There was hard authority etched into his face. She could see that his temper was being tested. She sat down, not out of fear. No, something much worse than that. Jemma did as her brother indicated because she knew that she was behaving poorly.

Like a brat.

It was harsh yet true. Guilt rained down on her without any mercy, bringing to mind how many times she had staged such arguments since her father died. It was a hard thing to recall now that he was gone.

Her brother watched her sit and maintained his silence for a long moment. That was Curan's way. He was every inch a hardened knight. The barony he held had been earned in battle, not inherited. He was not a man who allowed emotion to rule him, and that made them night and day unto each other.

"Lord Barras went to a great deal of effort to ask me for permission to court you, Jemma."

"Your bride ran into his hands. That is not effort; it is a stroke of luck."

Her brother's eyes glittered with his rising temper. She should leave well enough alone, but having always spoken her mind, it seemed very difficult to begin holding her tongue.

"Barras could have kept Bridget locked behind his walls if that was his objective. He came outside to meet me because of you."

"But—"

Curan held up a singled finger to silence her. "And to speak to me of possible coordinated efforts beween us, yes but an offer from the man should not raise your ire so much sister."

The reprimand was swift and solid, delivered in a hard tone that made her fight off the urge to flinch. Her brother was used to being in command. His tone was one that not a single one of his men would argue with even if she often did. But that trait was not enhancing her reputation. She noticed the way his knights looked at her, with disgust in their eyes. When they didn't think she could hear them, they called her a shrew. She would like to say it did not matter to her, but it did leave tracks like claw marks down the back of her pride. Knowing that she had earned that slur against her name made her stomach twist this morning. Somehow, she'd not noticed until now, not really taken the time to recognize how often she quarreled with her brother. He was a just man.

"You are right, brother."

Curan grunted. "You admit it, but you make no apology."

Her chin rose and her hands tightened on the arms of the chair as the impulse to rise took command of her.

"Remain in that chair, Jemma."

Her brother's voice cracked like a leather whip. She had never heard such a tone directed at her before. It shocked her into compliance, wounding the trust she had in her brother allowing her to do anything that she wished. The guilt returned, this time thick and clogging in her throat.

"Has Bridget complained of me?" Her voice was quiet, but she needed to know if her brother's wife was behind her sibling's lack of tolerance.

"She has not, but I am finished having my morning meal

ruined by your abrasive comments on matters concerning your future. You may thank the fact that my wife has been at this table every day for the past six months as the reason for this conversation not happening before this."

Bridget, her new sister-in-law, had taken one look at the morning meal and turned as white as snow. No doubt her brother was on edge with concern for the wife who had told him to leave her alone in one of the very rare times Bridget raised her voice in public to her husband. Curan had slumped back down in his chair, chewing on his need to follow his bride when Jemma had begun to berate him.

Her timing could not have been worse.

But hindsight was always far clearer.

"I will not speak against our father and his ways with you, Jemma. However, you will not continue as you have. You were educated well, just as my wife, and yet you spend your days doing nothing save pleasing your whims. You have refused to see Barras every time he has called upon me as thought the match is beneath you, it is not." Her brother paused making his displeasure clear. "Well, madam, I believe a few duties will help you place some of your spirit to good use. Curan drew in a stiff breath. "I will not force you to wed, because that was our father's wish. Yet I will not tolerate anyone living in this castle who does nothing to help maintain it. You may have the day to decide what you prefer to do or on the morrow. I will have a list of duties given to you. Food does not appear from thin air, and you shall help make this fortress a decent place to reside."

Her brother stood up and strode away, several of his knights standing up the moment their lord did to follow him. Conversation died in the hall and the sounds of dishes being gathered up for washing took over. Jemma watched the maids and cringed. Shame turned her face red, for she noticed more than one satisfied smile decorating their lips.

Standing up, she left the hall, seeking out the only living creature that she could trust not to lecture her.

But that was only because a horse could not talk even if she often whispered her laments against its velvety neck.

In the dim light of the stable, she moved down the stalls until she found her mare. The horse snorted with welcome, bringing a smile to her face, but it was a sad one. Jemma reached out to stroke the light gray muzzle, the velvety hairs tickling her hand. Storm had been her constant companion since her father's death and she realized that she had never really dealt with that parting. Instead she'd refused to admit that her sire's departure from this life had cut her to the bone.

Instead of grieving, she had become a shrew, irritating everyone around her, and escaping to ride across her father's land while the rest of the inhabitants toiled at all the tasks required to maintain a castle keep.

Curan and the others labeled it selfish but in truth it was running. She had swung up onto the back of her horse and ridden out to avoid facing the fact that her father was dead. It had never been about escaping her chores or thinking the match with Barras beneath her, she had sought out the bliss of not thinking at all which removed the need to grieve from her mind. She simply ignored the fact that time was passing, choosing to remain locked in a few hours that never progressed. That way, she didn't have to face the sadness that threatened to reduce her to a pile of ashes.

Barras . . .

The burly Scot was something else that she liked to avoid thinking about, yet for a far different reason. He looked at her as though he wanted to touch her. Even now, a shiver rippled down her spine at just the memory of the way his eyes traveled over her curves, tracing them, lingering on them while he eyes narrowed and his lips thinned with hunger. Some manner of sensation twisted in her belly and it set her heart to moving faster but she was unable to decide just what it was. Or maybe she had merely avoided naming it to remain locked in her fairy bubble where she didn't have to face the grieve that wanted to assault her.

Don't miss DEAD ALERT
by Bianca D'Arc,
new this month from Brava.

Fort Bragg, North Carolina

"I've got a special project for you, Sam." The commander, a former Navy SEAL named Matt Sykes, began talking before Sam was through the door to Matt's private office. "Sit down and shut the door."

Sam sat in a wooden chair across the cluttered desk from his commanding officer. Lt. Sam Archer, US Army Green Beret, was currently assigned to a top secret, mixed team of Special Forces soldiers and elite scientists. There were also a few others from different organizations, including one former cop and a CIA black ops guy. It was an extremely specialized group, recruited to work on a classified project of the highest order.

"I understand you're a pilot." Matt flipped through a file as he spoke.

"Yes, sir." Sam could have said more but he didn't doubt Matt had access to every last bit of Sam's file, even the top secret parts. He had probably known before even sending for him that Sam could fly anything with wings. Another member of his old unit was a blade pilot who flew all kinds of choppers, but fixed wing aircraft were Sam's specialty.

"How do you like the idea of going undercover as a charter pilot?"

"Sir?" Sam sat forward in the chair, intrigued.

"The name of a certain charter airline keeps popping up." Matt put down the file and faced Sam as his gaze hardened. "Too often for my comfort. Ever heard of a company called Praxis Air?"

"Can't say that I have."

"It's a small outfit, based out of Wichita—at least that's where they repair and maintain their aircraft in a company-owned hangar. They have branch offices at most of the major airports and cater mostly to an elite business clientele. They do the odd private cargo flight and who knows what else. They keep their business very hush-hush, 'providing the ultimate in privacy for their corporate clients,' or so their brochure advertises." Matt pushed a glossy tri-fold across the desk toward Sam.

"Looks pretty slick."

"That they are," Matt agreed. "So slick that even John Petit, with his multitude of CIA connections, can't get a bead on exactly what they've been up to of late. I've been piecing together bits here and there. Admiral Chester, the traitor, accepted more than a few free flights from them in the past few months, as did Ensign Bartles, who it turns out, was killed in a Praxis Air jet that crashed the night we took down Dr. Rodriguez and his friends. She wasn't listed on the manifest and only the pilot was claimed by the company, but on a hunch I asked a friend on the National Transportation Safety Board to allow us to do some DNA testing. Sure enough, we found remnants of Beverly Bartles's DNA at the crash site, though her body had to have been moved sometime prior to the NTSB getting there. The locals were either paid off or preempted. Either option is troubling, to say the least."

"You think they're mixed up with our undead friends?" They were still seeking members of the science team that had created the formula that killed and then turned its victims into the walking dead. Nobody had figured out exactly how they were traveling so freely around the country when they were on every watch list possible.

"It's a very real possibility. Which is why I want to send you in undercover. I don't need to remind you, time is of the essence. We have a narrow window to stuff this genie back into its bottle. The longer this goes on, the more likely it is the technology will be sold to the highest bidder and then, God help us."

Sam shivered. The idea of the zombie technology in the hands of a hostile government or psycho terrorists—especially after seeing what he'd seen of these past months—was unthinkable.

"If my going undercover will help end this, I'm your man." He'd do anything to stop the contagion from killing any more people.

Sam opened the flyer and noted the different kinds of jets the company offered. The majority of the planes looked like Lear 35's in different configurations. Some were equipped for cargo. Some had all the bells and whistles any corporate executive could wish for and a few were basically miniature luxury liners set up for spoiled celebrities and their friends.

"I hoped you'd say that. I've arranged a little extra training for you at Flight Safety in Houston. They've got Level D flight simulators that have full motion and full visual. They can give you the Type Rating you'll need on your license to work for Praxis Air legitimately."

"I've been to Flight Safety before. It's a good outfit." Sam put the brochure back on Matt's desk.

"We'll give you a suitable job history and cover, which you will commit to memory. You'll also have regular check-ins while in the field, but for the most part you'll be on your own. I want you to discover who, if any, of their personnel are involved and to what extent." Matt paused briefly before continuing. "Just to be clear, this isn't a regular job I'm asking you to do, Sam. It's not even close to what you signed on for when we were assigned as zombie hunters. I won't order you to do this. It's a total immersion mission. Chances are, there will be no immediate backup if you get into trouble. You'll be completely on your own most of the time."

"Understood, sir. I'm still up for it. I like a challenge."

Matt cracked a smile. "I hear that. And I appreciate the enthusiasm. Here's the preliminary packet to get you started." He handed a bulging envelope across the desk. "We'll get the rest set up while you're in flight training. It'll be ready by the time you are. You leave tomorrow for Houston."

"Yes, sir." Sam stood, hearing the tone of dismissal in the commander's voice.

"You can call this whole thing off up until the end of your flight training. After that, wheels will have been set in motion and can't be easily stopped. If you change your mind, let me know as soon as possible."

"Thank you, sir." Unspoken was the certainty that Sam wouldn't be changing his mind any time soon.

And keep an eye out for
SEVEN YEARS TO SIN by Sylvia Day,
coming next month!

A listair Caulfield's back was to the door of his ware-house shipping office when it opened. A salt-tinged gust blew through the space, snatching the manifest he was about to file right out of his hand.

He caught it deftly, then looked over his shoulder. Startled recognition moved through him. "Michael."

The new Lord Tarley's eyes widened with equal surprise, then a weary half-smile curved his mouth. "Alistair, you scoundrel. You didn't tell me you were in Town."

"I've only just returned." He slid the parchment into the appropriate folder and pushed the drawer closed. "How are you, my lord?"

Michael removed his hat and ran a hand through his dark brown hair. The assumption of the Tarley title appeared to weigh heavily on his broad shoulders, grounding him in a way Alistair had never seen before. He was dressed somberly in shades of brown, and he flexed his left hand, which bore the Tarley signet ring, as if he could not accustom himself to having it there. "As well as can be expected under the circumstances."

"My condolences to you and your family. Did you receive my letter?"

"I did. Thank you. I meant to reply, but time is stretched

so thin. The last year has raced by so quickly; I've yet to catch my breath."

"I understand."

Michael nodded. "I'm pleased to see you again, my friend. You have been gone far too long."

"The life of a merchant." He could have delegated more, but staying in England meant crossing paths with both his father and Jessica. His father complained about Alistair's success as a tradesman with as much virulence as he'd once complained about Alistair's lack of purpose. It was a great stressor for his mother, which he was only able to alleviate by being absent as much as possible.

As for Jessica, she'd been careful to avoid him whenever they were in proximity. He had learned to reciprocate when he saw how marriage to Tarley changed her. While she remained as cool in deportment as ever, he'd seen the blossoming of her sensual nature in the languid way she moved and the knowledge in those big, gray eyes. Other men coveted the mystery of her, but Alistair had seen behind the veil and *that* was the woman he lusted for. Forever beyond his reach in reality, but a fixture in his mind. She was burned into his memory by the raging hungers and impressionableness of youth, and the years hadn't lessened the vivid recollection one whit.

"I find myself grateful for your enterprising sensibilities," Michael said. "Your captains are the only ones I would entrust with the safe passage of my sister-in-law to Jamaica."

Alistair kept his face impassive by considerable practice, but the sudden awareness gripping him tensed his frame. "Lady Tarley intends to travel to Calypso?"

"Yes. This very morning, which his why I'm here. I intend to speak to the captain myself and see he looks after her until they arrive."

"Who travels with her?"

"Only her maid. I should like to accompany her, but I can't leave now."

"And she will not delay?"

"No." Michael's mouth curved wryly. "And I cannot dissuade her."

"You cannot say no to her," Alistair corrected, moving to the window through which we could view the West India docks. Ships entered the Northern Dock to unload their precious imports, then sailed around to the Southern Dock to reload with cargo for export. Around the perimeter, a high brick wall deterred the rampant theft plaguing the London wharves, which increased his shipping company's appeal to West Indian landowners requiring secure carriage of goods.

"Neither can Hester—forgive me, *Lady Regmont*."

The last was said with difficulty. Alistair had long suspected his friend nursed deeper feelings for Jessica's younger sister and had assumed Michael would pay his addresses. Instead, Hester had been presented at court then immediately betrothed, breaking the hearts of many hopeful would-be swains. "Why is she so determined to go?"

"Benedict bequeathed the property to her. She claims she must see to its sale personally. I fear the loss of my brother has affected her deeply and she seeks a purpose. I've attempted to anchor her, but duty has me stretched to wit's end."

Alistair's reply was carefully neutral. "I can assist her in that endeavor. I can make the necessary introductions, as well as relay information it would take her months to find."

"A generous offer." Michael's gaze was searching. "But you just returned. I can't ask you to depart again so soon."

Turning, Alistair said. "My plantation borders Calypso, and I could use the expansion. It's my hope to position myself as the best purchaser of the property. I will pay her handsomely, of course."

Relief swept over Michael's expressive features. "That would ease my mind considerably. I'll speak to her at once."

"Perhaps you should leave that to me. If, as you say, she needs a purpose, then she'll want to maintain control of the matter in all ways. She should be allowed to set the terms and pace of our association to suit her. I have all the time in the world, but you do not. See to your most pressing affairs, and entrust Lady Tarley to me."

"You've always been a good friend," Michael said. "I pray you return to England swiftly and settle for a time. I could use your ear and head for business. In the interim, please encourage Jessica to write often and keep me abreast of the situation. I should like to see her return before we retire to the country for the winter."

"I'll do my best."

Alistair waited several minutes after Michael departed, then moved to the desk. He began a list of new provisions for the journey, determined to create the best possible captive environment. He also made some quick but costly adjustments to the passenger list, moving two additional travelers to another of his ships.

He and Jessica would be the only non-crewmen about the *Acheron*.

She would be within close proximity for weeks—it was an extraordinary opportunity Alistair was determined not to waste.

GREAT BOOKS, GREAT SAVINGS!

When You Visit Our Website:
www.kensingtonbooks.com

You Can Save Money Off The Retail Price
Of Any Book You Purchase!

- **All Your Favorite Kensington Authors**
- **New Releases & Timeless Classics**
- **Overnight Shipping Available**
- **eBooks Available For Many Titles**
- **All Major Credit Cards Accepted**

Visit Us Today To Start Saving!
www.kensingtonbooks.com

All Orders Are Subject To Availability.
Shipping and Handling Charges Apply.
Offers and Prices Subject To Change Without Notice.